CITY
of
SCOUNDRELS

**Center Point
Large Print**

Also by Victoria Thompson and available from Center Point Large Print:

Murder on Amsterdam Avenue
Murder on St. Nicholas Avenue
Murder in Morningside Heights
Murder in the Bowery
City of Lies
Murder on Union Square
City of Secrets
Murder on Trinity Place

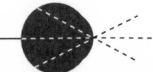

CITY

 of

SCOUNDRELS

Victoria Thompson

CENTER POINT LARGE PRINT
THORNDIKE, MAINE

To my daughter,
Ellen Thompson Nemetz,
who has always been a fighter

CITY
of
SCOUNDRELS

CHAPTER ONE

I hate this stupid war!" Elizabeth cried in frustration.

"Shhhh." Gideon glanced anxiously at the parlor door. Fortunately, it was tightly closed, even though it was highly improper for them to be alone in any room, even a perfectly respectable parlor. Gideon's mother thought an engaged couple deserved a little privacy, however, hence the closed door. "Not so loud. Someone might hear you."

"Do you really think your mother would turn me over to the League?" The American Protective League had thousands of civilian volunteers who were informally investigating enemy activities but who usually just reported their neighbors for being "unpatriotic."

"No, but I'm not too sure about the servants. People have been jailed for less, you know."

"I do know, although I'm sure *everyone* hates the war by now, so how can saying it be unpatriotic?"

"I have no idea, but it's not only unpatriotic. It's illegal, and the League has spies everywhere, so please be careful, my darling. I wouldn't want to spend our honeymoon in prison."

"If we ever even have a honeymoon. I still don't see why we can't go ahead and get married, war or no war."

Gideon sighed. "You know why, darling."

Elizabeth sighed, too, but much more dramatically. "Because you're too honorable to risk leaving me a widow."

"And possibly leaving you with a child you'll have to raise alone."

"You might be sorry for being so honorable, Gideon. The way this war is going, by the time it's over, I'll probably be too old to have children at all, and you'll wish we hadn't waited."

He smiled at that. "I'm sure you have at least a decade of childbearing years left, and the war can't possibly last that long. Now, stop fussing and kiss me before my mother decides we've been in here alone long enough."

A few minutes later, they broke apart at the sound of a discreet knock, and Mrs. Bates joined them, pretending not to notice how breathless they both were.

"Have you seen the newspapers?" Mrs. Bates asked. "They sentenced the suffrage demonstrators in Washington to ten days in the workhouse."

"Not the Occoquan Workhouse," Elizabeth cried in dismay. She and Mrs. Bates had spent time in that horrible place last fall for demonstrating for women's suffrage outside the White House.

"No, a different workhouse, but no better, I'm sure. They were protesting in Lafayette Square this time, right beside the White House. I'm sure the government is justifying it by saying demonstrating for women's rights is bad for civilian morale or some other poppycock."

"Shhhh, someone might hear you," Elizabeth said, jumping up to close the parlor door.

"Do you think the League has spies in our house?" Mrs. Bates asked in disgust.

"The League has members everywhere," Gideon said. "And I don't think they call them spies, Mother, so they might be offended if they heard you call them that."

"Whatever I call them, I hope I'm not harboring any in my own home."

"You never know," Elizabeth said, "and we can't take a chance of demoralizing our beloved doughboys with unpatriotic thoughts."

"I hope they aren't *your* beloved doughboys," Gideon said. "That's too much competition, even for me."

"Don't be silly. When you're a doughboy, you will be my only beloved one," Elizabeth said.

"I just wish you didn't have to go at all, Gideon," Mrs. Bates said.

"And you don't really have to. You could get yourself appointed as a Dollar-a-Year Man," Elizabeth said slyly.

"David did," Mrs. Bates reminded him, naming Gideon's best friend.

"And David will have to live with his decision, just as I have to live with mine." Gideon gave Elizabeth a disapproving frown. "I can't shirk my duty when so many other men have already paid the ultimate price."

"I suppose your mother and I are just selfish, Gideon," Elizabeth said. "We don't see any reason for you to pay the supreme price."

"If women ruled the world, I suppose there wouldn't be any wars at all."

"Another good reason to give us the vote," Elizabeth said.

"You already have the vote, at least in New York State," Gideon said.

"Yes," his mother said wearily, "and that's lovely, but a state here and there is not enough. All American women must have the vote."

"So you can put an end to this war?" Gideon guessed.

"Or at least elect people who will," she replied.

"I wonder if they really do pay those men a dollar," Elizabeth said to change the subject. Thinking about Gideon going to war was simply too dreadful.

"Who, dear?" Mrs. Bates asked absently.

"The Dollar-a-Year Men. Do they really get a dollar a year?"

"I think that's just an expression," Gideon said.

"I don't think they get any salary at all. David would know. Why don't you ask him?" he added with a mischievous grin.

Elizabeth pretended not to notice the grin. "I'm not sure David and I are actually speaking yet."

"Really?" Mrs. Bates said in surprise. "I thought he'd forgiven you for breaking your engagement to him."

"He apparently told Gideon that he was actually relieved that I did." She glanced at Gideon, silently daring him to confirm it, which he knew better than to do. "But I think his pride was a bit bruised, and you know how sensitive men can be about matters of the heart."

"Indeed I do," Mrs. Bates said.

"But apparently, many men have extremely strong stomachs," Gideon said, "which is what I imagine it takes for the Dollar-a-Year Men to give a speech in theaters at intermission and make people feel guilty because they haven't bought enough Liberty Bonds or knitted enough socks or saved enough peach pits for the war effort."

"Don't forget bandages, dear," Mrs. Bates said with only a hint of sarcasm. "Heaven knows, I've rolled miles of them."

"And bandages. David is welcome to serve our country as he sees fit, and I will serve it as I see fit."

Elizabeth didn't dare meet Mrs. Bates's eye.

13

Neither of them could bear the thought of losing Gideon, no matter how honorable it might be.

A few days later, Gideon's law clerk showed a handsome young soldier into his office. His uniform had obviously been tailored to fit him and had been smartly pressed, which was unusual. "Corporal Thomas Preston," Smith announced before leaving, closing the door behind him.

Gideon shook the soldier's hand and invited him to sit. "Where are you from, Corporal Preston?"

"Upstate," he said vaguely. "You're not serving?"

"I was too old for the earlier drafts, but they'll get me this time. I'm just waiting to be called up."

Preston nodded. "Raising the age limit to forty-five will get a lot of fellows."

"Indeed it will. I hear General Pershing wants a million more men over there."

"That should put an end to the Boche pretty quick."

Gideon shook his head. "Nothing about this war has been quick, but let's hope you're right. Now, what can I do for you, Corporal?" he asked, although he was pretty sure he already knew.

"The army tells me I need to make a will before I ship out."

Most of the boys didn't really need one, but

14

Preston looked as if he might. "I know that's what they're advising, and you probably also know our firm is preparing wills free of charge for the boys. It's our contribution to the war effort."

"I heard that, which is why I chose your firm, even though I can easily afford to pay for your services."

Which explained the tailored uniform and confirmed Gideon's suspicions. "That isn't necessary."

"In my case, it probably is. My will must be a little complicated because my situation is complicated, and I don't want any misunderstandings later if I . . . well, if I don't return."

Gideon nodded his understanding. "What do you mean by 'complicated'?"

"First of all, because of the war, I am a man of means."

"Why 'because of the war'?"

"My family owns Preston Shoe Manufacturing. We were doing quite well for the past twenty-five years or so, and when my father passed away about five years ago, he left me a third of the company."

"Who owns the rest?"

"My older brother, Fred, and my stepmother, Delia, each have a third. Fred is the president of the company, and Delia and I just collect our quarterly dividends."

"You aren't involved in the company at all?"

15

"I suppose that was my family's expectation, but I was still in school when my father passed. Then I turned twenty-one last winter, so I was eligible for the draft this past June, right after I graduated from Cornell, so I haven't had a chance to go to work yet." Working in an industry essential to the war effort could have provided a deferment. Why hadn't Fred offered his brother that opportunity? Or maybe Tom was too honorable to take it.

"I see. So you're a college man. I'm surprised you didn't go to officers' training."

"They wanted me to, but . . ."

Gideon waited, knowing how people detested silence and would often fill it with information they wouldn't ordinarily reveal.

After a moment, Preston said, "I didn't think a man as young as I am should be ordering men to their deaths."

Gideon nodded, understanding completely. "They made you a corporal, though."

"I went to a training camp in the summer of nineteen fifteen. One for college men."

"Ah, yes, the preparedness movement." As soon as the war started in Europe, several retired American generals had seen a future need for officers if America entered the war. They started a series of private summer training camps for college men and others for businessmen. "Did they teach you to be a leader?"

16

Preston chuckled at that. "They mostly just taught us to march. Did you go to a Business Men's Camp?"

"A Tired Business Men's Camp, you mean?" Gideon replied, giving it the sarcastic moniker the public had bestowed. "No, I didn't."

"You'll probably want to go in as an officer, anyway. Most of the older fellows do. I hear they're opening some new training schools because they need so many new officers."

To replace the ones being killed by the score, but Gideon didn't say that to this innocent young man who might still think war was mostly honor, glory and parades. "I'll probably just do what they tell me to do. Now, explain to me why your will must be complicated. Your situation sounds pretty straightforward."

"It would be ordinarily, I suppose. Did I mention that Preston Shoes has a contract with the army now?"

"No, you didn't, but I'd guessed as much since you said you were newly wealthy."

"Fred worked really hard and probably bribed a few politicians to get the job, and he's made a fortune. Although . . ."

Gideon clamped his lips together and waited again.

Preston glanced at the door as if to make sure it was still closed. "Now that I'm in the army, I've heard things."

"Things about what?"

"The shoes. The ones issued to the soldiers. They . . . The soldiers call them 'chicken skins.' Because they fall apart so easily."

"They're poor quality, you mean?"

"That's putting it mildly. I know the shoes I was issued were awful."

"I'm sure the army has contracts with many different shoe companies," Gideon tried. "Maybe the pair you got was made by a different one."

"You're probably right, and I would hate to think . . . Well, anyway, Fred is running the company, and there's nothing I can do about it now. When the war is over . . ."

Gideon let that pass. A lot of things would or wouldn't happen when this cursed war was over. "So you are now a wealthy man, courtesy of the U.S. Army. I'm assuming you want to leave someone your share of the company as well as the money you've made. Your brother?"

Preston smiled, but the expression held no mirth. "I already have a will that does that. Fred took me to have it drawn up the minute he realized I'd be drafted."

"And you've changed your mind?"

"Not exactly. I've gotten married."

"Married?" Gideon echoed in surprise and then managed to say, "Congratulations."

"Thank you. I know. You're thinking I'm crazy to get married just before shipping out but . . ."

The color rose in his beardless face, and he dropped his gaze. "Well, there's a baby, you see."

Gideon nodded knowingly. "I do see. Then you've done the right thing."

Preston smiled his mirthless smile again. "I don't think Fred or Delia would agree. She's not . . . well, she's not the sort of girl they would approve of."

"What sort of girl is she?" Gideon asked, carefully keeping all hint of judgment from his tone.

Preston's entire face seemed to light up at that. "She's wonderful. Not like anyone I've ever known. She doesn't care what other people think, and she always tells the truth, no matter how unpleasant it might be."

Gideon ostentatiously moved a pad of paper from the side of his desk to the center and unscrewed the top of his fountain pen. "And what is her name?"

"Rose O'Dell," he said proudly, instantly revealing why Preston's family would not have approved. She was Irish and probably Catholic into the bargain. Either of those would make her socially unacceptable to the Prestons. "Well, Rose Preston now. I have the marriage certificate if you need to see it."

Preston reached into his uniform jacket pocket, but Gideon shook his head. "No, I'll take your word, Corporal. If there's ever a question, your marriage is registered, I'm sure."

19

"Of course it is."

"Good. Then all I need to know is how you would like your estate to be distributed in the event of your death."

"That's just it. I don't want it distributed at all. I want it all to go to Rosie. And the baby, of course, except I don't think you can leave money to a baby, can you?"

"You can, but it's not a good idea. Presumably your wife would use her inheritance to support herself and your child, so leaving it all to her would ensure your child's welfare. Is that what you want?"

"Yes, that's exactly what I want. Fred won't like it. He won't like any of it, but I'm married now, and there's nothing he can do to change that."

"Does he want to change it?" Gideon asked uneasily.

Preston flinched just a little. "He doesn't actually know. That I'm married, that is. I'm shipping out in a few weeks and with the baby . . . We didn't have much time, and I didn't want Fred interfering."

"I see. Does Fred know your wife?"

"Oh no. How could he? She's from the city, after all, and Fred hardly ever comes to New York."

"How did *you* come to know her?" Gideon asked, still trying to sound merely conversational.

20

Tom Preston wouldn't be the first young man tricked into marriage by a girl looking for the main chance.

"I met her at a dance. At Camp Upton out on Long Island. They had lots of dances for us, to keep our spirits up, I guess. Girls would come out from the city on the train. It's not far, and the girls thought it was their patriotic duty to cheer us up."

Rose O'Dell had done some serious cheering up if she was expecting a baby, but Gideon didn't mention this. "And fun for them, too, I suppose."

Preston smiled sheepishly. "I suppose so, although I imagine there're plenty of dances in the city, too."

But not dances where an Irish Catholic girl like Rose O'Dell could meet someone like Tom Preston. Gideon wondered if she really was expecting a baby. Not that it mattered now. She'd married him. "So let me make sure I understand your intentions. You wish to leave your entire estate, which means all of your possessions as well as your share of Preston Shoes, to your wife, Rose O'Dell Preston. Is that correct?"

"Yes, and make sure to mention that the will I made a few months ago is no longer valid."

"Do you have the signed copy of that will?"

"Oh no. Fred kept it. It would be safer, he said."

"Is Fred also named the executor of your estate in that will?"

21

"Yes, although I wasn't really sure what that meant."

"Just that he's the person who is legally bound to make sure the terms of the will are followed exactly."

"I see."

"Do you want to name him executor of this will, too?"

"Oh no. Not if that means he's in charge of it. He won't want Rosie to get anything at all. Could you be the executor?"

"We typically don't name anyone from the firm in particular, but you could have our law firm serve as executor. I will do it if I'm available, but hopefully you won't need an executor for many years, and I might be retired by then."

Preston smiled at that. They both knew that it was possible neither of them would survive the war, which was why Preston was here in the first place. "That sounds fine. And your firm will look after Rosie and make sure she gets everything she's entitled to?"

"Of course."

Preston sighed with obvious relief, and for the first time, his smile was genuine. "Thank you, Mr. Bates. You've made it a lot easier for me to serve my country."

"Most of the young men who come here for a will don't really own much of value, so we made up a standard form that we just fill in with their name and the names of their beneficiaries. That way they can just sign it and be on their way. Your will is a little more complicated, though, and will take longer to draw up."

Preston reached to pull out his pocket watch, but military uniforms did not provide for pocket watches, probably because they wouldn't be practical in the heat of battle. Chagrined, he pushed back his sleeve and consulted his army-issued wristwatch. "I'm still getting used to this," he said, indicating the watch. "They tell us all the regular army fellows wear them, and so do all the real he-men."

Gideon smiled at that. Wristwatches had always been thought to be a silly affectation, so the doughboys still had mixed feelings about them.

Preston checked the time. "I have to be back at the base in a few hours, but I can wait until then, if you think it will be ready."

"It will take a few days, so there's no need to wait."

"That's fine, then. Just tell me when to come back, and I'll ask for a pass to return to the city."

"We can also keep the signed will here in our office, if you like."

"Oh no. Rosie already said she wants to keep it herself. It's not that she doesn't trust you, but . . ." he added hastily.

"But she feels more secure holding it herself. I understand," Gideon said. "We'll keep a copy, of course, but the signed will is the only one that is valid. You might explain to your wife that it would be far safer with us."

"I'll try, but you don't know Rosie," Preston said fondly. "She's the bravest girl I know."

Gideon thought that was probably true.

"Besides," Preston continued, "she feels pretty safe in the apartment I rented for her. They've got a doorman, and nobody can get in unless you live there."

"That was thoughtful of you."

"I couldn't have my wife living in a rooming house, could I? I paid the rent for a year and set it up so she can draw money from my bank account. That's where Fred sends my quarterly dividends."

"And the army sends your six dollars and thirty cents a month in army pay," Gideon added with a grin.

"Oh, I get almost eight dollars a month now that I'm a corporal," Preston said with a laugh. "So you see, Rosie will be fine until I get back."

And with that will, she'd be fine if he didn't get back, too. Gideon shouldn't judge her, though. Maybe this truly was a love match. Preston seemed smitten, at least. Gideon only hoped Rose O'Dell returned his affection.

"You should probably give me your wife's address, too, for our records. With any luck at all, the war will be over long before your lease is up and that will be your address as well."

Gideon could only hope the war would end that soon and that this fine young man would live to see it.

Elizabeth decided she should have been happy to be seated between the two people she loved best in the world—her fiancé, Gideon, and her best friend, Anna Vanderslice. They were, after all, enjoying an evening out by watching a moving picture. *Ali Baba and the Forty Thieves* was as far from New York and the Great War as one could get without leaving the planet, and they could forget the real world for at least an hour or two.

Or they should have been able to do that, but during the four-minute interval while the projectionist changed the reels, the lights came up, an American flag dropped from above to hang in front of the screen and a man came out to deliver his speech about how they could support the war effort. Dollar-a-Year Men who did this had been dubbed Four Minute Men.

No one actually groaned aloud—League spies were everywhere—but an unmistakably dissatisfied rustle went through the crowd as he reached the center of the stage. Only when Gideon made a little strangled sound did Elizabeth really look at the man, and then she recognized him, too. "Anna!" she whispered in outrage.

Anna smiled back, clearly unrepentant. "I know David will appreciate our supporting him."

David Vanderslice was Anna's brother and Gideon's best friend since childhood and Elizabeth's former (and fake) fiancé from last year. David didn't know he'd been a fake fiancé, and with any luck, he never would.

"You picked this film on purpose," Elizabeth hissed into Anna's ear.

"Shhhh. You're not supposed to talk during his speech."

Elizabeth gave her a murderous glare, which only made Anna smile more gleefully, and when Elizabeth glanced at Gideon, she saw him covering his mouth to smother a laugh. By then David had launched into his speech about why they should buy Liberty Bonds and Thrift Stamps to support the war effort. He threw in some descriptions of the devilish Huns committing atrocities that were probably fictional, and he closed with a plea for all of them to observe Meatless Mondays and Wheatless Wednesdays, because food would win the war.

Because an army traveled on its stomach or some such nonsense, Elizabeth remembered, although she thought an army probably really traveled on trucks and ships and mostly on its own feet. She'd be sure to point that out to David the next time they spoke.

Which turned out to be quite soon because the

film had no more than started up again than David made his way down the darkened aisle and took the empty seat beside Anna. He leaned over and nodded to her and Gideon. Gideon nodded back, and Elizabeth smiled. David didn't smile back.

Elizabeth managed not to sigh, although nobody would have heard her over the swelling chords of the organ that provided a musical backdrop to the silent film. She turned away under the guise of having to watch the screen and read the title cards that appeared in between each scene and explained what was happening in the film or told what the characters were saying. One did need to watch carefully and read the cards, although following the laughably simple plot wasn't really that hard.

She should have been grateful that David was here. He'd certainly join them for dinner afterward, and that would give them both an opportunity to talk and pretend nothing had ever been awkward between them. David would certainly be best man at her wedding to Gideon, if that day ever came, so she would be glad to be on good terms with him again. She was sure she would be.

She was going to give Anna a good pinch for doing this.

Elizabeth eventually managed to forget about David and enjoy the rest of the film. As it ended, the organ music swelled to deafening levels before dying away completely to allow the audience to applaud. As the only live performer present, the organist took his bows, although Elizabeth suspected little of the appreciation was really directed at him.

"David, good to see you," Gideon said when the audience began to rise to leave the theater. He reached around Elizabeth to offer his hand and David reached around Anna to clasp it, reminding Elizabeth how fond Gideon was of David.

"Likewise. They're keeping me pretty busy with my war work," David said. "I was glad Anna suggested meeting you here. Elizabeth," he added with a polite nod.

"So nice to see you, David," Elizabeth said, and it was. David was a handsome man and very nice to look at. Elizabeth made it a rule to tell the truth as often as possible now that she was engaged to Gideon, who never lied.

"Will you join us for supper?" Gideon asked.

"I was hoping you'd ask."

They made their way out of the theater and down the street to a Chinese restaurant. Elizabeth loved its exotic decor, with the marble dragons guarding the doors. When they were seated and had ordered, they started to discuss the film.

"Did you see the beginning, David?" Elizabeth asked.

"I've seen it at least ten times. I could probably quote all the title cards from memory."

"I thought it was so clever the way Ali Baba opened that huge door," Anna said. "I wonder how they did that."

"I especially liked the way Morgiana drowned the forty thieves in the oil," Elizabeth said.

Did David choke just a little? Elizabeth was sure he had. Gideon didn't even bother to cover his laugh.

"Do you get paid for being a Four Minute Man?" Elizabeth asked.

"I beg your pardon?" David said, a little affronted.

"I know you get paid a dollar a year for being a Dollar-a-Year Man, so how much extra does a Four Minute Man get paid?"

"Elizabeth is teasing you," Gideon said, giving Elizabeth a pleading look. Poor David never knew how to take Elizabeth. "How long have you been giving the speeches?"

"A few weeks. It's important work, but it wears on a man. Nobody likes hearing about the war in the middle of a moving picture they came to see in order to forget the war."

Elizabeth certainly hadn't, but she didn't embarrass Gideon by saying so. "What other things are you doing for the war?"

"I've been overseeing the army contracts in the state, making sure that the equipment all gets to the ports and is shipped out in a timely manner. It's a lot harder than you can imagine."

"I'm sure it is," Gideon said. "It must be a nightmare trying to fight a war when you're thousands of miles and an ocean away from your supplies. Tell me, do you oversee the contracts for shoes?"

"Shoes?" David echoed as if he'd never heard the word before. "I suppose so. We have so many suppliers. Most of the companies that make clothes and shoes have switched to making uniforms for the troops."

"Do you also check the quality of the goods being produced?" Gideon asked.

Now Elizabeth knew Gideon wasn't just making conversation. She turned to David expectantly.

"Oh no," he said. "I suppose they have inspectors for that sort of thing. But I'm sure no patriotic American would produce poor-quality equipment for our troops."

For a minute Elizabeth was afraid Gideon wasn't going to challenge that naïve assumption, so she said, "Are you thinking of something in particular, Gideon?"

"Yes, I am. David, are you familiar with the term 'chicken skins'?"

"No. What is it?"

"That's what the soldiers call the shoes the army issues to them, because they fall apart so easily."

"That's terrible," Anna said.

"It would be if it were true, but I can't believe it is," David said. "Where did you hear this?"

"From a soldier who came into my office today to have a will drawn up."

"Oh, well, you know how soldiers are . . . or maybe you don't. They like to complain, don't they? At least that's what I'm told. They complain about the food and the quarters and the uniforms and their pay. Everything really. Nothing ever suits them, so I'd take whatever a soldier tells you with a grain of salt."

"Ordinarily I would," Gideon said with his usual tact, which was one of the things Elizabeth admired him for. He'd never criticize his dearest friend for choosing public service over combat, even though Elizabeth thought David was a bit pompous for presuming to understand the soldiers. "But this particular soldier is part owner in a company that manufactures shoes, so his opinion carries a little more weight than someone else's might."

"I suppose it does," David said thoughtfully. "That's very disturbing."

"Can you do something about it?" Anna asked.

"I . . . I don't really know. I mean, certainly I will pass along your concerns, but . . ."

"But what?" Elizabeth had no patience with his attempt to placate her.

David's helpless expression told her everything she needed to know. "You have no idea how complicated it is. No one really knows who is in charge of anything. I send reports to someone who sends them to someone else. Mistakes are made but never corrected. Shipments are late or lost completely, and no one ever finds them."

"Shhhh," Gideon said, glancing around. No one seemed to be paying attention to them, but you never knew. Elizabeth glanced around as well. Was that strange-looking man in the corner watching them? He jumped to his feet, and for one horrible moment, she thought he was going to approach them, but he only waved to someone behind Elizabeth. In another moment a woman hurried past their table to join him. Elizabeth sighed with relief.

"I shouldn't have brought this up in a public place," Gideon said. "I'm sorry."

David had blanched, only too aware of what might happen to him for admitting the war wasn't being run as efficiently as it might have been.

"So, Anna," Elizabeth said brightly, "when does school start?"

Anna brightened in turn. "*School?* You make me sound like I'm in pigtails. I'll start *college* in just a few more weeks."

Elizabeth glanced at David and was gratified to see only a tolerant smile instead of disapproval. Or maybe he was just grateful that she'd changed the subject.

"Anna always was the smart one in the family." David gave his sister an affectionate look.

"I know she appreciates your support," Elizabeth said quite sincerely.

"I certainly do."

"I just hope her education doesn't scare off all her suitors," David said.

"All the young men are in the army, so no one has any suitors at the moment," Elizabeth pointed out, although every one of them except David knew that Anna would never be interested in marrying any of those young men.

Their food arrived then, distracting them from any further talk of Anna's marriage prospects. Gideon found a few safe topics of discussion that would not draw the attention of any lurking League members that took them through the rest of the meal.

Elizabeth and Gideon parted from David and Anna on the sidewalk outside, and Gideon found a cab so he could see Elizabeth home. The August heat had faded somewhat by this late hour, so the air coming in the cab's windows was almost cool. Gideon slipped his arm around her, and they snuggled contentedly as the cab made its way through the city streets.

"That soldier I saw today just got married," Gideon said.

Elizabeth straightened immediately so she could look him in the eye. "He did? And did he convince you it was a good idea?"

"There is a . . . a baby involved," he said rather primly.

Which was, of course, Gideon's biggest reason for not marrying her before going into the army. She couldn't resist teasing him, though. "Is that what it would take? Because I feel fairly certain—"

"Don't go making any babies in my cab," the driver called from the front seat, which sent them both into gales of laughter.

"Don't worry, my good man," Gideon said when he could. "No babies will be made tonight."

"I hope we didn't shock you," Elizabeth added.

"Not a bit. You wouldn't believe the things I hear. I'm glad that soldier did the right thing by his lady, though."

"So am I," Elizabeth said softly to Gideon.

But Gideon didn't smile.

"What is it?" she asked.

"Nothing. Not really. I just . . . I can't shake the feeling that I should have done something more for him."

"More than make his will, you mean?"

Gideon nodded.

"But what else could you do?"

Gideon had no answer.

"So are you registered?" David asked. He'd stopped by Gideon's office because yesterday,

September 12, was the date they'd both had to register for the draft.

"Of course I am. How about you?"

David settled back into the comfort of one of the chairs provided for clients. "I am, and I got a deferment, although they warned me I'm still eligible for the draft if they need more men. It's not too late, Gideon. I can still get you appointed to some board or other."

"Thank you for the offer, but you know my position on this."

David shrugged. "Your mother asked me to mention it to you, just in case you'd changed your mind."

"I'm certainly not excited about going, but . . ."

"But you feel it's your duty. I understand. And I'm the sole support of my mother and my sister, and just between us, I don't think Anna is really interested in getting married, so I'm probably going to be supporting her for the rest of my life."

Gideon leaned back in his chair and bit his tongue. At least David had finally noticed Anna's lack of interest in marriage. "But after she gets her college education, she can have a profession, so she'll be able to support herself."

"That's what she tells me, but you know a woman can never earn as much as a man."

He was right, of course. "Still, if she only has

herself to support, she can do all right. Look at Elizabeth's aunt Cybil."

"I suppose, although I don't see Anna as a college professor."

"She could be a social worker or another kind of teacher."

David looked like he was going to argue the point, but a disturbance in the hallway outside Gideon's office distracted them both.

"What on earth?" Gideon muttered, rising instinctively just as the door flew open.

"I'm so sorry, Mr. Bates," Smith was saying as he unsuccessfully tried to stop a very angry gentleman from barging into Gideon's office.

"Are you Bates?" the man demanded.

"Yes, and who are you?" Gideon demanded right back.

That seemed to startle him. Perhaps he had expected Gideon to be as intimidated as Smith appeared to be. He glanced uneasily at David, who had also risen and was glaring at him in marked disapproval. The man took a moment to straighten his suit jacket. "I am Frederick Preston."

The name was vaguely familiar, although Gideon knew he'd never seen this man before in his life. "And what is your business here, Mr. Preston?"

Preston. Suddenly Gideon remembered. Tom Preston, the soldier with the pregnant wife and

36

the brother named Fred, who would not approve.

Preston squared his shoulders as if bracing for a fight. "I understand my brother had you draw up a last will and testament for him some weeks ago."

"What business is that of yours, Mr. Preston?"

Preston glanced at David again and said, "My brother is dead, Mr. Bates."

CHAPTER TWO

All of them stood for a moment in stunned silence, including Preston, who seemed just as shocked by his bald statement as his audience. Gideon finally found his voice and wasn't at all surprised to hear his true regret reflected in it. "I'm very sorry, Mr. Preston. Tom was a fine young man." Another tragic loss in this horrible war. Surely, the poor boy could not have been on the battlefield for more than a week.

For some reason, Gideon's tribute seemed to anger Preston, but he finally remembered his manners. "I didn't mean to barge in on you like this, Bates, but your man insisted I needed an appointment to see you, and my business is rather urgent."

Smith was a strong supporter of appointments. "And as you can see, Mr. Smith was quite correct to insist since I was already engaged." He nodded at David, who glared at Preston with just the proper amount of disapproval.

"Yes, I . . . I see that." Preston apparently couldn't decide whether to be apologetic or continue to be outraged. Gideon guessed he wasn't used to apologizing.

"It's obvious this gentleman is grieving for his brother and is not responsible for his behavior," David said, allowing just the least hint of censure to creep into his otherwise polite response. Preston had the grace to flush. "We can continue our business another time, Mr. Bates."

"That's very generous of you, Mr. Vanderslice," Gideon said, echoing David's formality. No sense giving Preston the idea that they were friends who had just been chatting. Gideon wanted Preston to feel as guilty as possible for being such a lout. "Smith, would you see Mr. Vanderslice out, please?"

"Of course, sir."

David glanced back when he reached the door and was out of Preston's view. The look he gave Gideon warned him he'd want a full report on this rude fellow later. Gideon would be only too happy to give it.

"Please sit down, Mr. Preston, and tell me how I may be of service to you," Gideon said when Smith had closed the door behind himself.

Preston sat in one of the armchairs Gideon had arranged in front of his desk for the comfort of his clients. Preston took a moment to look around, as if judging Gideon's importance by the opulence of his office. If that was his standard, he should be impressed. All the offices at Devoss and Van Aken were tastefully decorated in the dark, heavy woods and velvets that typically indicated prosperity and permanence to clients.

Gideon used the opportunity to study Fred Preston in return. The man appeared to be at least ten years older than Tom, and he'd obviously spent a large portion of his war profits with his tailor. The expensive suit did little to improve one's impression, however, since Fred Preston's scowl must have been as off-putting to everyone else as it was to Gideon.

Finally satisfied, Preston returned his gaze to Gideon, who had taken his own seat behind his imposingly large desk. "Like I said, I heard you made a will for my brother."

But the attorneys at Devoss and Van Aken did not jump right into business without observing the usual amenities. "Your brother was indeed a client of mine. May I ask the details of his death? I came to like him very much and deeply regret that his life was cut short."

Preston's face twisted a bit, but Gideon couldn't tell what emotion had inspired the reaction. He might just still be angry at Smith. "I don't really know any details. I'm not the one who got the message from the army."

And of course he wouldn't have been, not when Tom had a wife. "How did you come to hear the news, then?"

This time Preston's expression signaled distaste. "Some woman came to see me. At my place of business. She said she was Tom's *wife,* although I don't believe that for a second. Tom was a fool, but he'd never marry a chippie like that, I can tell you."

"Are you saying the army notified this lady instead of you?"

"She received a telegram, yes," he reluctantly admitted.

"So the army, at least, believes her to be your brother's wife."

"Maybe they do, but I never will."

"I assume Mrs. Preston told you that Tom had been killed in combat."

Preston winced at the "Mrs. Preston." "So *that woman* told me. She said Tom's dead, and he'd made a will leaving her everything. Is it true?"

"I'm afraid I cannot discuss my clients or their affairs with you, Mr. Preston."

"But I'm his brother. I have a right to know."

"Even beneficiaries don't have a right to know what is in a will unless the person who made the will chooses to tell them, but if your brother is indeed dead and has a valid will, it will be filed for probate. At that point, it becomes public, and you can find out everything you want to know."

"My brother does have a valid will. I took him to our family attorney the moment he told me he was going into the army. I could have gotten him a deferment, of course. We own a shoe factory. Did he tell you that? Of course he did.

It's an essential industry, and I would have given him a job so he didn't have to risk his neck, but no, he had his head all full of guns and glory." Preston pulled out a handkerchief and wiped his brow. The day was comfortably cool, but he must have worked up a sweat muscling his way into Gideon's office.

"Do you know where that will is, Mr. Preston?"

"Of course I do. It's in my office safe. I know how important these things are. But if there's another will, a newer one . . ."

Since Preston hadn't really asked a question, Gideon did not reply, leaving it to Preston to fill the silence.

"Is there a newer will?" he finally asked.

"As I explained, I cannot discuss my clients with you, Mr. Preston."

"That hussy said there was. She said Tom wanted her to get his share of the business and that he got it all fixed up before he shipped out. She said you did the will for him. That's why I'm here. I came all the way down from Pough-keepsie to find you."

"I understand that you're concerned about the disposition of your brother's estate. Your concern for your brother's widow does you credit, but if you want to be of assistance to her, may I suggest that you speak directly with her?"

"I'm not concerned with her at all, Bates. I thought I'd made that clear. She's a gold-digging whore, and I'm not giving her a penny of my money."

"No one expects you to, I'm sure, and in any case, she won't be getting any of *your* money."

"Preston Shoes is my company, Bates, and my brother intended for me to have his share when he died."

"Then his last will and testament will reflect that, won't it?"

Preston jumped to his feet, his fury turning his face scarlet. "I can see you're not going to be any help to me, so I'll have to take matters into my own hands. You haven't heard the last of this."

Gideon was very much afraid he hadn't.

"What are you going to do?" Elizabeth asked when Gideon had told her and his mother about Fred Preston's visit to his office that afternoon. He'd been so quiet at dinner that they'd both known something was wrong and insisted he tell them. Elizabeth wanted to weep when she heard about poor Tom Preston.

"I sent Tom's widow a note of condolence and offered to assist her with filing the will or whatever else she might need. It's a little awkward because I've never met her. I asked Tom to bring her with him when he returned to sign his will, but she didn't come for some reason. So, of course, I don't want to give the impression I'm trying to force her to use my services."

Poor Gideon. How awful it must have been to have so many rules to follow. "Darling, perhaps you and I should pay a condolence call on her."

"Elizabeth is right," his mother said. They were seated in the family parlor, enjoying after-dinner coffee. Mrs. Bates was in her favorite rocking chair while Gideon and Elizabeth sat as close together on the sofa as propriety allowed. "If you've never met her, you can't expect her to have any confidence in you, and she must be feeling very much alone."

"Alone and terribly ignorant of what she needs to do to secure her inheritance," Elizabeth added. "I know I wouldn't have the slightest idea what to do. At the very least, you can explain what needs to be done."

"I assume her husband provided some kind of income for her while he was away," Mrs. Bates said. "Will that continue now that he's dead?"

"I hadn't thought of that," Gideon said, his forehead wrinkling in that way Elizabeth loved because it showed how concerned and serious he was. "He arranged for an apartment for her and paid a year's rent, he told me. He also gave her access to his bank account."

"I assume his army pay will cease now," Elizabeth said.

"She'll get a small widow's pension, I assume," Gideon said, "but a corporal's pay is less than eight dollars a month, so the pension will be tiny."

"Eight dollars a month!" Mrs. Bates exclaimed in outrage. "Who on earth decided that was enough to pay a man willing to give his life?"

"No amount is enough for that, Mother, but we don't do it for the money," Gideon said.

Neither woman had an answer for that. Elizabeth finally swallowed the lump in her throat and said, "How soon do you think we should call on Mrs. Preston?"

"She should get my note in tomorrow's mail, so I'll wait for her reply. She might just come to see me. I invited her to do just that if she felt the need, and if she doesn't . . ."

"If she doesn't, we'll go to see her," Elizabeth said.

"You don't need to go," Gideon said, "although it's kind of you to offer."

"If Mrs. Preston is as unsophisticated as you say, she'll feel more comfortable if I'm with you. It will seem more like a friendly gesture than a business meeting."

"Elizabeth is right. You don't want to intimidate the poor girl. She's probably terrified after her encounter with this Fred," Mrs. Bates said. "I certainly hope he didn't say the same horrible things to her that he said to you."

"I'm very much afraid he might have," Gideon said. "He seems to believe that the income from his shoe factory rightfully belongs to him."

"Does he know about the baby?" Elizabeth asked, suddenly remembering.

"He didn't mention it, so I'm guessing Mrs. Preston didn't tell him."

"I wonder why," Mrs. Bates said with a frown.

"I can think of one reason," Gideon said grimly.

"What is it?" Elizabeth asked although she didn't think she wanted to know.

"Because there isn't a baby."

"There isn't? Did she lose it?" Mrs. Bates never assumed the worst of people.

"Not that I heard, but I couldn't help thinking when Tom told me why they'd married so quickly that perhaps there was never a baby to begin with."

"You mean, she may have lied to trap him," Elizabeth said.

Gideon shrugged. He didn't like to think the worst of people, either, in spite of all the evidence to the contrary. "A poor girl meets a rich boy. He's lonely and homesick, and he'll soon be leaving to fight a war, so he imagines himself in love, and when she says she's carrying his child . . ."

"He wouldn't be the first to be tricked that way," Elizabeth said. "But what if you're wrong. What if they really were in love and there really is a child?"

"Yes, we mustn't judge this poor woman, certainly not without at least meeting her," Mrs. Bates said.

"And I can think of a much better reason why Mrs. Preston wouldn't tell Fred about her baby," Elizabeth said. "She wanted to protect the baby and herself."

"You don't think he'd harm them, do you?" Gideon asked in alarm.

"Don't tell me you didn't think of that, too."

"Of course he didn't think of that," Mrs. Bates said, "because he'd never think of something like that himself."

"It's certainly a possibility, though," Elizabeth said. "And from what you said about Fred Preston, I wouldn't rule it out."

"In that case, I guess it's a good thing he doesn't know about the baby. I just wish Tom had convinced his wife to let us keep his will in our office."

"But you have a copy, don't you?" Mrs. Bates said.

"A copy isn't a valid will. Only the signed original is. I've heard of more than one case where a disinherited child was the first one into the house after an elderly parent died and the will was never found."

"What happens in that case?" Elizabeth asked.

"If someone dies intestate—that means without a valid will—then the law dictates who inherits. It's a simple formula that pays no respect to the wishes of the deceased. In the case of a parent who dies leaving only children as his heirs, all of them would inherit equal shares of his estate."

"Including the one he wanted to disinherit," Elizabeth guessed.

"Exactly. If Tom died intestate, his wife and child would inherit all of his estate by law, which would be what he wanted anyway, but in this case, Tom already had a will he made just a few months ago and it leaves everything to his brother. That's why I'm anxious to get Tom Preston's newer will filed for probate."

"What's 'probate'?"

Gideon waved away probate's importance. "That just means it's examined by a judge to make sure it's legally valid, but once it becomes a matter of public record, it can't just disappear."

"So Mrs. Preston will be safe."

"Her legal rights will be protected. I'm not sure what else we can do to make her really safe, though."

Elizabeth didn't like the sound of that. Unfortunately, Gideon was correct, so they would just have to wait for Mrs. Preston to respond to his note.

Gideon didn't really expect to hear from Mrs. Preston the next day, Saturday, since she wouldn't have received his note until that morning. He tried not to think about her over the rest of the weekend, but on Monday morning, he told Smith to bring in his mail as soon as it arrived in case she'd replied.

To his relief, she had. She invited him to call on her at one o'clock that day. He pulled out his pocket watch and checked the time. Only a few hours and he would know if he could help Mrs. Preston in any way. With any luck, he'd be able to, and that would assuage the lingering sense of guilt he felt whenever he thought of Tom Preston and wondered what else he could have done for him.

He considered telephoning Elizabeth, but he no longer needed the fiction of a condolence call to see Mrs. Preston, so he decided to simply go by himself. The apartment building Tom Preston had chosen for his bride was the enormous Ansonia on Broadway between Seventy-third and Seventy-fourth Streets. The building had more than three hundred apartments. No wonder Mrs. Preston felt safe here. Not only did it have a doorman, but the lobby also held a bank, a bookstall, a cigar shop, a telegraph office, a doctor and a dentist. A huge fountain was home to real live seals. With meals being served in the seventeenth-floor conservatory, one would hardly ever need to leave.

The doorman directed Gideon to the front desk, where visitors were announced via an internal telephone system. "Mrs. Preston is expecting me. We have an appointment for one o'clock,"

Gideon told the officious-looking young man. When the young man looked at him in apparent disapproval, Gideon added, "I'm her attorney."

"I see. Yes, Mrs. Preston arrived home a few minutes ago. I'll ring her and announce you."

Gideon waited while the clerk used the internal telephone, but after a few minutes, he turned back to Gideon. "That's odd. She doesn't answer."

"Are you sure she's home?"

"Oh yes. She just picked up her key a few minutes ago."

"Are you positive? You must have a lot of tenants in this building. How can you keep track of all of them?"

The young man's officiousness dissolved into sheepishness. "Mrs. Preston is rather memorable. She's . . . not like most of our other tenants."

Gideon might have guessed that. "So you're sure she arrived home. Could she have stopped off somewhere first?" Gideon glanced meaning-fully at the shops surrounding them.

"She might have except she'd gone out for lunch—she often eats here, in the conservatory upstairs, but today she went out—and when she returned, she mentioned she needed to go back to her apartment right away. Probably because of your appointment."

"Try her again." The young man did so, but his frown told Gideon she still wasn't answering. That guilt Gideon had been feeling over Tom

Preston congealed into anxiety, although he couldn't have said why. "Perhaps I should go up and check on her."

"I couldn't possibly allow you to—"

"Then go with me."

The clerk frowned, perplexed. "But I can't leave my post."

"Then let me go. Look." He pulled Mrs. Preston's letter from his pocket. "She told me to meet her at one o'clock. If she doesn't want to see me, she doesn't have to open the door, but I . . . I just have a feeling something isn't right."

Plainly, the young man shared his concern. He gave Gideon the apartment number. "I'll keep trying to reach her," he called as Gideon hurried to the elevators.

Gideon tipped the operator a quarter to take him straight up without stopping. By the time he reached the sixth floor, his anxiety had turned to fear, and he found himself dashing down the hallway after the elevator operator pointed him in the right direction.

An odd noise, like something heavy hitting the other side of the wall, startled him. He was running now. "Mrs. Preston!" he shouted as he reached her door. He knocked but the door was ajar and flew open at his touch. "Mrs. Preston, are you here?" The door opened into a hallway, and he cautiously strode in. "Hello. Anyone home?"

Another loud thump and a grunt, and a large

man suddenly filled the hall and shoved Gideon so hard, he hit the floor before he even knew he'd been pushed. Pain exploded everywhere, and the shock stunned him for an instant. Two thick legs vaulted over his prone body and clattered away down the hall.

"Hey there, stop!" Gideon shouted as he struggled to his feet. He lurched to the doorway just in time to hear the stairwell door slam shut. He started after his assailant, but his knees threatened to buckle, and he had to grab the doorframe to keep from falling again. Muttering a curse at his weakness, he realized he'd never catch the assailant, but someone needed to check on Mrs. Preston. "Hello, Mrs. Preston?"

He made his way gingerly down the short entry hall, holding the wall for support, and glanced into the parlor. The sparsely furnished room was empty, but he heard a moan from the other direction. He pushed away from the wall and lunged down a connecting hallway where he saw a woman lying on the floor.

Gideon knelt beside her. "Mrs. Preston, can you hear me?"

To his relief, her eyelids fluttered, but when they lifted completely, they widened in terror, and she cried out.

"No, it's all right! I'm not the man who attacked you. I'm Gideon Bates, the attorney. That other man is gone."

"Gone?"

"Yes, he ran out when I got here. Are you all right? Did he hurt you?"

"I . . ." She reached up and grabbed her throat, which Gideon could now see was red and chafed. Good heavens, had the man tried to strangle her?

"Don't try to talk. Can you sit up?"

With Gideon's help, she managed it, but plainly the effort cost her. Before Gideon could ask her anything else, they both jumped at the shrill ring of a telephone bell.

"Harry," she croaked. "Front desk."

Gideon nodded his understanding and went in search of the internal telephone. Following the sound, he located it on the wall near the front door. "This is Bates, the attorney," he informed Harry. "Mrs. Preston has been attacked by an intruder."

"An intruder? Is she all right?"

"She needs a doctor, so send one right up and find a policeman and send him up, too."

Gideon hung up on Harry's sputtered response and hurried back to Mrs. Preston. The color was coming back to her cheeks, but she still looked quite a bit the worse for wear, although that didn't distract from her appeal. She wasn't what was typically called beautiful, but she was striking, with large dark eyes and creamy white skin. Her hat had fallen off in the struggle and pulled most of her hairpins with it, leaving her thick dark hair to tumble every which way. She brushed it impatiently out of her face when Gideon reached her.

"I told Harry to send up a doctor and a policeman."

"No police," she said, her voice a little stronger now.

"You'll need to report this."

The look she gave him said that she disagreed, but she said, "Help me up."

"Are you sure? You might be injured."

"He hit me in the face and tried to choke me, but I can still walk if you help me get up."

Now Gideon could see a bruise already darkening along her jawline. What kind of a man would punch a woman in the face? He gave her what assistance he could, given his own shaky condition, and together they made their way to the parlor, where he saw her seated in the lone armchair.

"Can I get you something? A glass of water?"

She smiled grimly at that. "Only if it has a shot of whiskey in it."

Well, well, Mrs. Preston was indeed a very different sort of lady. He cast about for something with which to fulfill her request, and she finally pointed to a cabinet along the far wall. He found a bottle and two glasses and poured them each a dram.

She took the glass with both hands, neither of

which was quite steady, and downed the amber liquid in one gulp. Not to be outdone, Gideon downed his as well.

"Did you know him? The man who attacked you, I mean," Gideon asked, taking the glass from her unresisting hands and setting it down on a nearby end table.

"No." She rubbed her throat again. "He tried to choke me to death."

"I can see that. I hate to make you talk, but can you tell me what happened?"

"He was here when I got here. The door wasn't locked, even though I always lock it when I leave. With Tommy gone, I try to be careful. So I thought that was funny, but I wasn't scared until I heard a noise. I should've run out again, I guess, but . . ."

"Was he lying in wait for you?" If the intruder's intent had been to rape her, that was what he would have been doing.

"No, he was in the bedroom."

"The bedroom? What was he doing in there?"

"Searching."

"Searching for what?"

"I . . ." She rubbed her neck again. "I think I'd like some water now."

Gideon found a small kitchen at the end of the hall, passing two bedrooms and a dining room on his way. A small servant's room opened off of the kitchen. Tom Preston had chosen a place where he and his family could live quite comfortably. So sad that he wouldn't be coming home to enjoy it.

He found a glass and filled it from the tap. On his way back, he looked more closely into the bedrooms and saw the one that was obviously the master bedroom had been ransacked. Drawers had been pulled out and their contents tossed onto the floor. He took the water into the parlor, and she drank it thirstily.

"Do you know what he was looking for?"

"No. I don't have anything valuable here, not even any money, just a few dollars in my purse. I use the bank downstairs whenever I need something."

And why would someone choose this particular apartment out of the more than three hundred in this building? Or any apartment in this building at all for that matter, in broad daylight with so many people coming and going who might notice someone who didn't belong? And why would he have started his search in her bedroom?

Probably because people didn't hide important papers in their living rooms.

The guilt that had been nagging at Gideon now blossomed into dread. "Do you keep anything important in your bedroom, Mrs. Preston?"

"No, just my clothes and . . ." To Gideon's horror, her expression told him she'd just realized what he had most feared. "And Tommy's will."

She jumped up from the chair and moved with surprising speed out of the parlor and down the hall. He'd taken only a few steps to follow when she emerged from the ransacked room holding an empty tin box, the kind in which poor people stored valuables they wanted to protect from fire. The flimsy lock had been no match for the beefy hands of Mrs. Preston's assailant. She held it up so he could see it was empty.

"Your husband's will was in that?"

"Yes, and our marriage certificate. He stole them! He stole them both! What will I do now? I can't even prove we were married!" she wailed.

"That's not a problem," Gideon assured her, taking her arm and gently leading her back to the chair. "Your marriage is registered at the courthouse. You can always get a replacement certificate."

"And you have a copy of Tommy's will. He told me you do," she said, looking up hopefully as she still clutched the empty tin box.

"Yes, but—"

Mercifully, the sound of men's voices in the hall distracted them before Gideon had to tell her the awful truth.

"Mrs. Preston?" Harry called.

"We're in here," Gideon called back.

He went to greet Harry, who had brought along a fortyish man with an impressive set of side-burns and a black leather doctor's bag.

"I'm so sorry this happened, Mrs. Preston," Harry was saying as the doctor went straight to where she was sitting and set his bag on the floor beside her chair. "I don't know how . . . I mean, nothing like this ever happened before."

Gideon suspected it might never happen again, either, but he didn't say so. "Did you send for a policeman?"

The doctor was gently removing the tin box from Mrs. Preston's hands and asking her where she had been injured.

Harry was trying to watch them and respond to Gideon's questions at the same time, with unsatisfactory results. "What? Oh yes. I sent the doorman to find someone. Was it a burglar?"

"Yes, although Mrs. Preston said she didn't keep anything of value here."

"Why would someone try to rob her then? And why pick her apartment when we've got so many that are . . . bigger?"

Gideon guessed he actually meant they were "the homes of much richer people." Gideon would have wondered that, too, if he still believed the man had been an ordinary burglar. Since he had no answer, he gave none, instead watching the doctor minister to his patient.

Mrs. Preston and the doctor spoke softly as he examined her jaw and her neck and looked in her throat. He listened to her heart and took her pulse. Then she leaned in and whispered something in his ear, laying a hand protectively over her stomach as she did.

Gideon didn't need to hear what she'd said. The hand on her stomach told him she'd revealed she was with child. Naturally, she'd be worried after an attack like that. So Gideon's suspicions were wrong, and he found himself glad of it. Tom might have left the world too soon, but at least he hadn't been deceived. But someone had just stolen his child's legacy, and Gideon knew he was at least partially to blame.

"Hello?" another voice called, and Gideon went to meet the policeman who had finally arrived. Harry followed closely on his heels. Between the two of them, they explained what had happened. By that time, the doctor had completed his examination and recommended that Mrs. Preston get some rest.

The policeman asked a few questions, but Mrs. Preston had little information to give him. She didn't know the man, had never seen him before, had no idea why he had chosen her apartment, and probably wouldn't recognize him if she saw him again, or so she claimed. Plainly, she didn't like the police at all, or more likely, she just didn't trust them. In any case, the cop mumbled something about a detective coming to see her later to get more details and left. By then the doctor was gone, too, leaving Gideon and Harry to comfort the stricken woman.

"Is there someone you'd like us to send for?" Gideon asked. "A friend to sit with you?"

"I . . . No, I can't think of anyone." She glanced at Harry and frowned, as if she wished him gone.

"Harry," Gideon said, "would you step out into the hallway a moment so I can consult with Mrs. Preston?"

Harry didn't like it, but he did as Gideon requested.

When they were alone, she said, "It was Fred, wasn't it?"

"Who attacked you?"

"No," she snapped, impatient with his stupidity. "Fred sent him. To get the will."

"We don't know that for certain, of course." Gideon couldn't forget his legal training. "But it does seem likely."

"And he got what he wanted, didn't he? But you've got a copy of the will, so it's just like the marriage certificate, right?"

"Not exactly," Gideon said, using the soft voice he used when breaking bad news to a client. "Only the signed copy of the will is valid."

"What does that mean?"

"It means that under the law, if we can't produce the signed copy of the will Tom made leaving everything to you, then his earlier will is the one that will stand, leaving everything to his brother."

"But I'm his wife!" she cried, tears filling her eyes. "It's not right."

"No, it isn't. The law often isn't fair, I'm afraid." A truth he'd only recently accepted.

"Isn't there anything I can do? Tommy wanted to take care of me. Of *us*." Her hand went to her stomach again.

"I know he did, and . . . Well, there are some legal steps we can take, a lawsuit perhaps, although a man would have to file it on your behalf, since women can't instigate lawsuits. But even if we do sue him, these things take time. In the meantime, you need to be safe."

"I'm safe now, aren't I?" she said bitterly. "He's got the will."

"But I don't think he knows about the baby. You didn't tell him, did you?"

She perked up at this. "No, I didn't. I thought . . . Well, I didn't think he deserved to know."

"Good. But it's not a secret you can keep forever, so you need to be safe while we see what we can do. Is there someplace you can go? Do you have family somewhere?"

"No." The word seemed to echo in the quiet apartment, telling Gideon more than he wanted to know about this woman.

"All right. Let me telephone my mother. She'll know of . . . of something. I'll leave Harry here to guard you. Is that all right?"

She nodded.

Harry, of course, was more than happy to guard Mrs. Preston, but when Gideon reached the telephone in the lobby and placed his call, he discovered that his mother was not at home and not expected back until that evening.

When he made his way back upstairs, he told Mrs. Preston, "My mother was out, so I telephoned my fiancée. She's on her way over, and between us we'll figure out how to keep you safe."

CHAPTER THREE

E lizabeth could hardly believe that Gideon had telephoned her to ask for help. Of course, she was more than a little annoyed because he hadn't taken her with him to visit Mrs. Preston in the first place, but the fact that he'd turned to her now inclined her to forgive him his earlier lapse in judgment.

She'd always been curious about the Ansonia, too, so the opportunity to see the enormous apartment building firsthand also made her willing to excuse Gideon's remarkable error. She took a moment to look around the luxurious lobby, with its richly wood-paneled walls and ornately gilded ceilings, and marvel at all the conveniences available and the fact that they had live seals in the fountain. Then she made her way over to the front desk, where a harried young man was attempting to look dignified. He would have had more success if he hadn't been fruitlessly trying to grow a mustache.

"I'm here to see Mrs. Preston," she told him.

"Are you Mr. Bates's fiancée?" he asked with obvious relief. "I should probably take you up myself." He leaned across the counter and whispered, "There may be a dangerous man in the building."

Elizabeth nodded solemnly, having gathered as much from Gideon's cryptic telephone call, and she allowed him to come out from this sanctuary and escort her to the bank of elevators. The operator took them to the sixth floor, and the clerk led the way down the hall and around the corner to one of many doors that opened into the many apartments on this floor. He rapped loudly and said, "It's me, Harry."

The door opened, and Gideon stepped out and looked up and down the hallway, as if searching for that dangerous man, before letting his gaze settle on her. "Thank you so much for coming, Elizabeth."

His obvious relief banished any trace of annoyance she might still have been feeling, and she allowed him to usher her into the apartment.

"Is there anything I can do?" the clerk asked.

Gideon assured him there was not and sent him on his way. Meanwhile, Elizabeth had found the parlor and saw a young woman lying on the sofa. Gideon or someone had fetched a pillow for her head, but she still looked remarkably uncomfortable.

Like Elizabeth, she wore a dark skirt and a white shirtwaist, which was practically a uniform for women in the warm weather. Mrs. Preston's clothes weren't quite the same quality as Elizabeth's, but she supposed Mrs. Preston was used to buying her wardrobe in a department store. Mrs. Preston herself was about what Elizabeth had expected, pretty enough to attract male attention and fulsome enough to promise all manner of fleshly delights. In short, a lonely soldier's dream.

"Hello. I'm Elizabeth Miles, and you must be Mrs. Preston," she said, stepping into the room.

Mrs. Preston took in Elizabeth with one glance, evaluating her in return, and said, "Pleased to meet you."

She didn't sound pleased at all, but Elizabeth figured being attacked in your own home gave a person the right to be a little grouchy.

Gideon came in then. "I see you've met."

"What happened?" Elizabeth asked him, then turned to Mrs. Preston. "How badly are you hurt?"

"Not badly, the doctor said," Gideon hurried to explain. "He choked her . . . the man, not the doctor. The doctor said to rest her throat as much as possible for a few days."

"He choked you?" Elizabeth asked her in outrage. "You mean, he tried to *kill* you?"

Fury flashed in Mrs. Preston's dark eyes, and she nodded grimly.

Elizabeth turned to Gideon. "And you saved her?"

"Hardly. I merely arrived in the nick of time. Scared him off, I guess, and then he ran."

"Oh, Gideon, I'm sure you're far too modest. Mrs. Preston owes you her life, and that's that. Now, what service is it you thought I could perform, since you have already dealt with the worst of it?"

"She lives here alone."

Which seemed perfectly ordinary to Elizabeth. "Perhaps if you tell me exactly what happened, I will understand. You were rather vague on the telephone."

"Because the operators are always listening in," Gideon said, "and I didn't want the Ansonia to get a bad reputation or for Mrs. Preston's attack to end up in the newspapers."

"Of course, but I think it's safe to tell me now."

So he did, as briefly as possible.

"Oh, my poor darling," Elizabeth said when he'd finished. "Are you hurt?"

"Not at all," he assured her testily. "But he did manage to steal Tom Preston's will."

"Oh dear."

"And of course he tried to strangle Mrs. Preston, so if that was his real goal, she won't be safe living here by herself."

Elizabeth turned to Mrs. Preston, who had been following their conversation with avid attention. "Do you think he came here to murder you?"

She winced at Elizabeth's bluntness, but she said, "I don't think so. He was really surprised

66

when he saw me. I don't think he expected me to come home when I did."

Elizabeth turned to Gideon. "He probably tried to kill her so she wouldn't be able to identify him."

"So he might come back to finish the job, if that was his intention. In either case, she's not safe here."

"Do you have any family who could take you in?" she asked Mrs. Preston.

"She doesn't," Gideon replied for her. "I already asked, which is why I telephoned Mother, but she wasn't home, so . . ." He shrugged.

Elizabeth planted her fists on her hips. "Are you saying I wasn't your first choice?"

Gideon saw his error immediately. "You are always my first choice, darling, but my mother has a lot more experience with . . . with . . ." He gestured helplessly.

"With rescuing endangered matrons?" Elizabeth supplied helpfully.

"Yes."

"I doubt it, although I'm sure she'd be extremely good at it if the need arose," she added for Mrs. Preston's benefit. "I, on the other hand, do have a bit of experience rescuing people, so I know exactly what we should do. Is it safe for you to be moved?"

Elizabeth was gratified to see Mrs. Preston lay her hand protectively over her stomach. At least the baby was real. She hoped Gideon had noticed. "The doctor said I should rest, but I think that's just because my head aches. That feckin' rat bag socked me in the jaw before he choked me."

Rat bag? Mrs. Preston certainly had a colorful vocabulary. "You poor thing. Do you feel up to a ride in a taxi? After we get where we're going, you can lie down and sleep until morning if you like."

"Do you really think—"

"Yes, I do think you'll be in danger here, and even if you disagree, are you willing to take a chance of that man coming back?"

Mrs. Preston winced, and Elizabeth knew she'd made her point.

"You just rest. I'll pack your things."

Gideon had watched this exchange in amazement, and he followed Elizabeth to the ransacked bedroom, stopping just outside the doorway, as was proper. "Where are you taking her?" he whispered.

"To Cybil's." Which was where Elizabeth lived as well. "She's got several spare rooms that she keeps for when her starving-artist friends are really starving and need a place to stay. She can stay there, and I can keep an eye on her. Besides, Fred Preston doesn't even know I exist."

"You think Fred was behind it?"

"Of course. Who else would break into someone's apartment and only steal a piece of paper? Don't you agree?"

"Yes, I do, but I was hoping I was leaping to irrational conclusions."

Elizabeth had found a cheap cardboard suitcase and laid it open on the bed. She began to sort through the clothing strewn around the room for the essentials. "What are you going to do about all this?"

"The mess?" he asked in obvious confusion, glancing around the room.

"No, about the *situation*," Elizabeth said, frowning her disappointment in him.

"Oh, I had a policeman up here. They're going to send a detective to investigate."

"And he will do absolutely nothing, especially if Fred Preston spreads a little money around, and I'm sure he will. No, what are *you* going to do about it?"

"I haven't figured that out yet. My, uh, legal options are limited."

"What are they?" Elizabeth scooped up another armload of clothes and began to fold and pack them.

"If Tom had died without a will, his wife and child would have inherited everything, so Mrs. Preston would be justified in suing the estate for support, at least until the child turns twenty-one."

"How long will that take?"

"A while, and of course, there's no guarantee she'll win."

"And even if she does, she won't be as rich as Tom intended, not if she just gets *support*."

"True. Of course, if we could prove Fred was behind the attack on Mrs. Preston . . ."

"But we'd need the police for that, wouldn't we?"

Gideon frowned. "If we hoped to prevail at trial, yes."

"So it's up to us."

"Us?"

"Yes, and by that, I mean you, with my help."

"Elizabeth, a woman was almost murdered here today."

"Which is the only reason I'm allowing you to be in charge. I knew you'd be too protective to let me do it. There now," she added, having managed to fit Mrs. Preston's entire wardrobe into the suitcase. "I just need to check in the bathroom."

This room was across the hall, and she was back in a moment with a collection of toiletries, which she stuffed into the corners of the suitcase before closing and latching it.

"Can that extremely nervous fellow at the front desk round up a cab and have it waiting for us when we get downstairs, do you suppose?" she asked Gideon.

"I'm sure he can."

While they waited, she managed to stuff Mrs.

Preston's unfortunate hats into one hatbox—maybe she would let Elizabeth advise her about buying some more tasteful accessories—and help Mrs. Preston rearrange her hair and replace the hat that had fallen off in the attack.

"Who is Cybil?" Mrs. Preston asked when she'd secured her hat with a long hatpin.

A lot of good it had done them to whisper. "My aunt. I live with her, too."

"So I heard. Where is she?"

"In Greenwich Village. She's a professor at Hunter College. No one will ever look for you there."

"A woman professor? I never heard of such a thing."

Elizabeth imagined there were a great many things Mrs. Preston had never heard of. She was about to be exposed to a lot of them at Cybil's house.

Gideon saw them safely to Cybil's house, and Elizabeth sent him back to his office to begin whatever actions he decided to take on Mrs. Preston's behalf. No one was at home, since Cybil and her dear friend Zelda were still at the college. Elizabeth got Mrs. Preston settled in one of the upstairs guest rooms.

By then the bruise on her jaw had darkened, and she truly looked exhausted. Elizabeth helped her get undressed and tucked her into bed.

"Don't go," Mrs. Preston said when Elizabeth started to leave. "Can you sit with me awhile?"

Elizabeth got the chair from the dressing table and moved it over beside the bed. "I'm sure you must be very frightened, after what happened, but you're perfectly safe here. My aunt and her friend will be thrilled that you've come to visit. They have a salon every Monday evening—that's when a bunch of people get together to talk—so there will be a lot of people in the house tonight, but no one will bother you up here. You're free to join us if you like, but I imagine you'd rather rest. And don't worry. They aren't a rowdy bunch. Mostly they just argue over poets."

"Why would anyone argue about poets?"

"I have no idea. I didn't have a chance before, but I'd just like to say how very sorry I am about your husband."

To Elizabeth's dismay, Mrs. Preston's eyes instantly filled with tears. "He was too good for this world, my Tommy."

"Mr. Bates thought very highly of him," Elizabeth hastily continued, "and considering how he went to all the trouble to make a new will, Mr. Preston must have loved you very much."

"It's not what you think."

Elizabeth was pretty sure it was exactly what she thought, but she said, "I don't know what you mean."

"Me and Tommy. He was a swell, and I'm a

nobody. That's what his brother called me, a nobody, and that was one of the nicer things he called me. But I know you think I tricked Tommy into marrying me."

"It's really none of my business," Elizabeth said with uncharacteristic honesty.

"But I need your help, so you need to understand. I loved Tommy."

"I'm sure you did," Elizabeth said, back to lying again.

"Not at first," she clarified, tears filling her eyes once more. "I met him at a dance out at the camp. Did you ever go to one of those dances?"

"No."

"They'd have them every Saturday for the recruits. Some of my friends had been going out for them, so I decided to try it. We'd take the train. It was only an hour. A bit of fun. What was the harm?"

Elizabeth nodded. What indeed?

"I'd only been a few times when I met Tommy. He was different from the other boys. You could tell just by looking at him. He talked real nice and had manners, and he could dance like an angel. Never stepped on my foot, not once."

He probably did stand out in a crowd of raw recruits. Gideon had said he should have been an officer, but he'd chosen not to be.

"He liked me right off, too. I don't know why he picked me out of all the girls. I wasn't the prettiest one, not by a long shot, but he liked me best. Maybe because I listened to him. I don't know, but my friends, they said I should try to hook him. You could tell he had money, and where would I ever meet another man like that? Not one who looked twice at me, I mean."

Elizabeth didn't think she wanted to hear the rest of this story. "Shouldn't you be resting your throat?"

"It doesn't even hurt anymore. So I let him do it. That's what my friends said would hook him. Then I could tell him there was a baby and he'd marry me. He'd have to if there was a baby. I didn't love him. Not then. Not yet, at least. But after we did it, he . . . he didn't even wait. He said we had to get married right away. He said it was the right thing to do, so of course I said yes. This was my chance, and I wasn't going to miss it. Lucky thing, too, since there really is a baby, or at least there is now."

So Gideon had been right, at least about part of it. "But you said you didn't love him *yet*."

"Not at the start, but he was so good to me. Nobody was ever so good to me, Miss Miles. He thought I was funny and smart and clever. Even when I did something wrong or said something awful, he'd just laugh. I told him I was sorry I wasn't a real lady, not like you." Elizabeth managed not to wince, since she wasn't a real lady, either. "But he said he didn't care. He said he'd had his fill of real ladies and what he wanted was me."

By that point, she was sobbing, and Elizabeth pulled out her own handkerchief and offered it to her guest. Then she went to fetch a glass of warm water with some honey in it, which Mrs. Preston drank gratefully.

When Mrs. Preston was calm again, Elizabeth said, "You should get some rest now."

But Mrs. Preston caught her hand when she would have turned away. "I loved him—I really did—and I'm going to take care of his baby and be a good mother to him. You'll see."

"I know. Go to sleep now. I'll bring you up some supper in a little while."

Elizabeth closed the door quietly behind her and went downstairs to await the return of her housemates so she could explain their visitor's presence.

Gideon was a bit surprised to see Elizabeth greeting people as they arrived for the salon that evening. He'd half expected her to still be tending to Mrs. Preston. As usual, he had escorted Anna to the salon. She really enjoyed these affairs, especially since she had decided to attend college. Gideon only attended as an excuse to spend the evening with Elizabeth, who was no more interested in the literary discussions than he was.

"Gideon told me all about your new house-guest," Anna was saying after greeting Elizabeth. They were still standing in the foyer, where they would have a bit of privacy until the next batch of guests arrived. They always seemed to arrive in groups.

"Did you tell her everything?" Elizabeth asked in some surprise.

"It seemed the wisest course," Gideon said, hanging his straw boater on the hat tree. "I figured it would save you the trouble. How is she?"

"She slept most of the afternoon and then she ate a little supper. I would have tried to convince her to come down for a while this evening except her face is terribly bruised and I knew she wouldn't want people asking her questions. She hasn't even met Cybil and Zelda yet, although they're quite anxious to see her."

"Poor thing," Anna said. "Imagine being nearly killed and driven out of your own home. So what are you going to do for her?"

"Besides keep her safe for the moment, you mean?" Elizabeth asked. "I'm not sure what we *can* do for her."

Gideon wouldn't have believed it if he hadn't seen these two in action before. They both looked like butter wouldn't melt in their mouths, and yet they were conspiring against him right in front of him and without even planning it out ahead of time. He sighed in exasperation. "I told you, I will do what I can, but I can't guarantee anything."

"Maybe you can convince this brother . . . What's his name?" Anna asked ingenuously.

"Fred," Elizabeth supplied.

"Perhaps you can convince Fred to honor his brother's will after all," Anna concluded.

"That will certainly be my first step," Gideon said.

"Although," Elizabeth said with apparent innocence, "if he hired someone to break into Mrs. Preston's apartment and steal the will in the first place, he must be determined to cheat her out of getting anything at all from Tom's estate."

"In which case," Anna said, "he probably isn't going to be interested in doing anything for her as a mere favor."

"The threat of a lawsuit might make him more cooperative, though," Gideon said. "A jury could award Mrs. Preston one-third of the company, as Tom intended, whereas he might be able to buy her off with a much smaller settlement that would still allow her to live in comfort."

Elizabeth gave him a pitying look. "But that would require Fred Preston to be a reasonable man. Do you think it's possible Fred Preston is a reasonable man, Anna?"

"Not for a moment."

"I'm also afraid a jury of men would take

Fred's side and decide Rose is a gold digger who doesn't deserve anything at all, so your lawsuit would gain her nothing," Elizabeth said.

"But he probably wouldn't think of that, at least not right off, and most men will usually do whatever is necessary to save themselves trouble," Gideon reasoned, "which is why I have to at least offer him that opportunity."

"I guess we can't argue with that," Elizabeth said.

"No, we can't, although if I were you, I'd go ahead and figure out what you'll do when Fred Preston refuses to save himself some trouble," Anna said. "Is Jake coming tonight?"

"I never know what that boy is going to do," Elizabeth said.

Gideon blinked at the sudden change of topic. "Since when are you interested in Jake?"

"I find him fascinating," Anna said. "He claims to hate these gatherings, but then he'll drop in and stay for hours."

"He's probably looking for potential marks," Elizabeth said. She didn't have a high opinion of her half brother's intellectual curiosity.

"But nobody here has any money."

"Maybe he doesn't know that," Gideon said.

"Maybe, but I think he comes because he likes the women here," Anna said.

"I hope you aren't leading him on," Elizabeth said.

"Oh no. I already told him I'm not interested in men, but I don't think that's what intrigues him about us. I think he genuinely enjoys listening to us talk about ideas."

"Really?" Elizabeth said in wonder. "Jake? My *brother,* Jake?"

"The very same."

As if they'd summoned him, Jake Miles stepped through the front door at that moment, having not bothered to knock. For the first time since Gideon had known him, Jake wore a conservative suit instead of the loud checks he usually favored, although he still had his straw boater pushed back so the brim stuck almost straight up, the way the dashing youngbloods wore them. "What's this?" he asked, eyeing their little group with a grin. "If you're planning a job, count me in."

"Anna was just asking if you were coming tonight," Elizabeth said with a mischievous glance at Anna, who refused to be embarrassed.

"I've missed you the past few weeks. Miss Adams even asked about you," Anna said.

Gideon had to cover a smile. The octogenarian Miss Adams's interest was not something Jake would welcome.

"I've been busy. On a job," Jake added with a trace of pride.

Gideon could never approve of his future in-law's choice of a profession, but at least Jake seemed to have regained the confidence he'd lost after a con had gone very bad for him.

Jake turned to Gideon. "The Old Man says you're getting called up."

Gideon didn't dare look at Elizabeth. "That's right."

"The Old Man could get you off, you know."

"Yes," Elizabeth said with just a trace of sarcasm. "Poor Jake can't serve because he has flat feet."

Jake frowned. "No, I don't. I have a bad heart."

"You poor boy," Anna said without a trace of sympathy, since they all knew the army doctor who had found Jake's *bad heart* had been duly compensated.

"I don't want to get off," Gideon said. "I wish everyone would quit trying to convince me to shirk my patriotic duty."

"We just don't want you to die, dear friend," Anna said, patting Gideon's cheek. "Come on, Jake. Everyone is eager to see you."

Jake flipped his hat onto the hat tree next to Gideon's and obediently followed Anna into the parlor. Gideon started after them, dumbfounded by Anna's bald statement.

Elizabeth said, "I should check on Mrs. Preston," and hurried up the stairs. Was she crying? Dear Lord, how on earth was he going to get through this?

Elizabeth blinked furiously, determined not to cry as she rushed up the stairs to the one room into which she knew Gideon would not follow her. She hated to disturb Mrs. Preston, but she needed a moment to compose herself. After a perfunctory tap, she went on in without waiting for permission. With any luck, Mrs. Preston would be asleep anyway.

Mrs. Preston was not asleep. She was sitting at the dressing table, brushing her amazingly luxurious black hair. She wore a beautiful silk kimono over her nightdress and was a vision of loveliness. No wonder Tom Preston had been smitten. She turned in surprise when Elizabeth stepped into the room. Elizabeth closed the door and leaned against it for a moment while she composed herself.

"Are you all right?" Mrs. Preston asked.

"I should be asking you that."

"I know, but you look upset. Did something happen? Did that man—"

"No, nothing like that," Elizabeth hastily assured her. "I just . . . Someone reminded me that my fiancé is being drafted soon."

Mrs. Preston smiled sadly. "And you remembered what happened to my Tommy."

Elizabeth drew a shaky breath. "I don't know what came over me. I'm usually much better at controlling myself." She pressed her fingers to her eyes to stop the tears before they could fall.

"I didn't have any choice about it. Tommy was already in the army when I met him, and by the time I really started to love him, he shipped out."

"I think it's the waiting. We've known for months that they were going to raise the draft age, and Gideon just missed the cutoff the last time, so he was sure to be called up. I guess I was hoping the war would end before that happened."

"I wish it had ended before Tommy had to go. He didn't mind, though. He wanted to go. He said if Americans didn't fight, the Germans would invade us next. I don't know how they would've gotten across the ocean, but I guess they could've used ships or something."

"Gideon says we can't let anyone get away with invading another country for no reason. If we don't stop it now, the world will end in chaos."

"Where's that?"

Elizabeth smiled in spite of herself. "It's a very bad place. How are you feeling? No problems with the baby, I hope."

"No, nothing, thank heaven. My jaw is awful sore." She touched it gingerly as if to confirm her statement. "But my neck is better."

Bruises were forming there, too, but Elizabeth didn't mention them. "I hope the noise from downstairs isn't disturbing you."

"Oh no. It's kind of comforting having so many people around. There were a lot of people at the

Ansonia, too, but the walls are so thick, we can't hear each other."

"I suppose that's a good thing."

"Usually. Tommy said they built it that way so musicians could practice in their apartments without disturbing anybody else. I know I never heard any music the whole time I lived there, but it's no good if you need to call for help."

"I guess not, but you can call for help here, and everyone will hear you. Can I get you anything?"

"No. I . . . I was going to go back to bed when I finished brushing my hair. Tommy loved my hair." She touched the dark fall and sighed.

Better change the subject. "That's a lovely kimono."

"Tommy bought it for me. I hardly had any decent clothes when I met him. I worked in the shirtwaist factory, but they don't pay much, so . . ."

Was there no topic that wouldn't remind her of Tommy? Before Elizabeth could think of one, someone tapped on the door. Had Gideon followed her anyway?

Elizabeth opened the door a crack and was relieved to see it was only Anna.

"Is Mrs. Preston receiving visitors?"

"Who is it?" Mrs. Preston asked in alarm.

"My friend Anna. I think she would like to meet you, if you feel up to it."

"I suppose."

Elizabeth opened the door all the way, and Anna stepped in. Elizabeth introduced them.

"I'm very pleased to meet you," Anna said. "Elizabeth told me what happened. You must be very brave to have confronted that man in the first place."

"I think I was just foolish. I never thought about him hurting me. I was just mad because he'd messed up my bedroom."

"Do you think you'd recognize him if you saw him again?"

Elizabeth gaped at her in amazement. *"Anna . . . ,"* she tried, but Mrs. Preston was giving her question serious consideration.

"I think so. His ugly mug was the last thing I saw when I thought I was going to die. Oh, and I scratched him. On the cheek, I think, and both his hands when he was choking me."

"Did you tell the police this?" Elizabeth asked.

Mrs. Preston's expression told her what a foolish question that was. "Why bother? They aren't going to do anything. He didn't kill me, and he didn't steal anything valuable, so they don't care."

Which was exactly what Elizabeth had told Gideon. "But you could identify him if you saw him again."

"I think so. I'm not likely to see him again, though, am I?"

"If he works for Fred Preston, you might."

"I hadn't thought of that!"

"How will we find him, though?" Anna asked.

"We?" Elizabeth echoed with a grin.

"Well, you and Gideon, although you know I'll help if I can. You never let me do anything, though."

"Do anything about what?" Mrs. Preston asked.

"Sometimes Elizabeth helps Gideon with . . . with things," Anna said, catching herself when she saw Elizabeth's warning glare. "In any case, I'm sure Gideon will be able to convince Fred Preston to have a change of heart."

"That's because you never met Fred Preston. He's a jackeen who doesn't care about anybody but himself."

"Jackeen?" Anna echoed in confusion.

"It means he's not a nice person," Elizabeth explained. "Nevertheless, Gideon will try his best, and when that fails, we will find another way."

"We will?" Anna asked hopefully.

"By *we,* I meant *I* will."

"But you'll let me help."

"If necessary."

Anna turned back to Mrs. Preston. "She's lying, but I'll help if I can."

"It isn't nice to call someone a liar right to her face," Elizabeth said.

"I did it to Mrs. Preston's face, not yours."

"Oh, please, don't call me Mrs. Preston," she said. "My name is Rose."

"And since we're going to be great friends, please, call me Anna."

"And I am Elizabeth."

"At least she is Elizabeth today," Anna told Rose. "Sometimes she's someone else."

"Why is she someone else?" Rose asked in confusion.

"Because sometimes I need to be, but you don't have to worry about that. Gideon is going to take care of everything."

"I thought you expected him to fail," Anna said.

"He'll fail at his plan, because it can't possibly work, but he will succeed at my plan."

"What is your plan?" Rose asked.

"I don't have one yet, but it will definitely succeed. Now, you need to go back to bed and get some rest. Don't worry about anything, either."

They got Rose tucked up into bed and left her in a state of bemusement.

"Gideon sent me after you," Anna told Elizabeth when they were in the hall again. "He thought he'd made you cry."

"*You* were the one who made me cry, telling him we didn't want him to die."

"Oh dear, I'm so sorry! I didn't mean . . . I'm so, so sorry!"

"You should be. Everyone should be sorry that Gideon has to fight in this stupid war."

"Be careful. I might be working for the League."

"I'll take my chances. I suppose we should go back downstairs."

"And you need to put on a brave face. Gideon is having a very difficult time of it without you making him feel bad for doing what he believes is right."

"Yes, Mother. I'll roll extra bandages this week as penance."

"I'm serious, Elizabeth." And she was.

"I know, dear. I'm serious, too. I'll stop trying to convince Gideon to be a slacker, even though I just moved a young widow into my own house who will be a daily reminder of what could happen. I will really put on my brave face, but you have to promise not to remind me that he might die."

"I promise. Now let's go back downstairs before he thinks you've deserted him."

Elizabeth followed Anna down the stairs, but she couldn't help thinking that maybe her plan for helping Rose Preston should include getting Gideon arrested for something. Nothing serious, of course, but just enough to save him from the draft.

That could be the best plan of all.

CHAPTER FOUR

Gideon didn't really need advice on how to handle Fred Preston, but he knew if he sought it from Roger Devoss, senior partner in Devoss and Van Aken, he would be much more likely to get permission to travel to Poughkeepsie to confront Preston in person. Roger Devoss listened with great interest to Gideon's account of his dealings with the Preston brothers.

"As unpleasant as he may be, you have no proof this Fred Preston was responsible for the attack on Mrs. Preston," Mr. Devoss pointed out.

"That's true, of course, but if he wasn't responsible, he should be willing to at least discuss making a settlement with his brother's widow, for the sake of the child if for no other reason. That's why I feel I need to speak with him in person."

"I see. And who will pay for your time away from the office?"

This was always a concern at Devoss and Van Aken. "I assume that I will succeed in getting a settlement for Mrs. Preston. At that time, I will send her a bill for my services."

"But you may not succeed in getting the settlement."

"Then the firm will have to struggle through without those fees." Gideon was happy to note he did not sound at all sarcastic.

Mr. Devoss wasn't too pleased with this answer, but he couldn't take offense. Gideon brought more income into the firm than any of the other attorneys. "I suppose you'll also tell me it's the right thing to do for one of our fallen soldiers."

"I was hoping I wouldn't have to mention that, but yes."

Mr. Devoss smiled grimly. "Well, I can't have you reporting me to the League for being unpatriotic. All right, go to Poughkeepsie and see what you can accomplish with this fellow, but don't be disappointed if he refuses to help Mrs. Preston. If he's making as much money as everyone else in this war, he won't want to share it with anyone."

"And he's already annoyed with me because I wouldn't tell him about his brother's will, but I have to at least try. He might have calmed down by now, too, and he should also be grieving his brother. I'm hoping that will soften his heart at least a little."

"If he has a heart. The stories I've heard about these war profiteers . . . Well, no use complaining about something we can't change. Go to Poughkeepsie, and let me know what happens."

"Thank you, Mr. Devoss."

He waved away Gideon's gratitude. "How is your mother doing?"

Gideon couldn't help smiling. "She's well. She's very busy with her war work, of course. The suffragists are proving their patriotism by being the most industrious of all the volunteers for the war effort."

"I'm not surprised Hazel is at the forefront of the efforts."

"Neither am I. Oh, by the way, we were just saying the other day that we should invite you over for dinner," Gideon said, sure his mother would have told him to do this if she'd thought of it, even though she usually didn't like to encourage Mr. Devoss's interest in her.

"I would be honored," Roger said with obvious delight.

"Not on Meatless Monday or Wheatless Wednesday, of course. Perhaps Friday evening?"

"That would be fine. I shall look forward to it. And thank your mother for me."

"I certainly will." Whether his mother would thank Gideon in return remained to be seen.

Rose came down to breakfast in time to meet Cybil and Zelda before they left for the day. She was obviously quite interested in these *lady professors*.

Elizabeth's aunt Cybil was an imposing figure, statuesque with dark hair and the same blue eyes as her niece. Zelda, in contrast, was petite and blond. Today they looked quite ordinary in their dark skirts and shirtwaists, although Cybil preferred to dress more flamboyantly when she could. She compromised with a bright red scarf tied in a bow at her throat. Zelda, on the other hand, was always the prim and proper lady.

"Elizabeth said you're teachers," Rose said with some awe. "At a college."

"That's right, dear," Zelda said. "I teach literature, and Cybil teaches history."

"History," Rose said with a touch of contempt. "I never understood why we had to learn about all that old stuff."

Cybil smiled beneficently. "Because if you don't know the mistakes people made in the past, you're probably going to make the same ones all over again."

"And even still, people never learn, which is why we're fighting this horrible war," Zelda added.

"I thought we were fighting because the Germans are trying to take over Europe," Rose said with a frown.

"As various countries have tried to do time and again for centuries, always without success," Cybil confirmed with a sigh. "If they had only consulted me, I could have explained that the other countries would fight to the last man to stop them."

"Do you really think they'll fight to the last man?" Rose asked in alarm.

"Hopefully, they will come to their senses long before that," Zelda said, giving Cybil a warning look. "I'm afraid we need to be off, but we'll see you at dinner tonight, Mrs. Preston."

Elizabeth saw them out, making sure the front door was locked behind them. Not that she expected anyone to find them, but there was no sense taking chances.

"Your face doesn't look as bad as I expected it to," Elizabeth remarked when she rejoined Rose in the dining room.

Rose instinctively touched her discolored jaw. "It's still too bad for me to go out, though. What were you planning to do today?"

"Stay here with you, I suppose, in case you need anything. I don't think you have to hide in the house, though. As long as you don't go back to the Ansonia, no one is likely to find you and follow you back here. I have a hat with a veil that would cover your face, if you'd like to borrow it."

Rose simply stared at Elizabeth for a few moments. "Why are you doing this for me?"

Elizabeth opened her mouth to reply with something flippant, but she realized she had nothing flippant to say. "I . . . Because Gideon thought very highly of your husband and wants to see you taken care of, as your husband wished."

"But what does he get out of it? Nobody does something like this for nothing."

Ah, now Elizabeth understood. In fact, she understood only too well. Last year at this time, Elizabeth wouldn't have believed it, either. People—at least the people she knew—were only interested in doing whatever would benefit them. You might do a favor for a good friend or a relative, but only because that person could return the favor when you needed it. Nobody in his right mind went around helping total strangers. Well, she supposed she'd been vaguely aware that do-gooders did things like that, church people and the like, but only because they were trying to get into heaven or something. Normal people didn't act like that.

Except the normal people she knew now did it all the time. She'd actually done it herself recently. But how to explain it to Rose Preston?

"I think people like Gideon actually enjoy helping other people."

Rose frowned, obviously unconvinced. "Why?"

"It makes them feel good."

"He won't feel good when he has to talk to Fred Preston."

She was probably right. "Yes, but think how good we'll all feel if Fred Preston gives you part of Tom's estate."

Rose didn't look like she believed that would ever happen, but she said, "That would make me happy, but why would you care one way or the other? Or Mr. Bates, for that matter?"

Elizabeth needed only a moment to figure out what would convince Rose. "If Gideon gets Fred to give you a settlement, he'll send you a bill for his services."

"Oh, that makes sense."

Did it? Not really, but it was enough for Rose. Fortunately, Rose didn't ask again why *Elizabeth* was helping her, because she had no answer for that at all.

Poughkeepsie was an easy train ride from New York but so different from the city that it could have been in another realm. Gideon couldn't call Poughkeepsie a sleepy little town, since it wasn't little and it certainly wasn't sleepy. Large businesses had set up shop there because the river provided easy transportation for their goods, and a few millionaires had built mansions along the river north of town to offer an escape from New York's summer heat. Compared to Manhattan, it was a nice change. The war had intruded here, too, however. Posters encouraging men to enlist and women to support the war effort were plastered onto every possible surface, and every house had a kitchen garden patch now withering in the cooling September temperatures.

The Preston Shoes factory lay outside the city limits in an area bordered by farmland. The taxi driver informed Gideon that the trolley ran out there for the convenience of the workers, in case he needed a ride back to town. As he stepped out of the cab and walked toward the sprawling but rather drab building, Gideon began to question the wisdom of coming here with no appointment. What if Preston refused to even see him?

He paused for a moment to give the matter some thought. Oddly, he'd never faced a professional situation where he'd had any doubts about his welcome, which was probably why he hadn't considered the issue until this moment. A few times people had dreaded the news he brought, but that had not affected their willingness to meet with him. In this case, however, Preston might well turn him away, and he would lose what would probably be his only opportunity to make his case. Somehow, he had to compel Fred Preston to at least grant him an interview.

To his great surprise, he needed only a few moments of thought to hit upon the perfect plan. Elizabeth would be proud, if he ever told her, but he probably wouldn't. This wasn't going to be something he wanted to brag about.

Inside, the entry was rather dreary and businesslike, the work of the shoe factory merely a dull roar heard faintly through a large set of doors straight ahead through the lobby. A pretty young woman sat at the receptionist's desk and greeted him with a smile. Gideon noticed with a pang that a photograph of Tom in his uniform had been hung on the wall behind her, draped with black crepe. At least they were pretending to mourn him.

"May I help you?" the receptionist asked.

"I hope so," Gideon said, giving her his friendliest smile. "I'm Gideon Bates. I was . . ." He let his gaze drift to Tom's portrait for a moment and then go back to her. "I was Tom Preston's attorney."

"Oh," she said, her pretty face crumpling with grief. "Poor Mr. Tom. He was such a nice boy. Man, I mean. I forget he was grown-up. He was a boy when I knew him, and then he went away to school. . . ."

"I didn't know him long myself, but he seemed like a very fine fellow. He was married, did you know?"

"Married?" This was certainly news to her, and Gideon would have bet a week's pay it would be general knowledge in the shoe factory before the day was out. "No, I never . . . Who did he marry?"

"A young lady he met in New York, I think."

"They couldn't have been married very long, then."

"Not long at all, I'm sorry to say. But, of course, he provided for her, and I need to meet with Mr. Fred Preston to work out the arrangements. Is he in?"

She frowned. "Did you have an appointment?"

"I'm afraid not. I was in the area and hoped I might catch him in his office."

"I don't know. I'm not supposed to send anybody back unless they have an appointment."

"Why don't you ask his secretary if he'll see me? Tell her I'm Tom Preston's attorney and I'm here to see him to make arrangements for Tom's wife's settlement. If he's not available, I'll make an appointment and come back." By which time, everyone in Poughkeepsie would know about Tom's marriage.

The receptionist used the intercom box on her desk to contact Fred's secretary, which had the added advantage of broadcasting her voice not only to those who happened to be going through the lobby as she spoke but to anyone who might have been in the area of the secretary's intercom as well.

"He doesn't have an appointment," the secretary said through the box after the receptionist had explained Gideon's mission.

"But it's for Mr. Tom's wife."

"I didn't even know he had a wife. Does Mr. Preston know?"

"Oh yes," Gideon said at the receptionist's questioning look. "She called on Mr. Preston here, I believe."

The receptionist's eyes grew round. "I remember," she whispered to Gideon without pushing the button on the intercom to speak. "She didn't say she was Mr. Tom's wife, though."

"I'm sure she wanted to break the news to Mr. Preston in person. She also had to tell him his brother had been killed."

The girl nodded solemnly. "Mr. Preston was very upset that day."

"I'm sure he was."

"Dolores, are you still there?" the secretary's voice squawked through the box.

"Oh yes. Sorry. Mr. Preston does know Mr. Tom had a wife. Can I send this gentleman back?"

"Let me check with Mr. Preston first."

Gideon managed not to smile at the thought of Fred Preston's reaction. If he hadn't told the staff about Tom's marriage, he probably hadn't told anyone at all. That would only accelerate the rate at which the gossip spread. Why, people would wonder to one another, had Tom kept the marriage a secret? But even more interesting, why had Fred kept it a secret?

Although infuriating Fred Preston was probably the wrong way to start this interview, Gideon was gratified when Fred's secretary informed the receptionist that she could send Gideon back and Mr. Preston would see him.

Fred's secretary was a neatly dressed older woman who took great interest in Gideon, although she was perfectly correct in her demeanor as she escorted him into Fred's office.

Fred, as Gideon had expected, was livid but holding on to his temper with both hands, at least in front of his secretary. He asked her to close the door behind her, however.

Gideon braced himself for another dose of Fred's fury, but when it came this time, it was icy cold instead of hot.

"What do you want, Bates? I already told you, I'm not giving that woman a penny of my money."

Fred stood behind his desk. He had made no move to greet Gideon or shake his hand, and he had certainly not invited him to sit. Gideon merely smiled in reply and sat down in one of the chairs that had been placed in front of the desk for visitors.

"You've got some nerve coming in here like this and telling my secretary you represent Tom's wife," Preston said, silently surrendering to the visit by sinking back into his own chair.

"I didn't tell your secretary. I told the receptionist," Gideon said.

Fred winced, so Gideon knew he understood he now had no hope of containing the gossip. "What do you want?"

"I wanted to let you know that Mrs. Preston was attacked yesterday."

"Was she?"

He didn't sound nearly as outraged as he should have. Was that because he already knew or because he just didn't care? "Yes. She apparently surprised a burglar in her apartment."

"That's . . . too bad."

"Aren't you going to inquire as to her well-being?"

Fred glared at him across the expanse of his cluttered desk. "I assume she's still alive or you would have told me already."

"You'll be relieved to learn that she's alive and well, except for a few bruises."

"She actually encountered the . . . the burglar, then?" Fred asked. Did he seem surprised?

"Yes. He apparently tried to kill her."

"Surely not," Fred said with some alarm.

Gideon shrugged. "When a man puts his hands around a woman's throat and squeezes until she can't breathe, one must assume he means to kill her."

"That's . . . I can't believe it."

"Why can't you believe it? It happens with alarming frequency, I'm afraid."

"In New York City, perhaps," Fred scoffed.

"This happened in New York City."

"But you only have her word for it," Fred tried, still determined to doubt.

"Oh no, we have my word as well."

"Yours?"

"Yes, I had an appointment with Mrs. Preston, and I arrived just in time to frighten the man off before he could finish what he came to do."

Fred had paled noticeably. "How do you know that's what he came to do?"

Fred had him there. "You're right, of course. We can't know exactly what he *intended* until we find the man and question him, but he certainly *intended* to burglarize Mrs. Preston's apartment because that's what he was doing when she caught him. And he definitely tried to choke her to death because I saw it with my own eyes."

Preston's own eyes narrowed. "You saw the . . . the burglar yourself?"

"Only a glimpse, I'm afraid. But we did notify the police, and they will be investigating." Gideon usually made a point of telling the truth. In this case, he was afraid it was more wishful thinking that the police would investigate, though. "But none of this is why I'm here."

"My secretary said you are here to make arrangements for Tom's estate, but I can't imagine why you need to speak to me about it. You have Tom's will, don't you?"

Did he look a bit too smug? Gideon thought so. "Did I mention that the man who tried to kill Mrs. Preston also robbed her?"

"Robbed her of what?"

"Some important documents."

Preston considered this for a long moment. "Was his will, by any chance, among them?"

Now Gideon was sure he'd known all along. "I'm afraid so, but I do have a copy of the original, so we know what his intentions were toward his wife."

Now Fred relaxed back into his chair and smiled, lacing his fingers across the small mound of his belly. He was confident that he had the upper hand. "But I only have your word for it that Tom actually signed a copy of that will. Perhaps he changed his mind and decided not to sign it at all. Without the original . . ." This time Fred shrugged.

"The will was witnessed, and those witnesses can testify that he signed the original." Gideon looked meaningfully around Fred's office. The room could only have been described as utilitarian. It probably dated to his father's tenure here, and Fred had made no attempt to add opulence with his newfound wealth. Perhaps he understood the good people of Poughkeepsie would frown on such ostentation, particularly when it came from the sacrifices of their young men. And if he cared about their opinion in that matter, he probably cared about it in other matters as well. "Your brother wanted to provide for his wife, Mr. Preston, and she has no other means of support. Without your help, she will find herself destitute, so I will have no choice but to file a lawsuit against his estate."

"File all the lawsuits you like, Mr. Bates. I'd much rather give my money to lawyers than to that woman."

"Family squabbles like this are always unpleasant, Mr. Preston, but they are much worse when the newspapers get involved, as they would if we make the matter public in a court of law."

Fred squirmed in his chair, but he still refused to be cowed. "When the newspapers find out the kind of woman Tom married, I'm sure public opinion will shift to my side."

Gideon considered all the ways public opinion could be swayed and suddenly realized that keeping Rose's baby a secret was no longer in her best interest. "I'm not sure what kind of a woman you think your brother married, but Mrs. Preston is perfectly respectable. She is also the widow of a war hero who gave his life in the service of his country, leaving behind a bereaved wife and orphaned child who—"

"Child?" Preston echoed in horror. "What's this about a child?"

Gideon feigned surprise. "Didn't you know? Mrs. Preston is expecting. That's the main reason Tom was so determined to make a new will before being shipped out."

"He knew about . . . ? That she was . . . ?" Fred looked like he could hardly breathe.

"Of course he did. I'm sure people would wonder why your sister-in-law had to sue you to get support for your brother's child, particularly after your brother died fighting in the war and when everyone knows how well you've done with your government contracts. Why, it looks almost unpatriotic."

Fred Preston looked like he wanted to strangle Gideon, but he was obviously too well-bred— or too sensible—to actually attempt it in his own office. "I'll need some time to . . . to think about this and to consult with . . . with my own attorneys."

"Of course. I know you want to do the right thing for Mrs. Preston, to honor your brother's memory."

Plainly, he did not, but he said, "Certainly. Good day, Mr. Bates."

Elizabeth knew a moment of alarm when the doorbell rang that afternoon. Reminding herself that no one knew where Rose Preston was hiding, and in any case, hired assassins probably didn't ring the doorbell, she told Rose to stay out of sight in the parlor while she answered the door.

"Mrs. Bates," Elizabeth exclaimed happily, stepping aside to admit Gideon's mother. "What a lovely surprise."

"I should have telephoned to let you know I was coming, but from what Gideon told me, I assumed you and your guest would be staying home today."

"Yes, Mrs. Preston doesn't feel much like going out at the moment." Elizabeth escorted Mrs. Bates into the parlor where Rose had been waiting. Rose jumped to her feet in alarm, but Elizabeth quickly said, "This is Mr. Bates's mother. She's come to see how we're doing."

"Oh, for a minute . . ." Rose laid a hand over her heart and drew a calming breath.

"Who did you think I was?" Mrs. Bates asked.

"I . . . Tommy had a stepmother, you see. I thought maybe . . ." She shrugged helplessly.

"Do you think you have reason to fear her, dear?" Mrs. Bates asked as she removed her gloves and found herself a seat on the sofa where Rose had been sitting. She patted the sofa, indicating Rose should sit down again, which she obediently did. Elizabeth would have to figure out how Mrs. Bates got people to do exactly what she wanted without saying a word. It was quite a gift.

Elizabeth sat down in a chair nearby.

"I don't know if I should be afraid of her or not," Rose was saying, "but Tommy didn't like her much."

"And if she knows where Rose is, that would mean his brother knows, too," Elizabeth observed.

"Yes, I can see that would be a concern. How are you feeling after your ordeal, Mrs. Preston?" Mrs. Bates leaned forward to study Rose's bruised face more closely.

Rose touched it self-consciously. "I'm fine, I guess, except I jump at every noise now."

"A perfectly natural reaction, I'm sure. After

Elizabeth and I were released from prison, I kept waking up in the middle of the night trembling, sure I was back in that horrible place."

This admission clearly startled Rose, who gaped at Mrs. Bates in amazement. "You . . . you were in *prison?*" Her gaze darted to Elizabeth for a moment in disbelief before settling on Mrs. Bates again.

"We were arrested for demonstrating outside the White House for women's rights."

Rose's lovely forehead wrinkled with confusion. "What were you demonstrating that got you arrested?"

Mrs. Bates smiled with infinite patience. "We were marching on the sidewalk out in front of the White House. That's where the president lives, you know."

"What president?"

"The president of the United States. We were carrying signs asking him to support women's suffrage."

"You want women to suffer?"

Elizabeth had to cover a smile, but Mrs. Bates—bless her—did not even blink. "That's an odd word, isn't it? It sounds like suffering, but it actually means the right to vote in political elections. We were trying to convince President Wilson to support a law that would give women the right to vote."

"Why would you want to vote?"

Elizabeth had to admit it was a good question. She'd asked it herself when she was first learning about the women's suffrage movement.

Mrs. Bates smiled again. "Because politicians are elected, and they get elected by convincing people to vote for them. They convince people to vote for them by passing laws that help those people, but if women can't vote at all, no politicians are going to do anything to benefit us, are they?"

"I guess not," Rose said in that wondrous tone Elizabeth had heard other women use when they finally understood. "That President Wilson, he's the one got us into this war, isn't he? I've heard the soldiers complaining about him."

Mrs. Bates exchanged a glance with Elizabeth that reminded her that President Wilson was responsible for Gideon being drafted as well. "Yes, the president is the one who makes the decision for our country to go to war. Where did you hear soldiers complaining about him, dear?"

"At Camp Upton, out on Long Island. My friends and I would go to the dances they have for the soldiers."

"I'm sure that's a lot of fun for you and your friends." Elizabeth could tell from her tone, however, that Mrs. Bates didn't quite approve of such carrying-on.

"It was only an hour on the train each way, and we wanted to meet some soldiers. We tried going to the dances at the *Recruit*, but those were all sailors, and sailors aren't going to see any action, are they? Although now I kind of wish Tommy was a sailor because he'd still be alive, wouldn't he?"

"I'm so terribly sorry, dear." Mrs. Bates took Rose's hand and patted it while Elizabeth pressed a handkerchief into her other one.

Rose took a minute to compose herself, and when she had, Mrs. Bates said, "You said you went to dances at the *Recruit* . . . ?"

"The USS *Recruit*," Elizabeth said. "You know, that ship they built in Union Square?"

"Oh yes. I'd forgotten what they call it."

"I always thought it was a crazy thing to do, building a ship in the middle of the city," Rose said.

Mrs. Bates nodded. "I went to an event there once. They were trying to get us to buy Liberty Bonds, but I thought they only used it to train sailors."

"They mostly use it to *recruit* sailors, I think," Elizabeth said, "which would explain why they have dances there."

"That's right," Rose said, pleased Elizabeth had figured it out. "The boys come to the dances because the girls are there, and the sailors try to recruit them into the navy."

"But don't all the young men get drafted anyway?" Mrs. Bates asked.

"Into the army, yes," Rose said, confident on this subject at least. "But the navy has to get volunteers."

"I see." Mrs. Bates glanced at Elizabeth again. "Maybe we should convince Gideon to volunteer for the navy."

"He told me he gets seasick," Elizabeth said.

"I'm sure he'd get over it."

"Can't he get out of the draft somehow?" Rose asked, still dabbing at her eyes.

"He could, but he considers it his duty to go."

"Like Tommy did. I wonder if Tommy would have changed his mind if he'd known what was going to happen. I can't even figure it out. He'd only been over there a few weeks. How could he get killed so fast?"

Elizabeth didn't want to even think about it. "Mrs. Bates, did you come to offer us any advice?"

"Good heavens, I wish I had some, but I'm afraid I have very little experience with these matters."

"Even though we've both been in prison," Elizabeth confided to Rose, who smiled as Elizabeth had intended.

"How long were you in there?"

"Not long. President Wilson was afraid we would die after we went on a hunger strike, so he let us go," Mrs. Bates said.

"Hunger strike?" Rose exclaimed in wonder. "How could you do that?"

"Considering how bad the food was, it wasn't difficult at all," Elizabeth said.

"I did come at Gideon's request, however," Mrs. Bates said. "He asked me to tell you both that he was going to Poughkeepsie to see Fred Preston today."

"Oh dear," Rose murmured.

"I suppose he has to at least try to make him see reason," Elizabeth said.

But Rose was shaking her head. "That man hates me. I can see why Tommy didn't want to tell him we got married. The things he said to me . . ."

"You must remember that he was very upset that day," Mrs. Bates said. "Gideon told me you also had to tell him that his brother had been killed, which would have been very difficult for him to hear."

"Especially when he realized you were the one who got the official notification and not him," Elizabeth added.

"But I'm his wife," Rose said.

"Of course you are," Mrs. Bates said, "but he didn't know that. It was a lot for him to take in all at once, so if he behaved badly, we can understand it, even if we can't excuse it."

"And Gideon is giving him a chance to make amends," Elizabeth said, which was what Gideon would have said if he were here.

"And what happens when he refuses?" Rose asked.

"I'm sure Gideon has a plan," his mother said.

Rose obviously didn't share her confidence. She turned to Elizabeth. "You didn't think it would work, though."

"It might. Gideon is very clever," Elizabeth said loyally.

"Yes, he is," Mrs. Bates said with a knowing smile. "And I'm sure he and *Elizabeth* will figure out something."

CHAPTER FIVE

Usually, Gideon wanted to spend as much time with Elizabeth as possible, but this evening was different. At least Fred Preston hadn't refused to even consider helping Rose, although Gideon was certain he wouldn't do so without a fight. Maybe his attorneys would advise him he'd be foolish to make his family's business public with a court case that would be the talk of the state. On the other hand, Fred had also been correct in predicting that the press would paint Rose as a gold digger and worse. Women always got the brunt of these things, and in this case, Rose even looked like a gold digger because she sort of was initially.

Twilight had settled over the city by the time he reached the big old house in Greenwich Village. Elizabeth answered the door, and her smile of greeting almost made him forget why he'd come. Then she kissed him, and he did forget, if only for a moment.

"You poor thing," she said. "Are you just back from Poughkeepsie?"

"I'm afraid so."

"Have you eaten?"

"Yes, I got something on the train."

"Come on inside, then." She escorted him into the parlor.

Cybil and Zelda were sitting with Rose, who looked a little better than she had the last time he'd seen her, even if the bruises on her face were turning odd colors. He greeted them all, and Cybil made an excuse for her and Zelda to leave him alone with Elizabeth and Rose.

When they'd gone, Elizabeth sat down beside Rose on the sofa and Gideon took one of the many chairs scattered around the room, sinking into it wearily.

"Fred isn't going to give me anything, is he?" Rose said.

"He's considering his . . . his options," Gideon said. "He was adamant that he wouldn't do anything for you at all until I told him about the baby."

"You told him?" Rose asked in alarm.

"Yes. I know I should have discussed it with you first, but . . . Well, let me explain my thinking. I made sure the receptionist and his secretary knew that I'd come to make arrangements for Tom's widow."

"Why did you do that?" Rose asked, horrified now. "It's nobody's business!"

But Elizabeth said, "Oh, I see." She turned to Rose. "Men like Fred Preston are often very worried about their reputations. They don't want to be seen in a bad light, and if people heard that he'd cut off his brother's widow without a penny, they'd think poorly of him."

"Especially because Tom was a war hero," Gideon continued. "So I made sure the word would get out."

"But he didn't care, did he?" Rose said.

"Not as much as I had hoped," Gideon admitted. "Not even when I mentioned a lawsuit and how interested the press would be in learning about his private business, so that's when I realized he needed to know about the baby."

"And how did he react?" Elizabeth asked.

"He was surprised, as I'd hoped he would be, and a bit disconcerted. A man might scorn his brother's wife, but his brother's child is an entirely different matter."

"He's not getting his hands on my baby," Rose said, laying a protective hand over her belly.

"Of course he isn't," Elizabeth said, giving Gideon a chastening glance for even suggesting such a thing, even though he hadn't.

"No, we won't allow that, but he could be persuaded to provide for you both, I think. In fact—if it's any comfort to you—he seemed genuinely shocked when I told him you were almost killed in the attack."

"Why would he be, since he was the one sent that goon after me?"

"I do believe he sent that goon, as you call him,

because he wasn't at all surprised to hear you'd caught a man burglarizing your apartment, but he obviously had no idea the man had attacked you, much less how serious the attack was."

"He probably just sent the man to steal the will while you weren't home," Elizabeth said. "Businessmen like Fred Preston don't usually solve their problems with murder."

Rose didn't look completely convinced. "But killing me *would* solve his problems and get rid of the baby, too."

"I'm hoping that his knowing about the baby will actually protect you. The child is his flesh and blood, too."

"Ugh, what an awful thought," Rose said with a shiver.

"And we certainly won't assume he feels protective toward the baby until we know for sure," Elizabeth said. "So you'll stay here for the time being."

"I can't stay here forever, though."

"I'm sure I'll hear from Fred Preston very soon," Gideon said. "He wanted to consult with his own attorneys, and they are bound to advise him to settle with you. It's the only sensible course to take."

"And once he's made a settlement, he won't have any reason to hurt you, will he, Gideon?" Elizabeth asked.

"No. I'll make sure the money is tied up in such

a way that he can't reclaim it even if something happens to you."

"Can you do that?" Rose asked with a skeptical frown.

"Attorneys can do all sorts of interesting things," Elizabeth said with an adoring smile that made Gideon feel a little better about this whole thing. But only a little.

"Yes, we can," he confirmed with only slightly less confidence than Elizabeth had expressed. "Tell me, is Fred married?"

"No, he's not," Rose said. "Does that matter?"

"Maybe. I was thinking I might also ask him to make your child his heir. I'm sure Tom would want that."

"I told you attorneys can do all sorts of interesting things," Elizabeth said.

Rose seemed unimpressed. "I'll just be happy if he can keep us both alive."

The next day Gideon was surprised when his clerk interrupted his perusal of some estate documents. He knew he had no appointments scheduled, and Smith usually discouraged anyone with the temerity to arrive without one.

"Excuse me, Mr. Bates, but a lady is here to see you. She said it's concerning Mr. Thomas Preston's estate, and I know you're assisting his widow."

"Did the lady give her name?" Could Rose have

come to see him? Surely not, at least not alone. Elizabeth would never have allowed it.

"She is Mrs. Frederick Preston Senior."

Ah, the stepmother then. Why on earth was she here? "She's alone?"

"So it appears."

"Well, then, send her in."

Gideon rose and went to greet Mrs. Preston as Smith escorted her into his office.

She seemed surprised when she saw Gideon, but he was used to that reaction. People expected attorneys to be middle-aged with gray hair and a paunch. For his part, Gideon was surprised because he expected stepmothers to be evil harpies. Mrs. Preston might well have been an evil harpy, but she disguised it well. She wasn't much older than Fred Preston, if Gideon was any judge, and her lush figure was enhanced by a walking suit that might well have come from Paris before the war. If Fred hadn't spent his war profits on sprucing up his office, Mrs. Preston had certainly spent hers on sprucing up her wardrobe.

Gideon introduced himself and offered her a seat. "Can I get you something to drink? Some tea or coffee?"

"I would like a glass of water, if you don't mind. I'm afraid I'm not used to the city."

Gideon nodded to Smith, who slipped away to fetch the water. "I'm sure it can be overwhelming if you aren't used to it." Mrs. Preston, for her part, didn't look a bit overwhelmed. "What can I do for you, Mrs. Preston?"

"First of all, I must apologize for my stepson's behavior yesterday. He told me about your encounter, and I'm afraid he has let his grief over losing poor Tom affect his manners and his good nature."

"I assumed he was not himself," Gideon said tactfully. Surely, Fred wasn't *always* a heartless cad.

"It's kind of you to excuse him. I did speak to him about it, and we have discussed this unfortunate situation and how best to deal with it. You'll be glad to know we realize we must accept responsibility for Tom's wife, no matter the circumstances of their marriage."

This was a pleasant surprise. "So you are prepared to honor Tom's wishes?"

"Oh, I hardly think that's a good idea. What would a girl like that do if she were suddenly given a fortune? All sorts of people would try to take advantage of her, and that wouldn't be in her best interest at all. But she is part of our family, as is her child, so we are prepared to offer her and her baby a home with us for as long as she lives."

Gideon seldom found himself speechless, but this was one of those rare occasions. How fiendishly clever! Nothing could have been more natural than for Tom's widow to go live with his

118

family. They couldn't be faulted for following the wishes Tom had set out in his only surviving last will and testament, even though it did effectively disinherit his wife and child, and by taking in the widow and orphan, they were showing true Christian charity toward them. Rose and her child would never want for anything, or so Fred and his stepmother would claim. If Gideon wasn't certain that Fred Preston had hired a henchman who was to steal Tom's true will and who had also almost murdered Rose in the bargain, he'd have been thrilled by this offer.

"How very generous of you," he finally managed.

"It's really the least we can do, isn't it? We are fortunate that we have the means to give this young woman our support."

Gideon took a moment to completely reconsider his opinion of Mrs. Preston Senior, because the unreasonable hothead with whom Gideon had met yesterday had surely not been the mastermind of this scheme. "Tom told me your factory was able to get a contract to provide shoes for the army."

If Mrs. Preston was surprised by the change of subject, she didn't show it. "I really don't know anything about the business except what Fred tells me over the dinner table, but I do know things are going well for us. Fred was honored that his company was selected."

Gideon was sure he was, just as he was sure Mrs. Preston knew far more about everything than she pretended. "I'll have to discuss your offer with Mrs. Preston, of course." Not that Rose would ever consider moving in with Fred Preston and his stepmother.

"I can't imagine she'll refuse. When Fred told me she'd actually been *attacked* . . . Well, I can assure her she will be perfectly safe in Poughkeepsie."

Gideon didn't even bother to respond to that. "What if she doesn't want to live in Pough-keepsie?"

Mrs. Preston seemed astonished at such an idea. "Why wouldn't she? Fred told me she has no resources of her own, and without Tom to support her, how will she manage? With a child, too?"

"I'm just imagining how difficult it will be for her to leave the city, which is the only place she's ever lived, and move to a town where she knows no one, not even the people she'll be living with."

"Beggars can't be choosers, Mr. Bates," Mrs. Preston said with a rather pinched smile. "And she needs to be thinking of her child's future. What kind of life can she give him?"

"She can give him a perfectly fine life if Tom's family would honor his wishes and provide for her and the child. Really, Mrs. Preston, aren't you

120

at least a little hesitant to bring a perfect stranger into your home?"

"Should I be, Mr. Bates?" she asked coyly.

Was she flirting with him? Once again Gideon reconsidered his opinion of Mrs. Preston. She was a handsome woman who had probably used her charms to snag the elder Mr. Preston when he was widowed. Nothing wrong with that in a world where women had very few opportunities outside of marriage. In fact, Rose had done the same thing with Tom. But now Mrs. Preston lived with her stepson, who was probably closer to her age than her late husband had been. A stepson who didn't have a wife of his own, which opened up other possibilities. "Rose Preston is a very attractive young woman."

Plainly, this was not at all what she had expected to hear. "What does that mean?"

Leaning forward and folding his hands on his desktop, Gideon assumed the earnest expression he used when he had to break unpleasant news to a client. "Am I correct in assuming that you still reside in the Preston family home?"

"Of course I do." She was getting angry now. Good.

"And your stepson lives there, too."

"I can't imagine what business it is of yours, but yes, he does."

"And you will be bringing an attractive young woman to live there with you."

"I will be there to chaperone, of course. It will all be completely proper."

Gideon nodded his understanding. "Yes, yes, I'm sure it will be. I was only concerned because . . ." He looked away as if loath to discuss it.

"You are beginning to annoy me, Mr. Bates. Pray tell me why you are concerned."

"As you may have gathered, Tom had not known his bride very long before they married."

"How could he have? He'd only been gone from Poughkeepsie for the three months of training before he was shipped out."

"But that was enough time for her to capture his heart and marry him."

"What does that have to do with anything?"

"Nothing, of course, but have you considered that his brother might also find her . . . appealing?"

Plainly, this had not occurred to Mrs. Preston, and now that it had, she was not best pleased. "That's . . . ridiculous."

"Also, Tom and his brother must be somewhat alike. I did see a family resemblance. Mrs. Tom Preston may find his brother attractive in the same way."

"So which is it?" she snapped. "Is Fred supposed to fall hopelessly in love with her or she with him?"

"I have no idea. Perhaps both."

The color was blooming in her cheeks. "I can assure you Fred would never . . . He can hardly stand the sight of that woman."

"Then why is he so anxious for her to live in his house?"

This time Mrs. Preston was the one struck speechless.

While she struggled, Gideon added, "Really, Mrs. Preston, that's hardly a convincing argument for Rose Preston to move in with you. I can't imagine she'd feel welcome under those circumstances."

Mrs. Preston's face was scarlet now, and she rose imperiously from her chair. "I don't particularly care if she feels welcome or not. This is the only offer she will receive from us. If she doesn't want to end up begging on the streets with her child strapped to her back, she'll take it."

With that, she stormed out, leaving the door hanging open. Smith appeared a few moments later, frowning in consternation at his visitor's abrupt departure. "Is everything all right, sir?"

"Oh yes, Smith. It seems Mrs. Preston got some bad news she wasn't expecting. I'm sorry if she was rude to you."

"Not at all. She simply showed herself out the door, which is rather out of the ordinary, so I assumed she was upset."

She wasn't the only one. "Smith, would you

telephone Miss Miles and ask her if it's convenient for me to call on her this afternoon?"

"Certainly, sir."

Elizabeth could hardly believe what Gideon was telling them. She and Rose had gathered with Gideon in Cybil's cluttered parlor again while he described Mrs. Preston's visit to his office.

"How very clever," Elizabeth said when he had explained their invitation.

Rose frowned. "Why is it clever? I just think it's mean. They figured out a way of getting out of giving me my money."

"It's clever because they outfoxed poor Gideon."

"Poor?" Gideon protested, laying a hand on his heart as if mortally wounded.

"I'm sorry, darling, but they did outfox you. You see," she explained to Rose, "Gideon figured he could embarrass Fred into giving you a settlement. He wouldn't want his friends and neighbors to think he was the kind of man who would abandon his late brother's wife and child."

"But that's exactly the kind of man he is," Rose said in exasperation.

"Yes, it is, but as I said, most people want others to think well of them, and when people get a little money, they want it all the more."

Rose frowned. "Why?"

"So they'll get invited to parties and . . . Oh,

124

it's all just too silly, but believe me, to people in society, it's all vitally important. But Fred figured out a way to protect himself."

Gideon stopped her with a raised hand. "I'm not convinced Fred figured it out."

"Really?" Elizabeth asked.

"Yes, really. I can't imagine he even cares what people think, or at least not very much, but his stepmother probably does."

"Women do tend to care about those things more."

"And Mrs. Preston strikes me as a woman who cares very much."

"You'll have to tell us more about her, darling," Elizabeth said, leaning forward eagerly.

"I told you, she's the widow of Tom and Fred's father."

"What does she look like? How old is she? And she must be quite smart if you think she came up with this plan."

"She's . . . well-dressed," he hedged.

"Tommy said she was only five years older than Fred," Rose offered. "Which still makes her pretty old."

"Still far short of forty, though," Gideon said a little defensively.

"She's a handsome woman, too, or Gideon would have called her 'matronly' or something like that," Elizabeth confided in Rose.

"My mother would disapprove of my judging

a female by her appearance," Gideon reminded her.

"As would I," Elizabeth said, "but in this case, we need to form an opinion of this woman since she is obviously very involved in what's happening. Why did you decide she was the one who had come up with the plan?"

"Because it's a woman's solution. Fred was content to cheat Rose out of her inheritance and send her on her way, but someone who cared about their reputation came up with an alternative that would save them embarrassment and still not cost them or particularly benefit Rose, either."

"But they don't really want me moving in with them, do they?" Rose asked. "Because they hate me and because I'm trash, according to Fred."

"If it makes you feel any better, Mrs. Preston apologized for Fred's behavior," Gideon said.

"It doesn't make me feel better at all," Rose said. "And you can't apologize for somebody else. Even I know that."

"No, you can't," Elizabeth said. "So we must ask ourselves why Fred and his stepmother came up with this idea if they really don't want you moving in with them."

"That's easy," Gideon said. "So they can tell their friends and neighbors that they did offer Rose and her child a home with them but that she scorned their generous offer and went off on her own."

"Which would mean that they didn't believe Rose would accept their offer," Elizabeth said. "But they had to have considered the possibility that she would."

"But I wouldn't, not ever," Rose insisted.

"Never say never," Elizabeth said. "You don't know what you'll do if you're desperate enough. Right now you've got Tom's money and a lovely apartment, but I'm guessing Tom's income from the factory will stop now, and sooner or later you'll run out of money. What will you do then?"

"I'll . . . I'll get a job, I suppose. I was working in the shirtwaist factory when I met Tommy."

"And who will take care of your baby?"

"I . . . I don't know," she finally admitted.

"Just as I thought. It's one thing to be on your own and quite another to be on your own with a child. And the Prestons may have counted on you having no other choice but to come to them."

"But why would they want me to?"

"Yes, why, Elizabeth?" Gideon asked uneasily.

Elizabeth looked at both of them, unable to believe neither of them had realized the darker side of Mrs. Preston's offer. "That man who broke into the apartment tried to kill you, Rose."

Instinctively, she touched her throat. "You don't think . . . But they couldn't . . . Not in their own house!"

"Surely not!" Gideon exclaimed. "Rose is right. They couldn't harm her in their own house."

"I'm not saying it's true. I'm just saying it's a possibility, and they've certainly tried it once already, even though it might not have been planned. At the very least, it got them to thinking, and with Rose out of the way, they wouldn't have to worry about a lawsuit or a scandal or anything else."

"But if Rose died, they'd have a completely different scandal," Gideon said.

"Not necessarily. Women do die in childbirth. They might spare the baby out of a tenderness for Tom, but Rose is the real threat here. And if they didn't want to wait for the baby to be born and didn't care about the baby at all, Rose could simply become ill and pass away."

Elizabeth watched in dismay as the color drained from Rose's face. "I never thought . . ."

"I'm so sorry," Elizabeth cried, seeing her distress. "I didn't mean to frighten you." But of course she had meant exactly that, because Rose needed to understand the terrible danger she was in. She just hadn't intended for Rose to faint. "Are you all right?"

"You could have been a little more diplomatic," Gideon whispered fiercely as Elizabeth jumped up and helped Rose to lie prone on the sofa, lifting her feet and finding a cushion for her head.

"I don't know a diplomatic way to tell someone her life is in danger," Elizabeth whispered right back.

"I can hear you," Rose said weakly. "And you're right. I should've thought of it myself."

"I'm sure Cybil has smelling salts around here somewhere," Elizabeth said, casting about helplessly.

"I'm fine. I just need a minute," Rose said, sounding a little stronger.

"Maybe a glass of water," Gideon said.

Elizabeth hurried off to fetch it. When she returned, Rose's color was much better, and she sat up on her own to drink the water.

"I'm so sorry," Elizabeth said again.

"Stop it," Rose snapped. "I need to know the truth, and now I need to know what to do next."

Elizabeth looked up and met Gideon's gaze.

"Don't look at me. My ideas have nearly gotten Rose killed," he said.

"It wasn't your idea for Rose to keep Tom's will at her apartment," Elizabeth pointed out generously.

"So it's *my* ideas that almost got me killed," Rose said with a sigh.

"Let's not waste any time casting blame," Elizabeth said. "The real villains are Fred and his stepmother." She turned to Gideon. "You didn't finish your story. How did you leave things with Mrs. Preston?"

"Oh, I almost forgot, although, now that I think of it, I probably just gave Mrs. Preston another reason to . . . uh . . . to not want Rose around."

Elizabeth managed not to sigh. "Just tell us."

Gideon motioned that she should sit back down next to Rose, and he took his own seat as well. "I got this idea. . . . Really, Rose planted the seed when she told me Fred wasn't married, and while I was talking with Mrs. Preston, I realized she and Fred share a house."

"Is that so unusual?" Elizabeth asked.

"For a grown man to share a house with his widowed stepmother? Probably not, unless she's only a few years older than he is and a very handsome woman."

"I told you she was a handsome woman," she said to Rose.

"Not what you'd call a beauty, but she's . . . interesting," Gideon admitted.

Elizabeth considered this for a moment, then turned to Rose. "Did Tom ever mention anything about this to you?"

"Not exactly. He did mention that he didn't like Delia much. That's her name, Delia. He never called her 'Mother,' even though he was still pretty young when his father married her."

"And what about Fred?"

"Tommy didn't talk about Fred much. I didn't understand it at first. I thought maybe he didn't like Fred, either, but I finally realized that he just didn't like saying things that made Fred look bad."

"Things like what?" Elizabeth asked.

"Like how Fred seemed to get along too well with Delia. 'Thick as thieves' was what he said once. I didn't know what he meant then, but now I think I do."

"So maybe I was right to be suspicious," Gideon said.

"Oh dear," Elizabeth said.

Gideon gave her a sympathetic glance. "Yes, well, I decided to test the waters a little with Mrs. Preston . . . Delia . . . so I pointed out that Rose is an attractive young woman."

Rose brightened at that. "Thank you, Mr. Bates."

Gideon colored a little, but he continued bravely. "And I mentioned how Tom had only needed to know Rose a short time before deciding he wanted to marry her, which I felt indicated a man might fall in love with her rather quickly. Then I pointed out that Fred and Tom were brothers, and maybe Rose would also find Fred appealing because of that."

"Not likely," Rose sniffed.

"I didn't really think so, either," Gideon admitted, "but I didn't see any harm in suggesting it to Mrs. Preston."

"Gideon, did you lie?" Elizabeth said, feigning shock.

"Not at all. Stranger things have happened."

Elizabeth turned to Rose. "One of those stranger things would be Gideon telling a lie."

"Really?" Rose marveled. Plainly, her world included the normal use of prevarication, which was good to know.

"Really. So how did Mrs. Preston receive this suggestion from you?" she asked Gideon.

"She was not at all pleased, and she left my office in a huff."

"A huff?"

"Well, she didn't slam the door, but Smith was quite distressed that she didn't wait to be shown out."

"Poor Smith. He bears his burdens bravely."

"Who is Smith?" Rose asked.

"Gideon's law clerk. He's a lovely gentleman, but don't ever try to see Gideon without an appointment. You have been warned."

Rose solemnly nodded her understanding.

"So Mrs. Preston and Fred may have an . . . *unusual* relationship," Elizabeth mused.

"I felt I had to discourage her somehow from wanting Rose in her house," Gideon said. "She may eventually realize I was only bluffing and the very thought of a romance between Rose and Fred is absurd, but that will take some time. Meanwhile, we can figure out our next step."

"Don't you know our next step?" Elizabeth asked.

"Not yet," Gideon said with a sigh, "but I have a feeling you're going to explain it to me very soon."

"Thank you so much for coming, Anna," Elizabeth said the next morning as she ushered Anna Vanderslice into the parlor.

"I'm happy to help," Anna said. She wore a brown skirt and a white shirtwaist with a jaunty blue scarf tied in a bow at her throat. A straw hat completed her ensemble, making her look exactly like the schoolgirl she had denied being only a month ago. "Good morning, Rose. You're looking well."

"Thank you," Rose said.

"And so are you." Elizabeth eyed Anna critically. "What have you done to yourself?"

"Not a thing. Maybe being happy makes me look different."

"Why are you happy?" Rose asked.

"Because I'm learning such marvelous things."

"Anna is a student at Hunter College."

Rose made a face. "I always hated school."

"College isn't like regular school. It's exciting and different, and everyone there is so smart."

"I wouldn't like it, then. I'm not smart," Rose said.

"Don't be so sure," Anna said. "I didn't think I was, either, but after a few days in college, I think I'm brilliant."

"That's interesting," Elizabeth said. "Maybe I should go to college, too."

"Maybe you should. Where are you off to today?"

"I need to see the Old Man," Elizabeth said, "and I didn't want to leave Rose alone."

"I don't think I'll be much protection for her," Anna said. "And don't forget I have classes this afternoon, so I have to leave by twelve thirty."

"Do I need protection here?" Rose said.

"Of course not. I was just afraid that if I left you here alone, you might get bored and go out somewhere, so Anna is going to entertain you."

"I wouldn't expect too much entertainment," Anna told Rose, who smiled.

"I won't."

"So what do you need to see your father about?" Anna asked.

"What do you think? Gideon asked Fred Preston to do the right thing, but of course he won't. Then Fred's stepmother offered to let Rose move in with them so they could look after her."

"Good heavens, is that a good idea?"

"Absolutely not. Rose can give you the whole amazing story while I'm gone."

"And you think your father will be able to figure out some way to help Rose?"

"No, but he might be able to figure out how to get some money out of Fred Preston, which will accomplish the same thing."

CHAPTER SIX

Elizabeth had worn a hat with a veil in a feeble attempt to conceal her identity as she made her way down Twenty-eighth Street to Dan the Dude's Saloon. Not that she planned on entering the saloon itself, but she also didn't want anyone to see her slipping down the alley to the side door, either. It wasn't likely she'd be recognized, but she did have to think about her reputation now that she and Gideon were engaged. Or, rather, she needed to think about Gideon's reputation, since she didn't really have one with the society people who mattered in this city.

But no one seemed to notice her as she made her way to the nondescript side door. She rapped out a series of knocks, and after a few moments, the viewing panel in the door slid open, and someone peered out suspiciously. That suspicion lasted only a second, however, when Elizabeth lifted her veil. The door instantly opened to reveal a fireplug of a man with a face like a dried-up potato.

"Good morning, Spuds," she said, stepping inside.

"It's good to see you, Contessa."

Elizabeth smiled at the honorific the other grifters had bestowed upon her after a particularly harrowing experience. "It's good to see you, too."

"You threw me for a minute with that veil. I didn't expect no widows to be coming to call."

"I should hope not. Is the Old Man here?"

"For a while. He's got an . . . appointment this afternoon." Which meant he was helping someone with a con.

"I won't keep him long." Elizabeth made her way into the large room at the rear of Dan's Saloon, which served as a gathering place for the grifters of the city. A grifter who wasn't on a job would be keeping late hours while he spent his ill-gotten gains on questionable amusements, so the place was nearly deserted at this time of the morning. One fellow looked up from a lazy game of solitaire and greeted her warmly. She returned the greeting, and the sound of her voice brought the Old Man out of his office.

He was as dapper as usual in a tailor-made suit with a fresh carnation in his lapel. His silver hair was brushed back from his forehead and his bright blue eyes sparkled with pleasure at the sight of her.

"Lizzie, what brings you to this disreputable establishment?"

"I need to see my disreputable family," she replied cheerfully.

"Well, Jake isn't here, but I'll be happy to

accommodate you. Come in. Can I get you something? It's a little early for a drink, but I'm sure Dan can come up with some sarsaparilla or something."

"Nothing for me, and I won't keep you long. I may have a job for you, though."

He gave her a mocking scowl. "You're not trying to save someone again, are you?"

"As a matter of fact, another widow is in trouble."

"Where on earth do you find these people, Lizzie?"

"It isn't difficult. People are always trying to take advantage of women."

He winced just slightly, although she knew he made a point of never cheating a widow. "All right. Come into my office and tell me all about it."

When she'd told him everything, he leaned back in his chair. "A war profiteer, eh?"

"But all completely legal, and we don't know for sure if he's sending the army poor-quality shoes. All we know for certain is that he's cheating Rose out of her share of the profits."

"Do you have any idea how much these businesses are making from the war?"

"Not exactly, no."

"Millions. This Fred is ripe for the picking. He might be the biggest score I make this year."

"Most of it has to go to Rose," she warned him.

He waved away her concern. "He'll have plenty to go around. I'll need to do some research, though. Did you have anything particular in mind?"

"I don't know enough about Fred yet, I'm afraid, but I figured the best con man in the city would have some ideas."

"Did you say *the city?*"

"Oh dear, did I insult you? The best in the *country.*"

"Let's see, then. From what you told me, Fred might be tempted by a beautiful young woman."

"But if he's involved with his stepmother—"

"If he's involved with his stepmother, they could never marry, so he's looking at a life without a wife and children. Some men might be satisfied with that, but most wouldn't be. Even if he doesn't want children, he'll be flattered if a younger woman pays him some attention. I'm guessing the stepmother keeps him on a short leash because she doesn't want anyone stealing him away."

"But if that's the case, how will this *beautiful young woman* make herself known?"

"We'll figure that out. The question is, are you willing to participate?"

"You mean, is Gideon willing to allow me to participate?" she said.

"Surely, you don't let him control you."

"Of course not, but he does worry about my

safety, and someone has already tried to murder Rose Preston."

"No one will have any reason to harm you, except perhaps the stepmother, and by the time she figures that out, you'll have disappeared."

"Then you *do* have an idea."

He raised a hand to end her speculation. "Not really. Not yet. But this . . . We'll make your Rose a rich woman."

"That's what I'm counting on."

Gideon had been pleased to find Elizabeth had come to have dinner with him and his mother that evening. For some reason he'd expected they could forget Rose Preston and her problems for one night, especially when his mother was thoughtful enough to leave them alone after supper. But he should have known better.

"I saw the Old Man today."

He did know better than to groan. They would need the Old Man's help, after all. Still, no matter how charming and helpful Mr. Miles was, Gideon could never completely approve of a man who made his living by cheating people. "I'm sure he saw the potential in Fred Preston."

"Obviously. In fact, I don't think I've ever seen him quite so impressed."

"What is he going to do?"

"He's not sure yet," she said, and although Elizabeth was the most skilled liar he had ever met, he could tell she wasn't telling him the whole truth. He decided to let it pass, though. He'd probably find out the rest of it soon enough, and he figured he was happier not knowing in the meantime. "But he'd like to speak with you, to find out everything you know about Fred and his business."

"I don't know very much."

"You may know more than you think, from things Tom said. He can come to your office, if that's all right."

"Of course it's all right. Should I warn Smith that he's your father?"

"His name will give him away, unless he uses a fake one."

"That's not a good idea. He may want to see me another time, and everyone in the office would wonder why he was using different names."

"Oh, and they'll see him at our wedding, too."

"Yes, although he may need to wear a disguise."

That amused her. "Why would he have to wear a disguise?"

"Because David and his mother know him as General Sterling."

"Haven't you explained all that to David yet?"

"I haven't found it necessary. It was difficult enough explaining that I was going to marry his former fiancée."

"I'm sure he thinks you're insane to take me on."

That made Gideon smile. "Don't underestimate him. He can certainly understand the appeal."

"Why, Gideon, are you saying I'm irresistible?" she asked coyly.

"I certainly find you so, and you must be if you ended up engaged to David when he never even proposed to you."

"I suppose you're right, although I'm sure David has no idea he never proposed."

"If he does, he never mentioned it to me. I only know it because you told me. But how did we get on this subject? I thought we were talking about Rose Preston and her problem."

"The Old Man is going to come to your office."

"Oh yes. I'll tell Smith. But I still don't know how he thinks I can help."

"Don't worry. He knows you won't help him with the con. He just wants your impression of Fred and what his weaknesses might be. For example, do you think he might have a penchant for the ladies?"

"Not from the way he treated Rose. If that's how he speaks to women, it's no wonder he isn't married."

"But Rose is a special case, isn't she? She's a distinct threat to him. Maybe he's actually very charming."

"He's not charming at all."

"Then maybe he thinks he is. That's even better."

Gideon didn't like the gleam in her lovely blue eyes one bit. "Are you planning to take part in this . . . this thing?"

"Call it a job, darling, and I have no idea. We'll have to see what the Old Man comes up with. Now, kiss me before your mother comes back."

"Why would your father care anything about helping me?" Rose asked the next morning when Elizabeth told her the Old Man was coming to meet her.

"He's a grifter." When that elicited only a blank stare, Elizabeth added, "A con man."

Rose's lovely eyes widened in understanding.

"And he's not really interested in helping you, but if he can figure out a way to get money out of Fred for you, he'll keep some of it for himself."

Obviously, that made perfect sense to Rose. "But how do I know he won't cheat me, too?"

"Because he's my father and I'll make sure of it. But he does make it a policy not to cheat widows. He doesn't have many rules, but that's one he never breaks."

"Fred should take a lesson from him."

"Indeed he should."

"So what does your father want with me?"

"He wants to ask you about Fred."

"I don't know anything about Fred."

"But you do. Tom told you things about him,

and you met with him. You know more than you think."

Luckily, the doorbell rang before Rose could argue any more. The Old Man wore one of his tailor-made suits, and today his carnation was red. He bowed over Rose's hand as if she were royalty, and Elizabeth could see she was impressed. When they were seated comfortably in Cybil's parlor with lemonade to sustain them, he leaned back in his chair and said, "Have you always lived in the city, Mrs. Preston?"

"I guess so. That's all I remember, anyway."

"Does your family still live here?"

She shook her head. "They don't live any-where. My mother died when I was thirteen. I had a brother, but he got run over by a trolley when he was six."

"What about your father?"

"He left when I was small. I don't really remember him, and I don't know if he's alive or dead. I don't much care, either."

"I'm sorry to hear it. I'm afraid not all men are as responsible as we would like them to be. So you've been on your own since you were thirteen?"

Rose shrugged as if that were nothing out of the ordinary. "I suppose so."

"That must have been hard," Elizabeth said, remembering that she had lost her own mother at the same age. The Old Man had sent her to live with Jake and his mother, who was the Old Man's mistress. She'd deeply resented him for it at the time, but now she realized how very different her life might have been had she been left alone in the world at that age.

"Everything is hard," Rose said, "even when it seems like it won't be. When Tommy asked me to marry him, I thought my troubles were over, and then somebody tried to strangle me."

"I'm terribly sorry about that, Mrs. Preston, but let's see if we can't do something to make your life a bit easier in the future," the Old Man said. "Lizzie tells me that Fred Preston objected to your marriage."

"He did more than object. I wondered why Tommy didn't want his family there when we got married, but when I met Fred, I understood."

"Do you think Fred's objections were to you in particular, or would he have objected to anyone his brother chose?"

Rose frowned. Plainly, she had never considered this, so she took a minute to do that now. "I think maybe it was me. I mean, he called me all kinds of names and said I tricked Tommy just to get his money, so maybe if I was rich, too, he wouldn't have minded so much."

"I suppose he was very fond of his brother."

"I don't think so."

The Old Man perked up at that. "Why?"

"Tommy said they weren't close. Fred was

144

ten when Tommy was born. He always thought Tommy was a nuisance."

"Maybe he was jealous because the new baby got all the attention," Elizabeth suggested.

"Tommy did say they spoiled him. Because he was the youngest, I guess. Whatever it was, Fred never liked him much."

"Did Tom like Fred?" the Old Man asked.

This made Rose frown again. "He never really said, but . . ."

"But what?"

"He seemed a little afraid of him . . . or maybe he was just afraid of what he might do. That's why he didn't tell him we were getting married, I guess."

"Was he just worried about displeasing his brother, do you think? Or was he genuinely afraid?"

"I . . . I don't know." Rose rubbed her forehead as if it were starting to ache.

"I'm sorry to distress you, my dear," the Old Man said with such sincerity that even Elizabeth believed him. "Let me put it another way. Do you think Tom admired his older brother, the way children do when they have a much older and more accomplished sibling?"

"Oh, I see what you mean," she said. "No, he didn't admire Fred at all. He was angry about the way he was running the company. Something about the way he was making the shoes."

"What about them?"

"Well, a soldier's life is pretty awful even before he gets to the war, and one of the things they complain about a lot is the shoes. Tommy took that personal because his family makes shoes, you see."

"I imagine soldiers are pretty hard on their shoes, though, with all that marching," the Old Man said.

But Rose shook her head again. "It was more than that. The soldiers were always hearing rumors about what it was like over in France. The real fighting, I mean. How bad things were and all that. Tommy didn't care. He was happy to do his part, no matter how bad it was, but one thing that really upset him was when somebody told him General Pershing's army sometimes left bloody footprints in the snow because their shoes fell apart."

"How awful," Elizabeth said.

"Indeed," the Old Man said, "and I can see Tom would have taken that to heart."

Rose nodded vigorously. "I said maybe those weren't shoes that his company made, but he said, 'I know my brother.' That's all he said, that he knew his brother, so it made me think he didn't *admire* Fred, like you asked."

"How very perceptive of you, my dear," the Old Man said. "Do you think he ever spoke to his brother about it?"

146

"I don't know if he ever had the chance."

The Old Man nodded sagely. "What do you know about the stepmother? What's her name?"

"Delia. I know she was a good bit younger than Tommy's father. Tommy was still in school when they married, but he never thought of her as a mother."

"Is she pretty, do you think?"

"Not to hear Tommy tell it, but he'd be loyal to his own mother, wouldn't he?"

"What about Fred? I don't suppose he thought of her as his mother, either."

"Not hardly! He was a grown man when she married his father."

"Did Tom ever give you the idea there was anything inappropriate about Fred's relationship with Delia?"

"No, he didn't."

"But didn't Tom say they were 'thick as thieves'?"

Rose glanced at Elizabeth, obviously surprised Elizabeth had remembered. "He did, but I thought he just meant about . . . about business things."

"Is Delia involved in the company?"

Rose opened her mouth to reply but nothing came out. She stared at the Old Man for a long moment, and then she said, "I don't know. I mean, she's a woman, isn't she?"

"As far as we know," the Old Man allowed with a small smile.

"And women don't run companies, do they?"

"Not usually."

Rose wrinkled her nose. "But now that you mention it, Tommy said something once. . . . I don't even remember what it was, but he thought Delia might be controlling Fred somehow."

"Do you mean controlling Fred or controlling the company?"

"I don't know. Both maybe."

"Do you think Delia was really the one who objected to your marriage?" Elizabeth asked.

Plainly, Rose hadn't considered this possibility, either. "Maybe, but why should she care?"

"Families always seem to care about such things, even if they don't particularly like each other," Elizabeth said.

"Rich people are funny," Rose said.

"Indeed they are," the Old Man said.

"Oh," Rose said suddenly. "I just remembered. She's German, too."

"Who is? Delia?" the Old Man asked.

"Yeah. She wasn't born there or anything, or at least I don't think so, but that's where her people are from."

"Lots of people in America are of German descent," Elizabeth said.

Rose shrugged. "You wanted to know everything."

"Did Tom have the impression that Delia's sympathies lie with Germany in the war?" the Old Man asked.

"He just said they didn't want him to join up, her and Fred. Tommy could've got out of it, you know. Lots of rich men do."

"Yes, even though the government took great pains to make sure that couldn't happen in this war the way it did during the War Between the States."

Elizabeth had to cough behind her hand when she remembered Jake had been excused from the draft because of a mythical heart ailment.

The Old Man pretended not to notice. "Did Tom think their reluctance for him to go into the army was because of their love for him or because they didn't believe in the cause?"

"He never said, but I think Fred just didn't want his brother to go into the army as an enlisted man."

"Why did Tom do that, do you think? I'm sure he could have gotten a commission."

"He was sick of being privileged, he said. He wanted to really fight."

"He sounds like a fine young man," the Old Man said, although Elizabeth was pretty sure he really thought Tom a fool for fighting someone else's war.

Rose cocked her head and stared hard at him, as if she didn't quite believe him, either. "So,

Elizabeth said you're going to steal some money from Fred."

That amused him. "I'm sure she didn't say that."

"No, I did not," Elizabeth assured him.

"Well, something like that. She said you're a grifter."

"Such an ugly word. I merely relieve dishonest men of their excess cash. I consider it a redistribution of wealth."

"Why do you want to redistribute some of it to me?"

"Because Lizzie asked me to, and because Fred Preston might be the most deserving dishonest man I've encountered recently."

"You're right there. What are you going to do to him?"

"I haven't quite decided yet."

"Can I help?" Rose asked hopefully.

"How do you think you can help?"

"I don't know, but I'd sure like to see Fred get what's coming to him."

"I'm sure you would, but Fred probably knows that already. We don't want him to think you're behind this."

"But if you think of something, I'm willing. I . . . Well, I wasn't always Mrs. Thomas Preston."

The Old Man smiled beatifically at her. "I will keep that in mind."

· · ·

Gideon had been expecting a visit from his future father-in-law, and as instructed, Smith escorted him in with great ceremony. Gideon's clerk was quite fond of Elizabeth, and apparently, this fondness extended to her relations.

"Thank you for seeing me, Gideon," Mr. Miles said. "I've just come from meeting with Rose Preston—Elizabeth sends her regards—and I believe I have a clearer picture of Fred Preston now," he said when he was comfortably seated in Gideon's office.

"What do you need from me, then?"

"Let me tell you what I learned from Mrs. Preston and compare that with your own knowledge and impressions. Mrs. Preston said she does not think the brothers were close or that they cared for each other very much."

"Tom did give me that impression. Fred is a lot older, of course, so they wouldn't have had a lot in common growing up."

"Would you say Tom admired Fred?"

"Looked up to him, you mean?" Gideon considered the question for a moment. "I can't speak for his feelings when he was younger, but Tom had definitely begun to question his brother's integrity when I met him."

"Something about the shoes he made for the army, was it?"

"That was at least part of it. Tom was afraid his

151

brother was producing poorly made shoes, but I got the impression there was more to it. Fred didn't want Tom to join the army, either."

"But he was going to be drafted regardless."

Gideon smiled in spite of himself. "We both know he wouldn't have had to serve if he didn't want to go."

"That's true," Mr. Miles said without the slightest hint of guilt. "Did you ever hear Tom express any sympathy for the Germans?"

"What?"

"Sympathy. Warm feelings. Regret that he was going to fight them."

"Absolutely not."

"Think about it. Are you sure?"

Gideon opened his mouth to protest, but then he realized Mr. Miles wouldn't be asking if he didn't have a good reason. "Do you think Tom was a German sympathizer?"

"Not really, but did you know the stepmother is German?"

This wasn't exactly a shocking revelation. Half the people in New York City were German. Probably half the people in the country were, too. Gideon thought back to his encounter with Mrs. Delia Preston. "She doesn't have an accent."

"Lots of German people don't, if they grew up here."

"And Delia isn't a German name."

Mr. Miles shrugged. "Names can be changed."

"What are you insinuating?"

"Nothing at all. I just wondered if I should report her to the League," Mr. Miles said with a wicked grin that told Gideon he was joking.

Gideon didn't grin back. "But you're thinking you can use that in some way. What did you have in mind?"

"Some sort of investment, I think. Fred is probably too conservative to risk his ill-gotten gains in the stock market, but he may be interested in expanding his business. The war will probably drag out for another year or two, at least, so there's plenty of time to make another fortune."

"I heard Pershing wants a million more men by next spring."

"I heard two million, and someone must feed and clothe them. Fred will understand that. It's nice that I know about the German step-mother, though. Lizzie thinks there's something between them, and even if there isn't, she'll be an influence."

"I hope you aren't going to involve Elizabeth in this little scheme of yours."

"There is nothing *little* about it, and I hope you aren't going to start telling Lizzie what she can and cannot do, because I can assure you, there is no better way to ensure that she will do exactly the opposite."

"But if it's dangerous—"

"Lizzie is my daughter. I'd never put her in danger."

Gideon sighed. "I know *you* wouldn't, but that doesn't mean things won't go wrong. They did the last time."

"And everything came out just fine. Really, Gideon, you worry too much."

And Mr. Miles didn't worry enough. "I hope you don't expect me to play a role in any of this."

"My dear boy, I respect your principles and wouldn't think of asking you to violate them."

"You did the last time."

"On the contrary, your principles were the reason your participation was required. Admit it. You didn't have to compromise yourself in the least in that situation."

Gideon wanted to grind his teeth because Mr. Miles was absolutely right. "Just keep that in mind," he said lamely.

"I most certainly will. As to Elizabeth, she will do what she wants, as usual. I know I'm not really qualified to give advice, but I do know my daughter, and you'd be well-advised to allow her to make her own decisions."

"I've already learned that from bitter experience."

Mr. Miles smiled his sympathy. "I didn't raise her to be a fool, Gideon. If there's one thing a grifter knows, it's how to get himself—or herself—out of a difficult situation."

"I certainly hope so."

Mr. Miles nodded his approval. "Now, tell me your impressions of Fred and Delia Preston."

"Roger, I'm so glad you were able to come," Mrs. Bates lied to Roger Devoss as she and Gideon welcomed him into her parlor on Friday evening.

Elizabeth knew Mrs. Bates hadn't been pleased to learn Gideon had invited him, but he was, after all, Gideon's employer, so she couldn't very well rescind the invitation.

"I was honored to be invited," Mr. Devoss assured her, and plainly he was. He'd long had a fondness for Hazel Bates that she did not return with equal fervor, which was why she didn't like to encourage him.

He really wasn't a bad specimen, Elizabeth decided. He was about the same age as Mrs. Bates, and he seemed fit enough. Like many men of his age, his hair was mostly gray, but he still had most of it, which was a plus. He was a substantial man, but not really fat, and he obviously earned a good income. A widow of a certain age could have done much worse.

"You know my fiancée, Miss Miles, I believe," Gideon said.

"Of course. How delightful to see you, Miss Miles."

They chatted for a bit about the weather and the

war news, which was relentlessly bad, until the maid summoned them to dinner.

"I'm afraid our entertaining isn't up to my usual standards, Roger," Mrs. Bates was saying as Mr. Devoss escorted her to the dining room.

"Gideon was careful not to invite me for a Meatless Monday or a Wheatless Wednesday," he said.

"Even on the days when we can serve meat and bread, we find ourselves just making do, I'm afraid," Mrs. Bates said. "Apparently, all the good cuts of meat are going to the army nowadays, as well they should."

"At least we hope so," Gideon said.

"Nothing is too good for our boys," Mr. Devoss said. If anyone here was a spy for the League, he was safe.

They took their seats, and the maid served them their soup.

"I wanted to thank you, Mr. Devoss," Elizabeth said, taking the bit in her teeth, "for allowing Gideon to travel to Poughkeepsie on behalf of Mrs. Preston."

"Think nothing of it, Miss Miles," he said graciously. "Mrs. Preston is our client, after all. I'm surprised you know so much about it." Was that disapproval in his voice?

"Mrs. Preston and I have become friends. In fact, she has been staying with me until we feel it's safe for her to return to her own home."

"Oh, I had no idea." He glanced at Gideon with definite disapproval. "I'm sorry you had to become involved. If only Gideon had been able to persuade Mr. Preston to cooperate . . ."

"I'm afraid I wasn't surprised that he didn't," she continued, ignoring Gideon's uneasy glances. "In my experience, most people don't share their money voluntarily."

"You're young to be so cynical, Miss Miles," Mr. Devoss said.

"Not cynical," she said with a smile. "Just realistic."

"Elizabeth is right, I'm afraid," Mrs. Bates said loyally. "And like Mrs. Preston, women too often find themselves cheated or abandoned with no recourse, which is why it's so very important for our government to give women the vote."

Mr. Devoss couldn't hide his surprise at this sudden change of topic. He tried a placating smile. "But you do have the vote."

"Yes, here in New York, but most women in other states are not so fortunate. We need a constitutional amendment to protect us."

"I . . . I'm sure most men try very hard to . . . to protect the ladies. It's our God-given duty to look after the fairer sex, after all." He smiled magnanimously, as if he thought he'd solved the whole problem of female inequality.

"Unfortunately, not all men fulfill that duty," Elizabeth said before Mrs. Bates could beat her

157

to it. "Mr. Preston has already provided the lie to your argument."

"I'm not sure how giving women the vote will change men like Mr. Preston," Mr. Devoss said.

"It won't, of course," Gideon said quickly. "But if women had more legal rights, men like Preston wouldn't be able to take advantage of them so easily."

Plainly, Mr. Devoss didn't want to argue. "I'm just old-fashioned, I guess. I'd like to see women safe and protected in their natural sphere of home and hearth."

"And yet," Mrs. Bates said without giving Elizabeth a chance to draw a breath, "the government has called on females to take the jobs left vacant by the men they have drafted to fight, doing things no one had ever thought them capable of before."

"Well, yes, but it's an emergency, isn't it?" Mr. Devoss said reasonably.

"Of course it is, but women have proven we can do the work of men if given the opportunity. And not every woman is fortunate enough to marry and find herself secure for life."

"After the war, many women will also find themselves *unable* to marry because so many young men have not returned from the war," Gideon said, making Elizabeth wince. He rarely mentioned the possibility of dying in battle, and hearing him mention it now took her appetite completely away.

"Yes, I've, uh, seen the casualty lists," Mr. Devoss admitted uneasily.

"Oh my, how did we get on such a dreary topic?" Mrs. Bates said. "Let's change the subject, shall we?"

"You're a Four Minute Man, aren't you, Mr. Devoss?" Elizabeth asked brightly, which wasn't much of a change of subject.

"Why, yes, I suppose I am, although I only present at clubs and such. I mainly encourage people to buy Liberty Bonds. I know Gideon has fulfilled his duty in that department, and I hope you have, too, Miss Miles. You know, you can pay it off over time. Five dollars a week, and in ten weeks, you'll have purchased a fifty-dollar bond. Think of all the good that will do for our boys."

Before Elizabeth could think of a reply worthy of such a request, Mrs. Bates said, "Elizabeth has already done her duty. Haven't you, dear? She bought a thousand-dollar bond the very first time she was asked."

Gideon, to his credit, covered his mouth and coughed to conceal his bark of laughter, while Mr. Devoss simply gaped at her.

"I hoped it would help end the war before Gideon had to go and fight," Elizabeth said as demurely as she could manage, because that had truly been her reason. "But you see how effective it was."

"I, uh, yes, well . . ." Mr. Devoss couldn't quite meet her eye. Usually, only millionaires and businesses bought such large-denomination bonds. "I believe I have underestimated you, Miss Miles."

"I make that mistake almost daily," Gideon said.

The maid came in to remove their soup bowls and serve the next course, giving Mr. Devoss time to recover his composure.

When they had been served and the maid had retreated, he said, "It is also my honor to serve as a member of the American Protective League."

Plainly, he expected them to be impressed. Elizabeth was not, although she tried not to show it. "I'm glad you warned us, Mr. Devoss. I'm afraid I'm often critical of the war that will take my fiancé away from me and into grave danger."

"I'm very sorry to lose Gideon to the army, too," Mr. Devoss said, "but how can we win the war if our young men don't fight it? You should be proud Gideon is so willing to serve."

"Of course we are," Mrs. Bates said quickly, "but we don't have to be happy about it. I had no idea you had involved yourself with the League, Roger. I'm having a difficult time picturing you hunting the city for spies."

"That's not what we do at all," Mr. Devoss assured her.

"Then what do you do?" Elizabeth asked.

He smiled the condescending smile that set her teeth on edge. "We are simply loyal citizens who keep an eye out for anyone who expresses anti-American views."

"Or pro-German views," Elizabeth guessed.

"Yes, that, too."

"Or people who are involved with labor unions or the Irish or . . . who else does the League consider a threat?" Elizabeth asked.

"Now, Miss Miles, you've been listening to rumors. We are merely volunteers helping out our Justice Department, which is seriously under-staffed, by reporting anything we think would be of interest to them."

"Like all those slackers the League picked up in that big raid?" Mrs. Bates asked sweetly.

The color rose noticeably in Mr. Devoss's neck. Earlier that month, members of the League had accosted virtually every man in the entire city who appeared to be of draftable age, demanding they prove their draft status. "We identified almost two hundred draft dodgers in that raid."

"And how many men did you detain in total?" Elizabeth asked, just as sweetly.

"About sixty thousand, wasn't it?" Gideon said when Mr. Devoss didn't answer.

"We may have been a bit overzealous that day, I'll admit," Mr. Devoss said.

"I should say. I was fortunate to have my identification with me," Gideon said.

"But we must be vigilant," Mr. Devoss argued. "Do you know how many young men from New York enlisted in the German army when the war first started?"

"But America was neutral then," Mrs. Bates reminded him.

"Yes, but some of our German residents may not be neutral now. We can't take any chances."

"I'm sure the government is very grateful for your help, Mr. Devoss," Elizabeth said, but she was thinking how convenient it would be if they could turn Fred Preston in as a German spy. Too bad he wasn't German like Delia.

CHAPTER SEVEN

Elizabeth was facing another day of trying to keep Rose Preston from dying of boredom when someone rang the doorbell. Cautiously, she went to see who was there and sighed with more than one kind of relief when she saw Anna Vanderslice on the front porch.

"What a surprise!" Elizabeth exclaimed, practically pulling Anna inside. "Don't you have classes today?"

"Of course not. It's Saturday," Anna said, laughing at Elizabeth's eagerness.

"Is it? I've lost track. One day is pretty much like another around here."

"Didn't Miss Miles and Miss Goodnight stay home this morning?"

"As a matter of fact, they were already gone when we got up. They probably went to the market or some other place that opens at the crack of dawn."

"Good morning, Miss Vanderslice," Rose said from the parlor doorway.

"Good morning to you, too, Rose, and I told you to call me Anna. I've come to entertain you once again, although I'm afraid I used up all my tricks the last time, so you'll probably be sorry."

"Never," Rose declared stoutly.

"Come in," Elizabeth urged her. "It's such a beautiful day. Maybe we can go for a walk, at least. I'm sure Rose is going crazy cooped up here all the time."

The three of them went into the parlor and settled themselves.

"I take it that you've seen no sign of potential assassins," Anna said.

Elizabeth gave her a sour look. "Please, don't use that word in front of Rose."

"Do you really think I'm that fragile?" Rose asked in feigned outrage.

"You're in a delicate condition," Elizabeth said. "We can't be too careful."

Rose sighed dramatically. "I suppose, but a word is hardly likely to do me in. Tell us what's happening out in the world, Anna."

"Nothing particularly noteworthy. There's a war, but you've heard about it already. Oh, and there's some kind of flu going around."

"Flu?" Rose asked.

"Influenza. Remember, Elizabeth, I had it back in the spring? A lot of other people did, too. It wasn't too bad, although I do hate to be sick, but it's back now, with a vengeance. Several of the girls at Hunter got it. Two were so sick, they went to the hospital."

164

"Oh dear, that doesn't sound good," Elizabeth said.

"I know. It's early in the season for it, too. Usually, people don't get the flu until the weather is cold."

"At least I'm not in danger of getting it," Rose said sadly. "I never leave the house."

"Since you've been here almost a week without anyone trying to kill you," Anna said with her usual diplomacy, "you really need to go out for some air. We can walk over to Washington Square and look at the fountain, at least."

"Someone might see Rose," Elizabeth objected.

"I can wear your veil," Rose said.

"Or one of your wigs," Anna said.

"Wigs? Why would Elizabeth have wigs?" Rose asked with a frown.

Elizabeth sighed. "Because I sometimes want to change my appearance. But I hadn't thought of a wig for Rose. That's brilliant, Anna. Let's go upstairs and see what we can do."

An hour later, they'd turned the lovely Rose into a middle-aged dowager, much to her delight. Elizabeth had borrowed some items from Zelda's wardrobe to complete her ensemble, and they were just about to set out when the doorbell rang again.

This time Elizabeth could see it was a man, but a quick peek revealed him to be her brother, Jake. "What are you doing here?"

He grinned. "How would you like to go for a ride in my motorcar?"

"You don't have a motorcar."

"I do today, so you'd better take the chance to ride in it while you can."

"May I bring my friends along?" Elizabeth asked, gesturing to where Rose and Anna stood in the foyer watching them.

"Of course. Hello, Miss Vanderslice. Nice to see you."

"Nice to see you, too, Mr. Miles. Have you met Mrs. Preston?"

He'd already removed his straw boater, and he sketched a respectful little bow. "Pleased to make your acquaintance, ma'am." He turned back to Elizabeth. "The Old Man said we need to find a business to buy."

"Is this part of his scheme?" Anna asked in delight. Elizabeth half expected her to clap her hands in glee. At least Rose was being circumspect.

"We'll see," Elizabeth said, hoping to quell her enthusiasm. "And Mrs. Preston wanted to be included, so here is your chance, although I'm afraid it won't be as exciting as you expected."

"Anything that gets me out of the house is exciting," she said.

The ladies gathered their hats and gloves and then followed Jake out to the street, where he had parked his very impressive automobile.

"Where on earth did you get this?" Elizabeth asked as she and the other ladies admired the red touring car. Its four large wheels and the spare mounted prominently on the driver's door sported white-walled tires and elaborately entwined spokes. The seats were upholstered in rich tan leather. In deference to the lovely weather, Jake had lowered the top.

"You'd better ride in the front, Rose," Elizabeth said. "Because of your, uh, hair." Having Rose's wig fly off would have defeated all their efforts to disguise her.

Jake made a face at his sister behind Rose's back. "She's not what I expected," he whispered while Rose took her seat. Ah, if he only knew!

Anna and Elizabeth climbed into the backseat and they set out.

"What kind of a business are we buying, Mr. Miles?" Anna called.

"It could be anything. We'll have to see what's available."

"Are you looking for something Fred Preston might buy?" Rose asked.

All three of her companions turned to her in surprise, and they almost hit a wagon before Jake recovered himself.

"Watch where you're going," Elizabeth cried. "And yes, something Fred would buy. Do you have any ideas, Rose?"

"Not shoes," she said.

"Why not?" Anna asked. "Isn't that his business?"

"Which is why he doesn't need another place to make shoes. If he wants to make more shoes, he can just do it in his own factory."

"What makes sense, then?" Elizabeth asked.

"How about clothes?" Anna said. "They go along with shoes, don't they?"

"Nobody is making clothes now, though," Jake said. "Everything is for the war."

"Uniforms, then," Anna said, willing to compromise.

"Which they make in clothing factories. So where are there factories in the city?" Elizabeth asked.

"I used to work in the shirtwaist factory on Twenty-third Street," Rose said.

"Then we'll start on Twenty-third Street," Jake said, making a turn that had the rest of them madly clutching the sides of the car.

Traffic was moving well since it was the middle of the day, and they quickly reached the neighborhood where Rose's old job had been. They cruised slowly along, examining each building for a possibility.

"What's that?" Anna asked as they approached a large building on which someone had painted some anti-German slogans. Several windows were broken, and glass still lay on the sidewalk. Debris and trash littered the whole area.

Jake pulled over, and they all stared. The sign over the front door read Adolph Hirsch Clothing Manufacture. Someone had painted a black X over it.

"What happened here?" Anna asked of no one in particular.

"I don't know, but let's find out," Jake said. "Lizzie, you take Mrs. Preston, and I'll take Miss Vanderslice. We'll walk around the neighborhood and see if anybody can tell us."

Elizabeth noticed Jake had taken Anna for himself. Even though he knew she could have no interest in him, she was far more attractive than Rose was at the moment. If Rose minded, she didn't let on. The two couples set off in different directions.

"Your brother thinks I'm an old lady," Rose said with a smug grin when they were out of earshot.

"I guess your disguise works."

"I could go anywhere like this."

"But someone who knows you already might recognize you. Your voice would give you away at least, so don't go thinking you can fool Fred or Delia."

"I won't, but I could probably fool that goon who tried to murder me."

"Let's hope you never see *him* again. Look, there's a tea shop. Let's go in."

The shop had only two other customers, a pair of ladies who appeared to be mother and daughter. Elizabeth and Rose sat down at a nearby table, and Elizabeth wondered if she and Rose looked like mother and daughter, too. They ordered tea and some lemon squares. When the waitress returned with their things, Elizabeth said, "On the way here, we passed a building with some awful things painted on it. Do you know what happened there?"

"Oh, that's Hirsch's place. The other night, a group of men marched down there with torches. They were with the Protective League. They claimed Hirsch was on the Germans' side or something, and they tarred and feathered him. When the police came, they locked him up."

"They locked *him* up?" Elizabeth repeated, sure she had misunderstood.

"Yeah, he's German, so they locked him up."

"They're going to sentence him to twenty years in prison," the older lady at the next table said. "He's a German spy."

"They say he helped plan the Black Tom explosion," the younger woman said with smug satisfaction.

Rose gasped, as well she might. Black Tom Island, just across the Hudson River in New Jersey, had been an ammunition depot where tons of munitions were stored before being shipped to France. Now it was just a big black hole after it had been blown to bits almost a year before the United States had even entered the war.

"But the Black Tom explosion was an accident," Elizabeth said.

"That's what the government said, but nobody really believed it," the older woman said. "Now we know Hirsch planned it all."

"That's awful," Rose said. "He deserves to go to prison."

"Everyone thinks so," the older woman said. "We are so ashamed that he was in our neighborhood all these years, but how could we have known?"

"Who is going to run his business now?" Elizabeth asked.

The two women exchanged a glance and shrugged. Elizabeth looked at the waitress, but she said, "What does it matter?" and walked away.

She was right. It might matter to the employees and to Mr. Hirsch's family, but for what Elizabeth had just thought up, it really didn't matter a bit.

"Hirsch was smuggling guns to the Germans," Jake reported when they all met back at the motorcar later. "He had a submarine that would come up the East River and take them out, with no one the wiser."

"That's ridiculous," Elizabeth said. "How did it get past the mines?"

"Are there mines in the East River?" Anna asked in alarm.

"Who knows? But I meant the mines the British set up out in the ocean so the Germans can't ship anything in."

"I don't know anything about mines," Jake said, not pleased that Elizabeth had called his information ridiculous. "But that's why they threw Hirsch in prison."

"We heard that he was the one who blew up Black Tom," Rose said.

"Now who's ridiculous?" Jake said. "That was an accident."

"And now I wonder what Mr. Hirsch is *really* guilty of," Elizabeth mused.

"Being German is my theory," Anna said. "It sounds to me like this is all just ordinary gossip and nobody really knows why poor Mr. Hirsch was arrested."

"You're probably right, Anna. Who told you about the gun smuggling?" Elizabeth asked her brother.

"We spoke to some fellow and his wife. They were out for a stroll, and they were sure he'd smuggled guns or something out of the country."

"Although he did say that was only what he'd heard," Anna qualified.

"Now that you mention it, the ladies in the tea shop had also only *heard* that Mr. Hirsch had blown up Black Tom. I guess it will all come out at his trial," Elizabeth said.

"No, it won't," Rose said with more authority

than Elizabeth thought she had a right to. "Official secrets. The newspapers can't print things like that. It's bad for morale. They never print anything bad."

Except the casualty lists, Elizabeth thought.

"How do you know so much about it?" Anna asked, obviously impressed.

"The soldiers talk."

"When do you talk to soldiers?" Jake asked with a frown.

"At the dances. I've been going to dances at the camps for months, and all those soldiers want to talk about is the war."

Jake's confusion was comic. He obviously couldn't figure out why a middle-aged matron had attended the dances held for the soldiers or why the soldiers would have been dancing with her. Elizabeth held up a hand to Anna, who caught her meaning immediately, and they waited silently while he worked through it.

Finally, Jake squinted and leaned down for a closer look at Rose's face. "Lizzie fixed you up."

Rose smiled in delight. "And you couldn't tell."

Jake shook his head. "The Old Man said you were a looker, so I was pretty disappointed when I saw you today. I thought he must be getting senile."

"That's good. Maybe nobody else will notice her, either," Elizabeth said. "Now, why don't you take all of us to lunch, Jake, and I'll tell you an idea I've got?"

"I should probably go home," Elizabeth said the next day when she and Gideon had finished Sunday dinner with his mother. As usual, they had attended church together and returned to the Bates home for dinner. Normally, she stayed on until supper, but now she had responsibilities and was feeling guilty. "I hate leaving Rose alone all day. I know Cybil and Zelda will look after her, but she's not really their responsibility."

"I'm sorry that she's yours, darling," Gideon said. "If I could think of a safer place for her, I'd move her in an instant."

"I know, and I don't really mind, but she can't stay with me forever. I certainly hope the Old Man comes up with an idea soon." Which he would, since it would be her idea.

"Someday I'm going to insist that you explain to me why you call your father the 'Old Man,'" Mrs. Bates said.

"And someday I will tell you," Elizabeth replied with a grin.

The doorbell rang, startling them.

"Who could that be?" Mrs. Bates asked with a frown. "Gideon, are you expecting anyone?"

"No, Mother, I'm not."

So they waited while the maid answered the door and escorted the Old Man into the parlor.

"Mr. Miles," Mrs. Bates said with obvious pleasure. Really, Elizabeth was going to have to have a talk with her. The Old Man was charming, but Mrs. Bates shouldn't be falling under his spell. "Please, come in."

"I'm sorry to disturb you, Mrs. Bates, but I needed to speak to Lizzie and Gideon privately, and this is the one place I knew I'd find them together. I hope you don't mind the intrusion."

"Not at all. Can I offer you some refreshment?"

When they had dispensed with all the courtesies and the Old Man had a glass of lemonade to refresh him, Mrs. Bates withdrew with obvious reluctance.

"Is this about the Prestons?" Elizabeth asked when Mrs. Bates was gone.

"Of course it is. I wanted to thank you for working with Jake yesterday. He told me about his excursion with you and your friends."

"Excursion?" Gideon asked with a frown.

"Jake took Anna, Rose and me out for a drive in a beautiful red motorcar."

"Whose motorcar?" Gideon asked. He knew Jake well.

"A friend's," the Old Man said vaguely. "At any rate, they were able to locate exactly what we were looking for, and now I have a plan. I just need to know if either of you are going to be involved."

Elizabeth glanced at Gideon and was surprised

to see he wasn't quite as horrified at this prospect as she had expected. Instead of objecting outright, he said, "What did you have in mind?"

"I want to present Preston with an opportunity to buy a clothing manufacturing company at a bargain rate. A man with his contacts should be able to obtain a government contract to produce uniforms, which would result in an enormous profit for him."

"I don't suppose the person from whom he will buy the factory actually owns it," Gideon said without a trace of irony.

The Old Man merely smiled.

"What would you need from us?" Elizabeth said as if she had no idea.

"I need a roper. I could just use Jake or someone else I know, but I was thinking Preston might be suspicious if an opportunity suddenly presented itself so soon after his encounter with his brother's widow. I thought perhaps a softer approach would be wise."

"And by 'softer,'" Gideon said, "I assume you want to use Elizabeth." He did not look pleased.

"A damsel in distress is always appealing and never threatening."

"But Preston has already demonstrated that he has little sympathy for ladies in distress."

"He won't need to have any at all for my purposes."

"Oh, I see," Elizabeth said, and of course

she did. "Preston won't really want to help me, but he'll see an opportunity to profit from my misfortune."

"That is what I had in mind," the Old Man confirmed. "You were always the quick one, Lizzie."

"What exactly did you want Elizabeth to do?" Gideon asked, still not pleased.

"Just to rope him," Elizabeth said. "That means I tell him the tale and get him interested and vouch for the inside man. Then I introduce them, and my part is done."

"If everything goes according to plan," the Old Man said. He didn't mention that the roper got a generous share of the profit, which would go to Rose, of course.

"But nothing ever goes according to plan, does it?" Gideon said. "And what would Elizabeth do to 'rope' him?"

"Simply present herself in a situation where her distress and her unfortunate situation would most naturally be revealed. I was thinking an attorney's office would be just the place."

"No, Father," Elizabeth said. "You can't use Gideon's office for something like this."

"I suppose you'd expect me to play some role in all of it, too," Gideon said, ignoring her protest.

"A small one. I wouldn't expect you to lie, of course." The Old Man knew Gideon well, too.

"What *would* you expect me to do?"

"Gideon, you can't be serious," Elizabeth said. "What would Mr. Devoss say?"

"He isn't likely to know anything about it," Gideon said. "But if you're going to meet Fred Preston, I'm going to be there to make sure you're safe." He turned back to the Old Man. "Now, tell me what you have in mind."

Gideon couldn't believe how easy it had been to get Fred Preston back to his office. All it had taken was a telegram saying Rose Preston was considering the invitation to move to Pough-keepsie and live with her brother-in-law and his stepmother. Gideon had to wait a few days—Fred had to impress upon Gideon that he was a busy, important man who couldn't just drop everything at a moment's notice—but late on Wednesday morning, Fred arrived right on schedule.

"This had better be worth my time, Bates," Preston said without observing the usual pleas-antries. Behind him, Smith winced in dismay before making his discreet exit.

"I hope it's worth my time as well, Mr. Preston. You can't think my employer is happy to see me spending time on an estate that is now worthless."

This took Preston aback, as Gideon had expected, and he sat down without another word of complaint.

"Are you seeing much flu up your way?"

Gideon asked pleasantly as he took his own seat behind his desk.

"I . . . A bit. I saw the posters at the train station when I came in. It must be worse here."

"We have more people, I suppose. The posters went up a couple days ago. You'd better read them and do what they say. They'll arrest you for spitting on the sidewalk now."

"Arrest? What kind of a place is this?"

"A careful one, but it's still much more interesting than Poughkeepsie, I'm sure. Are you planning to stay over? You could see a show while you're here."

Fred Preston didn't look like the type of man who enjoyed shows. "I thought they'd closed the theaters."

"They talked about it, but they decided not to. Instead they've got the Four Minute Men delivering speeches on how to avoid getting the flu. It's rather strange."

"That is strange, but I'm not staying. I have a company to run, after all, and I need to get back."

"Of course you do. So let me begin by apologizing to you. I'm afraid I let my temper get the best of me at our previous meetings, but we're both reasonable men, and I think we can come to some kind of understanding." This wasn't a lie. Gideon thought they should be able to, although he very much doubted Fred Preston would ever cooperate.

For his part, Preston seemed placated. He actually relaxed a little in his chair. "I'm sure we can, Mr. Bates. I know you're hampered with a hysterical client, but if anyone can make her see reason, you can."

"I'm afraid I wasn't as polite as I could have been to your stepmother, either, but she did take me by surprise with your offer to provide a home for Mrs. Tom. Once I had an opportunity to consider it, however, I recognized your generosity and could see the many advantages." The advantages, of course, were negated by the possibility that they could murder Rose with impunity, but there was no sense in mentioning that.

"Your telegram said Rose is going to accept our offer," Preston said with some satisfaction.

"I said she is *considering* it," Gideon corrected him. "She knows how you feel about her marriage to Tom, though, so she needs some reassurances that she won't be made to suffer at your hands."

"Suffer? In what way?" Preston asked with credible astonishment. "Oh, I suppose I was a little harsh with her when she arrived on my doorstep out of the blue and told me she'd married Tom in practically the same breath that she told me he was dead. Is it any wonder I was less than tactful? Who could blame me for thinking her an adventuress? I was overcome

180

with grief at finding out my only brother was dead."

"I'm sure I can understand your distress," Gideon said as tactfully as he could manage. "And of course you didn't know about the child then."

That made Fred flinch. "Yes, well. The child does change things."

"I suppose that's why your stepmother decided to take Rose in."

Fred started a bit at that. "We both decided it."

"I'm sure you did. I suppose I just assumed it was something a woman would think of first."

Fred had no comment to that. "So is she coming or not?"

"She would like a little assurance. After all, you could change your mind and put her out at any time."

"Why would we change our minds?"

Gideon thought that a disingenuous question, but he said, "Perhaps you'll find it difficult to live together. She's a stranger to you, after all, and Mrs. Tom's, uh, background is much different from yours."

"If you mean she's a common little . . ." Fortunately, he caught himself before saying something Gideon could not forgive. "She's common. Yes, we understand, and we're prepared to make allowances. In fact, I think living with

181

Delia—that's my stepmother—will be a good influence on her."

"That's possible," Gideon granted. "Mrs. Tom would also like to have an allowance so she isn't completely dependent on you for everything."

"If I pay the allowance, she'll still be dependent on me," Fred pointed out acidly.

"That's true, of course, but at least she wouldn't have to ask every time she needed some little thing."

Fred grinned at that. "I suppose she's feeling the pinch now that I've cut off Tom's dividend payments."

Gideon hadn't even thought of that. "Have you?"

"Of course. Tom is dead, so as soon as I learned of it, I told our bookkeeper to stop sending the checks."

"Were you sending them directly to him?"

"Not after . . . Well, I suppose it was after he married. He requested that I send them to a bank in New York instead."

Probably the bank in the lobby of the Ansonia, which would have made it relatively easy for Fred to figure out where Rose lived. And once Rose had spent whatever money remained in Tom's account, she would be penniless. Fred had her exactly where he wanted her. "I'm sure Mrs. Tom wouldn't expect an allowance as generous as Tom's income was, but surely a man as successful as you are could afford a few hundred dollars a year in spending money for your brother's widow and child."

"Certainly, I could, but I don't see any reason why I should. We'll provide everything she needs."

Gideon would never advise any client to accept a situation like that, although he realized that women did so every day when they married. When she became a wife, a woman gave up all rights, even to property she had owned before the marriage, and put herself completely at the mercy of her husband. Gideon could honestly say he'd never entrust any woman's welfare to Fred Preston.

"Mrs. Tom will be disappointed, I'm sure," Gideon said, "but I'll relay your response to her. I suspect she'll want to meet with you and your stepmother before making her final decision."

"Delia and I will be happy to meet with her, although traveling back and forth to the city is rather tiresome and time consuming for us. Perhaps Rose could travel to Poughkeepsie next time."

To Poughkeepsie, where Preston's goon would have a much easier time of it if he wanted to attack her again. "Perhaps," Gideon said.

"Really, if this is the only reason you wanted to speak to me, I must insist that you make the trip to me the next time," Preston said, warming to his outrage. "I'm a busy man, and with the war on—"

The door burst open, and Elizabeth rushed in. She looked so desperate, Gideon almost forgot why she was there.

"Oh, Mr. Bates, you must help me. What on earth am I going to do now? They're saying my father will go to prison for twenty years and—" She stopped dead, having just noticed Fred Preston, who, like Gideon, had automatically risen to his feet when she entered. "I'm sorry. I didn't know you . . ." She gestured helplessly at Fred.

Smith had hurried in behind her. "I'm sorry, sir, but she insisted . . ."

"Quite all right, Smith. I'll take care of Miss—"

"Don't say my name!" she cried with a panicked glance at Fred. "It's too . . . humiliating." To Gideon's horror, she burst into tears.

"Smith, would you get Miss . . . get a glass of water, please? Here, sit down." He guided her to the empty client chair beside Preston's. She'd pulled out a handkerchief from somewhere and was weeping into it. "I'm sorry, Mr. Preston," he said, giving the man a glance.

Preston looked perplexed and annoyed, so he probably wasn't the type to offer his assistance to a damsel in distress. They'd been right about that, at least.

Smith returned with a glass of water, which

Elizabeth gratefully sipped. "I didn't mean to bother you, Mr. Bates, but I didn't know whom else to turn to."

"I already told you, I can't help you. A man who has . . ." He glanced at Preston, who wasn't bothering to hide his interest. "A man in that position should have a criminal attorney."

"I know, I know," she said, "but you've been so kind to me, and my father always said that if anything happened . . ." She glanced at Preston again and seemed to catch herself. "But he also said we should never air our dirty laundry in public." She forced a smile and dabbed at her eyes one last time. "Please forgive me, Mr. Bates, and Mr. . . . ?"

"Preston," he replied with a very curt nod.

"Mr. Preston. You must think me terribly rude for barging in like that. I'll just . . . I should go."

She cast Gideon a hopeful look, but he merely took the water glass from her hand and made no move to stop her. "If there's anything that I *can* do, don't hesitate to ask," he said.

She thanked him with a wan smile and made her exit, apologizing one last time for interrupting their meeting. For a long moment after she left, neither he nor Preston said a word. Then Preston said, "What was all that about?"

"I . . . Well, as you probably guessed, the young lady appears to be in serious difficulty, but I couldn't possibly discuss it, I'm afraid. I can't discuss my clients' business with other people. I'm sure you understand."

"Of course, but . . . Such a lovely young woman. I can't imagine how she could be in any trouble."

"She isn't, or at least not personally, but . . . Well, it's confidential. You wouldn't want me telling strangers about your situation with your brother's widow, would you?"

"No, of course not." He glanced at the door through which Elizabeth had disappeared, and Gideon thought he looked a little wistful. Elizabeth had that effect on men, but Gideon certainly didn't like seeing her have it on Fred Preston.

"So, where were we?" Gideon asked.

Preston needed another moment to remember himself. "You were going to explain to Rose why I won't be giving her an allowance and why it would be in her best interest to come to Poughkeepsie."

That wasn't exactly what he'd agreed to do, but Gideon nodded. "Yes, and if she agrees, I will bring her to Poughkeepsie to discuss the details with you and your stepmother."

He shook hands with Preston and summoned Smith to see him out. Once he was alone, he sank down into his desk chair and sighed. That had gone well, or at least he thought it had. Now all he had to do was worry about the rest of it.

CHAPTER EIGHT

Elizabeth hadn't been able to get much of a feel for Fred Preston during their brief encounter, although she did notice he hadn't seemed particularly taken with her charms. Gideon, she knew, would have behaved exactly as he had even if he'd never laid eyes on her before, jumping to assist and comfort her. Just as he'd done the very first time they'd ever met, she remembered. He also would have done the same for any female in distress, even if she weren't young and pretty. As for Fred Preston, well, she was going to put him to the test once more.

She took up her position on the sidewalk outside the offices of Devoss and Van Aken, pulled out her handkerchief and waited. She didn't have to wait very long. Fred Preston appeared, pausing on the stoop to adjust his straw boater before proceeding on his way. Elizabeth took this opportunity to sob into her handkerchief in an effort to get his attention.

Fred glanced at her, then hesitated and looked around. Was he checking to see if he was observed? Did he hope someone else was coming to assist her? Would he simply ignore her completely? She made it more difficult for him by looking up and meeting his eye. She gave him her most entreating gaze, and as she had hoped, he moved toward her, even though he seemed less than enthusiastic about it.

"Excuse me, miss, but can I summon a cab for you or something?"

Thank heaven he had been properly brought up, no matter how disagreeable he might be otherwise. "Thank you, Mr. Preston. You are very kind." She dabbed at her eyes but continued before he could turn away to perform his duty. "Pardon me for asking, but are you an attorney, by any chance?"

"Me? No, not at all. I'm a businessman." He turned toward the street in search of a cab.

"What kind of business are you in?" she asked with too much interest.

He heard the tinge of desperation in her voice, a sound that must have touched a chord that mere pity or common courtesy would have ignored. "I . . . Shoes. I own a factory that makes shoes."

"Do you really? Oh, Mr. Preston, forgive me for being so forward, since we hardly know each other, but perhaps you could advise me."

He didn't look very eager to do any such thing, but at least he didn't run away. "Advise you about what?"

"You see, my family owns a factory, too. We make clothes. Or, rather, my father does. Did. He used to make men's suits, but most recently, he had a contract to make uniforms for the army."

"Yes, well . . ." He was looking for that cab again.

"Beth, is this man bothering you?" Jake asked, hurrying to her side. He had done a good job of transforming himself into Karl, a factory worker, and he looked very German with his blond wig and mustache.

"What? Oh no, Karl, not at all. This is Mr. Preston. He owns a shoe factory."

The two men eyed each other suspiciously.

"How nice for him," Jake said. "Why are you talking to him on the street, Beth?"

"I was just going to ask his advice about what I should do with our factory now that Father can't manage it. . . ." Her voice broke again, but she caught a glimpse of Fred Preston before burying her face in her handkerchief. She finally had his interest.

"You can't be going around asking total strangers for advice, Beth," Jake said.

"But I'm not a total stranger," Preston said, suddenly quite willing to be friendly. "I was just introduced to this lady in Mr. Bates's office, although she refused to divulge her name."

"As well she might," Jake muttered. "Beth, we should go."

"But, Karl, I was going to ask Mr. Preston for help."

"What do you think he's going to do? Buy your father's company? After the trial, you'll be lucky to give it away."

"Oh, Karl, don't say that," she cried, and burst into tears again.

This time Fred Preston could not have been more solicitous. "This young lady is in no condition to go anywhere. Perhaps a cup of tea would help. There's a tea shop just down the street where she can rest and regain her composure."

"Thank you, Mr. Preston," Elizabeth said between sobs. "Karl, you'll accompany us, of course."

"Of course," Jake said with little grace.

Elizabeth took Preston's arm, leaving Karl to follow behind them. She'd managed to stop sobbing by the time they reached the tea shop. Mr. Preston got all of them seated at a table and ordered a pot of tea for them. Karl was understandably sullen while they waited for the tea, and Preston didn't press her until it had arrived and she had taken a few calming sips.

"I don't mean to pry into your private affairs, you understand," Preston said at last, "but if I can be of some assistance, it would be my great privilege to help."

Karl glared at him, unimpressed, but Elizabeth said, "You are so kind. I hate to burden you with my problems, but I've received so much advice from friends that I don't know whom to believe anymore. I thought perhaps someone who isn't personally involved might be able to see things more clearly."

Preston gave her what he probably thought was his most charming smile, although it made him look a little like a simpering snake. "I will certainly try, although I can't help at all until you tell me your situation."

"Beth, you don't have to tell him anything," Jake said. "What if he's one of them?"

"One of whom?" Preston asked with interest.

"It's too late to worry about that now, isn't it?" she chided Karl sharply, then turned to Preston. "I told you that my family—well, my father really—owns a company that manufactures clothing. A few days ago, a mob descended on the business and my father was arrested." She glanced around to make sure no one was listening, then leaned in closer and lowered her voice. "My father is German, you see. He came here when he was only fifteen, and he worked very hard, and now he owns his own business. He loves this country, but his parents still live in Germany. He has tried to get them to move here many times, but they always refused to leave the Fatherland. Now, with the war, it is impossible, but things are very difficult for them over there, so he sends them money. He has always supported them, but now . . ." She had to pause to collect herself. "Now they

191

say he is giving aid and comfort to the enemy."

Jake made a sound of disgust.

"I see," Preston said, although she could not tell from his tone exactly what he thought he saw.

"I know it sounds terrible, sending money to Germany when they're killing our young men, but my grandparents are just two old people who might starve if my father doesn't help them. How can it be against the law to support your own parents?"

"And yet it is," Preston said. "This is a very serious matter."

"We know that only too well, Preston," Jake said, not bothering to hide his anger. "And now you see that there's nothing you can do to help. Beth, we should go."

"But I haven't asked Mr. Preston what I should do," Elizabeth protested.

"I don't think there's anything you *can* do for your father," Preston said.

"I know that, but what about the company? The army is going to cancel our contract. Isn't that what they said, Karl?"

Jake nodded reluctantly.

"I'm sure they will. They won't do business with a traitor," Preston said, making Elizabeth sob again.

"But if my father goes to prison and the company goes out of business, I'll . . . What will become of me? My mother died years ago, and I don't have any other family. I'll be penniless."

"Really?" Preston asked with way too much interest. "Didn't your father put anything by?"

"I suppose so, but . . . Mr. Preston, let me be frank with you. I had once hoped to make a good marriage, but now my father has been branded a traitor. He may go to prison."

"He most certainly will go to prison," Jake said grimly, earning a black look from Elizabeth.

She shivered but continued. "I can no longer expect any man of principle to take me as his wife, so I must plan to be alone for the rest of my life. If I hope to avoid destitution, I need to sell my father's business."

"But who would buy it now?" Jake scoffed, getting another glare from Elizabeth, which he ignored. "No one wants to be associated with a traitor, and even if you could find someone willing, they'd never pay you what the company is worth."

Preston nodded, clearly understanding their predicament even better than they did themselves. "You said your company had a contract with the army."

"Yes," Jake said. "We'd just started making uniforms. With this month's draft, they're going to need thousands more, but they won't do business with . . . with us anymore."

"They'd continue the contract if someone else took over the company, though," Elizabeth said eagerly. "Isn't that what they told you, Karl?"

"Not me. They don't talk to me," he said sourly.

"Karl—Mr. Weber—is only our foreman," she explained to Preston with another chastening glance at Jake. "They would have spoken with Mr. Lange. He's the manager."

"And did they tell this Lange that they would continue the contract if someone else owned the company?" Preston asked. Elizabeth could actually see the greed glittering in his eyes.

"You'll have to ask Lange," Jake said, clearly fed up with this discussion. "And what does it matter? Nobody is going to buy it now. Have you seen the building? It's covered with anti-German slogans. The workers won't even come near it, so who would make the uniforms even if we did get the contract back?"

"I don't think that will be a problem. Thousands of people have come to the city to find war work. We could get all new workers if necessary."

"We?" Jake asked with a threatening frown. "When did this become your problem?"

Preston gave her his simpering-snake smile again. "When this young lady asked for my help. I'm sorry, miss, but I still don't know your name."

"Hirsch," she said in a whisper, looking around to make sure no one had overheard.

"As your friend here points out, Miss Hirsch, this is not really any of my business, but I would

194

not be able to live with myself if I failed to help you when it was within my power to do so."

"How can you help her?" Jake asked, even more skeptical than before.

"I . . . Well, as I told Miss Hirsch, I own a factory that makes shoes. In Poughkeepsie. I also have an army contract, and as you will no doubt surmise, I have done very well. I've been wanting to expand my business, but opportunities are limited, because everyone else is doing well, too, and no one is interested in selling out at any price."

"But would you be brave enough to . . . to deal with this situation?" Elizabeth asked, a quaver in her voice.

"Dear lady, it would be my honor."

"You don't have any idea what you're getting into," Jake said.

Beth could have slapped him, although Elizabeth thoroughly approved. "Karl, how can you speak to Mr. Preston like that when he's trying to help?"

"You are fortunate to have friends who look after your interests, Miss Hirsch," Preston said amiably. "Mr. Weber is right to be skeptical, and quite frankly, I cannot make any promises until I know a bit more about the situation, but I would be happy to speak to . . . Mr. Lange, is it?"

"Yes, Mr. Lange. He will know everything. Oh, Mr. Preston, how can I ever thank you?"

"I haven't done anything yet, Miss Hirsch. Now, tell me how I can arrange to meet with Mr. Lange."

"You said your business was in Poughkeepsie, Mr. Preston, but do you by chance live in the city?"

"I'm afraid not, but I was planning to be in town for a few days on business."

Elizabeth almost smiled at that. He hadn't intended to stay in the city another moment when he left Gideon's office, which she knew because she'd been eavesdropping on the conversation before making her entrance. "If you'll tell us which hotel you're staying at, we can send you a message. Would tomorrow be all right for you, or do you have appointments already scheduled?"

"Nothing that can't be changed, I'm sure." He gave her the name of a hotel.

"Karl and I will go to find Mr. Lange right away and see when he is available. You'll hear from him as soon as we can make arrangements. Oh, Mr. Preston, you have given me hope."

"I'm glad to hear it, Miss Hirsch. And don't worry about a thing. I'm sure we can come to an agreement that will satisfy everyone."

Elizabeth felt sure that was almost true.

"I believe Smith has a successful future ahead of him if he chooses to pursue a life of crime," Gideon informed her when he found her waiting for him in his parlor at home later. She and Jake had been visiting with his mother while they awaited his arrival.

"Have you involved poor Smith in your machinations?" his mother asked, plainly delighted to think so.

"He was only too happy to do whatever Miss Miles asked of him," Gideon said with a feigned scowl. "I believe he is besotted with her."

"With Lizzie?" Jake scoffed.

"Many men find me irresistible," Elizabeth informed him.

"Only because they don't know you very well," Jake said.

"Then I suppose it's a blessing that Smith doesn't know me very well," she said. "At any rate, I thought he performed his part magnificently."

"He told me later that he found it quite enjoyable, too," Gideon said.

"Compared to what he normally does, I'm sure he did," his mother said. "What part did he play?"

"He simply had to pretend that I had burst into Gideon's office unannounced and be suitably outraged."

"Fortunately, Smith has gotten a lot of experience with people bursting into my office unannounced since I met Elizabeth, so it wasn't difficult for him," Gideon said.

"Had no one ever burst into your office before?" Elizabeth asked in wonder.

"Never. Devoss and Van Aken frowns on bursting."

"Or anything resembling excitement at all, I imagine," his mother said.

"What a sorry place that must be," Jake said. "You should come to work for the Old Man, Gideon. It would be a lot more fun, and you'd make more money, too."

"Thank you, Jake. I will give your offer some serious consideration."

"Especially if Mr. Devoss fires you for allowing such unseemly behavior at the office," Elizabeth said.

"If I'm able to bring in a fee for managing Tom Preston's estate, he will forgive me anything," Gideon said. "So how did you do with Fred Preston?"

Jake gallantly got up from where he'd been sitting beside Elizabeth on the sofa so Gideon could take his place, and moved to a chair nearby. Gideon sat down and took Elizabeth's hand in his, wishing his mother and Jake weren't here so he could take the rest of her into his arms.

"He fell for it," Elizabeth said, "although not because he was blinded by my charms."

"I'm glad to hear that."

"Another man who doesn't find you irresistible, Lizzie," Jake said with some satisfaction.

She stuck her tongue out at him.

"Fred strikes me as one of those single-minded men who refuse to be distracted from their sole purpose in life, which is to make as much money as he can before he dies," Gideon said in her defense.

"And once he realized I might be able to help him reach his goal, he did suddenly become interested in me," Elizabeth said.

"I don't know how you do it, Elizabeth," his mother said. "I'd be so nervous, I'd probably give myself away in the first minute."

"I don't know about that," Elizabeth said. "I've seen you lie with the best of them."

"What?" Gideon exclaimed, seeing his own shock mirrored on his mother's face.

"Whatever do you mean?" his mother asked in obvious dismay.

"Every time you say, 'How nice to see you,' when it isn't nice at all. Or 'You look lovely in that hat,' when it's hideous, or 'I'd love to come to your party,' when you know it will be a total bore."

"But everyone does that," his mother protested.

"Quite naturally, too, which proves you'd be a good liar, because you already are."

"Should I take that as a compliment?" his mother asked uncertainly.

"Oh yes," Jake said. "That's about the nicest thing I've ever heard her say to somebody."

Everyone laughed at that, and when they'd regained their composure, Gideon said, "What happens next?"

"The Old Man will go to Preston's hotel to meet with him."

"Does that mean your part in this is done?" Gideon asked hopefully.

"Most likely, although you never know. Nothing ever goes exactly the way you plan it."

"But that's the fun of it," Jake said.

"Fun?" his mother echoed in obvious disbelief.

Jake shrugged unapologetically, and Gideon didn't bother to explain. Obviously, these things were fun for Jake and Elizabeth, however harrowing they might be for Gideon.

"Just promise me that you'll never be alone with Fred Preston," Gideon said in all seriousness.

"I wouldn't even consider it," Elizabeth said, "although I don't think Fred is the real danger. He had to hire someone to rob Rose's apartment, remember."

"I wish we knew who that was," Gideon said.

"Let's just hope we never encounter him," Elizabeth said, "and we have no reason to think we will. Fred Preston isn't going to need to frighten anyone into taking his money."

"Gideon said you're going to make him think he's buying a factory," his mother said. "What will you do when he tries to take possession of it, though?"

"You worry too much, Mrs. Bates," Elizabeth said.

"Yes, you do," Jake added with a flirtatious grin. Why was Jake flirting with his mother? "First of all, we won't be anywhere around when Fred tries to take possession of the factory, and secondly, that probably won't even happen."

"But if he's going to buy it . . ." she tried, but Elizabeth was shaking her head.

"As I said, things hardly ever go as planned. Something is bound to happen that will disappoint his expectations."

"But you will keep me informed," his mother said. "This is all so fascinating."

"Of course," Elizabeth said.

Gideon couldn't tell if she was lying or not and thought it better if he didn't know. He cleared his throat, drawing everyone's attention. "I got some news today about my enlistment."

Elizabeth's grip tightened on his fingers, and her beautiful blue eyes filled with alarm. At least what he had to say would banish it. "They're closing all the training camps for the entire month of October because of the flu."

"The flu?" his mother said. "Why would they close them because of the flu?"

"It's running rampant through the camps, and they can't send sick soldiers to France, so they've suspended the draft until this thing runs its course."

"What does that mean for you?" Elizabeth asked.

"It means I won't have to report for training until November."

The alarm was indeed banished, replaced by joy. "And three more months of training before you go to France. Maybe the war will be over by then."

He smiled, but he knew it would look stiff because it felt stiff. "Maybe it will be," he said, but he was pretty sure it wouldn't be.

"I'll never understand Gideon," Jake remarked as he and Elizabeth left the Bates house in search of a cab.

"Why? Because he's in love with me?" Elizabeth asked in amusement.

"That, too, but I meant I'll never understand why he'd want to be a lawyer."

"He makes a very good living as a lawyer, and he never has to worry about being arrested."

"Most of the lawyers I know worry about that all the time," Jake told her with what sounded like pride.

"But Gideon doesn't, and I must admit, it's comforting to know I won't ever have to visit him in jail."

"That was all a big mistake," Jake said a little defensively.

"I know. I helped you get out of it, didn't I?"

Plainly, Jake didn't like being reminded of his youthful indiscretions.

"You did very well with Preston," she said when they reached the corner.

Jake had been scanning the street for a cab, but that stopped him, and he turned to Elizabeth with a frown. "What does that mean?"

"It just means you did very well with Preston."

"What were you expecting?"

She heard the challenge in his voice and refused to rise to it. Jake had been badly beaten a few months ago after a con went bad, and for a while, he'd been unable to work. The Old Man had told her Jake had lost his nerve. Part of her thought anything that got him out of the life would have been a blessing, except she knew Jake too well to imagine him earning a living doing honest work. "I was expecting you to do well, and you did. I'm a lady now, Jakie, and ladies say nice things."

"Don't call me Jakie, and saying nice things is very unnatural for you."

"As is being a lady, but here we are. Is that a cab?"

Jake flagged it down, and they climbed in. The driver was wearing one of the surgical masks the government had started giving out to help protect people from the flu.

Should she get one? She shook off the thought.

Jake gave the driver the address of Cybil's house in Greenwich Village.

"So I'm not going with you to see the Old Man?" she said.

"You said yourself your part is over."

She knew a pang of disappointment, sharpened by anger that Jake felt he had the authority to make that decision. But he was right. She really shouldn't be going around town conning people when anyone might see her and wonder why she was in the company of strange men. She shouldn't even have taken this small role, although nothing could have stopped her except maybe the Old Man absolutely refusing to tell her what he was up to. Jake was right. Conning people was fun, and when she and Gideon were married, she'd never be able to do it again, so one last time couldn't hurt, could it?

The Old Man made Fred Preston wait until the next afternoon for their meeting. He wanted to make Fred more anxious, and he also needed time to perfect a disguise that would make it difficult for Preston to identify him later. The downtown hotel, the Old Man couldn't help noticing as he checked his disguise in a foggy lobby mirror, was second-rate. Fred apparently didn't believe in throwing his money away on expensive lodging. Fred was waiting in the lobby for him, as the desk clerk informed him when he asked for Preston. The two men shook hands, and Fred suggested that they move to a far corner of the lobby where they were not likely to be overheard.

The Old Man thought this silly. They could still easily be overheard, but Fred was probably not willing to spend a few cents on a drink, so going to a restaurant or some other place where they would have to pay was out of the question. Preston, he could see, would be an easy mark. His unwillingness to part with his money for little things also indicated a greedy nature that would make him vulnerable to the promise of a big score.

"I don't know what Miss Hirsch told you," the Old Man began, letting Preston see his reluctance to discuss this subject at all.

"She said her father owns a factory that was making uniforms for the army."

"Yes. That's no secret."

"But there was some trouble, and the old man was arrested."

"Mr. Hirsch is innocent. He would never do the things he has been accused of."

"The girl said he was sending money to Germany, so that means he wasn't innocent."

"To his parents only, to keep them from starving. That cannot be wrong."

"It is if it's against the law. Look, Lange, I don't care what the old man did. That's between him and the government. What I care about is the girl said she needs to sell the company because her father is going to prison."

"Miss Hirsch does not know how business works."

"Well, I do, and I know that the army is going to cancel their contract with Hirsch, and nobody else is going to do business with a traitor, either, so Hirsch might as well board the place up if he's not planning to sell out."

"I do not know what Mr. Hirsch plans to do. I have not been allowed to visit him. No one has."

"The girl said you would know all about it," Preston said, not bothering to hide his irritation. "I've been sitting around here waiting for you since yesterday because I thought we could do business."

"What business is it you want to do, Mr. Preston?"

"I thought it was pretty clear. Hirsch can't run his factory if he's locked up. Nobody else can run it for him because he's a traitor."

"No one has proved that yet."

"But they will, and when they do, things will be even worse. I'm willing to take the factory off his hands right now. I already have government contracts, so they'll be happy to do business with me."

"Why are you so eager, Mr. Preston?"

Preston frowned, annoyed again. "I'm a Good Samaritan. I want to help Miss Hirsch."

The Old Man didn't bother to hide his contempt. "How fortunate Miss Hirsch was to meet you, then."

"All right, I want to make a buck just like the next guy, but I'd be doing her and her father a favor. If they just close the place up, they'll get nothing, and I'm ready to pay them cash."

"Cash?"

"I told you, I have government contracts. I'm doing very well, and I want to do even better. It's my patriotic duty to supply the troops."

The Old Man managed not to laugh at that. Instead he frowned. "I told you, I cannot speak for Mr. Hirsch."

"Then go see him. Tell him I'm willing to buy him out."

"The company is worth a million dollars, maybe more. Can you pay that much in *cash?*" the Old Man said with a sneer.

But Preston laughed in his face. "Maybe it was worth that much a month ago, but it's not worth anything now. I'm willing to give him a hundred thousand, but that offer won't be good for very long."

"A hundred thousand? The factory and equipment alone are worth more than that."

"But the factory alone can't make anything. You've got to have workers and contracts. Nobody is going to work for Hirsch, and nobody is going to buy from him. So you tell him you've found somebody to save his skin."

"I do not know how quickly I can speak to him."

"Then I'm not waiting around. If you want to make a deal, come and see me in Poughkeepsie." He handed the Old Man his card. "Don't wait too long, though."

Fred Preston was feeling very good about himself by the time he got back to Poughkeepsie. He'd telegraphed Delia to wait dinner for him, since he saw no reason to spend another night in New York when he could eat and sleep for free at home. His father had taught him the virtues of frugality—something Tom had never really mastered, he was sure.

Or Delia, either, for that matter.

She was waiting in the parlor when he got home, and she told him to close the parlor doors behind him. She looked calm and composed, her beauty a mask she wore comfortably to conceal the emotions that ran deep inside her and that could erupt at any moment. Fred had to tread carefully.

"What did that attorney say about Tom's widow?" she asked without so much as a hello first.

"He said she is considering our offer."

"You mean, she'll come to us?"

"I got the feeling she knows it's her only choice, but she's holding out for an allowance."

"What kind of an allowance?" There it was, that little edge of temper.

"He didn't say exactly, but pin money, probably."

"Probably? Didn't you ask him for an exact amount?"

"Why bother when we aren't going to give her anything at all? You said yourself, she needs to be completely dependent on us." He realized he needed a drink and moved to the sideboard to pour himself one.

"But we will probably have to promise her something to get her here."

"Then we'll promise. What does it matter?"

She waited until he had poured some whiskey into a glass and taken the first sip. He could feel the warmth settle into his stomach. In a few moments, it would spread. "Why did you stay overnight in the city?"

She had tried to sound nonchalant, but he heard the edge again, the sharp point of her anger peeking through.

"I had some business."

"What business?"

He'd considered not telling her at all, but why not? She had never respected him, certainly not when it came to his business acumen, so this was a chance to prove her wrong. "I came across a chance to buy a clothing factory."

"Clothing? What kind of clothing?"

"Men's suits ordinarily, but army uniforms currently. The owner is German-American, and he was just arrested."

"Arrested? Who is he? What's his name?"

The anxiety in her voice startled him, but then he remembered that she was German-American, too. Born here, but still, the Germans were very proud of their heritage. Most of them continued to speak German at home and subscribed to German-language newspapers and went to German churches and relaxed at German social clubs. A lot of that had ended—or at least gone underground—with the start of the war, but still . . . "Do you think he's someone you know?"

She frowned at the sarcasm in his voice. "What is his name?"

"Adolph Hirsch. I went by the factory to take a look at it. It's right in the city. A nice little place except for the broken windows and the anti-German slogans someone painted on the walls. I can pick it up for next to nothing, and Hirsch already has a contract with the army. We can do what we're doing here with the shoes: use the cheapest materials and charge the army twice what they should be worth and—"

"How did you find out about this Hirsch?"

"What?" he asked to stall.

"You heard me. Who told you about him?"

"I . . ." But he couldn't think of a lie fast enough. "I ran into his daughter."

"Hirsch has a daughter?"

So she did know him. Those Germans all stuck together. "Apparently. I doubt anybody would claim to be his kid if she wasn't, what with him being arrested for treason and all."

"Where did you *run into* her?" She didn't bother to hide her contempt, and it set Fred's teeth on edge, as it always did.

"At the lawyer's office. She's one of his clients, or, rather, her father is. I got the whole story from her, and then I arranged to meet with the manager, a fellow named Lange."

"What did he tell you?"

"He didn't think Hirsch would want to sell out, but I don't think he has any choice." Fred paused and smiled before revealing his triumph. "I offered him a hundred thousand for the whole business."

"No one would accept an offer like that. It's insulting," she sniffed.

"Of course it is, but beggars can't be choosers, can they? He'll take it and be grateful. He's got his daughter to think of."

"You need to speak to Hirsch himself."

"The manager Lange, he said Hirsch couldn't have visitors."

"Then we need to see this daughter. We need to see her right away."

CHAPTER NINE

"Gideon, what a delightful surprise!" Elizabeth exclaimed when she opened the front door to him. "And in the middle of a workday, too. Has Mr. Devoss finally fired you?"

"No such luck," he said, slipping an arm around her waist and kissing her while he had the chance.

Rose allowed them a few moments before clearing her throat from where she waited in the parlor doorway. They broke apart and Gideon managed not to scowl at poor Mrs. Preston, who was being remarkably patient while they tried to sort out her situation.

"I suppose you're here for Rose," Elizabeth said. "Do you have news for her?"

"Actually, I'm here to speak to you. You warned me things don't always go as planned, and I think something has already gone wrong. I received a telephone call from Fred Preston this morning. He and Delia want to meet with Miss Hirsch."

He could see from Elizabeth's frown that this was an unforeseen development, as he had already suspected.

"They want to meet with her and not me?" Rose asked.

"That's right," Gideon said. "I did mention you, of course, but I said you weren't quite ready to meet with them yet. You're still hoping he'll change his mind about your allowance."

"But if he wanted to see Elizabeth, why did he telephone you?" Rose asked.

"I guess because he knew she was my client and didn't know any other way to contact her."

They were all still standing in the foyer, so Elizabeth ushered them into the parlor, where they sat and stared at one another for a long moment, considering this new development.

"Did he tell you why he wanted to see Miss Hirsch?" Elizabeth finally asked.

"I asked him, of course, and all he would say was Delia wants to meet her."

"How very strange."

"She's German, remember," Rose said.

Gideon frowned. "What does that have to do with—"

"Oh no," Elizabeth said. "What if she knows Hirsch somehow? Germans tend to live close to other Germans, and they have all those social clubs."

"And Italians live close to other Italians, and Chinese people live close to other Chinese people. And she's from Poughkeepsie, after all," Gideon said.

Elizabeth turned to Rose. "Do you know if she's from Poughkeepsie originally?"

Rose shrugged. "I don't think Tommy ever mentioned where she was from."

"Oh, I see," Gideon said. "What if she's from New York, and Adolph Hirsch is her godfather or something."

"I doubt it's that bad," Elizabeth said, patting his hand. "If it was, she would've known immediately that the story we told Fred was a lie. Well, at least some of it was. Hirsch was really arrested, after all."

"He might even have a daughter, too," Rose said helpfully.

"We can hope," Elizabeth said.

Gideon frowned. "But if Delia knows Hirsch . . ."

"We don't know that she does. We don't know anything yet," Elizabeth said.

"So what do we do?" Gideon asked.

"I'll go see the Old Man first and get his opinion, but I'll probably have to meet with them."

"Then I'm going with you," Gideon said, trying to ignore the anxiety prickling up his spine.

"I don't think that's a good idea," Elizabeth said. "You might have to lie."

"Don't be silly. I can lie if I have to," he lied.

She just gave him a pitying smile. "The Old Man will go with me. And we'll make them come here. Maybe we'll meet in your office. Would that make you feel better?"

"A little."

"Good. We'll even let you arrange it, since you were the one they contacted."

"When will you go see your father?"

"I can telephone the saloon and see if he's available now. If he is, I can have him come here, if you like."

Luckily, Mr. Miles was available, and he arrived at Elizabeth's just in time for lunch, which Rose had thoughtfully prepared because cooking was the only thing keeping her from going insane with boredom.

"Cybil and Zelda and I will miss her terribly," Elizabeth confided as they sat down to the minor feast.

"So why do you think the Prestons want to meet Elizabeth?" Gideon asked their guest before anyone could distract him with small talk.

Mr. Miles gave his question careful consideration as they passed around a plate of ham. "It could just be because Delia is the brains of the team. We already considered this, which is why we approached Fred alone."

"So she'll ask the hard questions that Fred is too stupid to think of," Gideon guessed.

"Not necessarily. She could just be jealous. Remember, you teased her yourself with a suggestion that Fred might be attracted to Rose here, as any man would be." He smiled beneficently at her, making her blush.

"Do you really think she'd be jealous over Fred?" Elizabeth asked.

"I didn't get that impression," Gideon said, "although she was obviously upset at the thought of Rose stealing his heart."

"Maybe she's just worried about another woman influencing him," Mr. Miles said. "If she's telling him what to do, then she'd be worried if he fell in love with another woman who might influence him more."

"I see," Elizabeth said. "She'd lose her power over him."

"Or at least some of it," Gideon said, seeing it now himself. "And we've introduced two new women who might possibly win Fred's heart." He gave Rose and Elizabeth a beneficent smile of his own. His didn't elicit any blushes, though.

"I wonder if that's what Delia is thinking or if she just wants to hear Miss Hirsch's story for herself," Elizabeth said.

"We won't know for sure until we meet with her," Mr. Miles said, "but Lizzie is right. I should be with her. That would be natural, since I'm in charge of the factory during her father's absence."

"What will she want to know?" Elizabeth asked.

"She'll want to know if you speak German," Rose said, surprising everyone. At their gaping stares, she added, "All Germans speak it when they're together. That way they can talk about you without you knowing it."

"I don't know what they talk about, but Rose is right," Elizabeth said.

"But that's not so true anymore. They've outlawed people speaking German in public," Gideon said.

"That's right. They don't even teach it in schools since we got into the war," Elizabeth said. "But surely Hirsch's daughter will speak German. His plant manager, too. How do we explain that they don't?"

"The same way we explain why Hirsch's daughter has red hair," Mr. Miles said, nodding at Elizabeth's auburn locks.

"And how do we do that?" Gideon asked.

Mr. Miles shrugged. "I don't know, but we'll figure something out."

Saturday was usually quiet at the offices of Devoss and Van Aken. The attorneys only worked a half day, if at all, and the clerks usually left by noon as well. Smith stayed until he had shown Fred and Delia Preston into the conference room, where Elizabeth, Gideon and the Old Man were waiting.

Elizabeth found Delia Preston a revelation. Gideon had hinted she was attractive, and while she wasn't conventionally beautiful, she was a striking woman who made the most of her natural advantages. Her buxom figure was encased in a perfectly fitted navy blue walking suit that Elizabeth wouldn't have minded owning herself. Her raven locks were glossy and carefully arranged beneath her very pretty hat. Her dark eyes seemed to take in all of them at once, leaving nothing unnoticed.

Gideon greeted the Prestons and introduced Delia to Miss Hirsch and Mr. Lange, who had also risen when she entered. The Old Man wore a wig of salt-and-pepper hair cut in a haphazard style, an impressive mustache, and gold-rimmed spectacles. His suit was cheap and ill-fitting, and he somehow managed to even look a bit shorter than he was.

Delia greeted Elizabeth in German, and Elizabeth recoiled in horror. "English, please. The League is everywhere, and someone might hear us."

Delia said something else in German, probably pointing out they were not in public, but Elizabeth shook her head. "I'm being watched. I cannot take any chances."

"She's right," the Old Man said. "The government has had someone following her ever since her father was arrested. I don't know what they think she is going to do, but we cannot do anything suspicious. Besides, if we speak German, Mr. Bates will not understand us."

"And neither will I," Fred said with just a touch of irritation.

"Very well, then," Delia said, although her expression reflected her annoyance as well. "As you wish."

Gideon invited them to take the empty seats at the table. Gideon sat at the head, with Elizabeth and the Old Man on one side. Fred and Delia sat across from them. Delia had not taken her eyes off Elizabeth since they'd entered the room, but if she was hoping to disconcert her, she was failing.

Elizabeth smiled politely. "I'm a little confused as to why you are here, Mrs. Preston. Are you going to be a partner with Mr. Preston in purchasing my father's business?"

"Not at all," Delia said. "I have no interest in your factory."

"Why did you wish to meet with me, Mrs. Preston?"

"I . . . I am acquainted with your father."

Even though she'd been expecting something like that, Elizabeth's nerves tingled. How well did she know him? And did she know his family? She wondered how Gideon was reacting, but she dared not look to see. "Is that so? How do you know him?"

"We . . . I don't know him well. I don't get to the city very often, but we met once or twice at social functions, I believe."

She was lying, although Elizabeth couldn't

imagine why. "I don't believe he ever mentioned you."

"He wouldn't have. It was a very casual acquaintance."

Which probably meant she didn't know much, if anything, about his family. They could hope, at least. "I suppose you were as shocked as I to hear he had been arrested."

"Yes, I was. One hears rumors, of course. The press would have us believe all German-Americans are saboteurs, but we all know otherwise."

"My father loves the Fatherland, but he would never betray America," Elizabeth said.

"Why was he arrested, then?" Fred asked with just a little too much glee.

"Mr. Hirsch was sending money to his elderly parents," the Old Man said quickly, as if jumping to Elizabeth's defense.

"Things are very hard in the Fatherland," Delia said. "People are making great sacrifices to support our army."

"*Our* army?" Gideon asked mildly. "Do you consider yourself a citizen of Germany, Mrs. Preston?"

She stiffened at that. "Heritage is very important. I'm sure you understand such things, Mr. Bates."

"That's true," Gideon said, "but this country— the country you live in—is at war with Germany.

Surely, heritage becomes less important in a situation like that."

"You are correct, of course. I'm sorry if I suggested otherwise. I'm afraid I get very emotional over these things."

"Do you have family still in Germany?" the Old Man asked.

"I'm sure that's none of your business," she replied primly. "And none of this has gotten us any closer to the reason for this meeting."

"So perhaps you will tell us what the reason is, Mrs. Preston, since you appear to be the only one who knows it," Gideon said in that lawyerly tone that brooked no argument. Elizabeth could have kissed him.

If Delia was insulted, she gave no sign of it. "Very well. How much do you know about your father's business dealings, Miss Hirsch?"

Elizabeth glanced at the Old Man, as if for support, then turned back to Delia. "Nothing at all. Papa is very old-fashioned. He never speaks of business when he is at home."

"And he would never discuss it with a daughter, I assume. That is very typical."

"Is there some reason you are asking about Mr. Hirsch?" the Old Man asked.

"If we are going to buy his business, we want to know as much as we can about him," Fred said, obviously impatient at having been left completely out of the conversation until now.

"But Mrs. Preston says she knows Mr. Hirsch," Gideon said.

"Only socially," Fred said before Delia could reply. "She doesn't know anything about his business."

Delia glared at him, but he wasn't paying her any attention.

"Is there some matter of particular concern to you?" the Old Man asked. "I can assure you the business is in perfect order."

"Is that really true, though?" Delia asked.

"Well," the Old Man hedged, shifting nervously in his seat, "except for the army wanting to cancel its contract with us, I suppose. I'm sure you would like to examine our books before making a commitment, but the government seized them when they arrested Mr. Hirsch." They actually had no idea if this was true or not, but it was an excellent excuse for not having them to show.

"Do you have any reason to believe something is amiss?" Gideon asked the Prestons.

Delia shrugged one rounded shoulder. "Miss Hirsch says her father is merely supporting his parents, but some Germans are doing much more than that."

"Do you think my father is really guilty of treason?" Elizabeth asked with credible outrage.

"That is not for me to decide," Delia said. "I am merely interested to know if he has been

222

supporting Germany and if others at the company have been doing it, too."

"I can assure you, no one has done anything of the kind," the Old Man said. "I didn't even know about Mr. Hirsch's parents until he was arrested."

Delia was unmoved. "But if he was doing something illegal, he isn't likely to have confided in you, is he? And if you were helping him, you aren't likely to admit it, either."

The Old Man jerked as if she'd slapped him, thoroughly insulted. "How dare you accuse me of such a thing!"

"Delia, really . . ." Fred was obviously chagrined but also not brave enough to actually challenge her outrageous accusation.

"I'm sorry you are insulted, Mr. Lange," Delia said without the slightest hint of regret, "but I'm sure you have experienced the suspicion that all German-Americans have lived under ever since the war began. Miss Hirsch herself refuses to speak the language for fear of being thought unpatriotic."

"But most German-Americans are completely loyal to America," Elizabeth said.

"Are they, Miss Hirsch? Can you really speak for *most* German-Americans?"

"Delia, why are you being so rude?" Fred asked in dismay, but she didn't even glance at him.

"What are you saying, Mrs. Preston?" Gideon asked impatiently. "If you don't want to be involved with Miss Hirsch and her father for fear of being branded a traitor, then—"

"Oh no, that's not it at all. I simply wanted to see Miss Hirsch's reaction when I suggested her father might be a little too loyal to his native land."

"And are you satisfied that I am not a German agent, Mrs. Preston?" Elizabeth asked acidly.

"Reasonably," she replied with a smirk. "But I wonder if we might speak in private, Miss Hirsch. Woman to woman, as it were."

Elizabeth hadn't foreseen this possibility. She glanced at the Old Man. He was too good at this to panic, but he didn't bother to hide his suspicious frown.

"Miss Hirsch has already told you she knows nothing about her father's business," he said.

"I have nothing to ask her about her father's business." Delia was still smirking. "I would merely like to chat with her for a few moments. Alone."

Elizabeth could sense Gideon's alarm, so she didn't spare him a glance. "I'm sure the gentlemen will excuse us for a few minutes, then."

Judging by their expressions and the deliberate way they rose from their chairs, none of the men wanted to leave, but Elizabeth simply waited, keeping her gaze locked on Delia Preston's, until the men had closed the door behind themselves.

Delia said something to her in German.

"I told you—"

"Yes, you did, but it's not because you're afraid someone might hear, is it? You don't speak German, do you?"

Elizabeth drew a steadying breath. "No, I do not. I never learned."

"And why is that? Your father wasn't ashamed of his heritage, was he?"

"Not at all, but my mother . . ." Elizabeth looked away guiltily.

"She *was* ashamed?" Delia guessed.

"Yes, but not . . . She wasn't German. She didn't speak it herself, and she didn't want me mistaken for a foreigner." Now she'd find out how much Delia really knew about Hirsch's family.

"How *patriotic* of her," Delia said sarcastically.

"You have no right to criticize my mother."

"I wouldn't think of it."

"Is that why you wanted to speak privately? So you could make me admit I don't speak German?"

"Of course not." She glanced at the door, as if checking that it was still tightly closed. "I told you I know your father."

Oh no. Elizabeth braced herself to hear they were lovers or something equally troublesome.

Instead Delia said, "You need to know that your father is not a loyal American."

This was not one of the troublesome things

Elizabeth had been prepared to hear. "What are you talking about?"

"Those fools who volunteer for the American Protective League aren't always wrong. Sometimes they suspect someone who really is . . . *unpatriotic.*"

"Are you saying my father is a traitor? I don't believe it!" Elizabeth was glad to hear she really sounded suitably outraged.

"Believe what you like. I'm just warning you not to be shocked by what he will probably be accused of."

Elizabeth frowned. *"Probably?"*

For the first time, Delia Preston's confidence slipped just a bit. "I do not know what they have learned about him, but . . . Adolph Hirsch is loyal to Germany and to the German cause. That is all I can say."

The Old Man might have been too experienced to panic, but Elizabeth couldn't help the chill of alarm that raced down her spine. "How can you know this about him? You said you were only slightly acquainted. You didn't even know about me." And nobody else did, either, of course.

"We make it a point not to know very much about each other, Miss Hirsch. That way we can't be forced to betray any information about our . . . colleagues." Frantically, Elizabeth tried to figure out what a loving daughter would say in this situation, and then she realized it was probably no different from what she would say if the cops arrested the Old Man. "Is there evidence? Should I be looking for something and destroying it before they find it?"

Mrs. Preston smiled approvingly. "You are a good daughter, Miss Hirsch, but I do not know. It would do no harm to look through his papers, the ones he keeps at home, and burn anything that looks odd to you."

"Is there someone at the factory who is . . . is also involved? Someone who would know what to look for? Someone I should warn?" No, spying was not so very different from grifting at all.

"There is someone, but I do not know who it is. Your Mr. Lange, perhaps, but he will never admit it now, and Hirsch will never betray him."

At least Elizabeth knew it wasn't Lange. The Old Man was as ignorant of this as she! Elizabeth lifted a hand to her forehead, as if she were overcome with emotion. "Whatever will I do? Why have you told me all this?" She felt the sting of tears and let her eyes fill. She'd always been able to weep on demand.

"I have told you because your father was doing something very important, and he is the only one who knows . . . Well, he is the only one who knows certain important information. You must see him and find out for us."

"Us? Is Mr. Preston in on this, too?" Elizabeth didn't even have to pretend to be shocked.

"Certainly not, but I am not doing this alone."

"I didn't think you were, but what's to stop me from going to the League myself and reporting you, reporting *all* of you?"

"Your father. If you report us, he will undoubtedly be implicated. They will want to know how you learned of us, and you will have no other explanation. But if you keep our secret, no evidence against him will be discovered and he will be released, just as thousands of others have been released after being falsely accused by their friends and neighbors."

She was probably right. The self-righteous League businessmen who had volunteered their services to the Department of Justice's Bureau of Investigation had often used their powers to accuse anyone of whom they simply didn't approve. People were publicly humiliated, imprisoned and then quietly released a short time later when no evidence was found. Could that happen to Adolph Hirsch? Elizabeth and her cohorts had invented his "crime" of sending money to his aging parents, but who knew what he had really been up to?

Well, apparently Mrs. Preston knew.

"Are you sure they'll find nothing to accuse my father of?" Elizabeth asked, dabbing at her tears.

"I can promise it. I just need a name. Adolph

will know it, and you must convince him to give it to you."

"Who is this person? How is he involved?"

"You don't need to know that. Your father has protected you, and the less you know, the less you can reveal if you are caught."

"Caught?" Elizabeth didn't have to feign her alarm.

"By the League. They would question you but release you when they discover you know nothing of importance."

That was cold comfort to Beth Hirsch, and even colder comfort to Elizabeth Miles. "I see. But they told me I cannot see my father."

"Bring Mr. Bates and tell the authorities you are trying to sell your business and you need his signature."

"That makes sense." Elizabeth tried to think of what else she wanted to know. "When I have it— the name, I mean—should I tell you?"

"Yes. Have Mr. Bates telephone us to set up another meeting to discuss our purchase of the business, but do not mention anything we have discussed here with anyone."

"But—"

"Not anyone. Your Mr. Lange may be involved or he may not be. If not, he must know nothing of this. Remember, your father's life depends on this."

"His life? Surely not!"

"His freedom depends on it, and do you really think he could survive twenty years in prison?"

Having never met the man, Elizabeth couldn't judge, but it did seem unlikely. "I won't tell anyone."

"Good. Now, dry your tears. You are fortunate that your face doesn't blotch when you weep. Are you composed?"

"Yes, I think so."

Delia rose and opened the door as a signal that the men could return. Gideon was the first one through the door, and his gaze went instantly to Elizabeth, who gave him what she hoped was a reassuring smile.

"Is everything all right?" he asked.

"Perfectly fine," Delia replied cheerfully. "Thank you for indulging me, Mr. Bates. I feel Miss Hirsch and I now know each other much better."

The Old Man came around the table and took his seat beside her, leaning in solicitously. "Are you all right?" he asked with just the amount of concern a loyal family retainer would have shown.

She patted his arm reassuringly. "Of course. Mrs. Preston merely wanted to make sure I understood what selling the business would mean for me."

"I hope she convinced you not to sell at all," the

Old Man said, giving Fred Preston a disgruntled frown.

"You know we have no choice," Elizabeth said with apparent regret.

The Old Man nodded grimly. "We have been discussing terms, and Mr. Preston would like to see the factory before giving us his *revised* offer." The Old Man must have been doing some bargaining. "I will take him there now."

"Will they allow you back in?" Elizabeth asked.

The Old Man simply smiled. "No, but I have my ways, and you cannot expect Mr. Preston to buy a pig in a poke, can you?"

"No, you cannot," Fred said. He hadn't even sat back down. "Delia, why don't you go shopping or something while Lange and I visit the factory? I'll meet you back at the hotel later."

Delia's carefully controlled expression did not change, but she couldn't contain the spark of irritation in her eyes at his curt dismissal.

"How long are you staying in the city?" Gideon asked.

"Just for the night," Fred said. "Delia wanted to see a play or something." Plainly, he thought that a waste of time.

"Miss Hirsch, may I get you a cab before we go?" the Old Man asked.

"No, I, uh, I need to speak with Mr. Bates about something. I'm sure he'll take care of me."

The Old Man nodded. "Mrs. Preston, may we find you a cab?"

"Yes, please. Thank you for arranging this meeting, Mr. Bates. Miss Hirsch has indicated she would like this matter settled quickly, so I look forward to seeing you again soon."

The Old Man went out with the Prestons, and when they were gone, Gideon carefully closed the door behind them. "Is your father going to break into the factory?" he asked in amazement.

"I'm sure someone has already picked the lock for him. He's not good at that."

"How reassuring. What did the stepmother want with you?"

"Oh, Gideon, this is so strange, I don't even know how to tell you."

He sat down in the seat the Old Man had vacated and took her hands in his. "Then just tell me."

"Adolph Hirsch is a German spy."

The way Gideon jerked in his chair, Elizabeth knew this was the last thing he'd expected to hear. "How do you know that?"

"Because Delia just told me he is."

"But . . . Maybe she just assumed because he was arrested—"

"No, she knows him. Remember, she said so. She . . . I think she must be a spy, too."

Poor Gideon obviously did not want to believe any of this. "What *exactly* did she say to you?"

Elizabeth told him, trying to remember it *exactly*.

"That's . . . interesting," he managed when she was finished.

"Isn't it? What do you suppose they do in New York? Spies, I mean. It's not like they can report on what the American army is doing or anything like that."

"I have no idea, but they must be doing something to help Germany or they wouldn't be here. Maybe it's sabotage."

"What could they sabotage? We're thousands of miles away from the war."

"I don't know. They could blow something up, I suppose."

"Could they have blown up Black Tom?"

Gideon sighed. "It's possible, but I don't know how you'd prove it. With so many tons of explosives in one place, something was bound to set it off sooner or later, and I can't imagine there was much evidence left afterward to find."

"But there have been other explosions in other places, too."

"At munitions factories, yes, but when you're making things with dynamite, accidents happen."

"Oh, Gideon, this is wonderful."

"Wonderful?" he echoed incredulously. "We've just discovered a nest of German agents right here in our city."

"Delia is actually in Poughkeepsie, but no

matter. You're right. She's working with some other people doing heaven knows what to undermine America. If nothing else, we don't even have to feel guilty about conning her, too."

Gideon opened his mouth, but nothing came out.

"See," she said, "even you can understand that."

"So is Fred Preston a German spy as well?" he asked uneasily.

"Well, no. I specifically asked, and Delia seemed insulted that I would suggest such a thing. Clearly, he isn't good spy material."

"What *is* good spy material?"

"I have no idea, but Fred definitely isn't it."

"So we justify cheating Fred because he's a terrible person and Delia because she's a spy."

"Yes. This is very exciting news."

Plainly, Gideon did not think it was exciting news at all. "If you say so."

"Oh, Gideon, I'm sorry you had to be involved in this, but don't forget, we're doing it to help Rose."

"I do try to remind myself of that every so often."

CHAPTER TEN

G ideon and Elizabeth had just finished telling his mother what they had learned at their meeting with the Prestons when Mr. Miles arrived. The maid brought him in, and Gideon noticed he had a surgical mask hanging around his neck.

"When did you start wearing one of those?" Elizabeth asked, jumping up to greet him.

"Since they're handing them out on practically every street corner," he said. "Everybody has them on now or, I should say, everyone who is out. The streets seem deserted, although what seems like deserted in New York would probably be crowded anyplace else."

"I was supposed to be rolling bandages today," Mrs. Bates said, "but they canceled because so many of the ladies are down with the flu."

"Several of my, uh, associates have it, too," Mr. Miles said, "but it seems like it's only the young fellows who get it."

"Perhaps this is one time it's better to be old," Mrs. Bates said, earning a smile from Mr. Miles.

"Let's hope so," he replied.

"Was Fred pleased with his tour of the factory?" Gideon asked.

"Oh yes. He was quite impressed. Apparently, Hirsch keeps the place in good running order." He turned back to Gideon's mother. "Have they told you what we're up to, dear lady?" Why did he think he could call Gideon's mother "dear"?

"Yes, although I don't think you know the most interesting part of it yet," she replied. "Sit down, and I'll get us all some lemonade."

"What is the most interesting part?" he asked Elizabeth, folding himself into the most comfortable chair in the room. "Something fair Delia said to you in private, I'm sure."

"You'll never believe it," Elizabeth predicted, and then she told him.

"I *don't* believe it," he declared. "Why would Delia tell you something like this?"

"Because Adolph is a spy, and she thinks I'm Adolph's daughter," Elizabeth said.

"And because she needs help getting in touch with Adolph," Gideon said. "They're obviously planning something, and we need to stop them."

"Do we?" he asked with some amusement, which made Gideon's hackles rise.

"Gideon, darling, we can't stop them if we don't even know how to start them," Elizabeth said.

"What?"

"We can't help them at all because I'm not

really Adolph's daughter and I can't really get in to visit him. Even if I could, he isn't likely to give me any information about his spying, is he?"

"Oh, I guess not."

"So we don't really need to worry about any of that spying stuff, do we?" Mr. Miles said.

"Of course we do, because we can probably use it to get some money out of Delia, too," Elizabeth said.

Mr. Miles gazed at Elizabeth with so much fatherly pride, Gideon expected her to blush. Instead she looked annoyed that he seemed amazed at her brilliance.

"Do you have a plan, my dear?" he asked her.

"Of course I have a plan. Well, maybe not a complete plan, but I have an idea. Gideon thinks the Germans aren't really spying because there isn't very much happening here that they could spy on."

"I didn't say that," Gideon said, pretty sure he hadn't.

"Maybe not, but you did say you thought they were engaging in sabotage here."

Had he? He thought not, but it was useless to argue.

"Sabotage?" Mr. Miles repeated thoughtfully. "Do you think they're blowing things up?"

"Remember Black Tom?" Elizabeth said.

"That was an accident."

"Maybe it was, and maybe all the other

explosions in other places were accidents, too, but what if they weren't? What if there is a secret group of German spies planning to blow up . . ." She gestured helplessly, apparently unable to think of what the Germans might want to blow up.

Gideon couldn't think of anything, either, at least not anything that might affect the outcome of the war.

Mr. Miles came to their rescue. "The Statue of Liberty?"

"The Statue of Liberty was already damaged by the Black Tom explosion," Gideon said. "They say we might never be able to walk up into the torch again."

"Why would anyone want to walk up into the torch?" Elizabeth asked, genuinely mystified.

"I don't know, but lots of people used to do it," Gideon assured her.

"Well, maybe not the Statue of Liberty," Mr. Miles allowed. "How about one of the banks on Wall Street?"

"I don't think it matters what they want to blow up," Gideon said, "since we aren't even sure that they want to blow up anything at all."

"But they probably want to blow up something, because that's what saboteurs do, isn't it?" Elizabeth continued. "In order to do that, wouldn't they need money?"

"Money for what?" Gideon asked.

"I don't know. I've never been a spy, but surely they have to pay all the spies. They'd need to buy bombs and probably bribe people to not notice when they planted them."

"Lizzie, you may have a future as a saboteur," Mr. Miles said, showing his fatherly pride again.

"It's just common sense. Let's see if we can figure out how much that would cost."

"Why would we need to know how much it costs?" Gideon asked, thoroughly confused now.

"Because we need to know how much to ask Delia for. Remember, she gets a third of the profits from the Prestons' business. She's probably going to get half now that Tom is dead and they've cheated Rose out of her share."

"Maybe we can get her to buy part of Hirsch's place," Mr. Miles said.

"I didn't think so," Gideon said. "Fred indicated this was his deal with his money, so I couldn't understand why Delia was with him today."

"And I actually asked her, and she said she isn't interested in Hirsch's business, but now we know she had her own reasons for coming," Elizabeth said. "All we have to do is figure out how spies would act and then inform her we need a lot of money to do whatever it is she's expecting Adolph Hirsch to do."

"No," Gideon said, knowing he had to stop this before things got completely out of hand.

"No to what, darling?" Elizabeth asked, turning

her adoring gaze on him, but he wasn't going to be distracted.

"We can't get mixed up with a bunch of German spies. We can't help them blow something up."

"We won't help them blow anything up," Elizabeth said. "They're going to give us money to buy bombs and such, but we aren't actually going to buy them."

Gideon wasn't about to admit he'd really thought that for a moment. "I know, but we can't be associated with spies. What if they get arrested? The League's volunteers are everywhere. Sooner or later somebody is going to report Delia Preston just because they're jealous of her clothes or something."

Elizabeth smiled in delight. "You noticed her clothes? They're magnificent, aren't they? But even if they do arrest Delia, she isn't going to implicate *us*. In fact, she wouldn't tell me anything at all about their plans in case I do get arrested. If I don't know anything, I can't be found guilty of anything."

"But they really are guilty of something. They should be arrested," Gideon argued, "preferably before they really do blow something up."

"We can certainly arrest them later," Elizabeth said. "In fact, I think we should let Mr. Devoss do the honors."

"Devoss?" Mr. Miles repeated in amazement. "Is he a member of the League? Oh, of course he is. Doing his patriotic duty, no doubt. Yes, indeed, he must be the one who uncovers their little nest of vipers and brings them to justice."

Gideon rubbed the bridge of his nose because his head was starting to ache. This was not at all how things were supposed to go. "Elizabeth . . ."

"I have no intention of putting myself in danger," she assured him without even waiting to hear his protest. "And think about it. We'll be doing a wonderful thing for our country by ruining all their plans."

"After you've cheated them out of their money," Gideon recalled.

"Money they would only have spent on doing their spy work, so that's another wonderful thing."

"So what is your idea, Lizzie?" Mr. Miles asked just as Gideon's mother returned with the promised lemonade.

When they had all been served, she told them.

"This is insane, Elizabeth," Gideon said, not for the first time as they walked down the street. He had to speak up because they were both wearing the white surgical masks that everyone was being asked to don in hope of stopping the spread of the flu throughout the city.

"What's the worst thing that can happen?" she asked as they reached the visitors' entrance to the Tombs. New York had built a new city jail

241

about fifteen years earlier to replace the old, crumbling one that had been designed to look like an Egyptian tomb. The new jail had been built to resemble a French château, with lovely crenellated towers, but it was still known as the Tombs and probably always would be.

"The worst thing that can happen?" Gideon echoed. "I'm having a difficult time deciding between incarceration and execution."

"Don't be silly, Gideon. Nobody is going to do either one of those to us. We just want to visit a prisoner."

"But he isn't allowed visitors."

"We don't really know that. We made it up, remember?"

"Of course I remember," Gideon said, although he wasn't certain if he did. He was having a difficult time keeping it all straight. Obviously, he wasn't cut out to be a con man—knowledge that would once have given him cause for pride but now filled him with terror.

"Just don't say I'm Hirsch's daughter. I'm your secretary, remember?"

Elizabeth Miles didn't look like any secretary Gideon had ever seen, but he decided not to mention it.

The place was crowded. Apparently, Sunday afternoon was a prime time for people to visit the prisoners. Amazingly, the guards didn't even blink when Gideon introduced himself as an attorney and announced he wanted to see Adolph Hirsch.

"Who's she?" the guard asked through his mask, giving Elizabeth a look that was a bit short of respectful.

"My secretary. She is going to take notes."

"Secretary, huh?" Plainly, he didn't think she looked like one, either. "Whatever you say. You're a brave man, taking on a German traitor as a client."

Gideon couldn't help himself. "No one has proven he's a traitor."

The guard shrugged. "Can't trust them Germans. They all stick together."

After they were processed, they were escorted to a large room where visitors met with inmates huddled together around small tables so no one could overhear their conversations.

"That was easy," Elizabeth whispered to Gideon while they waited for Adolph Hirsch to be brought in. They'd pulled off their masks, thinking it rude to use them inside.

"What if he refuses to see us?"

"Why would he? He'll at least be curious as to why a lawyer he never met has come to visit him."

Just as she predicted, the guard soon escorted a middle-aged man into the room. The guard wore a mask but not Hirsch. The prisoner looked around, obviously confused, frowning when the guard brought him to the table where they sat. He was an ordinary-looking man with a long, pointed chin and sad eyes. His brown hair was thinning and mussed, as if he hadn't combed it, and his mustache was badly in need of a trim. He looked particularly pathetic in the striped uniform that hung on his thin frame.

Gideon rose and introduced himself. Hirsch shook hands awkwardly, since his wrists were manacled. Then he turned his sad gaze to Elizabeth.

"This is . . ."

"His secretary," she said with a polite smile. She'd pulled out a small notebook and a pencil and appeared poised to take notes.

The guard put Hirsch into a chair at their table and moved away. When he was gone, Hirsch whispered, "Who are you, and why are you here?"

"Mrs. Preston sent us," Elizabeth said.

Hirsch frowned. "Della?"

"No, Delia," Gideon said, thinking there was some mistake.

"Her real name is Della," Hirsch informed them with some satisfaction. "Della Schmitt."

Mr. Miles was right. Names could be changed.

"You know her, then?" Gideon asked.

Hirsch nodded once, his sad eyes a little angry now at the mention of Della Schmitt. "Why did she send you?"

"She said . . ." Elizabeth looked around to make sure no one was paying them any attention. "She said you are the only one who knows something important. A name."

Suddenly, Hirsch was no longer the sad little man in manacles. His back straightened and his gaze sharpened and his lips tightened. "What name is it you wish to know?"

"We aren't sure," Elizabeth said. "Mrs. Preston just told us to find out. We don't even know why she needs to know, but she said it's very important."

"But who are you, and why did she send you?"

"She couldn't come herself, obviously," Elizabeth said. "Mr. Bates really is an attorney, although he's not a criminal defense attorney."

"I can't defend you or even advise you," Gideon felt compelled to explain. "I'm just doing Mrs. Preston a favor."

"A favor? You have come to a prison to see a man accused of treason as a *favor?*"

Gideon had known this wouldn't be easy.

Elizabeth, however, seemed pleased that it wasn't. "You're right to question us. We're strangers to you, but Mrs. Preston knows us and trusts us. We've worked with her before. That's why she sent us." She glanced around again, then leaned in closer. "We know all about Black Tom and the other . . . accidents. We helped provide . . .

information and materials. Mrs. Preston asked us to help when she heard you'd been arrested. She's confident that they won't find anything to charge you with, but in the meantime, the work must go on. You understand that, don't you?"

Gideon had half expected Hirsch to start denying everything and begging the guard to take him away from these crazy people, but instead his gaze narrowed and he studied both of them more carefully than he had before. "Yes, I understand," he said after a long moment.

"Is there anything we should, uh, remove from your house or your office? Anything they might not have found when they arrested you?" Elizabeth asked.

"That is an odd question," Hirsch said suspiciously.

"Is it? Mrs. Preston suggested you'd want to get rid of anything that might be used against you," Gideon said.

Elizabeth nodded. "But of course if your family has already taken care of it, then—"

"I have no family," Hirsch said.

"Then we are more than happy to take care of things for you," Elizabeth said.

"We are simply trying to help you," Gideon added.

"I think I will take my chances."

Gideon couldn't blame him.

"Will you at least tell us the name?" Elizabeth said. "Mrs. Preston is very anxious to contact him."

"If she is so sure I won't be charged, why is she in such a hurry?"

That was something Gideon hadn't even thought to wonder. He really wasn't cut out for this.

"We don't know," Elizabeth said quite honestly, and then continued to almost tell the whole truth. It was amazing. "We assume there is some urgency about the . . . project. She indicated she needed to get in contact with someone right away, but you were the only one who knew his identity. We can understand that you don't trust us with his name. We are all in great danger, as we see from your arrest, so you don't want to betray your cohort, but perhaps you can give us a clue that will be meaningless to us but enable Mrs. Preston to identify the man."

But Adolph Hirsch sat back in his chair and shook his head. "I have no reason to believe Mrs. Preston is involved in anything untoward. I suspect that you are government agents sent here to trick me into confessing to something illegal, but you are wasting your time. I don't know what you are talking about. I have done nothing to betray America. I am innocent, and they will certainly discover that soon and release me."

Gideon was outraged. "You can't really believe—"

247

Elizabeth grabbed his arm to silence him. "It's all right, Gideon. Mr. Hirsch is right not to trust us. I guess if Mrs. Preston wants this information, she will have to visit Mr. Hirsch herself."

Gideon thought he saw a spark of alarm flicker across Hirsch's face, but it was instantly gone. "We thank you for your time, Mr. Hirsch."

"Not at all. This has been most interesting," he said with a tiny smile.

"I hope you have hired an attorney to assist you."

"Gideon," Elizabeth said with a trace of impatience, "Mr. Hirsch doesn't need our advice."

She was right, of course.

They didn't dare speak until they had made their way out of the Tombs and were standing on the street corner. "I can't believe that man," Gideon fumed.

But Elizabeth hushed him. "Mr. Devoss has compatriots all over the city," she whispered. "Wait until we get home."

He nodded grimly and hailed a cab. They had replaced their masks, and Elizabeth noticed the driver wore one as well. Gideon gave him the address, and they sat back as the cab headed north to Elizabeth's home. Gideon took her hand and squeezed it, probably trying to reassure her, although she didn't feel the need for reassurance.

This was shaping up to be a very interesting situation indeed.

"What's going on?" Gideon asked, leaning forward to see as the cab slowed. All the other traffic had slowed, too, as it moved past a small crowd gathered on the sidewalk.

"Looks like somebody's lying on the sidewalk," the driver said, craning his neck to peer into the crowd. "It's likely the flu."

"The flu?" Elizabeth said, able to see for herself now that some man lay on the pavement. "Surely, somebody wouldn't fall down in the street because they have the flu."

"Yes, ma'am, they would. I seen it before. It takes people like that sometimes. They'll be just walking along, perfectly fine one minute, and then they fall down dead."

Elizabeth saw her own disbelief reflected in Gideon's eyes, but then they were past the small disturbance and on their way again. "I had no idea it was so serious," Elizabeth whispered.

"I knew there had been some deaths. A few clients have notified us, but nothing like this."

Stunned, they rode the rest of the way in silence. Rose welcomed them enthusiastically when they arrived, distracting them from their dark thoughts of people dying from the flu, and ushered them into the parlor.

"How did it go? Did he think you were spies?"

she asked eagerly. Elizabeth had told Rose this morning what they were going to do.

"No, he didn't," Gideon said. "It was a complete waste of time."

"How can you say that?" Elizabeth asked. "We found out all sorts of valuable information."

Poor Gideon looked confused. "How can you say *that*? He didn't trust us, he didn't give us the name we were looking for and he didn't even admit he was a spy."

"He most certainly did," Elizabeth said. "If he wasn't a spy, he would've been outraged and furious at us for even suggesting such a thing. And he admitted he knows Delia."

"Della."

"Who's Della?" Rose asked.

"That's Delia's real name," Elizabeth said.

"Oh my," Rose said.

Elizabeth grinned. "Indeed. He wasn't pretending, either. He really knows her. He knows she's a spy, too."

Gideon frowned. "But he said—"

"That he didn't believe she was a spy," Elizabeth finished for him. "I know, but he was lying."

"How do you know he was lying?" Gideon asked.

"Because he knows a woman who has already admitted to me that she's a spy and sent us to get information from him. That proves he's a spy, too. He's suspicious of us, though, as well he might be."

"He did say he thought we were government agents trying to trick him into confessing," Gideon allowed.

"But what made Delia or Della or whatever her name is think that he'd trust two people he'd never seen before?" Rose asked.

"She didn't. She thinks I'm Hirsch's daughter, remember, so of course he'd trust me."

"We should have told *Hirsch* you were his daughter," Gideon said mildly. "Maybe he would've given us the name."

"What a good idea, Gideon," Elizabeth said without a trace of irony, squeezing the hand she held.

He simply rolled his eyes while Rose giggled.

"So what can you do now, since he wouldn't tell you the name of the other spy?" Rose asked.

"That's easy," Elizabeth said. "We give Delia or Della the name of the spy."

After much debate at Cybil's house that evening, they decided that the Old Man should make the next move. Elizabeth gave him a sealed note to deliver to Delia Preston, and he took the train to Poughkeepsie on Monday. He'd taken a later train so he would arrive at the Preston home at suppertime.

The house was about what he'd expected. One

251

of the largest on a street of stately homes where the elite families of the city lived, it boasted what must have been a lovely garden that was now dying back as fall set in. A sprawling porch still held an array of wicker furniture on which the family could catch the evening breeze. He strode up and rang the bell. A maid answered and told him Mr. Preston hadn't arrived home yet. Mrs. Preston agreed to see him while he waited, however, which suited his purposes perfectly.

She met him in a well-furnished parlor. She looked as attractive as ever, and the Old Man couldn't help admiring the curves that her tailor-made gown accentuated. "Mr. Lange, what a surprise. I don't think Fred or I expected to see you again so soon."

"Miss Hirsch was fortunate enough to be allowed a visit with her father yesterday. She followed your suggestion and took Mr. Bates with her as her attorney, so they admitted her. I did not see any reason to delay informing Mr. Preston of his decision about selling his company."

"So Miss Hirsch has seen her father," Delia mused, probably wondering why she hadn't had Gideon telephone her.

"Yes. Oh, I almost forgot. She asked me to give you a message."

"A message?" Delia's gaze had sharpened, and her tone was wary until he pulled the envelope out of his pocket and presented it to her. She checked to make sure it was sealed. "Thank you, Mr. Lange."

"I admit I'm curious as to why Miss Hirsch is sending you private messages," he said.

"I believe I mentioned that I am acquainted with Mr. Hirsch. I had asked her to give him a personal message for me, and I believe this is his reply."

"Still, it's dangerous for her to be carrying secret messages from him," the Old Man said. "She might get in trouble."

"With whom?" Delia asked with remarkable innocence.

"With the League. With the government. With anybody who believes Mr. Hirsch is a spy, and if they think she's helping him—"

"But he isn't a spy, is he? Or at least Miss Hirsch assured me that he isn't. In any case, no one will know she sent me this message, and even if they find out, it's harmless."

The Old Man frowned his disapproval, but he was spared from having to reply by the sound of Fred Preston's arrival. The Old Man rose to his feet when Fred entered the parlor, and he noticed Delia quickly tucked the envelope into her pocket, out of sight. For once Fred was smiling, probably because he expected some good news from his visitor.

"Lange, you're a fast worker."

"I saw no reason to delay."

"And what did Hirsch say to my offer?"

The Old Man glanced at Delia. "Maybe we should discuss this privately. I'd hate to bore Mrs. Preston with talk of business."

"And I would hate to be bored," Delia said with forced cheer. "I'll withdraw and leave you gentlemen to it. I have some correspondence to attend to anyway." She was undoubtedly anxious to read the message he'd brought. "Will you stay for supper, Mr. Lange?"

"Thank you, Mrs. Preston, but I must be on my way, I'm afraid."

"Very well. It was lovely to see you again."

When she was gone, Fred closed the parlor doors behind her. "Does that satisfy you? Now, what did Hirsch say?"

The Old Man pretended reluctance. "I'm afraid he is not interested in selling the company to a stranger."

Fred's anticipatory smile faded. "Did you remind him that he's not in a position to be choosy?"

"He understands his position completely."

"But . . . Wait. You said he doesn't want to sell to a *stranger*. Does that mean he's willing to sell to someone who isn't a stranger?"

The Old Man smiled. "I believe he is."

"Does he have somebody in mind?"

"Mr. Preston, I owe you a debt of gratitude. I

never would have thought of this if you hadn't explained to me why Mr. Hirsch should be willing to sell his business for a fraction of its worth."

"Thought of what?"

"Of buying the company myself."

Fred's expression went from shock to anger to amusement in a matter of seconds. His rude gaze raked his visitor, taking in his shabby suit and cheap shoes. "You? How could you afford to buy anything, much less a business, even at the price I am willing to pay?"

"I have a . . . a business deal. An important business deal. My brother and I are working on it, and when it is finished, I will have the money I need."

"What kind of a business deal could a man like you have going that would give you that kind of money?" His skepticism was obvious.

"I cannot tell you. It is confidential."

"Or imaginary. You're doing your employer a great disservice by refusing to help me buy his company."

"It is not imaginary. I will soon have the amount that you offered, and then I will convince Mr. Hirsch to sell to me."

"Are you saying he hasn't already consented?" Preston asked, perking up.

"He will when I have the money in hand. He does not believe I can get it, either."

Fred shook his head. "Well, when your deal falls through, be sure to let me know. How soon did you say you would have the money?"

"A few days at the most."

"I'd like to know how to raise a hundred thousand dollars in a few days."

The Old Man smiled wisely. "Maybe I will teach you when it is done."

Fred was only too happy to show the Old Man out, but Delia came hurrying down the hall to bid him farewell. "Mr. Lange, I hope you will give Miss Hirsch my regards," she said, coming close enough to slip something into his coat pocket. A neat trick. Could she pick pockets, too? An interesting thought.

Elizabeth and Rose had been preparing food for the salon that evening when Cybil and Zelda arrived home.

"Lizzie!" Cybil called, and Elizabeth instantly knew from her tone that something was wrong.

She hurried out to find Cybil easing Zelda into a chair in the entryway. Zelda's face was gray. "What's wrong?"

"I think it's the flu," Cybil said with a worried frown.

"Nonsense. I'm just tired," Zelda protested weakly.

"Help me get her upstairs," Cybil said.

"What is it?" Rose asked, having followed Elizabeth from the kitchen. Then she saw Zelda. "Oh dear."

"It's the flu," Elizabeth whispered to her. "Stay back."

Between them, Cybil and Elizabeth got Zelda upstairs, undressed and into bed.

"Should we send for the doctor?" Elizabeth asked.

"I'm not sick," Zelda insisted, but she was burning with fever and had curled into a fetal position.

"I'll do it," Cybil said, moving Elizabeth away from the bed so Zelda wouldn't hear, "but there isn't much he can do. Several of the girls at the school are sick, and we've had the doctor for them. He said to keep them warm and try to get them to drink liquids. He gave them morphine for pain if they needed it, and some of them were literally screaming if you touched them, but that's all he could offer."

"Should we take her to the hospital, then?"

"Some of our girls went, in the beginning, but they say the hospitals are getting full now. I think she'd be better off here. I'll stay home and look after her. I'm just worried about you and Rose."

"Especially Rose," Elizabeth said. "Because of the baby."

"Yes. We should probably send her away, but where?"

"I don't know. I don't think it's safe for her to

go back home yet, and besides, she'd be all alone there if she did get the flu."

"I suppose we should ask her what she wants to do."

In the end, Rose decided to stay there because even moving through the streets could expose her. Cybil forbade her from going near Zelda, so she stationed herself in the front hallway to turn people away if they arrived for the salon while Elizabeth tried to reach people on the telephone to warn them not to come.

She caught Gideon before he left his office. "You should come and stay with us," he said when she'd told him about Zelda.

"And bring it to you and your mother? That doesn't make sense. We'll be fine. Cybil isn't letting me or Rose near Zelda. Have you heard from the Old Man?"

"Not yet. I wish I knew what he has in mind."

Elizabeth smiled. "No, you don't."

CHAPTER ELEVEN

The Old Man came by late the next morning. He hadn't gotten Elizabeth's message about Zelda, but he seemed unconcerned about the threat of flu. He didn't even have a mask hanging around his neck today.

"Our fair Delia was thrilled to receive your note," he reported after Elizabeth had sent Rose to the kitchen to make some coffee. "And she's sent you a reply."

"Already? What did she say?"

"Do you think I'd read your mail?" he asked, affronted, but when he handed the envelope to her, she saw he'd already opened it.

She gave him a look and pulled the single sheet of notepaper from the ripped envelope. "I would love to meet your friend as soon as you can arrange it" was the important sentence amid a lot of "so glad to hear you're doing well" and other claptrap inserted to make it look like an innocent letter.

"How long do we keep her hanging?" Elizabeth asked.

"Keep who hanging?" Rose asked, carrying in a tray with the coffee things.

"Delia. She's anxious to meet the spy."

"But you don't know who the spy is."

"We don't need to."

"Why not?"

"You'll see."

"I wish I could be involved in all this," Rose said wistfully.

"Be careful what you wish for," Elizabeth cautioned, and turned back to her father. "When did you intend to see Fred again?"

"A few days. I have to allow time for my deal to fall through."

"If it falls through, how will it work?" Rose asked.

"That's all part of the plan," Elizabeth assured her. "Do you have everything ready?" she asked her father.

"Yes. Tim North has a setup in New Jersey. He already told me to bring Preston in when he's ready. I figured you should wait for him to be out of town before you meet with Delia. If they're separated, they can't figure out what the other is doing."

"Good idea. I guess you should send Jake over so we can finalize our plans."

"He's got his men lined up, too. I think he's got his nerve back, Lizzie."

Was that good news? Probably not, but she wasn't going to reform her brother. All she could do was set a good example, although running cons for a good cause probably wasn't the example he wanted.

The Old Man once again took the train to Poughkeepsie on Thursday morning. He got an early start because he was hoping to get Fred out of town before Lizzie and Jake got to Delia's house that afternoon. The station felt deserted, and not many people were making the trip today. Everyone wore their masks, and no one made small talk with strangers.

He found Fred in his office at the shoe factory, and Fred seemed pleased to see his visitor was not quite as cocky as he had been earlier in the week.

"So how did your deal turn out?" Fred asked, rubbing his hands together in anticipation.

"You asked me to tell you if I was not able to raise the necessary funds. I'm afraid that has happened."

"As I expected."

"Do not think that this will help you, however, Mr. Preston. Mr. Hirsch is still adamant. He will not sell his business to you at any price."

"I'm sure if I could speak with him, I could convince him—"

"But you cannot speak to him. They will only allow his family and his attorney to visit. I do have a suggestion that could benefit us both, however."

Fred's eyes narrowed suspiciously. "What kind of suggestion?"

"You are a businessman, so I know you will understand that what I am to tell you is confidential."

"Of course."

"It is also a way for me to make enough money to purchase Mr. Hirsch's factory and for you to also make a lot of money without having to do anything much at all. Would you be interested in an opportunity like that?"

"How much money could I make?"

"Perhaps a quarter of a million. Maybe even more."

Fred's eyes were no longer narrowed. "What kind of a deal could make that much money?"

"As I said, this is confidential."

"Yes, yes, go on."

"My brother, Dieter, was always the smart one in the family. He is the confidential secretary to a group of millionaire financiers. They have vast holdings in mines and railroads and municipal bonds. They travel around in a private railroad car, like a luxury hotel on wheels. Because they're so rich, they don't have to work, so they are avid sportsmen, hunting and fishing whenever they can. They are also very interested in the fight game. Are you interested in prizefighting, Mr. Preston?"

"Not particularly. I don't like throwing my money away."

The Old Man nodded sagely. "These millionaires have a physical-culture man, a fighter, who travels around with them. They arrange fights for him wherever they go, in mining camps and towns where they turn a blind eye to prizefighting, which is still illegal in most states, as you know."

"A blind eye, eh?"

"Yes. There are many such places. And this fighter never loses, so these men have won vast sums of money in private wagers."

"If you think I'm going to bet on a fighter, you're even dumber than I thought."

The Old Man smiled at the insult. "I would not suggest such a thing, but these men have sometimes won a million dollars on a fight."

"They won't be winning it from me," Fred said sourly.

"Of course not. I only tell you this so you understand how *our* little deal will mean nothing to them."

"So what is *our* little deal?"

"Several years ago, these men bought a three-thousand-acre tract of marsh land on the Delaware River in Pennsylvania. They built a lodge and used it for a shooting preserve. They'd go there and shoot when the ducks were so thick you could get them with a stick. Do you hunt, Mr. Preston?"

"No. I've never seen the appeal of sitting out-side for hours on a cold day just so I could kill something."

Maybe Fred wasn't as dumb as the Old Man thought. "A while ago, they were hunting at this lodge, and when they all gathered for dinner one evening, they realized one of their friends hadn't yet returned. They immediately went out searching, and they found him dead. Someone had shot him accidentally."

"Another good reason not to hunt."

The Old Man couldn't have agreed more. "Needless to say, they no longer wanted to go to this lodge. Too many sad memories, and they were never sure which of them had shot their friend, so the place has sat empty for a few years. They told my brother to sell it for whatever he could get. Then recently, my brother received a letter from a banker in Philadelphia asking if the land was for sale."

"Ah, now your story is getting interesting, but I still don't see how any of this can benefit me."

"You will. My brother got curious, so he went to inspect the land. Turns out, the large company that owns the adjoining land had ditched and tilled it, so the swampy land had drained, and now the property is rich farmland. The property they'd paid fifty dollars an acre for is now worth at least three hundred an acre."

The Old Man gave Fred a few moments to do

the multiplication and subtraction necessary to reach three-quarters of a million dollars. When Fred gave a low whistle, the Old Man continued.

"What I didn't mention before is that the fighter these men employed is a bit angry with them. Although he has earned them millions of dollars, they only pay him a modest salary."

"You mean, he doesn't get part of the purse?"

"No. Not only that, but his sister is very ill and needs medical care. He can't afford to help her on his salary, so he asked his employers for a loan. They refused."

Fred nodded, as if this were something of which he could approve. The Old Man let it pass.

"Not only that, but they treat him more like a servant than a valued employee, and my brother knows all of this and sees that he himself is treated much the same way. When he learned about the value of the land, a sum that would mean little to men as rich as these but which could change his life, Dieter asked me to help him find a buyer for the land."

"How would that help your brother?"

"We would find someone willing to buy the land from these men at fifty dollars an acre. Then that man would sell it to the banker for three hundred an acre and split the profits with Dieter and me. My brother would get half, and the buyer and I would split the other half."

Fred took a long moment to consider this and

do some division in his head. The Old Man could tell by the glitter in his eyes when he had finished his computations. "And did you find someone to buy the land for you?"

"Yes, but he wanted to keep fifty percent of the profit for himself and for Dieter to pay my part out of his share. This was not acceptable to us."

"But you'd get your share either way," Fred pointed out.

"My brother is the one who came up with the idea. He should get the larger share."

"All right, so your brother is the one who wouldn't deal with this other buyer, and now you're looking for somebody else to buy the land for you."

"I was very sorry for your disappointment, Mr. Preston. I had no idea that Mr. Hirsch would be so stubborn, but I feel that this simple business deal I am proposing would help make up for it in a small way, if you are interested. You will make a fortune."

"And you will get Hirsch's business for next to nothing."

The Old Man allowed himself a small smile. "That is my plan, yes. Of course, I do not know if you have the funds available. Perhaps you are not able to raise a hundred and fifty thousand dollars in cash."

Fred was insulted, as the Old Man had intended. "Of course I can. I'm a millionaire myself, or close to it. The war has been very good for business."

"So I have heard from Mr. Hirsch. Then you are interested?"

"I'm interested," he said, trying not to sound too enthusiastic, but his eyes gave him away.

"Of course, it is not my decision to invite you or not," the Old Man said quickly. "Dieter is the one who must approve you."

"Then take me to Dieter."

The Old Man hesitated. "He will be angry that I have told you about this. As I said, it must be confidential."

"Then don't tell him I know the whole story. Just tell him I've got some money to invest. In fact, tell him the truth: that you met me when I tried to buy Hirsch's business, and you thought I'd have the money for this project."

The Old Man hemmed and hawed and let Preston argue and plead until finally relenting after about an hour. By then Preston was ready to beg Dieter to take his money.

"When can I meet your brother?" Preston asked.

The Old Man checked his pocket watch. "If we leave today, I can arrange for you to meet him tomorrow. The men he works for will be in New Jersey for about a week longer."

"Good. I'll just need to stop off at home and pack a bag."

The Old Man smiled. That should get them out of town before Lizzie and Jake arrived to meet with Delia.

"We need somebody who speaks German," Elizabeth told Jake as they walked up to Delia Preston's front porch that afternoon.

"Don't worry about it."

"The Old Man said you had your people all lined up."

"Of course I do. That was the hard part. This part will be easy."

"Don't underestimate Delia. She managed to marry a wealthy man who left her very well-fixed. If she's helping German spies, you can bet she knows what she's doing."

"Don't underestimate *me*, Lizzie," he replied with a smirk.

Somehow she resisted the urge to stick her tongue out at him.

Elizabeth rang the bell and the maid admitted them. Delia had been expecting them since Elizabeth had sent her a telegram this morning.

"Miss Hirsch, I'm so glad you decided to stop by to visit."

Elizabeth shook her hand and indicated Jake, who looked very German again today in his blond wig and matching mustache. "May I present Karl Weber? He is a trusted employee of my father."

Jake had pulled off his hat and nodded a bit

awkwardly. "Pleased to meet you, Mrs. Preston."

"And I am pleased to meet you, Mr. Weber. Please, sit down. May I offer you some refreshments?"

They agreed to coffee and some pastries, and the maid went to fetch them. Until she returned, they made small talk about the weather and the war and the flu, which was hitting Poughkeepsie, too.

"Those masks are so uncomfortable, don't you think?" Delia asked. Elizabeth and Jake had worn them on the train.

"I just wonder if they do any good at all," Elizabeth said. "Nobody really knows how people catch it, after all."

Finally, the maid returned, and Delia instructed her to close the parlor doors behind her. They waited for a few moments, giving the girl time to get back to the kitchen. Then Delia said, "Mr. Weber, how long have you worked for Mr. Hirsch?"

"I don't really work for him. I mean, I do have a job at the factory, but that's only so I have a reason to be in the city."

"Why haven't you been drafted?" She tried to look disapproving.

"I have a bad heart," he said with a small grin.

"How very tragic. What do you know about what Mr. Hirsch was working on?"

"I don't think I want to know any more about

this," Elizabeth said sharply, setting her coffee cup down on the table. "Perhaps I should leave."

"Yes, perhaps you should," Delia said. "Mr. Weber will stay, of course, but you may want a breath of fresh air. You'll be very comfortable on the porch, I think."

Elizabeth gathered her things and let herself out. She managed one last glimpse of Jake and caught him smiling benignly. She found a comfortable rocking chair on the porch and sat down to wait.

When they were alone, Mrs. Preston turned back to Jake. Lizzie was right. He shouldn't underestimate her. "Where were we?"

"You asked me if I knew what Mr. Hirsch was working on."

"And do you?"

This was where it was going to get tricky. Jake stared down at his shoes for a tortured moment. "The truth is, Mrs. Preston, I don't. See, he wasn't going to tell me until closer to the time. He was afraid if I got caught, they'd make me talk."

"Then I'm not sure you'll be any help to us," she said icily.

"I do know it was sabotage," he said quickly, which was what he and Lizzie had decided to claim. "I mean, he told me that much. I just don't know what."

"Do you know *how?*" she asked, not satisfied but not shocked, either, so they'd been right about the sabotage at least.

"With a bomb, of course." Wasn't that what sabotage was? "I hope you don't expect me to build it, though. Mr. Hirsch was going to get it from somebody, I think, but I don't know who."

"You don't know very much, do you?"

"Mr. Hirsch is not a trusting man, Mrs. Preston. If you know him, you know that," Jake said, figuring it was true because spies certainly couldn't go around trusting people. "He recruited me, but I'm new to all this, and he didn't have time to train me very well. I was supposed to meet some other people so they could teach me what I needed to know but . . . So anyway, I don't have much experience."

"Yes, we lost all of our best people when America entered the war."

"What do you mean? Mr. Hirsch is still here," he protested.

"But many others fled the country," Delia said, which obviously still made her angry. "And those who remain have been afraid to act."

"I'm not afraid. Just tell me what needs to be done, and I will do it." Did he sound reckless and brave? That was how they'd decided a spy in Karl Weber's position would act.

To his relief, Delia smiled tolerantly. "I have no reason to question your courage or your

271

dedication, Mr. Weber. May I ask *why* you are so dedicated to the cause?"

"My parents are German. My whole family is. Or was. My parents died when I was little, and I grew up in an orphanage. I always knew I was better than those other kids, though. My parents had always told me Germans were the best race. When I finished school, I got a job with an old German, and I started going to the German clubs. I learned all about the Fatherland and my heritage, and when the war started, that's all everybody talked about. Germany was just trying to defend themselves and their allies, but England and France wouldn't let them be. Germany didn't have any choice but to fight. They couldn't just let England and France tell them what to do, could they?"

"Certainly not. How did you meet Mr. Hirsch?"

"At one of the German clubs. I'd said some things and . . . Well, people talk, don't they? I was going to be drafted, and Mr. Hirsch found a doctor to say my heart was bad. He said I could do important work if I could stay out of the army."

"And then he gave you a job?"

"Yes, in his factory. I wasn't doing much there, and he kept saying he was going to introduce me to some other people, but he had to be careful. He thought he was being watched."

"And he was." She studied him for a few

awkward minutes. Jake managed not to squirm by noticing that she was quite a looker for an older woman. She didn't seem interested in him that way, though.

Finally, he asked, "Do you know what he was planning?"

"I know generally what he was planning, but I do not know who was going to do the work."

"What do you know exactly?"

She pursed her lips and studied him again. "What do *you* know exactly?"

He smiled at that. "More than I've told you. You see, Mr. Hirsch told me not to trust anybody, either."

"And I don't trust you. Suppose I tell you something, and you tell me something in return. If we are impressed, we can tell each other more."

"All right. You start."

She shook her head, but she smiled and said, "J. P. Morgan."

"And Company," Jake added, figuring they wouldn't waste time trying to blow up just one man.

"That bank is financing the entire war," Delia said bitterly. "England couldn't afford a single bullet without their loans."

"Everybody knows that."

"So we need to disrupt them."

Jake nodded. This was easier than he could

273

have imagined. "A well-placed bomb would do that."

"But someone already tried blowing up a bank on Wall Street several years ago," she reminded him.

Jake vaguely remembered the incident, but he'd been a kid then. "I said 'well-placed.'"

"But who would provide such a bomb, and who would place it?"

"We have someone to build it. I met him before Mr. Hirsch was . . . arrested."

She jerked back in her chair. "Then you do know who has the bomb."

"He doesn't have it yet."

"Where is it, then?"

"It doesn't exist."

"Why not? Hirsch said he had everything taken care of."

But Jake shook his head this time. "Not yet. You see . . ." He looked away, toward the window, as if he were wishing himself miles away when in fact he was so very happy to be right here. "We don't have any money."

"That's impossible. Hirsch . . . We provided . . . He has plenty of money."

Jake couldn't help wondering who had "provided," but he just said, "Not anymore. The government took it."

"They can't take his money!" She was outraged that a German spy's American rights had been violated. Jake wished he could take a moment to enjoy the irony.

"Maybe not. Maybe they didn't actually take it, but he can't touch it, and neither can Miss Hirsch, which is one reason why she's anxious to sell the factory."

Delia waved Miss Hirsch's concerns away. "Hirsch had close to a hundred thousand dollars from us."

Jake didn't bother to hide his amazement. Karl Weber would have been amazed, too. "Where did he get it?"

"Not from the German government, if that's what you're thinking. They do not have J. P. Morgan's bank to lend them money, and we need to end this war before Germany is ruined."

"I agree, but who did give Mr. Hirsch the money? Maybe we can ask them for more."

But Delia was shaking her head, and this time she meant it. "We cannot ask for more when we have done nothing. Oh, why am I arguing about this with you? And why do you need money in the first place?"

"Well," Jake said, drawing it out as if he were reluctant to admit it, "our people have not been paid in months."

"Months?"

"Mr. Hirsch knew he was being watched. He couldn't start drawing a lot of money out of his accounts."

"How much do you need for that?"

"I don't know exactly. I'll have to find out. Miss Hirsch didn't tell me why we were coming here, so I didn't know I'd need that information."

"This is ridiculous. They should work without pay."

"It's hard to work when you can't eat and your landlord throws you out in the street."

Delia made an exasperated sound. "All right. Is that all?"

"The materials for the bomb, I'd guess."

"That can't be much."

"I don't know. I've never built a bomb. Have you?" he added hopefully.

"Don't be foolish. Anything else?"

"I told you, the bomb must be well-placed. That means it must be inside the building."

"So?"

"So somebody will have to be bribed to put it there."

"Do you have someone in mind?"

"Mr. Hirsch recruited someone, but he is naturally very nervous now that Hirsch has been arrested."

"So he'll want to be paid more."

"If he'll do it at all. Mrs. Preston, this is very dangerous, especially now."

"Which means you want to be paid more, too, I assume."

Jake smiled sheepishly. "I'm not a greedy man,

but when this is over, I might need to leave the country, too. We all might. That would be easier if we had some money."

"And where do you think I will get all this money?"

Jake looked around at the nicely furnished parlor. "I heard Mr. Lange say that you folks were doing really well with your government contracts."

"That is my stepson's company."

Jake feigned surprise. "Didn't your husband leave you anything?"

Color flooded her face. "That is none of your business."

Jake shrugged. "Maybe it is, if you've got the money to help us end the war. And when America surrenders, then Mr. Hirsch would get all his money back. He could reimburse you. In fact, I'll make sure he does."

"If you haven't left the country," she said acidly.

"If we're successful, everything will work out." Jake gave her his best boyish grin.

She didn't return it. "But only if we're successful."

"If we don't try, then Germany is going to lose, because America is going to send a million more men to the front in a few months. Does Germany even have a million more men to send?"

She frowned. "Yes, you are right. We must try,

but I cannot help if you do not know how much money you will need."

"I'll have to go back and talk to my, uh, friends. How should I let you know?"

"Did Hirsch have time to teach you the code?"

Code? There was a lot more to being a spy than he'd counted on. For a second, Jake's heart was in his throat, but he shook his head. "He didn't."

She made another sound, this time of disgust. "Tell Miss Hirsch to write to me. In her letter she will put a number. That number will be how many thousands you need."

"And you can get it? In cash, because we can't write checks for these things."

"I'm not an idiot. Of course in cash. But you will account for every penny."

"Of course."

"Where are we going?" Preston asked as they boarded the train.

"Trenton," the Old Man said.

"New Jersey? That seems like a funny place for millionaires to be vacationing."

"They aren't vacationing. They've got business there."

They took the train to New York City and then switched trains for the rest of the trip. As the Old Man had arranged, a man was waiting for them when they reached their New Jersey train.

"Mr. Preston, this is Sam Hooper." Sam was an impressive figure of a man. He'd been a fighter in his day, and he still looked the part. He carried two suitcases. One of them was his own, and one was for the Old Man. "I hope you don't mind, but Sam will be going with us. He's a fighter I'm training, and I need to keep an eye on him so he doesn't break training."

Preston was obviously impressed by Sam's physique. "He could be a good bodyguard, too."

The Old Man chuckled. Actually, that was about all Sam was good for now. Preston didn't seem to notice that Sam was past his prime and a bit out of shape for a fighter, though. Having a mark who knew nothing about the fight game was a definite advantage.

The train ride to Trenton was uneventful, and they checked into the best hotel in town. The Old Man got two adjoining rooms. "You can have one," the Old Man explained, "and I'll share the other with Sam so I can keep an eye on him." They had dinner in the hotel restaurant and then went to the bar. The Old Man sent Sam to bed, though, because he shouldn't be drinking while he was in training.

"I've got him scheduled for a big fight in Chicago next month," he explained to Preston.

"You're a man of varied interests, Mr. Lange. You surprise me."

"I have been hoping that Sam will win a big purse and free me to work with him full-time, but it is difficult when I don't have the funds to bet on him myself."

Preston grinned knowingly. "So that's another reason you want this deal to go through."

"Is it wrong to want to be a rich man, Mr. Preston?"

Preston allowed that it was not wrong at all.

Elizabeth didn't have to pretend she was nervous when Jake and Delia called her back into the house, but Delia seemed just as calm and composed as usual and Jake betrayed no hint of concern. Could he have done just fine? Anything was possible with Jake.

"Miss Hirsch, I must thank you for introducing me to this young man. I believe he will be very helpful," Delia said.

"I hope so," Elizabeth said. "You aren't going to need me anymore, I presume."

"Only a bit and it's completely innocent. Mr. Weber will explain it to you."

"I already told you, I can't be involved," Elizabeth said, hoping she sounded just slightly desperate. "If anyone even suspects . . ."

"How could anyone suspect you, my dear?" Delia asked with a condescending smile that Elizabeth wanted to slap off her face.

"Perhaps you've forgotten my father is in

jail and facing a twenty-year prison sentence."

"But they can't suspect you, or you would be there with him."

"Don't worry, Miss Hirsch," Jake said. "You won't be involved in anything illegal. Let's go, and I'll explain it all to you."

They took their leave of Delia, who still seemed very pleased with Jake and whatever arrangements they had made.

"Looks like you did well," Elizabeth said when they were safely down the street and could no longer be overheard.

"Of course I did, but nobody told me about any secret codes."

"Secret codes?"

"Yeah. I guess that's how spies talk to each other so nobody else catches on."

"Did she talk to you in code?"

Jake's eyes widened. "I don't think so. If she did, I didn't notice, but she did ask if I knew the code. I told her I was new and Hirsch didn't have time to teach me everything, though."

"Just like we planned. Good."

"Which is what saved me, but that means I can't send her a message of how much money I'll need, so she said you should write her a letter with a number in it. That number will be the amount we need."

"So all we have to do is figure out how much that should be," Elizabeth said with a smile.

The next morning, when Fred got up, he found Sam in his boxing trunks, doing calisthenics.

"What's he doing?" he asked the Old Man.

"I told you. He has to keep in shape. This is part of his training. I've already had breakfast, so I'll go over to see my brother and tell him I've found someone to help us with our project."

When the Old Man left, Fred was warily watching Sam shadowboxing in front of a mirror.

A little over an hour later, the Old Man returned with Tim North, who was going to pretend to be his brother, Dieter. The Old Man didn't think they looked much like brothers, but Preston didn't seem to notice. He introduced the men, and they gathered chairs in Fred's room so they could talk. Sam stayed in the room he shared with the Old Man, although they left the door open.

"I don't know how much my brother has told you about this," Dieter said, "but I have to be very careful because of my position with these men and the trust they have in me."

"Mr. Lange just told me that you need an investor to help you close a deal that will earn me a huge profit, so I'm willing to listen to whatever you have to say."

Dieter helpfully explained what the Old Man had already told him and mentioned how much money Fred Preston stood to make, even though his share of the deal was only one quarter of the profits. "I don't know if you have a bank account, Mr. Preston—"

"Of course I have a bank account." He named a bank in Poughkeepsie. "If you don't believe me, you can contact the president of the bank."

"I apologize, Mr. Preston," Dieter said with suitable humility. "We just need to be careful. Here is what I suggest. You should go to the local bank and arrange to draw on your account in Poughkeepsie. We don't know exactly how much my employers will agree to, but when we know, you can have that amount transferred here and placed to your credit."

"How much do you think it will take?" Preston asked.

"I'm guessing they will at least want to get back what they originally paid for the land, which was a hundred and fifty thousand, but they might want more. Will that be a problem for you, Mr. Preston?"

Fred was offended or pretended to be. "Of course not, but aren't either of you going to put up any money to purchase the land?"

"We could, but if my employers were to learn later how much the land was really worth, they would want to know why it had been sold so low. I will claim I had no idea of its true value, but I would have a difficult time explaining my ignorance if some of my money had been used to buy it. If the money is all yours, I can claim ignorance."

Just then Sam jumped up from where he had been relaxing on the bed in the other room and began to shadowbox.

"I see Sam is in good shape for the fight next month," Dieter remarked.

Fred watched the fighter uneasily, but the Old Man said, "Yes, I just wish I could get him a fight with a bigger purse."

"How soon can we resell the land once I've bought it from them?" Preston asked, reclaiming their attention.

"A day or two, probably," Dieter said. "The banker is very eager to conclude the deal."

"Won't he be suspicious that somebody else owns it now?"

"I doubt it," Dieter said. "We should go to the bank now and ask them to begin the process."

They left Sam doing jumping jacks in the next room.

"That man worries me," Fred said.

"He doesn't worry me," the Old Man said cheerfully. "Someday he's going to make even more money than our land deal."

CHAPTER TWELVE

"T here's nothing suspicious about this at all,"
Elizabeth said, but Gideon was sure everything about it was suspicious. "At least you don't
have to lie," she added.

Which was the only good thing about it.

She had summoned him to her house Friday
morning to explain what she needed from him,
and he didn't think it was a good idea at all.

"What if somebody sees Rose?"

"She'll be wearing a veil, and she's not going
to speak to anyone at the Ansonia, just to the
people at the bank." Which was in the Ansonia
lobby. "Nobody at the Ansonia will even know
she's been there, so there's no chance word will
get back to Delia and Fred."

"Explain to me again why Rose needs to see
the banker?" Gideon asked, even though he was
very much afraid he understood all too well.

Elizabeth glanced at the parlor door, making
sure they were alone. Rose was still getting
ready for their excursion. "We just need to know
how rich Delia is likely to be. Judging from her
clothes, she's pretty well-off, but maybe she
spends it all on her wardrobe."

"Tom Preston said she got a third of the business, just like he did."

"Then knowing how much Tom earned a year would be helpful, and Rose certainly has a right to know that, doesn't she?"

Gideon frowned. "Actually, she doesn't."

Elizabeth gave him the look that told him this was why she and his mother were fighting for women's suffrage. "Perhaps not legally, but certainly morally."

"You said none of this was illegal," he reminded her.

"Rose might not have a legal right to know her husband's finances, but it's not illegal for her to ask. She at least needs to know how much money is still available to her as his widow."

"How do I look?" Rose asked from the parlor doorway. She was dressed all in black with a veil over her face. Her own mother wouldn't have recognized her.

"Just lovely," Elizabeth replied. "Does Zelda need anything before we leave?"

"I looked in on her, and she said she's fine. She expects she'll be able to go back to the school on Monday."

"She should be careful," Gideon said. "Mother said a lot of people who have the flu think they're better, and then they get sick all over again." And died of pneumonia, he thought but didn't say because he didn't want to be too grim.

"I'm sure Cybil won't let Zelda go back to teaching before she's completely recovered, but she never was badly sick, at least not as sick as some of the girls at the college," Elizabeth said.

"She was lucky."

"Yes, she was. Are we ready?" Elizabeth asked.

They adjusted their masks, which only enhanced Rose's disguise, and set out. They walked over to Broadway to hail a cab. The driver of the first one that stopped challenged them before they could get in.

"Where are you going?" He was a middle-aged man behind his surgical mask, but his eyes looked very old.

"The Ansonia up on Seventy-third," Gideon said, a bit startled. He'd never had a cabdriver ask where he was going before allowing him into the cab.

"You're not going to some hospital, are you?" the driver replied from behind his mask. "I don't take sick people in my cab."

"We're all perfectly healthy," Gideon assured him.

"What about her?" He nodded at Rose. "She lose somebody to the flu?"

"No, the war," Gideon said softly, hoping Rose wouldn't hear, which was absurd, but he couldn't help trying to spare her whatever pain he could.

"All right, then," the driver said, and they climbed in.

"Do many people ask you to take them to the hospital?" Elizabeth asked the driver when they were on their way.

"The past week or so, yeah."

"If they're sick, why don't they send for an ambulance?" Rose asked.

"Have you tried to get an ambulance lately?"

"Well, no," she admitted.

"Too many people are sick. Hundreds. Maybe thousands. They can't get to all of them, even if they go day and night, and they can't do that because too many of their drivers are sick, too."

"That's terrible," Elizabeth said.

"This flu is terrible. Business is terrible. Lots of people are sick, and the rest are too scared to go anywhere."

Gideon exchanged a look with Elizabeth, wondering if they were foolish to be out like this. Never mind the danger to Rose if Fred found out where she was. The flu was everywhere.

"We'll be fine," she said behind her mask. "Look, there's nobody out to catch it from."

She was right. The usually teeming streets were practically deserted, and the cab encountered little traffic in the long drive up Broadway to the Ansonia.

To their surprise, no doorman held the door or greeted them when they entered the magnificent lobby, where no residents or shoppers lingered as they usually did. The fountain bubbled as usual, but even the seals seemed subdued today.

"Where is everybody?" Rose whispered in wonder.

"Hiding from the flu," Elizabeth said. "Is that the bank over there?"

She took Rose's arm, and Gideon followed them to the conveniently located office, which opened directly off the lobby. Inside, two tellers looked up when they entered, but the rest of the windows were empty. Gideon refused to think that the men had registered alarm at their entrance, but it was difficult to tell since they were wearing masks, too. He explained to one of them what they wanted, and they were ushered into an office in the rear.

The man there had been working without his mask, but he pulled it up when they entered and jumped to his feet. He seemed young to be a bank president, but then he introduced himself as the head teller.

"We were hoping to see someone more senior," Gideon said, trying not to sound annoyed.

"And I would love to take you to someone more senior," Mr. Feely said, "but everyone else has the flu."

Which explained the empty teller cages. "I see. Well, thank you for seeing us."

Mr. Feely invited them to sit down, and when he had sat down again, he said, "How may I help you today?"

"This is Mrs. Preston and Miss Miles, and I'm Gideon Bates, Mrs. Preston's attorney. Mrs. Preston's husband, Corporal Thomas Preston, has an account here on which she draws for her support."

Mr. Feely winced a bit, although reading his expression was difficult with half of his face covered. "Yes, of course. I was so sorry to hear about your husband, Mrs. Preston."

"Thank you," Rose said faintly. Gideon gave her a moment before continuing.

"As Mrs. Preston's attorney, I'm in the process of getting her affairs in order. She would like to know the balance of her account."

Mr. Feely nodded. "You realize, of course, that the account is in her husband's name, and not hers."

"Yes, but I believe he arranged for her to be able to draw funds from it at her discretion."

"I . . . If you'll wait just a moment, I can get the information on that account."

Mr. Feely went out a little more quickly than seemed polite.

"What's wrong with him?" Elizabeth whispered. They had put Rose between them, and she was also looking at Gideon for an explanation.

"He's probably not used to dealing with customers on matters like this," Gideon said, although he had an uneasy feeling about Mr. Feely's reaction, too. Something wasn't right.

Feely returned in a few minutes with a ledger. He didn't make eye contact with any of them. When he was seated behind his desk, he opened the ledger to a page he had marked, examined it as if to make sure it was the right one, then turned the ledger so they could see it as well. He had to clear his throat before speaking. "This account originally held well over a hundred thousand dollars."

Rose made a strangled sound, and Elizabeth gasped.

Gideon somehow managed to maintain his dignity. This amount would have been more than enough to support Rose and her child forever. Perhaps not in the style that Tom would have liked, but certainly in comfort. Why hadn't Gideon thought to check the account sooner?

"But," Feely continued gravely, "you will note that the balance available in the account now is zero."

"What?" Rose exclaimed in a very unladylike manner, pulling the ledger closer so she could see. "How could that happen? Who stole all the money that Tommy left me?"

Gideon and Elizabeth also leaned forward to look, and Gideon scanned the pages, hoping to find some clue.

"Nobody stole it," Mr. Feely said, apparently a bit offended at the implication. "We received a notice that Mr. Preston had, uh, passed away, and that his heir wished to secure the money in the account until his will could be probated."

"Fred," Rose said bitterly.

Gideon should have expected this, or he would have if he'd even imagined how much money Tom had provided for Rose. He felt like a fool. "But you haven't released the funds to him yet, I hope."

"Oh no, not without the proper paperwork."

"And did your instructions include any provision for Mrs. Preston's support?" Gideon asked, not bothering to hide his irritation.

"Uh, no, I'm afraid not. He did show me the will, which was enough for me to secure the account, though."

"But how am I supposed to live?" Rose asked, her voice breaking. "Tommy wanted to leave me everything."

Elizabeth took her hand and patted it. "Don't worry. We'll work something out."

"I'm sorry, but the bank has little choice in these matters. We must do what the law says," Mr. Feely said, obviously distressed to have caused Rose distress.

"Of course you do," Gideon said. He handed the man one of his cards. "Would you let me know if you receive any more instructions concerning Mr. Preston's account?"

"I . . . I suppose that would be permissible."

"It certainly would, Mr. Feely," Elizabeth

said, sounding as grateful as anyone could have wished. "I know Mrs. Preston would appreciate it very much."

Rose nodded vigorously, since she was now weeping too hard to speak.

"And so would I," Elizabeth added with apparently heartfelt sincerity, giving him her hand across the desk.

"I'm sorry, but what is your relationship to Mrs. Preston?" Feely asked, holding Elizabeth's hand much longer than Gideon thought proper.

"She is my dearest friend. I know you'll do whatever you can to help her. She's simply devastated by the loss of her husband, and now her brother-in-law is determined to leave her and her unborn child penniless and take Tom Preston's fortune for himself."

Mr. Feely blushed at the mention of the unborn child, but that didn't stop him from continuing to hold Elizabeth's hand. "Oh my, I had no idea. Are you saying that the will he showed me wasn't valid?"

"I'm afraid it may be," Gideon said in an effort to distract Feely from staring at Elizabeth. "Mr. Preston had a later will making provisions for his wife and child, but it has . . . disappeared."

"I see," Feely said, finally realizing he should release Elizabeth's hand. "How . . . unfortunate."

"But Mrs. Preston *is* fortunate to have Mr. Bates as her champion, so we hope everything will work out in Mrs. Preston's favor," Elizabeth said.

"I hope so, too, Miss Miles," Feely said quite fervently. At least Elizabeth had ensured that Feely would keep them informed.

Gideon thanked him and escorted the ladies out to the lobby. They didn't linger in case anyone going by might recognize Rose. They couldn't be sure Fred's henchman wouldn't try to finish what he'd started if he could find her. They quickly left the opulence of the Ansonia and had to summon a cab themselves since the doorman was still not in evidence.

This driver seemed grateful for their custom and just nodded when Gideon gave him the address in Greenwich Village.

"I can't believe what Fred did," Rose said when the cab pulled out into the sparse traffic.

"I should have foreseen that," Gideon said. "Most people would at least wait until the will is probated, though."

"He was probably afraid Rose would take all the money and disappear," Elizabeth said.

"I wish I'd thought of it," Rose said bitterly. "But I didn't have any idea how much money there was! Tommy just told me there was enough to last until he got home and that Fred would be making regular deposits, too, so I'd never have to worry."

"Did you at least find out what you needed to

know?" Gideon asked Elizabeth with little hope.

"As a matter of fact, I did," she assured him. "And it's very good news indeed."

Jake was waiting for them when they reached the house. He had his mask hanging around his neck, which gave him an oddly rakish air, as if he weren't really afraid of the flu and just wore the mask to be fashionable. Elizabeth wished he'd take it a little more seriously.

"How did you get in?" she asked.

"Zelda let me in. She says she's already over the flu."

"We hope so. Where is she?"

"She went back to bed."

Elizabeth gave him a pitying look.

"What did you find out?" he asked when they'd retired to the parlor.

"We found out that Tom Preston had 136,347 dollars and eighty-four cents in his account."

Rose muttered something, and Jake whistled. "Then why does Rose need our help?"

"Because Fred Preston is Tom's legal heir now, and all that money belongs to him," Gideon said. He was sitting next to Elizabeth on the love seat, so she took his hand and squeezed it comfortingly.

"I wonder if Tom had money someplace else, too," Jake said.

"It's possible, but if Rose can't claim it, it

doesn't matter," Elizabeth said. "The important thing to know is that Delia should have at least as much as Tom did."

"We call this establishing a mark," Jake explained to Rose, who had removed her veil and mask and looked quite fetching in her widow's weeds, probably because she was so angry at Fred that it made her eyes sparkle. "You somehow get him to reveal to you how much he's got available."

"Elizabeth already explained it to me. It's very clever," she added, instinctively knowing how important it was to stroke a man's ego.

"Now we just need to decide how much German spies might need to blow up J. P. Morgan and Company," Elizabeth said.

"I told Delia me and my people hadn't been paid for a few months," Jake said.

"What do you suppose the average wage for a spy is?" Gideon asked with only a trace of sarcasm.

"And how many of them are there?" Elizabeth added with a grin. "I'm inclined to be generous. I'd say ten thousand for that."

"I'm in the wrong profession," Gideon muttered.

"We need to buy supplies to build the bomb," Jake said.

"Another ten thousand," Elizabeth said. "Someone has to build it, and that requires special training and a secure place to work."

"The hardest part is getting the bomb into the building," Jake said. "We've got somebody lined up to do it—"

"You do?" Rose asked in surprise.

"No, Rose. We're just making all this up, remember?" Elizabeth said kindly.

"Oh yes. I guess I'm just excited."

Jake waved away her concern. "But it's a dangerous job, as I made sure Delia understood, and the man might have to leave the country later if the cops suspect him. Delia said a whole bunch of their spies did that when America got into the war. So probably we'll all have to leave, too. I'd say fifty for the fellow who plants the bomb."

Gideon actually gasped. "Will she believe that?"

"The man will have to go to a foreign country and support himself, so it's reasonable," Jake said, although Elizabeth had to admit it was actually pretty unreasonable. "We should get another fifty for whoever else has to go, too. If they know we're ready to take care of them, they'll be willing to take chances for us."

"Your concern for these men is admirable, Jake," Gideon said. Elizabeth was relieved to note he was joking now.

"Thank you, Gideon," Jake replied with a twinkle. He was enjoying himself immensely. "So how much are we up to now?"

"A hundred twenty," Gideon said before

Elizabeth could reply. "Delia will surely balk at a figure like that."

"She might," Elizabeth said, "but even if she only provides half, that will still be fine."

"So now you just have to figure out how to put that into a letter that won't get you arrested as a spy, Lizzie, and we wait for her to reply," Jake said.

"I don't think Elizabeth should be involved in this," Gideon said.

"I won't be *involved.* I'm just going to write Delia a letter telling her I thank her a hundred times for her support during these difficult days and am hoping I can return her kindness twenty-fold. Nobody can arrest me for that. Besides, I'm not even Beth Hirsch."

Gideon muttered something that might have been a curse.

"What's wrong?" she asked.

"I forgot the advice your father gave me."

"He gave you advice?" Jake asked gleefully. "This should be interesting. What did he say?"

"He said I should never tell Elizabeth not to do something."

Jake whooped at that, and even Rose laughed. Elizabeth didn't find it a bit funny. "Why would he say that?"

"Because, he informed me, that would ensure you'd do just the opposite."

"I wish that were true of you," she replied

tartly. "I'd tell you to be sure to enlist in the army."

That sobered everyone, even Jake, who quickly changed the subject. "Lizzie, if you want to write that letter to Delia now, I'll take it with me and mail it tomorrow."

"Will that give you enough time to contact all your people?" Gideon asked.

"Probably," Jake replied, cheerful again. "We need to finish Delia's part before Fred gets back from New Jersey."

"Why is Fred in New Jersey?" Rose asked.

"I'll explain it to you while Lizzie writes her letter," Jake said.

"And I will go back to my office and try to get some work done," Gideon said.

Elizabeth wished he didn't look so glum, but he was probably just worried about her. She only wished he would worry more about himself. At least they now had another month before he had to report to the army. A lot could happen in a month. Maybe she could convince him he had a bad heart after all.

The trip to the bank had gone well. Tim North and his pals had enlisted the local bank president in their scheme—Fred Preston was not their first victim and would not be their last—and he understood his role perfectly. He had examined Fred's credentials and assured him that he would contact the bank in Poughkeepsie and have a line of credit established as soon as the Poughkeepsie bank confirmed the amount in his account.

Fred seemed quite optimistic as they walked back to the hotel. "Are you sure the banker who inquired about purchasing the land was only willing to pay three hundred dollars an acre?" he asked.

"I think that was the minimum that it is worth," the Old Man said. "They might go higher. It's premium farmland now, after all."

"If I have to pay more than a hundred and fifty for it, I'll naturally want to sell it higher."

The Old Man thought Fred was being awfully greedy, since he'd certainly make a killing on this deal, but he was also willing to encourage that greed. "I'm sure we can negotiate whatever price you want. Dieter says the banker is very eager. He probably has buyers already lined up himself."

They had lunch in the hotel dining room. Sam joined them, and he ate heartily, since he was building himself up for the big fight in Chicago. After lunch, he kept Fred distracted with his shadowboxing and calisthenics. The Old Man had just started to wonder how he was going to keep Fred busy all weekend while they waited for the Poughkeepsie bank to reply to the Trenton bank when the telephone rang. The Old Man answered.

"Mr. Lange," the bank president said, and no one could mistake the triumphant tone of his voice. "The bank in Poughkeepsie has informed me that Mr. Preston has over eight hundred thousand dollars in his personal account. I've never had anyone get back to me so quickly. Apparently, Mr. Preston is one of their biggest depositors."

So Preston hadn't lied about almost being a millionaire. With the land deal, he'd cross that magical threshold and secure his fortune, so naturally, he was enthusiastic.

The Old Man thanked the banker and reported the good news to Fred.

"Telephone your brother and tell him," Fred said. "I want to meet with these financiers he works for as soon as possible."

Tim North was only too happy to arrange a meeting. The "financiers" would come to their hotel the next morning to negotiate the deal.

Tim North showed up at the hotel early on Saturday morning. The Old Man greeted his "brother" warmly, and Dieter returned his greeting enthusiastically. The Old Man had told him what the bank president had reported, and everyone was feeling quite optimistic, especially Fred.

"Now you're going to be meeting some of the wealthiest men in the United States," Dieter told them, "but you should treat them just like you would anybody else. They're really no better than you or I, and they hate it when people try to impress them or treat them like they're royalty or something. This is America, after all."

"Don't worry," Fred said. "I know how to conduct myself in business."

The Old Man had some extra chairs brought up, and the three businessmen arrived. They did look impressive. Mr. Sutcliffe was a distinguished gentleman of slender build with wavy silver hair and a Vandyke beard. Mr. Worthington was portly and bald with a tiny mustache and a cigar clenched in his teeth. Mr. Nash walked with a silver-headed cane, which he didn't appear to need, and wore his dark hair parted in the middle and heavily pomaded into place. He wore a fresh rose in his lapel. Dieter introduced everyone.

"All right, Lange," Mr. Worthington said to Dieter, "we're all here. Now tell us what the deal is."

"He's been very mysterious," Nash confided to Fred, who was practically squirming with anticipation.

"I'm sorry to keep you in suspense, gentlemen," Dieter said, "but this is a sensitive subject, and I didn't want to bring it up until I could be certain everything was in order. You'll remember that you instructed me to sell off your hunting lodge and the property that goes with it."

"Do we still own it?" Sutcliffe asked, somewhat distressed. "I thought we'd gotten rid of that cursed place after Horace died there."

"Yes, it's been years now," Worthington said. "What's taken you so long, Lange?"

"I've had a difficult time finding a buyer willing to pay what the land is worth," Dieter said. "I know you wanted to get back your original investment."

"We don't care about our investment," Sutcliffe said. "We just want to get rid of the place."

"Well, Mr. Preston is willing to pay the same price you originally paid for the land," Dieter said.

"And how much was that?" Worthington asked with no real interest.

"A hundred and fifty," Dieter said.

"Wait. We built the hunting lodge on it after we bought it. Will you have a use for that, Mr. Preston?" Nash asked.

"I, uh, yes. I plan to form a club and sell memberships," Fred improvised. The Old Man was impressed by how quickly he'd come up with that.

"The hunting there is excellent," Worthington said. "You should do very well with it."

Fred smiled at the approbation. He was probably actually considering opening a club, at least for the moment.

"We should get back the cost of the lodge, too,"

303

Nash said. "It's only good business," he added apologetically to Fred.

"I understand completely," Fred assured him, although he was frowning.

"How much did the lodge cost to build, Lange?" Sutcliffe asked.

"Fifty thousand," Dieter replied reluctantly, casting Fred an apologetic glance.

Fred winced, but he didn't protest. Plainly, he wanted these men to consider him an equal, and that meant not worrying about mundane details like how much something cost.

"So are we agreed we'll let the property go for two hundred?" Worthington asked. The others nodded. Worthington turned to Fred. "Then as soon as you can get the money, Lange here will take care of everything."

"I'll have to get an abstract first." Dieter turned to Fred. "I'm sorry, Mr. Preston, but we can't sell the land without one."

Plainly, Fred knew he was right, even though he wasn't happy about it. "How long will that take?"

"A few days. I might be able to get it done on Monday. Tuesday at the latest."

Fred didn't look like he relished the thought of being stuck in Trenton over the weekend. Before he could remark upon it, however, the connecting door to the other hotel room opened, and Sam started into the room. He stopped when he saw the group gathered there. He was wearing his trunks and looking a bit winded.

"Sorry. I didn't know you were having a meeting."

"This fellow looks like a boxer," Mr. Sutcliffe noted with approval.

"Yes, I'm training him," the Old Man said. "He's got a big fight in Chicago in a few weeks."

"Maybe your brother already told you, but we have a boxer, too," Worthington said.

"Do you?" the Old Man said, feigning surprise. "Who is he?"

"Kid North."

"I've heard of him, but I think my boy here can beat him."

Fred Preston's expression said he wasn't quite as sure, but no one paid him any mind.

"Why don't we find out, then?" Worthington said. "While we're waiting for the abstract, maybe we can arrange a match."

The Old Man smiled. "I'd be happy to arrange a match, so long as you are prepared to make a substantial wager."

"We'd like nothing better," Sutcliffe said. "Lange, draw up the articles of agreement."

After a few more pleasantries and some good-natured joking about which fighter was the best, the businessmen went on their way, leaving Dieter behind.

As soon as the other men were gone, Dieter

turned on the Old Man. "What do you think you're doing? They bet hundreds of thousands of dollars. We can't possibly come up with that kind of money."

"You and I can't, but Mr. Preston here will have the two hundred thousand he's transferring for the land deal. Mr. Preston, how would you like to double it even before you make the money on the hunting lodge?"

Preston's eyes were gleaming now. "I'd love it, but how can you be sure your fighter will win?"

"Oh, I see what you're thinking," Dieter said, exchanging a knowing look with his "brother." "Kid North has been wanting to get even with these men for a long time. They've made a fortune betting on his fights, but he only gets paid a pittance. His sister is really sick. She's got consumption, and he wants to send her out west for treatment. He asked for a loan from those men, but they refused, so I think he'll be more than happy to make sure that our man wins the fight in exchange for a couple thousand to help his sister."

"I see," Fred Preston said, nodding vigorously.

"The whole thing depends on us using your money to place the bets, though," the Old Man said. "Dieter and I would expect a cut, but you'd get the larger share."

"How much would you want?" Fred asked warily.

The two men exchanged a glance. "Twenty percent each," Dieter said. "That gives you sixty percent."

"I want seventy-five percent, and the two of you can split the other twenty-five."

The Old Man wanted to laugh at Fred's terms, but he managed to look appropriately disgruntled. "But we brought you into this."

"And without my money, you'd get nothing at all. Take it or leave it."

"We'll take it," Dieter said, giving the Old Man a warning look. "But even with all Mr. Preston's money, we still won't have enough to cover the kind of bets these men make. I've seen them go as high as a million dollars. How can you cover that with just two hundred thousand?"

"By pyramiding the bets," the Old Man said. "Have you ever heard of that?"

"No," Dieter said. "I don't know what you mean."

"It's simply a matter of moving the money around the right way. You can have yourself designated as the stake holder, can't you?"

"Of course. I usually am."

"All right. Then this is the way it works."

The Old Man explained it all in great detail, answering Dieter's questions. Fred Preston listened attentively, never batting an eye at how crooked the scheme was.

"Is that all right with you, Mr. Preston?"

Dieter asked when the Old Man had finished his explanation.

"Perfectly all right," Preston said happily.

Dieter nodded. "Then I'll draw up the terms and—"

"Wait a minute," Fred said. "I think I'd like somebody neutral to draw up the terms."

"Neutral?" Dieter echoed in apparent astonishment. "Are you insinuating that I would cheat you somehow?"

"Of course not, but I'm not familiar with this sort of thing, and you work for those men and are the brother of Mr. Lange here. Nobody is looking out for *my* interests."

"I see your point," the Old Man said quickly, before Tim could reply with something that might have put Fred off. "Why don't we ask somebody who has no ties to any of us?"

"That's what I was thinking," Fred said. "But I don't know anyone here."

"And if you did, we wouldn't approve of him," Dieter said sourly.

"How about that young lawyer we met with the other day? What was his name?" the Old Man said.

"Bates," Fred remembered.

"Yes, as I recall, he has no love for either of us," the Old Man said with more truth than he wanted to admit.

"And he's a real stickler," Fred said with a trace

of bitterness. "He might not want to be involved with a prizefight, but he'd make sure everything was fair. Do you think we can get him out here?"

"I'm sure he'll come," the Old Man said, giving his "brother" a look that told him not to worry. He pulled out his pocket watch. "We just won't tell him about the prizefight until he gets here. He may still be in his office. I'll try to reach him. Why don't you go to the bank before it closes, Mr. Preston, and ask them to transfer your funds so we'll have the money on Monday?"

Fred was only too happy to do just that.

When he was gone, Tim turned to the Old Man. "Who is this Bates?"

"He's engaged to my Lizzie, but don't get the wrong idea. He's as honest as the day is long, which is why he's perfect for this. I think we'll keep him around for the fight, too."

"An honest attorney?" Tim marveled.

"I know. It's hard to believe, but sometimes that can come in handy. Now, let's see if I can get him out here tomorrow."

CHAPTER THIRTEEN

Gideon couldn't decide if he was angry or relieved that Mr. Miles had summoned him to assist with his con. Helping him would violate every standard he had ever set for his life, but helping him would also help win Rose Preston what was rightfully hers from the man who had conspired to cheat her out of it. There must have been a name for this moral conundrum, but Gideon couldn't for the life of him figure out what it was.

In any case, this was not how Gideon had planned to spend his Sunday.

"Mr. Bates," Mr. Miles shouted when he saw Gideon get off the train at the Trenton station. He waved and hurried over to Gideon. "I hope you had a pleasant journey."

"I can't practice law in New Jersey," Gideon said by way of greeting. "I'm not licensed here."

"We just need you to draw up the terms for a prizefight." He gently guided Gideon toward a waiting taxi.

"A prizefight? How . . . ? What . . . ? I thought Fred Preston was going to buy Adolph Hirsch's business?"

"Heavens no. How could we sell Hirsch's business when we don't own it? Mr. Preston is going to bet on a prizefight."

"But prizefighting is illegal," Gideon said, more than a little outraged.

"Of course it is, so you won't technically be practicing law, will you?"

His logic baffled Gideon, who allowed himself to be prodded into the taxi while Mr. Miles loaded his bag.

"Why isn't anyone wearing masks?" Gideon asked.

"The flu must not be as bad here," Mr. Miles said. "Not as many people. I've booked you a room at the hotel where we are staying."

"I still don't understand why I have to stay over. Drawing up a contract won't take that long."

"We may need you for something else, so I thought it was easier for you to stay than to go home and then return."

"What else could you need me for?" Gideon asked suspiciously.

"Nothing that I know of, but Fred Preston seems to trust you, and we may need that later."

Gideon didn't know whether to be flattered or insulted by Fred's confidence in him, so he decided not to think about it.

Masks or no masks, the Trenton streets were quiet, too, and the desk clerk at the hotel did wear a mask. When Gideon had checked in and put his suitcase in his room, he joined Mr. Miles and Fred Preston in their rooms.

"This is our fighter, Sam Hooper," Mr. Miles said, indicating a well-built fellow who had been shadowboxing in the corner. He had hands as big as hams and his grip made Gideon wince. "And this is my brother, Dieter Lange."

Dieter Lange probably wasn't his brother, and that certainly wasn't his name even if they did happen to be related, because Mr. Miles's name wasn't Lange, either. Still, Gideon shook his hand and murmured something appropriate.

"You already know Mr. Preston," Mr. Miles added.

Fred Preston had the grace to look a bit uncertain of Gideon's goodwill. "Thank you for coming on such short notice, Mr. Bates."

He seemed relieved when Gideon shook his outstretched hand. "You're welcome."

Fred blinked in surprise at this bald reply. Gideon should have said it wasn't any trouble or something else to make Fred feel at ease, but Gideon didn't feel like putting him at ease. Fred quickly recovered, however, stretching his lips into a forced smile. "I don't think what we're asking you to do is too taxing."

"So I gathered, although I have never been involved in a prizefight before, so I'm not sure—"

"Don't worry," Dieter assured him. "I've done dozens of these. I'll tell you what needs to go in, and you will just need to make sure Mr. Preston's interests are protected. Once we've composed the contract, I'll get a stenographer to type it up, and we'll sign it tomorrow."

Someone had left a stack of paper and some pens on the desk, so Gideon took his seat. Gideon made a list of each of the items that Dieter indicated needed to be covered by the agreement, and then he set about composing a paragraph for each one. They agreed that it would be a fight to the finish between the two boxers for a purse of five hundred thousand dollars. Dieter Lange would be the referee and stakeholder. If either side failed to put up their share of the purse, all monies wagered would be forfeited, but each side would have twenty-four hours to raise its share of the purse. The match was to be held in a private gymnasium.

"Who provides the purse?" Gideon asked when he came to that part of the agreement.

"Each side puts up half of it," Dieter explained. "The winning side gets it all."

"So that's what you're putting up, Mr. Preston?"

Fred looked surprised. He turned to Mr. Miles. "No, I . . . I thought I was just going to provide money for the wagers."

"We don't need to worry about our share of the purse, Mr. Preston," Mr. Miles said. "Only the loser will have to pay it."

"But what if your fighter loses?" Gideon asked.

The other men all smiled.

"Our fighter isn't going to lose, Mr. Bates," Fred said.

Gideon couldn't believe this. "You're going to fix an illegal prizefight and then bet on it?"

"I believe you have summed it up quite adequately," Mr. Miles said with far too much satisfaction.

"I can't be involved in that," Gideon said, although he knew it was far too late to protest.

"You won't be," Mr. Miles assured him with all the honesty Gideon had learned to expect from him.

Someone knocked on the hotel room door.

Mr. Miles opened it, and another well-built fellow walked in. "Close the door before somebody sees me," he said anxiously.

Mr. Miles closed the door.

"Kid, we really appreciate this," Dieter said.

"No, I appreciate the chance to get back at those rats," the Kid said.

Gideon wondered who the "rats" were and what they could have done that was worse than this part of it.

Dieter introduced everyone. Preston seemed especially delighted to make the Kid's acquaintance.

"Why is he here?" Gideon whispered to Mr. Miles.

314

"They have to plan the fight."

The two fighters shook hands and began to discuss what they would do. Then they moved the furniture in the room to one side and began to practice. All the blows looked hideously real to Gideon but did no apparent damage. In fact, the two fighters seemed to be enjoying themselves immensely.

"We'll go for five rounds, and then Sam will knock me out in the sixth," the Kid explained.

"The fight is set for tomorrow afternoon, assuming your funds arrive by then, Mr. Preston," Dieter said. "We've booked a private gymnasium, and we will be the only ones there, so there's no danger the police will be notified."

"Sounds like you've thought of everything," Gideon said. No one seemed to notice the sarcasm in his tone.

"We have tried to, Mr. Bates," Mr. Miles said. "As soon as you've finished the contract, we'll go down to dinner, shall we?"

"We need a bomb," Jake informed Elizabeth the instant she admitted him to the house on Monday morning.

"A bomb?" she echoed in alarm.

"Yeah. Delia might want to see it, so I thought we should have one."

"I doubt she'll want to see it."

"Then we'll show it to her anyway. It won't

cost much. I thought we could get it from Mahoney's."

"Oh. Why didn't you say so?"

"I just did. I thought you and Rose would like to go with me," Jake said. "Unless you're too busy taking care of Zelda," he added hopefully.

"Oh no, Zelda is completely recovered from the flu." Against everyone's better judgment, Zelda had gone back to teaching that morning. Elizabeth hoped she would be all right. "And if you think I'm leaving you alone with Rose, you're crazy."

Jake tried to look innocent. "What are you talking about?"

"I'm talking about how attractive Rose must be since you know she'll soon be a rich woman."

"Don't worry about me," Rose said as she came down the stairs. "I can take care of myself."

"Mrs. Preston, you're looking lovely this morning," Jake said with all the charm he could muster. Elizabeth wanted to punch him.

"I know I do," Rose said sweetly. "What's this Mahoney's you're talking about?"

"It's a . . . Well, you need to see it to believe it."

"Can we go, Elizabeth?" Rose asked. "I'm so sick of being cooped up."

"Aren't you worried about the flu?" Elizabeth tried, wondering how it might affect a pregnant woman.

"Zelda had it right here in the house, and we're all fine," Rose reminded her. "And we'll all be wearing masks."

"You probably aren't in any danger anyway," Jake said. "Nobody else is out."

"All right," Elizabeth said. "I always enjoy going to Mahoney's."

They needed a few minutes to get their hats and gloves and masks. The walk over to Broadway was pleasant, although the good weather probably wouldn't last much longer. The leaves were already turning. Jake flagged down a cab, since they didn't want to risk being close to other people on a streetcar.

Mahoney's was a small storefront on Twenty-fifth Street, not too far from Dan the Dude's Saloon. The sign above the door read Mahoney's Electric, and the dusty window revealed an uninviting interior cluttered with intimidating-looking gadgets of all shapes and sizes.

A bell mounted above the door heralded their arrival. They could hear the sound of footsteps coming from above and down some unseen stairs.

Rose looked around in wonder. "What is all this?"

"No one knows," Jake said mysteriously.

A ferret-faced man of less-than-average height appeared from some shadowy place in the back and marched toward them, peering at them beneath his beetled eyebrows with great suspicion. "May I help you?" he asked in a tone that said he already knew the answer was no.

"Hey, Mahoney, how are you doing?"

Mahoney waited for Jake to give him the sign that con men used to tell others to pretend not to recognize them, but Jake just stuck his hands in his pockets and grinned. Mahoney turned his attention to the ladies, studying them as if he weren't quite sure they were really there.

"Mr. Mahoney, you remember my sister, Lizzie. And this is her friend Mrs. Preston."

"Pleased to meet you, ladies. Sister, eh? I'm surprised you admit it, Miss Miles."

Elizabeth gave him her best smile. "Sometimes I don't."

"So what brings you here, young Jake?" Mahoney asked, apparently delighted to welcome them now.

"We need a bomb."

"A bomb?" Mahoney echoed with the same alarm Elizabeth had used.

"Not a real one," Jake quickly explained.

"If you wanted a real one, you wouldn't've come here. What on earth do you need a fake bomb for?"

"Because we're not planning to blow up a very important building," Elizabeth said.

"Because we aren't really German saboteurs," Jake added.

Rose just grinned because she found this all so amusing.

Mahoney looked at them like they were crazy for a long moment. "You aren't with the League, are you? Trying to trick me or something?"

"Not at all. We're the ones who aren't blowing up the building," Jake said. "You are just building a bomb that won't explode."

"I never built a bomb before," Mahoney said doubtfully.

"The people who will see this one have probably never seen a real one, either, so they won't know the difference."

"I don't know. Gadgets are more my line."

"I can see that," Rose said, glancing around. "What do all of these things do?"

Mahoney looked up in surprise. "Nothing."

"What do you mean?" she asked, looking around again in amazement. "They must do something."

The display of equipment was indeed impressive. Machines small and large, square and oblong, jagged and sleek, simple and complex, with wires and gears and metal projections, were displayed in every possible space.

"I believe I can honestly say that none of these things even works at all," Mahoney said proudly.

"Then why do you sell them in your shop?"

Elizabeth covered a smile, and Jake didn't even bother to hide his laugh. "He sells them to suckers, just like we're going to do. Mahoney, I won't be bringing the mark in here. I'll just take the bomb with me."

"So I'll have to put it into a box."

"Yes, and don't make it too big or too heavy. Do you have anything you can use already made-up?"

"I might. Come in the back and take a look. What makes a bomb explode?"

"How should I know?" Jake asked.

"Dynamite," Rose called after them. "It comes in sticks, with a fuse sticking out the top."

Elizabeth looked at her in admiration. "How did you know that?"

"I don't know. Some soldier probably mentioned it. I've danced with a lot of soldiers, and they love talking about the war and bombs and all that sort of thing. Oh, Elizabeth, is this really going to work?" she added, her voice nearly breaking as her cheerful mood suddenly evaporated.

"Of course it is, Rose," Elizabeth hastily assured her. "My father has Fred in New Jersey right now, and they could be finished with him as early as tomorrow."

"But what if he figures it out and finds out I've gotten his money?"

"He won't. You'll see. Everything will be fine."

But Rose wasn't listening. Tears filled her eyes, and in the next instant, she was sobbing on

Elizabeth's shoulder. Elizabeth comforted her as best she could, and fortunately, Rose's crying jag lasted only a few minutes.

"Oh dear, I'm so sorry," she said, pulling out a handkerchief to mop up the damage. "I don't know what's wrong with me."

"I'd guess it's your condition. Women who are expecting do get emotional, I'm told."

"I miss Tommy so much. It's funny. I didn't even like him that much at first. He wasn't very exciting, but in the end, that's what I liked most about him. I know he would've been good to me, and he was so happy about the baby."

"This stupid war," Elizabeth said.

"What do you think, Lizzie?" Jake called as he emerged from the back room with a contraption about a foot square.

"I don't have no dynamite, but I remembered I heard you could set off a bomb with a timer, so I added this clock," Mahoney explained to the ladies.

Neither man seemed to notice Rose's red-rimmed eyes. She gazed down at the thing with the same amazement Elizabeth felt. It did look oddly dangerous with that wind-up alarm clock mounted on the side.

"It's got some porcelain tubes inside. We'll say that's where the dynamite is," Jake said.

A tangle of wires connected the tubes and appeared to connect the clock as well.

"I wish I was selling this to a real German spy. I could charge him a lot of money, but for you, Jake, only two hundred dollars."

"That's robbery," Jake said good-naturedly, "but worth every penny."

Mahoney found a wooden crate into which he packed the "bomb" and then nailed the top on. Jake happily settled up with him, and they went back to Broadway to hunt for a taxi.

"What are you going to do with that?" Elizabeth asked when they were on their way back to Greenwich Village.

"I'm not going to do anything. You're going to keep it for me until we hear from Delia that she has our money."

"And then what?"

"Then we show her the bomb and get the money from her," he replied cheerfully.

The typed agreement was delivered to Gideon's hotel room midmorning on Monday. He read it over and found it satisfactory. When he delivered it to Mr. Miles's room, he found that Miles, Fred Preston and Sam Hooper had rearranged the furniture in one of the rooms to accommodate what Gideon assumed would be the placing of the bets. He had no intention of staying around for that part of the negotiations, but he agreed to wait until the agreement was signed in case anyone had any questions.

A few minutes later, Dieter—or whatever his name really was—and the men posing as the millionaire financiers arrived, along with their fighter. Everyone was introduced to the people they didn't already know and, in a few cases, to men they weren't supposed to already know. Dieter read over the contract and signed on behalf of his employers. Fred Preston signed for himself.

Then everyone took their positions. Dieter sat at a table by himself. Fred sat at a desk in front of him and Sam Hooper sat at another table in front of Fred. On the other side of the room was a larger table, where the financiers sat. Mr. Miles had thoughtfully provided bottles of wine and glasses for them.

Fred had successfully drawn out two hundred thousand dollars from the local bank that morning, and he had the money in a satchel on the floor beside his desk. The satchel wasn't visible to the millionaires, who sat with their backs to the others and seemed oddly preoccupied with their own conversation. They had their money carelessly stacked on the table.

When everyone was in place, Gideon started for the door, but Mr. Worthington called out to him. "Why don't you join us, Mr. Bates?"

"Oh no, I—"

"Mr. Bates doesn't approve of gambling," Mr. Miles said.

"Nobody is asking him to gamble," Worthington said. "But he can enjoy a glass of wine with us."

The other two millionaires seconded the invitation, and Gideon found himself sitting with them while Worthington poured him a generous libation. They seemed very interested in him, asking him questions about his background and his law practice. Gideon was astonished that the betting was done almost as an afterthought, because the stacks of cash on the table made him very nervous and the sums involved made his head swim.

They opened the wagering with a fifty-thousand-dollar bet. The Kid carried the appropriate number of wrapped bundles from the financiers' table over to Sam Hooper, who tabulated the bets. Fred Preston pulled out an equal number of bundles of cash from his satchel, and Mr. Miles carried them to Sam for tabulation. Then they carried all the cash to Dieter Lange's table so he could count it.

This proved to be a laborious process, as Lange tore off the bands the bank had put on the bundles and counted out each one. Even though the bundles contained hundred-dollar bills, there were still quite a few.

After a few minutes of waiting while Dieter made slow progress through the stacks, Worthington said, "I don't think it's necessary to count all this money. It was counted by the bank and wrapped with the teller's initials on the wrapper. We're just wasting a lot of time."

"That's true," Sutcliffe said. "What do you men think?" he asked Fred Preston and Mr. Miles. They both agreed, and that was when Gideon realized that the packets of money the "millionaires" were betting with were probably boodle. He'd encountered this before. Con men would wrap up stacks of plain paper, using a real bill only on the top and bottom. That way a few thousand dollars could look like hundreds of thousands. No wonder they didn't want the bundles broken open for counting.

The betting continued. Gideon tried to pay attention to what was happening, with the Kid and Mr. Miles carrying stacks of money from table to table, but they were moving too fast, and the financiers kept distracting him with questions about himself. One thing he knew—the wagers were now almost up to half a million dollars.

Suddenly, Mr. Nash said, "Wait a minute, Kid. I think I gave you fifty thousand dollars instead of twenty-five thousand dollars as my part of that last wager."

"That's easy enough to check," Mr. Worthington said. "Lange, count the money and see if you've got twenty-five thousand dollars too much."

Gideon could easily understand how Nash might have made such a mistake, with so much money lying on the table, but when he looked up, he saw an expression of pure terror on Fred Preston's face. But Fred didn't know about the boodle, so why would he be terrified at the thought of counting the money?

That was when he realized that something else was going on, but he had no idea what it could be.

Before anyone could think about it, however, Dieter said, "There's no need to take the time to count all the money. Why don't we just put it all in a safe-deposit box and count it after the fight?"

"An excellent idea," Worthington said. "If our friends win, they can see if there's an extra twenty-five thousand dollars, and if we win, we can count it at our leisure. We'll keep one of the keys, and Mr. Preston can keep the other. Whoever loses will turn their key over to the winner."

Everyone agreed that Dieter's suggestion sounded like a good plan. Dieter packed all of the cash from the wagers into the satchel Fred had been using for his money. He picked it up and started for the door.

"Wait a minute, Dieter," Mr. Miles called. "You forgot something." He pointed to a bundle wrapped in newspaper lying under Fred Preston's chair. It turned out to contain a large quantity of cash.

"What's the matter, Lange?" Mr. Worthington

asked his embarrassed secretary. "Aren't you feeling well? Maybe I should go with you to make sure nothing happens to you." The two men left for the bank, with Dieter looking chagrined.

The other financiers then took their leave and went with Kid North to the gymnasium.

"We'll follow you as soon as Dieter gets back," Mr. Miles called after them.

"That went well," Fred Preston said when they were alone. "I don't think they suspected a thing."

"What would they have suspected?" Gideon asked.

Fred frowned, and Mr. Miles said, "Nothing you need to worry about, Mr. Bates. I know you didn't want to remain here for the wagering, but I didn't want to offend those gentlemen by insisting that you be allowed to leave."

Gideon didn't know whether to believe that or not. Maybe Elizabeth's father had intended all along that he should be there to witness whatever was or was not happening. Asking him about it wouldn't do any good, though. "I don't think I was too seriously compromised."

Mr. Miles smiled. "I'm glad to hear it."

"I'll get my things together for the fight, Mr. Lange," Sam Hooper said, and disappeared into the adjoining room.

"Let's get the furniture moved back while we wait for Dieter," Mr. Miles said.

They had moved the tables out into the hallway and put the room back in order by the time Dieter returned. He was hopping mad, too.

"What's the matter with you?" he demanded of Mr. Miles. "I knew I'd left that money under Preston's chair."

"Oh, I'm sorry," Mr. Miles said. "I thought you'd just forgotten it."

"I did, too," Fred said. "What's wrong?"

"What's wrong is that we're in a fine mess now. If I'd gone to the bank alone, I'd have kept both keys to the safety-deposit box, but Worthington said I might as well go ahead and give him their key, so now I only have one of them. Besides, I had two hundred fifty thousand dollars in that bundle under the chair to cover the purse, in case they ask for it. What are we going to do now?"

"Where is Worthington?" Mr. Miles asked.

"He went along to the gymnasium."

"Well, maybe they'll forget about the purse," Mr. Miles said.

"Is that likely?" Fred asked.

"I hope so," Dieter said, "but I doubt it."

"The agreement gives you twenty-four hours to come up with the money for the purse," Gideon reminded them.

"That's right," Fred said. "But it doesn't matter because our fighter is going to win, so they're the ones who will have to come up with it."

Gideon winced, but he had to agree, the scheme

seemed foolproof if the fight was really fixed. "I just want to know how you were able to match all those wagers." The last he'd heard, Fred was supposed to be buying Hirsch's company for a hundred thousand. Had they really gotten Fred Preston to give them almost half a million dollars?

"That was the really clever part," Fred said, clearly impressed. "I only had two hundred thousand, but Mr. Lange would take the money I handed him from my satchel and go to the fighter to record the bet. Then on the way to his brother's table, he would drop my share back into my satchel."

"How could he do that without being seen?" Gideon asked in horrified amazement.

"You were sitting right there in the room. Did you see him do it?" Fred challenged.

"I . . . uh . . . no, I didn't."

"And those other men weren't even paying any attention," Fred continued. "I was really scared he'd get caught until I saw him doing it right under their noses."

"So that means not only do you not have the money for the purse, but you also don't really have enough money in that safe-deposit box to cover the bets," Gideon said.

"That doesn't matter, either," Fred said, his good humor completely restored, "because our fighter is going to win."

Gideon had thought his opinion of Fred Preston couldn't get any lower, but he'd been wrong. The man was a complete cad. "But what if they want to count the money for some reason? If it's short, you'll forfeit all the money you wagered, no matter who wins the fight."

"You worry too much, Mr. Bates," Mr. Miles said. "Come along with us to the gymnasium. After all this, you don't want to miss the fight itself."

Ordinarily, Gideon didn't enjoy watching men beat each other senseless, but he had a feeling that the real entertainment would be happening outside the ring. He simply had to see how this would all work out, so he went with the other men to the gymnasium.

The place was deserted except for their group. One well-used boxing ring sat in the middle of the large room, surrounded by various pieces of equipment, punching bags and assorted mismatched chairs. The whole building was seedy and smelled of sweat and despair, but Gideon was apparently the only one who noticed. Kid North was already in the ring in his boxing trunks, warming up. Sam Hooper needed only a few minutes to change in the locker room.

While they waited, the financiers were chatting as Fred hung back with Mr. Miles and his brother. Suddenly, Worthington said, "We just realized we forgot about the purse."

"Say, that's right," Mr. Miles said. "We did forget. But do we really need it?"

"It's in the articles of agreement," Nash said. "The fight can't go on until it's covered, can it, Mr. Bates?"

"I . . ."

"According to the articles of agreement," Mr. Sutcliffe added, "you forfeit all the money you bet if you can't cover the purse."

"I can cover the purse," Fred said defensively. "Our share is two hundred fifty thousand dollars. I'll give you a check for it."

"I believe the agreement stipulates cash," Mr. Worthington said.

Gideon wasn't sure if Mr. Miles expected him to offer advice here or not, but Worthington had asked him directly, so he decided to reply, however belatedly. "The articles of agreement also give you twenty-four hours to raise the purse. Can both sides meet that requirement?"

"We certainly can," Nash said.

"And so can I," Fred said.

After a few more minutes of discussion, they decided to waive the prize money for now and go ahead with the fight.

By now Sam Hooper was in the ring warming up, too. Mr. Miles was his second, and Sutcliffe was second to Kid North. Dieter and Worthington were in charge of the clock, and they rang the bell for the fight to begin. Sam and the Kid started trading punches that looked far too convincing, not at all like the fake ones they'd been throwing at their rehearsal.

Gideon flinched time and again as blows landed, sending one or the other of the fighters staggering. The fight went on for two rounds, with both fighters landing plenty of punches and neither showing any effects. In the third round, Sam landed a blow that sent Kid North to the mat, but after a few seconds, he was up again. This happened twice more before the bell rang, ending the third round.

Gideon sat on one of the folding chairs near the ring between Mr. Nash and Fred Preston. Fred started taunting Nash. "It looks like my fighter is going to win, Mr. Nash. I'm sorry now I didn't bet more on him."

"The fight isn't over yet, Preston. Do you want to place another wager?"

"How much?" Fred asked eagerly.

"A quarter million?"

"I'll take that if you'll accept a check."

But Nash shook his head. "Fighting is illegal. I wouldn't want to be involved through a check."

The fourth round began, and this time, Sam knocked the Kid down with a solid blow that kept him down for a count of eight.

Fred Preston was fairly squirming in his seat and muttering to himself. Obviously, he would have bet everything he owned at that moment.

Gideon didn't feel a bit guilty for wishing Fred had been given that opportunity.

The Kid went down a few more times in the fifth round, but he managed to hold on. Gideon couldn't believe he wasn't really being beaten to a pulp. The punches looked far too real. If it had been up to him, he would have called the fight right then, but it wasn't up to him. All he could do was watch.

The sixth round began, and the Kid staggered out, apparently disoriented. Sam landed a terrific punch to the Kid's mouth, and blood flowed out and down his chin, onto his chest. Gideon was on his feet, screaming at them to stop the fight, but Fred and Nash were shouting, too, drowning out his pleas with their own cheers for their respective fighters. Everyone was shouting something, but the Kid managed to lurch to his feet once again. Sam danced around a few moments before drawing back his great right arm for the punch that would end the fight, but before he could land it, the Kid somehow managed to connect with a blow of his own that landed square on Sam's chin.

Sam fell backward, like a great tree, blood gushing from his mouth. Mr. Miles and Mr. Sutcliffe rushed to him. Mr. Miles had a towel and tried to stem the flow of blood, but it began to gush anew.

"He's having a hemorrhage," Mr. Miles said

frantically, trying in vain to stop the blood, but it continued to flow freely.

"We should call a doctor," Gideon shouted, but suddenly, Sam coughed and lay still.

Mr. Miles leaned down and put his ear to Sam's bloody chest. After a moment, he lifted his head and shook it gravely. "This man is dead."

CHAPTER FOURTEEN

Elizabeth and Rose convinced Jake to buy them lunch after their visit to Mahoney's. The restaurant staff seemed thrilled to have customers, since the place was almost deserted. Elizabeth and her companions could hardly keep a straight face when the few other customers glanced curiously at the box Jake had set carefully on the extra chair at their table.

After lunch, Jake dropped Elizabeth and Rose at home with the box. He carried it in and set it down on the hall table.

"What am I supposed to tell Cybil and Zelda that is?" Elizabeth asked.

"Tell them the truth," Jake suggested.

"That's probably not a good idea," Rose said.

"What are you going to do now?" Elizabeth asked Jake.

"I'm going to Dan's. We probably won't hear from Delia for a few days, so let me know as soon as she sends word that she has the money."

"Will you go to pick it up?"

"I guess that's what she'll probably suggest."

The doorbell rang, and through the frosted

glass of the front door, they could see a man's silhouette.

"Who could that be?" Jake asked with a frown. "Are you expecting Gideon?"

"No, and that fellow is too big to be Gideon. Rose—"

"I know. I'm going upstairs." Her face had gone pale, and she hurried up the stairs without another word.

When she was safely out of sight, Elizabeth opened the door. A large man dressed in a cheap suit and a derby hat stood on the porch. He looked to be in his thirties, with a pockmarked face and light hair that was in need of a trim.

"Are you Miss Hirsch?" he demanded, his small eyes narrowed in suspicion.

Could Delia have responded so quickly? And how had she known where to find Miss Hirsch? Had she put a return address on the letter? She must have. "Yes, I am," she said.

"Mrs. Preston sent me. She said to give you this." He held up a satchel.

"What is it?" she asked, even though she was pretty sure she knew.

"It's what you asked for, in your letter. She said to tell you to give it to Mr. Weber. He's here, isn't he? I saw him come in with you."

Had he been watching the house? But of course he had. He'd been waiting for her to return home. That meant he'd seen Rose, too!

"Yeah, I'm here," Jake said, coming forward.

"Where's that other lady who was with you?" he asked, peering over their heads into the hallway behind them.

"Don't worry about her," Jake said quickly. "She's just the landlady. She doesn't know anything about this. Miss Hirsch is just staying here while her father is, uh, locked up."

"I wish Mrs. Preston hadn't involved me in this," Elizabeth said in her most aggrieved tone.

"She wanted to get this taken care of, and she didn't know how to find Mr. Weber," the man said. "It's lucky he was here. Now you don't even have to worry about giving him the bag."

"Yeah, that was lucky," Jake said. "Do you know what's in the bag?"

"I know. Mrs. Preston, she tells me to be very careful. Now I tell you to be very careful." He handed Jake the satchel. "You will not contact her again until Mr. Hirsch is ready to repay her."

"Oh sure," Jake said, opening the satchel an inch to make sure it was filled with money. "Thank her for me, will you? And I'll be in touch."

"Not until after," he repeated.

"No, not until after."

The man nodded solemnly, then turned and made his way back down the porch steps.

"That was too easy," Elizabeth said, closing the door.

"It was certainly quick," Jake replied, pulling the satchel completely open.

"Did she give us what we asked for?" Elizabeth asked.

"I'll tell you when I've counted it."

He carried the satchel into the parlor and dumped the bundles of cash into a heap on the floor, then sat down next to it to count.

Elizabeth watched him thoughtfully for a few minutes, unable to shake her feeling of unease. Something wasn't right. Delia had agreed too quickly and supplied the money too easily.

"That was the man who tried to kill me," Rose said.

Jake and Elizabeth turned, startled, at the sound of her voice. She stood at the bottom of the stairs. Her face was chalk white. Jake jumped up to his feet, and he and Elizabeth went to her.

"Are you sure?" Elizabeth asked, although it made perfect sense that the same man who would deliver cash to German spies would also break into a poor widow's apartment to steal her husband's will and try to strangle her when he was caught in the act. No wonder Elizabeth had found him so disturbing.

"I watched him leave from my window upstairs. It was him all right. I'll never forget that face."

"Thank heaven you were wearing that veil outside so he didn't recognize you. He was watching the house and saw us when we got out of the cab," Elizabeth said.

Rose swayed slightly, and Elizabeth rushed to catch her. Jake jumped up and helped her get Rose into the parlor and seated on the sofa.

"I'm all right," she insisted. "I just . . . I was so scared there for a minute."

"You don't have to be scared anymore. This is almost over," Elizabeth assured her.

"Will it ever be over? Won't Fred and Delia always want me dead?"

Elizabeth exchanged a look with Jake. "Not always," she promised. "When this is over, you'll be free."

Jake went back to the parlor and started counting the money again, fanning every packet to make sure it was all real money. "And you'll be rich," he added cheerfully.

"This man is dead." The words seemed to echo in the sudden silence in the gymnasium.

They needed only a moment for the import of those words to sink in, and then pandemonium broke out. Nobody wanted to be involved with an illegal prizefight in which a man had died.

Mr. Miles scrambled out of the ring as quickly as he could and ushered Gideon and Fred aside. "We need to get out of here."

Fred was trembling from the shock, and he nodded vigorously.

"What about the dead man?" Gideon said, knowing they couldn't just leave him there. Surely, he'd been a friend of Mr. Miles's at least.

"Let the others worry about him," Mr. Miles said. "They have a lot more influence than I do, and I'm sure Mr. Preston doesn't want to be involved in something like this."

The only true part of that statement was that Preston didn't want to be involved. Gideon didn't want to be involved, either, and his every instinct told him to notify the police, but the police had probably already been paid off to look the other way. Gideon had no friends in Trenton, New Jersey, so left with no other option, he followed Mr. Miles and Fred Preston. The three of them rushed back to the hotel to pack.

"If we hurry, we can make the last train to New York," Mr. Miles said as they left Gideon to go to their own rooms.

Filling his suitcase took only moments, since he hadn't brought much. Then he went to the adjoining rooms the other men had shared to find them just closing their own suitcases. Mr. Miles had left Sam Hooper's things where they were, Gideon noted with a shudder.

Just as they were ready to leave, Dieter came rushing in.

He held up one of the safe-deposit box keys. "I'll get the other key from them. Then I'll take the money and meet you in New York."

"But you didn't win the fight," Gideon pointed out.

"No, but if I give them the money, they'll discover the shortage, and I'll lose my job anyway. I might as well just leave them now while I can get the money for a new start. As soon as I have it, we can meet and split it."

"What about the dead man?" Preston was still trembling.

"They've already decided to dress him in his regular clothes and dump his body down by the train tracks. The police will think somebody beat him up and left him there."

Fred moaned, and Gideon protested, but Dieter and Mr. Miles told him it wasn't his concern. He couldn't help Sam—a man in Gideon's position couldn't afford to be associated with a prize-fight—and they'd better hurry or they'd miss their train. Only the fact that Mr. Miles seemed so confident everything would work out enabled him to resist the urge to go directly to the police. Perhaps this wasn't what it seemed to be. Things Mr. Miles planned seldom were. That thought was all that kept him sane.

The train ride back to the city seemed endless to Gideon, who sat alone, brooding over the dead man and his own part in all this. Fred sat with Mr. Miles and fretted the whole way about the "murder" and the possible consequences.

"Those men aren't likely to implicate you, Mr.

Preston," Mr. Miles said. "If I know anything about them, they'll manage to cover the whole thing up, and you'll never hear another word about it. Now when my brother gets to New York, I'll telephone you and—"

"Your brother isn't coming to New York. When those men calm down, they'll demand a count of the money. Your brother will never be able to explain it, and he might as well kill himself."

Mr. Miles looked suitably distressed at the supposed fate of his fake brother. "Then I won't be able to buy Mr. Hirsch's business, and I don't even have my fighter anymore."

"You're just lucky you're not going to prison," Fred said.

When they reached New York, Fred wouldn't even shake hands with Gideon or Mr. Miles.

"If my brother does turn up, I'll let you know, Mr. Preston," Mr. Miles said.

"You do that," Fred said sourly, and headed off to find the train to Poughkeepsie.

When Gideon and Mr. Miles were outside and waiting for a cab, Mr. Miles said, "Good job, Gideon. You show real potential."

"How can you say that? A man is dead," Gideon replied furiously.

Mr. Miles gave him a pitying smile. "Have you learned nothing about grifting yet, my boy?"

Gideon gaped at him as he replayed the prize-fight in his memory. "But all that blood . . ."

"Cackle bladder. You remember that, don't you?"

How could he have forgotten? A rubber bladder filled with chicken blood and held in the mouth. But there had been so much of it! "So Sam isn't . . . ?"

"Dead? Not at all. As they say, he will live to fight another day."

Gideon wanted to slap himself upside the head. "Then the whole thing was fake?"

"Of course it was. I'm sorry I had to bring you in, my boy, but Preston was balking at the contract. He thought we might cheat him." Mr. Miles couldn't help smiling at that. "So I was able to recommend an honest attorney to protect his interests."

Gideon didn't know whether to be furious or relieved. "That's an elaborate scheme to set up just for Fred Preston."

"Yes, it is, but I didn't set it up. Tim North—otherwise known as my brother, Dieter—runs it. He gives me half of whatever I bring in."

"So all those men . . . ?"

"They all work for Tim, even Sam."

"But I thought the plan was for Fred to buy Hirsch's business."

Mr. Miles shook his head. "That was just to get his interest. I told him I was actually going to buy it, and I had a land deal that would've made me the money to do it, but I needed an investor and the deal would make him a fortune, too. That's how I got him to Trenton."

"Then why did you get him involved with the prizefight?"

"That was the goal all along. It's called the switch. You get a mark interested in one deal that might be a real business opportunity but a little bit shady. If he's willing to do that, you know you've got him, and you switch him to something really illegal, like a fixed prizefight. That's what we call it, the switch."

"But don't they want to stay with the original deal, the one that's only a little bit illegal?" How could his fellow man be so venal?

"Never," Mr. Miles assured him. "They actually forget all about it. You didn't hear Freddy even mention the land deal, did you?"

"Uh, no."

"Ah, here's a cab at last." Mr. Miles waved, and the cab pulled up to them. "Where can I drop you?'

"At Elizabeth's."

"Good. I'll go with you. She'll want to know how it went with Preston."

Cybil and Zelda had canceled the salon again for that evening. Too many people were sick, and it seemed foolish to bring any of them together for a social event. Besides, Zelda was exhausted after her first day back teaching. Cybil had put her straight to bed, and they were all worried about a relapse.

At a little after seven o'clock, while Cybil was upstairs with Zelda, and Elizabeth and Rose were cleaning up in the kitchen, the doorbell rang.

"Probably somebody who didn't get the word that the salon is canceled," Elizabeth judged. "You keep washing. I'll get it."

Leaving Rose in the kitchen with the dirty dishes, Elizabeth went to the front door. In the darkness, she couldn't see who might be out there, but she didn't think twice about opening the door. She had only a second to register who was there and to think she should have called out to ask who it was first before he punched her in the stomach and her whole body exploded with pain.

She was dying. She couldn't breathe, couldn't move, couldn't cry out, couldn't even think. Rough hands grabbed her when she would have fallen, and then she was flying or at least moving without any effort on her part. Familiar images flashed by. The porch post, the stairs, the sidewalk. Then she was in a dark place, and someone was doing something to her hands.

Elizabeth cared about none of this because she was so desperately trying to breathe. Her whole chest seemed paralyzed, and every organ in her body was screaming for air, and she couldn't get

345

her lungs to work, couldn't make air come in. She was dying, and this was how it ended, in a dark place where she couldn't breathe.

And then suddenly she could! She gasped, and her lungs convulsed, and she sucked in the blessed air but only one good gulp before her attacker stuffed something in her mouth, stopping it completely. A moment of sheer panic, until she realized she could still breathe through her nose, and while that wasn't quite as good as gulping the air had been, she could at least breathe. She wasn't going to die.

But then the whole world started shaking and rumbling or at least the part of the world she was in, that very dark place, which now that she had some air, her brain told her was a motorcar. The backseat of a motorcar. Someone had started it up, and now it was moving, and whoever had punched and nearly killed her was taking her away in it. She wanted to yell, but he'd tied a gag around her head to hold the rag he'd stuffed into her mouth, and her hands were tied behind her back. She wiggled and squirmed, trying to sit up, but a big hand reached over the seat and swatted at her.

"Stay down, or I'll hit you again," a voice said, and she remembered who it was. The man who'd almost killed Rose had almost killed her, and now he was taking her someplace she was pretty sure she didn't want to go to.

• • •

By the time the cab dropped them off at Cybil's house, Gideon had almost completely recovered from his terror at witnessing a man's "death" earlier in the day. Elizabeth would certainly tease him about his gullibility, but he would welcome it. He hoped he never got jaded enough to take things like that lightly. He'd need more time to get over his anger at Mr. Miles for involving him in this business, however. How much time, he couldn't begin to guess.

Cybil opened the door for them. "I'm sorry to say that we canceled the salon for this evening," she informed them with a sly grin. "I hope you're not too disappointed."

Mr. Miles hated attending the salons, as she well knew. "How is Zelda doing?"

"She went back to school today, so she's tired, but I think she's going to be fine." She turned and called toward the kitchen, "Elizabeth, Buster and Gideon are here."

Cybil was the only person alive who was allowed to call Mr. Miles by his childhood nickname.

Rose came out of the kitchen, frowning. "I thought Elizabeth was out here. She went to answer the door."

"I answered the door," Cybil said.

"No, I mean when the doorbell rang before.

She told me to finish the dishes, and she'd see who was there."

"When was this? I didn't hear the bell," Cybil said.

"A few minutes ago. Not very long."

Gideon knew he was being silly, but he felt an unmistakable prickle of unease. "Could she be upstairs?"

"I didn't hear her come up, but I'll go check," Cybil said. Plainly, she sensed his unease and shared it. She hurried up the stairs, calling for Elizabeth as she went.

"Who was at the door?" Gideon asked Rose.

Her eyes grew wide, and she clapped a hand over her mouth.

"What?" Gideon demanded. "What is it?"

"He was here, the man who attacked me."

"The one who broke into your apartment, you mean?" Gideon asked, rushing to her.

"Yes. I recognized him."

"And he was the one who rang the bell a few minutes ago?"

"No . . . I mean, I don't know, but he was here this afternoon."

"What was he doing *here?*"

"He brought the money," Rose said. "Delia sent him."

Mr. Miles muttered a curse. Gideon threw open the front door and ran out onto the porch. "Elizabeth!" he called, looking up and down the street frantically. But all was still, and his voice seemed to echo against the dark houses. If she had been out there, she was gone now.

When he went back inside, Cybil was coming down the stairs. "She's not up there."

"Rose," Gideon said, taking her arm and leading her into the parlor, "sit down and tell us everything that happened."

When she was seated, she looked up at them with terrified eyes. "Jake came by this morning and invited us to go to Mahoney's with him to buy a bomb."

"A bomb!" Gideon and Cybil echoed in horror.

"Not a real bomb," Mr. Miles said. "Mahoney's is a place that makes fake machines."

"Why would someone have a business making fake machines?" Gideon asked.

Everyone looked at him like he was crazy, even Cybil, and he realized how stupid his question really was.

"All right," he conceded. "Then what?"

"We had lunch and came back here. We'd only been here a few minutes when a man came to the door. Elizabeth sent me upstairs. She always makes me hide when someone comes to the door."

"So he didn't see you?" Gideon asked.

"No. Elizabeth thought he'd been waiting outside for her to get home, but she'd made me wear a veil, and we were all wearing the masks, so we don't think he recognized me."

"All right. What did he want?"

"He wanted to deliver the money that Delia sent."

"That was fast," Mr. Miles said. "She couldn't have gotten Elizabeth's letter until this morning."

"Elizabeth thought it was fast, too, but Jake was very happy. He counted the money, and he said she'd sent the whole amount he asked for."

"What did he say?" Gideon asked. "The man who brought the money, I mean. Did you hear what he said?"

"A little, and Jake and Elizabeth talked about it. He didn't say much, though. He said to be careful with the money, and Jake is supposed to let Delia know when Mr. Hirsch is ready to repay her."

"Who are all these people, Buster?" Cybil asked her brother.

"German spies."

"Don't tease me. I'm not in the mood."

"I'm not teasing. Delia Preston is a German spy, and so is Mr. Hirsch. Apparently, this man who delivered the money is their cohort."

Cybil still didn't believe it. "Gideon?"

"I'm afraid he's right. Delia Preston thinks she's financing some sabotage."

"Ah," Cybil said as if everything was now clear to her. "Hence the bomb."

"The fake bomb," Mr. Miles said.

"Of course it's fake, just like everything else you do," Cybil said angrily. "And now look what you've done."

"I haven't done anything, and no one has any reason to harm Lizzie."

"And yet she's missing," Gideon reminded him, furious.

"Who would have taken her and why?" Cybil demanded.

"It has to have something to do with all of this business with the Prestons," Gideon said. "Could they have figured out they were being tricked?"

"Not Fred," Mr. Miles said. "He was with us until half an hour ago, and it's far too soon for Delia to be having second thoughts. Besides, if this was revenge, they would have just killed Lizzie."

Gideon gave him what he hoped was a murderous glare. "That's comforting."

Mr. Miles turned back to Rose. "What was it that man said to Jake about repaying her?"

"He said to let Delia know when Mr. Hirsch was ready to repay her."

"Why would Hirsch repay her?" Gideon asked.

"Jake was going to tell her that Hirsch couldn't pay the other spies because the government was watching him too closely," Mr. Miles said. "That was why they needed cash from her. If she balked, he was going to promise that Hirsch would pay her back when he could."

"And Delia thinks Elizabeth is Hirsch's daughter," Rose reminded them.

"I can't believe this," Cybil said in exasperation.

"Nobody is asking you to, my dear," Mr. Miles said.

"But really, Buster, *German spies?*"

"We're hampering their efforts, Sissie. We should get a medal."

"This isn't getting us anywhere," Gideon snapped. "Would Delia have taken Elizabeth as . . . as—I don't know—collateral of some kind for her money?"

"It's possible," Mr. Miles said.

"Delia isn't very trusting," Rose offered.

"How long does she think she can keep a young woman a prisoner, though?" Cybil asked.

"They were going to keep me for heaven knows how long," Rose said.

"Dear heaven."

"Yes, well, I think we've established that Delia Preston is exactly the kind of person who would take a young woman captive as collateral for a debt," Gideon said. "Now we have to rescue Elizabeth."

"This wasn't part of the plan," Mr. Miles said with distinct disapproval, "but we may be able to move things a bit. Cybil, I need to use your telephone."

"Who are you going to call?" Gideon asked.

"Jake. He has everything we need, and he'll drive us to Poughkeepsie."

"He doesn't have the bomb," Rose said. "He left that here."

"How convenient," Cybil said.

Hours had passed. Elizabeth was certain of that. The car hit every bump in every road they traveled, too. She would be black-and-blue, she was sure, although that was the least of her worries. The first worry was wondering where her abductor was taking her. She was fairly certain it would be Poughkeepsie or someplace near.

This goon obviously worked for Delia and perhaps for both Fred and Delia. Why he had kidnapped her was a mystery, but he probably hadn't done it on a whim. Delia must have ordered it, since Fred was still busy with the Old Man and his fixed-fight scam. But why? As revenge for the cons? But they wouldn't even know yet that they'd been conned. So not revenge.

Delia would have some reason, however, and also some use for Elizabeth, so they probably didn't intend to harm her.

Or at least not more harm than being punched senseless and bound and gagged and carried away on the floor of a motorcar for hours, which in itself was more harm than Elizabeth ever wanted to endure again. Which still left her with the mystery of where they were going.

Surely, he wasn't taking her to Delia's house. She wasn't likely to keep a captive there, where any casual visitor might notice something amiss or hear her clanking around in her chains or whatever they planned to use to keep her subdued. But Delia would keep her somewhere nearby. That was only common sense. Elizabeth would point that out if Delia hadn't already considered it. At any rate, she would be a cooperative prisoner, at least until she found an opportunity to escape. Or Gideon rescued her, which she had every confidence he would try to do.

Elizabeth thought she might have actually dozed off, the rumble of the motor being somewhat soothing and her ordeal having taken a lot of her energy. At any rate, she woke right up when the motorcar finally pulled to a stop and the driver got out and opened the door.

"If you behave yourself, I won't hurt you," he said.

Elizabeth decided she would be very well-behaved. She let him help her out of the motorcar, since her muscles had stiffened and she had no strength left after being tied up so long. Her arms were numb, her stomach ached from the punch and every nerve in her body was screaming with distress.

She looked around and realized they were in a garage of some kind. Not a public garage, but one that had been converted from a stable that belonged to a private home. Could she be in Delia's garage? How lovely.

Her abductor held her roughly by the arm and directed her to the other end of the building, which contained a workbench and a door. The door stood open to what must be a storage area of some kind, although it was too dark to see. He shoved her through the door and slammed it behind her.

She stumbled and almost fell before hitting the wall opposite the door. The impact hurt, but she welcomed the pain. At least she was alive. The darkness was almost complete, but she could dimly make out an oblong shape against the sidewall that, upon inspection, proved to be a cot. Her hands were still tied and her mouth still gagged, but she now had the freedom to at least work at her bonds without drawing attention to herself.

She managed to use the rough wall to scrape the gag down over her chin so she could spit out the ball of cloth that had been stuffed into her mouth, which now felt as dry as cotton. She was eventually able to work up some moisture to ease the horrible stickiness. Before she could even think about the rope binding her hands, she heard voices and realized someone was coming.

She took her place standing against the wall opposite the door so she'd at least be facing her visitors.

The door opened, and a woman said, "Good heavens, didn't you even turn on the light?"

"You didn't tell me to," Elizabeth's abductor said.

"Must I tell you everything, Walter? Where is the string?"

A click and a bare lightbulb hanging from the ceiling filled the room with blazing light. Elizabeth cringed, slamming her eyes shut against the sudden, painful brightness. At least the place was wired for electricity.

"Miss Hirsch, I must apologize to you for the way you were transported here, but please believe me, you are our honored guest."

When Elizabeth opened her eyes a crack, she confirmed that the woman was Delia Preston. "Do you usually have to tie people up to convince them to visit you?"

"Walter, untie her," Delia said.

Walter marched into the room, and Elizabeth couldn't help cringing from him. He raised his hands in the sign of surrender, as if to show her he meant no harm, although he was a bit late with that sentiment. She turned so he could reach her bonds, and in a matter of moments, her hands fell free.

She couldn't help the moan of relief that

escaped her or the groan of pain as the blood rushed back into her numb hands.

"I'm terribly sorry. Walter can be somewhat of a brute, I'm afraid, but we couldn't take a chance that you would try to escape, so he had to tie you up."

As Elizabeth flexed her fingers, trying to massage them back to normal, she glanced around the room. There was indeed a cot on one wall and a small table and one chair on the opposite one. The table held a jug and a glass.

"Is that water?" she asked.

Delia nodded. "Walter."

He poured Elizabeth a glass, which she drank gratefully.

By then she'd also noticed the slop jar in the corner and realized that this might well have been the accommodations they had originally intended for Rose. Could they possibly have planned to keep an expectant mother in this horrible place? There wasn't even a window.

"Why am I here?" she asked when the glass was empty.

"You are to be my security," Delia said. "I gave Mr. Weber a very large sum of money, as you know."

"Yes, a hundred and twenty thousand."

"He told me your father will reimburse me, but I am not able to speak to Mr. Hirsch myself, since I cannot risk being associated with him, so I have decided to keep you as insurance. Surely, he will happily repay me when he knows it will also buy his beloved daughter's freedom."

Since Mr. Hirsch would have been quite surprised to discover he even had a daughter, Elizabeth doubted this very much, but she said, "He's charged with treason. He could be in prison for twenty years. Do you plan to keep me here for twenty years?"

"Of course not. He will be tried very soon. If he is found innocent, he will repay me, and you will be free. If he is found guilty, you will then be able to take over his business and his affairs."

"Meaning his bank accounts, I suppose."

"That's right. Either way, I will be repaid, and you will be released."

"My father will think it strange when I don't attend his trial," she tried. It was time to start crying because things were starting to look pretty hopeless for her. She let her eyes fill with tears.

"You will write to him and explain you are too upset to see him in that situation."

Curse Delia. She'd thought of everything. "You should be concerned about my well-being, then. Keeping me locked in this dump won't make me kindly disposed toward you."

"It's only temporary, as I said, and I can't very well keep you in the house. Fred would certainly notice."

"Just remind him I'm the daughter of an old friend who has been arrested for treason," she pleaded, letting the tears begin to fall, "and tell him I begged you to let me stay with you until the trial."

Delia found that amusing. "I appreciate your concerns, but we will do everything we can to make you comfortable here. Perhaps, if you are a model prisoner, I will trust you enough to move you to the house."

"Then you're just going to leave me here?" Elizabeth asked incredulously, her voice rising with only partially feigned terror. "What if I go mad? My father won't be happy about that, and nobody will let me run his business."

"You won't go mad." But happily, Delia didn't sound perfectly sure.

"Of course I will. Wouldn't you? Look at this place." She shuddered. "There're spiders! Thousands of spiders in here! I hate spiders! I'll go mad and start screaming. In fact, I feel like screaming at this very moment just at the thought of sleeping in this horrible place," she sobbed. "And what about *him?*" She waved her swollen hand at Walter. "How do I know he won't sneak down here in the night and have his way with me? I'm completely defenseless."

Walter looked highly insulted at the very suggestion, but Delia apparently believed her hysteria was real.

"I can't let you stay in the house. Fred just got home."

"But I'll be quiet," she promised desperately, somehow managing to control her sobs. "You can sneak me in after he goes to bed and explain it to him tomorrow. You must have a spare room. I won't make a sound, I swear, and I won't try to run away. In fact, I'll be grateful to be away from the city. I had to move out of my family home because of the reporters constantly badgering me. I was living in a boardinghouse. Walter will tell you."

Delia looked at Walter, who nodded grudgingly.

"Please," Elizabeth added, releasing a new flood of tears that spilled unchecked down her cheeks.

"You swear?" Delia asked.

"On my father's life."

She knew the Old Man wouldn't mind.

CHAPTER FIFTEEN

Gideon was sure they would never get to Poughkeepsie. Even though it was only a hundred miles from New York, the trip was taking forever. His only comfort was knowing that they weren't very far behind Elizabeth.

"They won't hurt her," Mr. Miles assured him again. He'd been doing that frequently, and Gideon wondered which one of them he was trying to convince. As unscrupulous as Mr. Miles was—and Gideon feared he had only begun to understand the depths of that trait in him—he did love his daughter.

Even Jake seemed concerned, for all the bickering he and Elizabeth did. He was driving like a madman, too, obviously as anxious as Gideon to find her. At this rate, they might even overtake Elizabeth and her abductor.

"At least tell me what you're planning," Gideon said. He was in the backseat of the red motorcar that Gideon thought was far too flashy for the mission they were on.

"I told you. We won't know that until we get there," Mr. Miles said from the front seat. "We have to see where she is and what the situation is."

"What was your original plan, then? You said you had one."

Mr. Miles glanced at Jake, who shrugged. "Our original plan was to have Jake and another spy be arrested while transporting the fake bomb."

"Arrested?"

"Not by real policemen," Jake said condescendingly.

"Oh, of course not," Gideon allowed. "But what would having them pretend to be arrested accomplish?"

"That would eliminate the possibility that Delia could recover any of her money, since she would never be able to find out what had happened to Jake and his friend."

Gideon remembered how effective that strategy had been once before in his dealings with Mr. Miles. "I see, but I don't understand how that plan will help us rescue Elizabeth."

"There was a bit more," Mr. Miles admitted. "A contingency, you might say, in case Delia became troublesome."

"And what was that?"

Mr. Miles explained, and Gideon sat back in his seat, finally able to at least hope they might be successful.

"That's a very nefarious scheme," he said in wonder.

"Is that a compliment?" Jake asked.

"I believe it is," Mr. Miles said with satisfaction.

362

・・・

"You must be quiet," Delia warned Elizabeth as they tiptoed up the back porch stairs. "Fred is in his study. I believe he is drinking. Something about a business deal gone wrong, but he is very upset, and I can't explain to him why you're here until he sobers up."

"I'm not interested in making any trouble for you, Mrs. Preston, believe me." Delia shouldn't believe her, of course. Elizabeth intended to make a lot of trouble for Delia before she was finished with her.

"I hope not. Walter can make you very sorry if you even try."

Elizabeth was sure of that.

They'd reached the back door of the house. "Don't say a word now. I'll take you up the back stairs to one of the spare bedrooms. It's right next to mine, so I'll hear you if you try anything, and Walter will be watching the house all night."

"Won't he get tired?" Elizabeth asked as if she were really concerned about the man who had kidnapped her getting enough rest.

"Walter knows his responsibilities. Do not test him."

The back door opened into the darkened kitchen, and the back stairs went up from there. Delia led her to one of the doors along the hallway and opened it. The room was furnished with a simple double bed, a washstand, a dresser and a clothes cabinet.

"The bathroom is across the hall," Delia told her. "Use it now while I stand watch, and then you'll have to stay in your room until I get you tomorrow."

Elizabeth made use of the bathroom, wishing she had a change of clothing. Being kidnapped was certainly inconvenient in ways she wouldn't have imagined. Her shirtwaist was dirty from the floor of the motorcar, and her skirt was hopelessly wrinkled. She didn't even have a brush to fix the ruins of her hair, and most of the pins had fallen out somewhere. If she was still here tomorrow, she'd demand Delia supply her with some amenities.

Delia was waiting outside the bathroom door when she came out. She handed her a folded nightdress. "You can use this tonight."

"Thank you. Perhaps I can send for my things from the rooming house tomorrow."

"Perhaps," Delia said, but Elizabeth was pretty sure she didn't mean it. "Now, give me your shoes."

"My shoes?"

"Yes. You won't get far barefoot."

"I won't get far alone with no money, either," Elizabeth grumbled, handing Delia her shoes.

Elizabeth went into the bedroom and closed the door behind her. She laid the nightdress on the bureau. She had no intention of getting undressed. Gideon would be coming for her the moment he discovered she was missing, and the Old Man would figure out where she was. They might not be back from New Jersey yet, though, so she was prepared to wait a day or two, but she would be ready whenever they came.

How would she let them know where she was, though?

The room had an overhead light and an electric lamp on the bedside table. She managed to move the lamp and the table over to the window, where the lamp would shine all night. Then she lay down on the bed fully clothed to wait. Exhausted by her travails, she fell asleep almost instantly.

"Jake went up and looked the place over a few days ago, just in case we had to use the contingency plan," Mr. Miles was explaining to Gideon. "There's a garage in back where they keep a motorcar."

They were parked down the street from the Preston house and could see it clearly, even in the dark. In spite of the late hour, a light still shone from one of the upstairs windows.

"The man who attacked Rose must work for them," Gideon said. "Maybe he's their chauffeur and that's how he got Elizabeth away so easily."

"I didn't see him when I was checking the place out," Jake said, "but there's a room over the garage where somebody lives, so that's probably him. There's also a storeroom in the garage. It . . . uh . . . it has a bed in it."

"A bed?" Gideon echoed. "Why would it have a bed in it?"

"I . . . uh . . ." Jake gave Mr. Miles a helpless look.

"Jake is very much afraid they were planning to keep Rose there, although we have no way of knowing that for sure."

"In a garage storeroom?" Gideon asked in horror.

"I don't think we need to feel bad about anything that happens to these people later," Mr. Miles said.

"Do you think they'll keep Elizabeth there?" Gideon asked, horrified anew.

"It seems likely, but if so, it will be relatively easy to get her out."

"What if the chauffeur is guarding her?" Gideon asked.

"Then we'll take care of him," Jake said, slapping something against his palm.

"What have you got there?" Gideon asked.

"A sap. One tap and our chauffeur will be in dreamland."

Gideon had read about the weapon used by criminals and police alike to deal with troublesome characters, but he'd never seen one up close. It was a leather strap about eight inches long with a lead weight on one end, and it looked like it would be very effective.

"What do we do?" Gideon asked.

"You, my boy, will try to stay out of the way," Mr. Miles said. "As you know, men in my line of work try to avoid violence in all its forms, but we do at least have some experience with it. Men in your line of work do not, however, so your job will be to follow us at some length and carry the satchel of supplies."

"I can be violent," Gideon protested. The very thought of facing the man who had abducted Elizabeth filled him with rage.

"I'd rather not put it to the test," Mr. Miles said cheerfully. "At any rate, bringing the satchel will be a tremendous help since Jake and I will be free to do whatever else is necessary."

He briefly outlined what they would do. Jake produced a flashlight, which he handed to Mr. Miles, and then Jake took the satchel from the trunk and entrusted it to Gideon.

"Can this blow up?" he asked, hefting the bag gingerly.

"No, or at least that's what I was told," Jake said.

Gideon did not feel reassured.

They set off through the darkness, moving quickly and fairly quietly. The very respectable neighborhood was fast asleep and silent. A dog barked in the distance, but that was the only sound they heard. The houses sat on large plots of ground, so the neighbors weren't likely to hear or notice them.

They moved up the side of the house, leaving a good ten feet between each of them as Mr. Miles had instructed. Jake was leading, and he had reached the back corner of the house, where he would stop and scout the yard for any sign of danger. Mr. Miles was somewhere in the middle, and Gideon had just reached the front corner of the house when he heard what sounded like a grunt behind him.

Every nerve in his body sparked in terror as an enormous arm clamped around his neck.

Elizabeth started awake, relieved beyond measure to discover herself in the unfamiliar bedroom instead of in the dark hole where she'd been dreaming Delia had thrown her.

She got up, moving carefully in deference to her abused body, and went to the window, but when she peered out, she could see nothing beyond the halo of light cast by the lamp that still burned. If her rescuers were coming, they hadn't arrived yet.

What had awakened her? A bad dream, which was understandable under the circumstances. Did she dare step out and explore the house? Surely, Delia and Fred were fast asleep by now. But then she remembered Walter, who most likely was still wide-awake and hoping she'd try something silly like an escape attempt. She lay back down and stared up at the ceiling, trying to calm her wayward thoughts into some sort of plan.

"And just where do you think you're going?" a voice Gideon didn't recognize growled into his ear.

Gideon didn't want to be rude, but he couldn't reply because the beefy arm around his neck was compressing his windpipe, and he couldn't speak or even breathe. He dropped the satchel, distantly wondering if that would make it explode, and started thrashing as violently as he could to attract the attention of his companions.

"Were you going to rob us, Mr. Burglar?" the voice said.

How long could a man live without air? Gideon really didn't want to find out. The fellow lifted him off his feet, so he started kicking backward, trying to land a shot to the man's kneecap or at least his shin. Then suddenly, the pressure on his neck released, and he gasped a lifesaving breath in the instant before he and his assailant went crashing to the ground.

Hopelessly confused, Gideon didn't wait for an explanation. He rolled away and scrambled to his feet just in time to see Jake slipping the sap back into his pocket.

"Thanks for finding this guy," Jake said. "Grab

one of his legs, and we'll drag him into the garage. Pop, get the satchel."

The chauffeur weighed a ton, but Gideon took joy in noticing how the man's head bounced against the ground as they dragged him what seemed like miles to the shadowy garage. Mr. Miles ran ahead and opened the doors for them. They did indeed find a motorcar inside.

"Where is that storeroom?" Gideon demanded the instant they were inside.

Jake pulled the flashlight from his pocket and flicked it on. He quickly located the door, which stood open. Gideon hurried over, but the room was empty. He muttered a curse. He'd been so sure they'd find Elizabeth here and her ordeal would be over. He heard footsteps on what must have been the stairs to the upper apartment, and in another minute, they returned.

"She's not up there, either," Jake reported.

"They couldn't have taken her far," Mr. Miles said, although Gideon thought he was once again trying to convince himself.

"How can you be sure?" Gideon asked.

"How many men do you think Delia employs to do her bidding? Someone would need to guard Elizabeth, who is clever enough to escape if given half a chance. If this fellow is here, then she must be, too."

"In the house, do you think?" Jake asked.

"We'll look. Jake, you stay here to guard this

gorilla and set everything up. Give him another tap if he wakes up."

"Shouldn't we tie him up, just in case?" Gideon asked.

"Not unless we have to. It has to look like he was at least partially responsible for what's going to happen."

Gideon nodded grimly and followed Mr. Miles back outside and across the backyard to the house.

"I doubt they'd keep her on the main floor. Someone might see her, so I'll check the cellar. You take the upstairs," Mr. Miles said.

"What if somebody wakes up?"

"Try not to let that happen, but if it does, you're a lawyer. Just talk your way out of it."

Gideon couldn't remember his legal training containing anything that would help him talk his way out of this situation, but Mr. Miles had already opened the door and gone into the kitchen. The door, Gideon was surprised to note, had not been locked.

Gideon found the back stairs easily enough. The stairs the servants used usually came down into the kitchen. The Prestons, it seemed, did not have live-in help, which was a blessing. Fewer people who might hear them banging around.

Gideon trod carefully up the stairs, happy to see the steps weren't particularly creaky. On the second floor, he found a hallway with several doors opening off of it. Unfortunately, all of them were closed. Then, to his horror, one of them opened, and Fred Preston came out of what was apparently the bathroom. He wore a dressing gown over his nightshirt, but it was hanging open, and he was holding his head in both hands, as if afraid it would flop off. He stopped dead when he saw Gideon frozen in the middle of the hall.

He peered more closely, trying to make Gideon out in the darkness. "Bates? Good God, what are you doing here?"

Gideon tried to swallow, but his mouth had dried up like a desert. "I, uh, I'm not really here. You're dreaming."

"Oh," Fred said meekly. "I should have known. I shouldn't have drunk so much. That fight . . . and the blood . . ."

"I know." Gideon meant it. "Go back to bed, Preston. You'll feel better in the morning."

Fred tried to nod, but ended up groaning and holding his head again as he shuffled back to his bedroom.

At least Gideon didn't need to check that one. Then he noticed the strip of light showing beneath one of the doors and remembered the room where the light had been burning, even though it was the middle of the night. It must have been either Delia or Elizabeth.

Could he convince Delia she was dreaming? Only one way to find out.

He went to the door and very carefully eased it open just far enough to see the figure on the bed. She bolted up and gaped at him.

"Gideon!"

He rushed in, forgetting to be quiet or cautious or careful, and threw his arms around her.

"Ouch!"

He released her at once. "Are you hurt? What have they done to you?"

"I'm fine, really, just a little bruised. Oh, Gideon, I knew you'd find me."

"It was your father really, but thank God we did. Come on, let's get out of here."

"Wait. Walter is out there lurking someplace."

"Walter?"

"He works for Delia and—"

"Is he the chauffeur?"

"He must be. Very large fellow."

"Jake took care of him. Come on."

"Who's Jake?"

They both looked up to find Delia standing in the doorway, wearing a frilly dressing gown and holding a lovely silver pistol. Gideon straightened very slowly. For a long moment, no one spoke.

"What are you doing here, Mr. Bates?"

"I think that's obvious, and I might ask you in return why you kidnapped this lady."

"I didn't kidnap anyone, and Miss Hirsch is a guest in my home, as she will tell you herself."

He glanced at Elizabeth, who merely smiled sweetly in return. "Then why are you pointing a gun at us?"

"I'm pointing a gun at *you,* Mr. Bates, because you are an intruder in my home."

She had him there. What had Mr. Miles said? Talk your way out of it.

"I'm a guest in your home, too."

"You're not my guest."

"He's my guest," Elizabeth claimed.

"I'm shocked that a respectable young lady would be entertaining a gentleman in her bed-room."

"Then you have every right to ask me to leave," Elizabeth said. "In fact, I'll be happy to do so." She jumped up from the bed, still smiling sweetly. "Mr. Bates, if you will escort me?"

"Nice try," Delia said. "Stay right where you are while I—*Ungh!*"

Mr. Miles had grabbed her from behind, and Gideon lunged forward, snatching the pistol. She fought him, refusing to release it, until he grabbed her wrist and pounded her hand on his knee. When the pistol clattered to the floor, he kicked it away.

"How dare you!" she cried, wrenching free from Mr. Miles's embrace. "Laying hands on me in my own house!"

"Don't worry. We're leaving now," Gideon told her.

"Where's Walter? What have you done with him?" she demanded.

"He's fine," Mr. Miles said pleasantly. "He's resting in the garage. Now, I think we need to make sure Mrs. Preston doesn't hinder us in our escape."

"I'll go find some stockings," Elizabeth said, handing Gideon the pistol on her way out.

Delia seemed to suddenly remember there was someone else in the house who could come to her aid. "Fred!" she cried without warning. "Fred, help!"

Mr. Miles sighed, reached over and clamped his hand around the back of her neck. Her expression of surprise lasted only a second before she went limp and slumped helplessly to the floor.

"What did you do to her?" Gideon asked in amazement.

"Nothing serious. Lizzie, hurry up with those stockings," he called. He turned back to Gideon. "Is Fred likely to wake up?"

"No. He was drinking pretty heavily this evening. The sight of all that blood unnerved him, or so he said."

"He said? You spoke with him?"

"You said to talk my way out of it."

"Here are the stockings," Elizabeth said, holding up a handful. She was also carrying some shoes.

"Gag her so she doesn't start screaming. She'll only be out a few minutes," Mr. Miles said.

"Gladly," Elizabeth said, dropping to her knees.

"Won't you suffocate her if you do that?" Gideon asked when he saw her stuff a whole balled-up stocking into Delia's mouth.

"No. That's what they did to me."

Gideon saw no reason to object, then.

Mr. Miles knelt down and began using the additional stockings to tie Delia's hands and feet while Elizabeth put on the shoes she had carried in. By the time Mr. Miles was finished, Delia was fully conscious and started frantically struggling.

"I've tied you very loosely," he told her. "You'll probably be able to free yourself without too much trouble in a few minutes, which is all the time we will need to get safely away. I advise you not to struggle too hard, or you'll tighten the knots."

She instantly stopped and glared at him murderously.

"Thank you so much for your hospitality, Delia," Elizabeth said as they left.

"Let's take Lizzie to the motorcar," Mr. Miles said, and Gideon was more than happy to oblige. While he was getting her settled in the backseat, Mr. Miles took a box out of the trunk. "Stay with Lizzie. I'll go get Jake and we can get out of here," he said, carrying the box away with him.

"Is that the bomb?" Gideon asked her.

"The fake bomb, yes."

"What's he going to do with it?"

"Probably leave it somewhere."

"Oh yes, to be found later." The plan was finally starting to come together, and Gideon could see the beauty of it.

After a wait of minutes that stretched like hours—surely, Delia had untied herself and was even now telephoning the police or something—they saw Jake and Mr. Miles running back to the motorcar. Jake started the car even before Mr. Miles had closed his door, and they were at the end of the street when they heard the explosion.

"I thought the bomb was a fake!" Elizabeth cried, peering out the rear window at the flames shooting up from the Prestons' garage. Lights were going on in houses up and down the street.

"It was," her father said with a big smile. "That explosion was Jake's doing."

"I just lit the fuse," Jake said modestly. "Bomber Morton supplied everything else."

"Somebody made you a real bomb?" Gideon asked in amazement.

"No, just a device that would make a big noise and start a little fire. I had to gather up some trash so it would catch and burn the shed."

"What about the chauffeur?" Gideon asked, trying to judge how bad the fire was as it receded in the distance.

"He'll get out okay."

"Drat. I was hoping he'd been blown to bits," Elizabeth said.

Gideon slipped his arm around her and pulled her close.

"Don't worry. He'll pay for snatching my little girl," Mr. Miles said. "We have some telephone calls to make as soon as we get back to the city."

No one had gotten any sleep at Cybil's house that night, so they were all awake when Jake pulled the car up to the curb out front. Cybil, Zelda and Rose all ran out, having heard the motorcar arriving, and they all burst into tears when they saw Elizabeth, bedraggled but safe and sound. Their hugs hurt a bit, but Elizabeth didn't complain. She was too happy to be back.

Gideon insisted on carrying her inside, much to everyone's delight, especially Elizabeth's. When he had deposited her on the sofa, the Old Man said, "Cybil, can you take care of Lizzie? We have some more business to attend to."

"Of course we can," Cybil said.

"Do you want me to stay with you?" Gideon asked Elizabeth.

"I would like nothing better, but right now I just want a hot bath and some sleep, and I'm sure you do, too."

"Yes, well, first I'm going to have a chat with Mr. Devoss."

"Are you worried about losing your job?" the Old Man asked in amusement.

"Not at all," Gideon replied with even more amusement. "Mr. Devoss is a member of the League. He will be very interested in reporting a group of German saboteurs."

"Then let's get Gideon where he needs to be, shall we, Jake?" the Old Man said.

The three most important men in Elizabeth's life took their leave. Gideon kissed her right in front of everyone, and even Jake managed to be sincere when he said he was glad she wasn't dead.

When they were gone, the other women took Elizabeth into the kitchen so Rose could prepare them all some breakfast while she told them all about her ordeal.

"But why did they blow up the garage?" Zelda wanted to know.

"They didn't really blow it up. It was just a loud explosion and a small fire. They did it to draw attention. Jake apparently had brought along some items used in making bombs and spread them out on the workbench. That's what the authorities will find when they put out the small fire."

"And that horrible man will be there, too," Rose said.

"Yes. They intended to implicate him by having him found nearby, and of course he lives above the garage, so he'd have to know what was going on there."

"But what will happen to Delia and Fred?"

"As far as we know, Fred isn't involved with the spy ring," Elizabeth said, "but Delia should be implicated. We'll have to see what the government chooses to do, but they're arresting people just because their neighbors heard them say something critical about President Wilson. I can't imagine that a woman with a bomb in her house wouldn't be suspected of something."

"I thought the bomb was in the garage," Zelda said.

"Oh, it was the fake bomb, wasn't it?" Rose said in delight. "That's why Jake took it with him when they went to find you, so you could leave it behind."

"Yes, the Old Man left it in her cellar, I think. At any rate, somewhere in the house. It should cause a sensation when it's found."

When Elizabeth had gobbled up the eggs and toast Rose had prepared for her, Cybil and Zelda sent her upstairs. Elizabeth had intended to take a bath first, but she headed straight for her bed instead, stripping off her clothes and letting them lie where they fell before crawling under the covers.

"You look very rough, Gideon," Mr. Devoss said when he looked up from his desk. "Where on earth have you been? We've all been very worried. Your mother telephoned me when you didn't come home last night—"

"I'm sorry, but it couldn't be helped. I was hunting down a German spy ring."

"What?" He had Mr. Devoss's full attention now.

"I've been trying to find out as much as I could about them before coming to you, and I can't tell you how I discovered these people without violating a client's trust, but I wanted to report it to someone I knew would take the information to the proper authorities."

"You can depend on me, but . . . Well, why don't you just tell me, and I'll save my questions for later?"

Gideon glanced over his shoulder to make sure the office door was closed. "The government recently arrested a man named Adolph Hirsch who owns a clothing factory here in the city. . . ."

As succinctly as he could, without revealing his sources, Gideon explained what he knew about Hirsch and Delia Preston's connection and Delia's intent to contact Hirsch's people and continue the work they'd started. "She has given someone over a hundred thousand dollars to place a bomb in J. P. Morgan's bank building. Last night there was an explosion and fire in Mrs. Preston's garage."

"Were they building the bomb in her garage?" Devoss asked in wonder.

"I wouldn't want to speculate. That's for the government to investigate. I'm just sharing what I know for a fact." Gideon was amazing himself with how easy it was to simply tell the truth about all of this.

"What about Fred Preston? He's your former client's brother, isn't he? Is he involved, too?"

"I don't believe so. I haven't heard anything, at any rate, but I'm sure the authorities will investigate and find out for certain." Gideon felt no guilt at all about causing Fred Preston some embarrassment and inconvenience. If he had to spend a few days locked up, he deserved it for what he'd planned for Rose.

"This is excellent information, Gideon. It's very difficult to learn about these secret groups. Do you think your informant would be willing to come forward and testify, if needed?"

"I'm sure my informant would not be willing to even be identified. I'm sorry, but you can understand how sensitive the situation is."

"Of course, of course," Mr. Devoss said, scribbling notes as quickly as he could. "I will report this immediately. The explosion happened last night, you say?"

"Only a few hours ago, in fact. It will be the talk of the town, I'm sure."

"Good, good." Gideon had rarely seen the old

man so excited about anything. He would win a lot of prestige for uncovering a German spy ring. Gideon was happy to gift him with it. "I think you should go home and get cleaned up and also let your mother know you're all right."

"I intend to, and I probably won't be back in the office today. I was up all night working on this."

"Take all the time you need, Gideon. I probably won't be able to tell you what happens as a result of this report, but perhaps you'll read about it in the newspapers."

Gideon dearly hoped so. As he left Mr. Devoss's office, he realized he was more tired than he'd thought. His head was pounding from lack of sleep, making him wish he'd asked Jake to wait instead of just dropping him off so he could drive Gideon home. But Jake and Mr. Miles had things to do as well, so he'd just have to find a cab, because he didn't think he could walk all the way home and the thought of catching a streetcar was overwhelming. At least the flu epidemic would make it easier to find a cab.

He hadn't stayed out all night in a long time, but he wouldn't have expected it to hit him quite this hard. Maybe he was getting old.

Elizabeth woke around three o'clock that afternoon and finally got the bath she'd been longing for. She winced at the number of bruises she discovered when she examined herself, but bruises would fade. She was grateful for many things that day, and one of them was that her injuries were only bruises.

Cybil and Zelda were still at the college, but Rose greeted her warmly when she finally came downstairs. "Let me make you a sandwich."

Elizabeth realized she was starving again, so she let Rose wait on her. "What will happen to me now?" she asked while Elizabeth sat at the kitchen table, watching her work.

"First of all, you'll get a large sum of money."

Rose frowned at that. She'd never quite believed all the grandiose plans Elizabeth and her family had been making. "How large a sum? I'll need to support myself for a while after the baby comes, until I can figure out how I can provide for the two of us."

"I don't think you'll have to worry about that for a while. You'll get nearly two hundred thousand dollars."

Rose gaped at her, and then she had to sit down. Elizabeth took over making the sandwich.

"That's even more than Tommy left me. How . . . ? What . . . ? Who . . . ?"

"Let me see if I can itemize it for you. The Old Man—my father—took Fred for two hundred thousand. He only gets half of that, which is his cut for bringing in the mark. Fred is the mark. He takes his expenses out of that, and usually he would keep the remainder for himself, but he said Tim was—Tim is the one who operates the . . . Well, he is the one who really took the money from Fred, who thought he was betting on a fixed prizefight. Anyway, Tim heard your story and chipped in twenty thousand from his end. The Old Man decided he could make do with twenty thousand for himself, so that leaves almost a hundred thousand for you."

"That's . . . a fortune," Rose said faintly.

"Not nearly as much as Tom would have been earning from the shoe factory if he'd lived, but at least you and the baby won't starve. That's not all, either. Delia was fairly generous herself. We got a hundred and twenty thousand from her. I get half of that because I was the roper. That means I steered Delia to them. Jake gets the other half. He pays his expenses out of that and keeps the rest for himself. So you'll get my sixty thousand, and Jake was embarrassed when the Old Man said he was giving up most of his share, so he's going to pitch in another twenty thousand. So that comes to around—"

"Almost a hundred and eighty thousand," Rose said in awe.

"If Fred and Delia had been fair with you, they could have settled for a lot less than that. Serves them right."

The telephone rang, startling them both.

"Maybe Gideon is awake and wants to come

for supper," Elizabeth said, jumping up to answer it.

She picked up the candlestick telephone, plucked the earpiece off the holder and held it to her ear. "Hello?"

"Elizabeth, is that you?" Mrs. Bates's voice sounded odd.

"Yes, is something wrong?"

"I . . . I'm very much afraid that Gideon has the flu."

CHAPTER SIXTEEN

Elizabeth couldn't find a cab, so she hopped on a streetcar. Usually, she avoided them when she was alone because mashers used the crowded conditions to sidle up next to a woman and grab her breast or some other part he had no right grabbing. Women would use a hatpin on men like that if the opportunity presented itself, but often you couldn't even tell which man was the guilty party.

Today, however, the streetcar was almost empty. The driver glanced at her with weary eyes above his mask, not even paying attention to whether she paid her fare or not. She took a seat at the very front. The conductor wandered down the aisle, nearly staggering as he tried to catch the hanging straps or the backs of the seats to steady himself. He looked terrible, his skin almost gray. Elizabeth realized she might have made a terrible mistake the moment before he fell, keeling over as if he had been pushed, although no one was near enough to have done that.

Elizabeth was halfway out of her seat when she realized she could do nothing for the man, short of helping him up, and there were others on the streetcar closer. But no one moved. They simply stared, and to her surprise, the man made no move to get up, either. He made no move at all in fact, and someone finally said, "Hey, driver, he's dead."

The driver said nothing. Didn't even turn his head. The streetcar rattled on to the next stop. Elizabeth sat there, frozen with fear. Surely, someone would do something, but no one did. Two of the other passengers got off without even glancing at the conductor. Before she could think what to do, the streetcar started again.

The driver still hadn't looked at the dead conductor. Was she imagining this? Was this another nightmare? Was she still asleep at Cybil's house? Or, worse, at Delia's?

But the streetcar stopped again, and she didn't wake up. She should get up. She should get off. She shouldn't be here. But when she started to rise, she glanced at the driver. She couldn't see his face, but his ear was blue. Not gray, not bluish, but deep blue. And his hand on the tiller was blue, too.

She was dreaming. She must be. People didn't turn blue.

And then the driver collapsed, as if he had been full of air that was suddenly released. He just crumpled to the floor where he stood.

Someone screamed. Was it her voice? She didn't know, and she didn't care. She jumped out of her seat and clambered down the steps, pushing the door open with both hands because the driver hadn't done it.

She should tell someone. She knew she should, but whom could she tell? The streets were practically deserted, and she didn't see a single policeman anywhere. And she had to get to Gideon because he had the flu, too, and he might collapse and die if she wasn't there to take care of him.

She ran the rest of the way to the lovely street where his family had lived for generations and trees were just starting to turn color and drop their leaves. The peaceful street where she and Gideon would live and raise their children when they were married. If Gideon came back from the war. If Gideon came back from the flu.

She was gasping when she finally reached his front steps. She had to pause and catch her breath. She couldn't go running in like some maniac. She had to be calm for Mrs. Bates. She had to be calm for Gideon. When she wasn't panting anymore, she climbed the steps and rang the bell.

Mrs. Bates opened the door herself. "Oh, Elizabeth, you shouldn't have come."

"Of course I should have come. How is Gideon?"

"He's burning with fever and shaking with chills."

"Have you called for the doctor?" Elizabeth

was taking off her hat and gloves. She was staying.

"I left a message but . . . So many people are sick. They couldn't say when he might come."

"We should take Gideon to the hospital, then."

"He won't hear of it. He says he just needs some rest."

"I'll go talk to him."

Mrs. Bates made no protest, and Elizabeth climbed the stairs and found Gideon's room. His mother had closed the drapes, even though the sun was almost down. Gideon lay curled on his side beneath a pile of blankets. As she approached the bed, she saw he was shaking. He hadn't seen her because his eyes were tightly closed.

"Gideon, darling, how are you feeling?" she asked because that was what you said to sick people even when you knew they were perfectly miserable.

His eyes sprang open, and his face contorted. "Don't come in here. You need to go home. I don't want you here."

He couldn't possibly mean that! "But you're sick. I'm going to help take care of you."

"No, you'll catch it," he rasped, which sent him into a fit of coughing.

How had he gotten so sick in only a few hours? He'd been perfectly fine when he left her this morning. Then she remembered the men on the streetcar. Surely, they hadn't been so very sick when they started work. If they'd been coughing and shivering in their beds like Gideon was, they never could have reported for duty.

Ignoring his frantic gestures waving her away, she went to his bedside and poured some water from the carafe into a glass and helped him sit up so he could drink it.

"You must go," he whispered when he lay back against the pillows, exhausted by the coughing and the simple effort of sipping some water. "Please, I'm begging you."

"Elizabeth," Mrs. Bates said from the doorway. "Come here. I want to talk to you."

Elizabeth hurried out into the hallway. Mrs. Bates closed the door so Gideon wouldn't hear them.

"He's terrified one of us will catch the flu, but someone has to take care of him. I'm his mother, so naturally, I will do it. Seeing you here is upsetting him, so I think it's better if you leave."

"Leave?" she echoed incredulously. "I can't leave you here to take care of him by yourself. You'll wear yourself down to a frazzle, even with the servants to help you, and . . . What is it?"

Mrs. Bates had flinched at something she'd said, but Elizabeth had no idea why. "Oh, nothing. I'm perfectly capable of taking care of my own son. No one can do it better."

She was hiding something. Elizabeth knew a lie when she heard one. What had she been saying?

"The servants," she remembered. "Wait a minute. Why did you open the door yourself when I arrived?"

"I was close, and . . . it just seemed sensible."

"Not when you're looking after your sick son." Elizabeth turned and ran down the back stairs to the kitchen. The room was dark and empty. "Hello? Where is everyone?"

The Bateses didn't keep a lot of servants, but the kitchen help and the maid lived in. No one answered her call, however.

Mrs. Bates had followed her down the stairs.

"Where are your servants?" Elizabeth demanded.

"They . . . left. They're afraid."

"Of course they're afraid. We're all afraid, but we can't just run away. I'm not going to leave you here alone to take care of Gideon."

"But he'll be so upset if he sees you."

"Then he won't see me. I'll just do the cooking and the washing and look after him when he's asleep, but I'm not leaving you. Have you had any dinner?"

"I . . . I'm not hungry."

"Nonsense," Elizabeth said. "Let me see what I can find. You go look after Gideon. I'll call you when it's ready."

She found a ham in the icebox and some potatoes, which she fried together. She also made a pot of coffee, which Mrs. Bates would need if she intended to sit with Gideon most of the night. Surely, the doctor would come soon and, if Gideon was really sick, send him to the hospital. That was where he'd get the best care, even if the hospitals were crowded. That was what hospitals were for, after all.

Elizabeth made Mrs. Bates eat and chipped up some ice to help cool Gideon's raging fever and brewed some beef tea to feed him to keep up his strength even though he couldn't eat. Near midnight, someone rang the doorbell. Elizabeth had learned her lesson about opening the door to just anyone, but at her shouted question, the doctor identified himself, and she let him in.

"Thank you so much for coming, Doctor," she said. He was a tall, slender man in a gray tweed suit.

"I'm sorry it's so late, but I've had so many patients today," he said. Indeed when he stepped into the light, he looked as if he hadn't slept in days. Dark circles made his eyes look bruised, and he had at least a day's growth of whiskers on cheeks usually shaved clean above his Vandyke beard.

"I'm Gideon's fiancée," she told him. "I came to help."

He nodded, almost as if he were too weary to form a polite reply. Mrs. Bates had heard the bell and was coming down the stairway. "Doctor, I'm so glad to see you. He's upstairs."

Mrs. Bates led the way, and Elizabeth followed. Gideon might not want to see her, but she wasn't going to miss whatever the doctor had to say.

"How long has he been sick?" the doctor asked, setting his black bag on the bedside table and opening it to remove his stethoscope.

Mrs. Bates answered his questions as best as she could while the doctor listened to Gideon's chest and looked into his mouth and eyes and ears. When he was finished, he put his instruments back into his bag, picked it up and walked out without a word.

Elizabeth and Mrs. Bates exchanged a puzzled look, then hurried after him. He stopped when he reached the hallway at the bottom of the stairs. "He has the influenza."

"We were already pretty sure of that," Elizabeth said.

Mrs. Bates wrung her hands. "Should we take him to the hospital? He seems awfully sick."

But the doctor was shaking his head. "Don't take him there. They don't have any room. All the beds are full, and people are lying on pallets on the floor in the hallways and the stairwells, and there's no one to take care of them. Half the doctors are sick and most of the nurses. There's no one to take care of him there and nothing we could do for him even if there was."

"What do you mean, nothing you can do for him?" Elizabeth cried.

"We don't know what this is. We've never seen anything like it before, and we don't have any medicine that helps. We bring people into the hospital and watch them die and then move somebody new into their bed until they die, too, and there's nothing we can do to help them. . . ."

To their horror, the doctor was weeping, great tears rolling down his stubbled cheeks.

"Stephen, good heavens, come in here and sit down," Mrs. Bates said, taking his arm and leading him into the parlor, where she conducted him to the most comfortable chair and made him sit.

"I'm sorry, Hazel," he said, pulling out a hand-kerchief to mop his face. "I don't know what came over me."

Mrs. Bates looked up at Elizabeth. "Dr. Simpson and I have known each other since childhood." She turned back to the doctor. "When did you last eat?"

"Hazel, don't—"

"When?" she insisted.

"I . . . I don't remember."

"Elizabeth, can you fix Dr. Simpson something?"

"Hazel, I don't have time to eat—"

"You can't help anyone if you collapse in the street. Elizabeth?"

Elizabeth hurried back to the kitchen and fried up some ham and eggs because they were quicker than potatoes. She called when they were ready, and Mrs. Bates brought him back to the kitchen.

Dr. Simpson muttered some halfhearted protests, but he ate everything on his plate and four pieces of toast with jam, which Mrs. Bates kept adding to the pile.

"Are there really no nurses at the hospital?" Elizabeth asked.

"Hardly any. So many are sick themselves. They fall down in the corridors and beside the beds. Some people are even holding nurses hostage if they are fortunate enough to get one to come to the house."

"Hostage?" Mrs. Bates echoed. "You mean, they won't let them leave?"

"They think a nurse can take better care of their loved one than they can, so they lock them up and keep them. But the truth is, Gideon is much better off here. There's no one at the hospital to feed him or bathe him, and as I said, there's nothing we can do for him there. I'll give you a prescription for morphine. The aches are almost unbearable for some patients. Don't give it to him unless he needs it, though."

"Of course," Mrs. Bates said.

"I've got to go now," he said.

"You can rest for a few minutes. Come back to the parlor. I'll light the gas fire, and you can have another cup of coffee before you go."

Elizabeth stayed behind to clean up, which only

took a few minutes, and when she was finished, she found them sitting in the parlor. Mrs. Bates had pulled over a footstool for the doctor, who was finishing his coffee.

"The worst part is that it's killing so many young people, Hazel. I think that's why the nurses are getting sick. They're mostly young women. In fact, I don't think I've had a single patient over sixty. Usually the flu takes the very young and the very old, but this . . . this is a scourge the likes of which we've never seen."

"I won't let it take my son," Mrs. Bates said.

Elizabeth slipped upstairs and tiptoed into Gideon's room. He was shivering, in spite of the blankets covering him and the gas fire blazing in the hearth. "Elizabeth," he murmured, "I told you to leave."

"I'm not really here," she said, remembering the story he had told them last night on the drive back from Poughkeepsie. He'd tricked Fred Preston. Maybe she could trick him. "You're just dreaming."

"That's good. I'm so cold."

"I'll warm you up," she said, and took off her shoes. She slipped underneath the covers and snuggled up to his back. His body felt like it was on fire, but he sighed with pleasure at her touch. After a few minutes, he stopped shivering and seemed to be resting.

She'd never given much credence to the stuff

they talked about in church, but she whispered a prayer to whoever might be listening, begging someone of higher authority to spare the man she loved so dearly.

Someone touched him, and he screamed because the pain was like a hot iron pressed against his flesh. He wanted to tell them not to touch him, not to move him, not to do anything at all but let him die because what was the point of being this sick if you weren't going to die?

He kept seeing Elizabeth, even though he knew she had gone. She told him she was a dream, though, whenever he asked, so he knew she wasn't there. He was glad. He loved seeing her beautiful face, but he couldn't stand the thought of her getting as sick as this and dying. No, he'd protect her from that, at least.

Someone was moving him again, wanting him to drink something. It was sweet and cool, and the pain of swallowing it was agony. He looked up to see who it was, but all he could see was the blood pouring out of his eyes. He knew it was blood because he heard them say the word over and over. Why was blood coming out of his eyes? And if it was, he'd surely die. No one could live after that, could they? He'd be glad to die because this would be over, but his mother would be so sad, and Elizabeth, he'd never get to marry her.

Poor Elizabeth had worried so about the war, but what did that matter now? And then he was there, in a dark place he knew must have been a foxhole, although why did they call them foxholes? He couldn't think. His head hurt too much to think. But he knew he was at the war somehow. Lights flashed that must be explosions. Did he have a gun? Did he remember how to shoot it? The enemy was coming, but they weren't men. They were animals, running across the field. Wild animals of every kind. Lions. Tigers. Creatures he didn't even recognize. Snarling and snapping and coming for them. He had a gun; he must have one. All soldiers got guns. But he couldn't find his anywhere, and the beasts were on him, tearing into his chest, and the pain was too great and he knew he'd never go home or see Elizabeth again.

Elizabeth had lost track of the days. Dr. Simpson had stopped by once. He looked even worse than he had the first time. He told them they were seeing more than a thousand new cases of flu in the city every day. No one knew how many people had died.

Anna had brought food a few times. The college wasn't holding classes, so she was trying to fill her time. They wouldn't let her in, since her family had so far been spared, but they accepted the food gratefully.

"I couldn't have done this without you," Mrs. Bates told Elizabeth one time as Elizabeth sent her off to get some rest because Gideon was in a morphine-induced stupor.

"How are families coping when all of them are sick?" Elizabeth marveled. It was all the two of them could do to take care of one man.

"Usually, people help their family and friends when sickness strikes," Mrs. Bates said, "but people are too scared of this. Thank heaven you stayed."

As if she could have done anything else.

Elizabeth went into Gideon's room. He seemed to be sleeping peacefully for the first time in days. She laid a hand on his forehead, bracing herself in case he screamed at her touch, but he didn't scream, and his forehead felt warm but not feverish.

She could have checked his temperature— they took it under his arm for fear he'd bite the thermometer in half if they put it into his mouth— but she didn't want to disturb him. Besides, she'd become adept at guessing his temperature just from how warm he felt. This was the coolest he had been since she'd arrived here Tuesday evening. What day was it now?

She could have checked the newspaper. Anna had brought them one last evening with their dinner, but it was downstairs, and she didn't have the energy to make the trip.

She sank down into the armchair she and Mrs. Bates had pulled up beside Gideon's bed. With a footstool, it served as a comfortable place to sit and even a makeshift bed if his caregiver could relax for long enough to fall asleep. She knew from the strip of light showing between the drapes that it was daytime, although that hardly mattered anymore.

"Are you a dream?" Gideon asked in a voice husky from disuse.

She started, looking at him in wonder. He'd hardly spoken a sensible word in days. "Gideon?"

"Are you really here?"

She slid off the chair and sank to her knees beside the bed. "How could I be? You wouldn't let me stay."

"I was a fool."

"You were very sick. How do you feel now?"

"Rotten."

She caressed his stubbled face. He could grow a respectable beard if he ever decided to.

"Was I bleeding?" he asked when she thought he must have fallen back to sleep.

Bleeding? Yes, he'd been bleeding. Blood pouring from his eyes and nose and even his ears. They'd thought for sure he'd die then, but he hadn't, and Dr. Simpson told them later that was common. As was vomiting and convulsing and delirium and excruciating body aches, which he had endured, and other even more horrible symptoms that, thank heaven, he had been spared.

"Bleeding?" she asked as if she'd never heard the word. "What a terrible dream you must have had."

"They were all terrible."

"They're over now, my darling," she promised rashly, "so just rest."

His eyes closed, and for once, his breathing seemed unlabored. The biggest worry about the flu was pneumonia. So far they'd seen no signs, but Dr. Simpson had warned them that some people got well and then a day or two later came down with pneumonia that killed them. When would they know Gideon was safe?

As he slept, she wept silently into the bed-clothes.

It was Saturday, or at least Elizabeth thought it was. Gideon had been awake for a few hours today, and he was doing so much better, they had started to hope. Elizabeth went to answer the doorbell and found Anna on the porch. She had been bringing them food, but her arms were empty today, and Elizabeth could see she'd been crying. Her eyes were red-rimmed and infinitely sad above her mask.

"What is it?" Elizabeth asked. "What's hap-pened?"

"May I come in? Just for a minute."

"Of course." Elizabeth stepped back, not wanting to get too close. She hadn't worn her mask to answer the door, and they'd been trying to protect Anna as best they could. "Tell me."

"It's . . . it's David."

"Oh no, has he got it, too?" Elizabeth asked, horrified by the thought.

"He's dead."

Elizabeth stared at her for a long moment, unable to comprehend the words she didn't even want to consider might be true. "Dead?" It was impossible.

Anna nodded, and the tears started rolling down her cheeks, although she didn't even seem to notice. "It was the strangest thing. He was going to his office yesterday. He was tired of being cooped up in the house, he said. Our neighbor, Mr. Phillips, was on his porch, and David stopped to say hello. Not close, you understand. No one stands close to people anymore, but David called out to him from the sidewalk. They chatted for a moment, and then David just . . . Elizabeth, he just fell over. At least that's what Mr. Phillips said. He was perfectly fine, and he just fell down, and when Mr. Phillips got to him, he was dead."

The cabdriver had told them all those days ago that he had seen this happen before, and those men on the streetcar . . .

"Oh, Anna, I'm so sorry." Elizabeth threw her

arms around her friend, and they wept together. Elizabeth's relationship with David had been complicated, and she would never have loved him the way Anna and Gideon did, but she loved both of them, so she grieved for their loss.

When Anna pulled away, she said, "Don't tell Gideon, at least not until he's better. I don't know when the funeral will be. So many people have died. . . . I only told you so you'd understand if I didn't come by. My mother is devastated."

"I'm sure she is. Oh, Anna, I wish there was something I could do for you."

"Just like I wished I could do something for you this week. Help Gideon when he finds out. That's what you can do."

"I will, I promise. And when he's well, we'll plan something in David's memory."

Elizabeth had to tell Mrs. Bates about David. She'd known something was wrong the minute she saw Elizabeth later. But they didn't breathe a word to Gideon until the following week when he was finally well enough to get out of bed and come downstairs for a meal.

His grief was heartbreaking to see, and Elizabeth knew a moment of guilt because she was so glad Gideon hadn't died.

Gideon and Mrs. Bates sent Elizabeth home on Monday. She'd made them swear to send for her if Gideon had a relapse or if Mrs. Bates got sick, and she found herself weeping when Jake escorted her out to the red motorcar.

"Whose motorcar is this anyway?" she asked when they were inside and she had dried her tears.

"I'm not sure," Jake said with a grin. "Did you hear about the Prestons?"

"No, I haven't heard a thing." She hadn't even thought of them during the long, dark days when Gideon had been so ill. "What happened?"

"They arrested Delia and that chauffeur fellow who kidnapped you."

"Walter."

"Yeah, Walter somebody. They found the bomb-making equipment in the garage with Walter. Somebody turned them into the League, and they found out Delia was connected to Adolph Hirsch."

"I'm sure Gideon explained all that to Mr. Devoss."

"This Hirsch got pretty mad when Delia spun a yarn about how Hirsch's daughter had carried information from him to her, since he doesn't have a daughter."

"I'm sure he was very confused."

"And Delia was furious because she claimed she'd given a bunch of money to Hirsch's people when they hadn't seen a cent of it, and then Hirsch claimed he never heard of the people who had taken the money."

"How shocking."

"Nobody could find a trace of the people Delia claimed she gave the money to, so naturally, they figured she was lying to protect the people she really gave it to."

"Have they been tried yet?"

"Not yet, but Gideon will probably be able to find out from his boss what happens to them. They don't report that stuff in the newspapers. In fact, they aren't even reporting on the flu. They keep saying it's nothing serious and don't worry if you get it, because it's just the flu."

"That's awful! And dangerous," Elizabeth said, furious. "People won't take precautions if they think it isn't serious."

"Oh, people know it's serious. Churches are holding funerals every hour. They can't hide that from people. But all the newspapers are reporting is some new battle in France that is supposed to rout the Germans once and for all and end the war."

"Do you suppose the Germans have the flu as well?" she mused.

"They must."

"Then maybe that will help rout them. Why can't the war end before Gideon gets called up?"

"Maybe it will, Lizzie," Jake said with uncharacteristic solemnity. "Maybe it will."

Cybil and Zelda were at the college when Jake delivered her to the house. Rose explained that they were helping nurse the students rather than teaching, since classes had been canceled because of the number of students down with the flu.

Rose made them lunch, and Elizabeth answered all her questions about Gideon's illness and Jake told her what he knew about the Prestons.

"I was wondering if you could take me to the Ansonia," Rose asked shyly when they had finished clearing away the luncheon things.

"Do you want to move back home?" Elizabeth said, thinking she couldn't blame Rose, even though they couldn't yet be positive she'd be safe there.

"Not yet. I mean, I'm still afraid Fred might send someone after me even though that fellow is in jail now, but I'm worried about the *money*." She said the word in a whisper, as if afraid someone would overhear.

"What money?" Elizabeth asked.

Rose glanced at Jake. "Mr. Miles brought over the money from the . . . from Fred and Delia the other day. I've got it in a satchel under my bed, but I've been terrified something will happen to it."

"And you want to put it in the bank," Elizabeth guessed.

"Yes. I thought about taking a cab or something, but I didn't want to be out all alone with so much money. What if somebody stole the bag?"

"Nobody would guess what you had in it," Jake

said, "but you're right. Anything could happen. How about if I drive you over?"

"And I'll go with you," Elizabeth said, giving Jake a look. "Just in case Jake tries to convince you to invest in some scheme of his."

"I'd never do that," he said with feigned outrage. "Don't forget, I donated part of my share to Rose."

"Something for which she will not be overly grateful."

Jake glared at her, but Rose interrupted.

"You don't need to go if you don't want to, Elizabeth. I'm not going to fall for any schemes."

"I know you aren't, but I wouldn't mind a little outing myself."

The streets were deserted, and the few pedestrians gave one another a wide berth.

"I'm feeling very reckless," Elizabeth said as the fancy red motorcar rumbled through the empty streets. She hoped they didn't see anyone lying dead on the sidewalk.

"I am, too," Rose said. "Reckless and rich."

They laughed at that, and it felt good to laugh. Elizabeth hadn't done it for far too long. At the Ansonia, no doorman greeted them this time, either, and no one was in the lobby. A lone clerk stood behind the desk, but he was talking on the telephone. They made their way to the bank, where Rose informed one of the two tellers that she wanted to open an account. She smiled when the teller gave her a condescending glance.

Since the bank had no customers at the moment, they didn't have to wait. Mr. Feely was deemed senior enough to handle Mrs. Preston's account.

"Nothing has changed with your husband's account, Mrs. Preston," he said with the proper amount of regret.

"I didn't think it had, but I've received a settlement from my husband's brother, and I'd like to open an account of my own."

He perked up at this. "It's irregular for a lady to open an account without a man to cosign, but widows sometimes do, so I can arrange that for you. If you have a check from Mr. Preston, I'll use that to open the account."

Rose exchanged a knowing glance with Elizabeth and Jake. "I'm afraid I have cash. I hope that won't be a problem."

"Not at all, Mrs. Preston." His tone had changed. If she had cash, it couldn't be very much money, but he was humoring her. "Do you know how much you would like to deposit?"

"I think I'd like to keep a little cash in case of an emergency, so I'll only be depositing a hundred and seventy thousand."

Mr. Feely's eyes didn't actually bug out, but it was a near thing. "Dollars?"

"Of course, dollars. If that's a problem, however, I can take my business someplace else," she added innocently.

"Oh no, it's not a problem at all. Let me . . . If you'll excuse me, I'd like to get our president. I'm sure he'll want to meet you." Mr. Feely hurried out of the room.

"I guess the president has recovered from the flu," Elizabeth remarked.

When they had finished their business at the bank, with the help of the bank president, who had personally handled Mrs. Preston's new account, they wandered out into the Ansonia's enormous lobby.

The seals were gone from the fountain, and the place had an abandoned air. Rose hadn't worn a veil today, since Walter was safely locked away, but they all were wearing their protective masks.

"I should probably check my apartment while I'm here since I don't have to worry about being seen anymore," Rose said.

"You might have some mail to pick up, too. You've been gone for a month."

"Has it only been a month?" Rose asked, and Elizabeth had to agree. It seemed far longer.

They went over to the desk, and the clerk who had been on the telephone greeted them enthusiastically. He probably didn't see many people nowadays. "How may I help you?"

"Hello, Harry," Rose said. She pulled down her mask so he could see her face.

"Mrs. Preston!" he exclaimed happily. "It's good to see you. We've been wondering if you'd come back here after . . . after what happened."

"I'll probably be back soon," she said, "but I had some business at the bank, so I thought I'd stop by and check on my place and see if I have any mail."

"You do have some mail, Mrs. Preston, and even a telegram. We would have forwarded it to you, but we didn't know where you were staying."

Rose's smile disappeared at the word "telegram." Everyone knew what that meant when you had someone in the war. But Rose had already received *that* telegram.

Harry didn't seem to notice her discomfort. He was too busy retrieving the mail that had been stuffed into the box for her apartment. He also handed her the key. "Just give it back to me when you're finished. Your rent is paid up for a long time yet, so whenever you're ready to come back, everything will be here for you."

They thanked him and had the elevator take them up.

"This is a really nice place," Jake remarked as they made their way down the hall to Rose's apartment. "I might look into this myself."

"They don't take bachelors without references," Rose informed him.

"I guess you're out of luck," Elizabeth teased him.

They found Rose's apartment exactly as they'd

left it four weeks ago. She still held the bundle of mail Harry had given her downstairs. She laid it on the hall table carefully, as if afraid it might explode.

"Don't you want to look at your mail?" Elizabeth asked.

Rose shook her head. "The last time I got a telegram, it was very bad news."

"Would you like me to read it for you?" Elizabeth asked.

"Oh yes," Rose said gratefully. "Thank you so much. If it's more bad news, at least you can break it gently, although I don't know how much worse the news could get with Tommy dead."

Elizabeth flipped through the stack of mail and found several letters from Tom Preston. How heartbreaking. He'd managed a lot of letter writing in his brief time overseas. She'd let Rose read them in private, and she'd read the telegram. She tore it open and scanned the typed letters. For a moment they made no sense. She had to read them three more times.

"What is it, Lizzie?" Jake asked.

"Rose," Elizabeth began carefully, "when you got the first telegram, what did it say?"

Rose frowned. "It said Tommy was missing."

"Missing? Just missing?"

"I know what 'missing' means. The soldiers talked about it all the time. The bombs, when they come down right where the men are, sometimes . . ." She closed her eyes and shuddered. "Sometimes there's nothing left of them, so they say the men are 'missing.'"

"Maybe you're mistaken about that," Elizabeth said.

Jake snatched the telegram from her fingers so he could read it himself.

"Mistaken about what?" Rose asked.

"About it always meaning the soldier is dead, because—"

"This says they found him," Jake reported, holding the telegram out for Rose to read.

"What?" She snatched it in turn and read the printed words. "They found him," she said in wonder. "He just got separated from his unit. He's not dead!"

Then she was laughing and crying, and Elizabeth was crying because she was so happy for Rose. "These letters are from him," she told Rose, handing them to her. "The most recent one was mailed only ten days ago."

Rose grabbed them and pressed them to her heart. "He's not dead!"

At least he hadn't been when that last letter was written, but Elizabeth didn't say that, and she shot Jake a look to make sure he didn't say it, either. "Let's sit down, and you can read his letters. Maybe he will explain what happened when he was missing."

Elizabeth sat down beside Rose on the sofa

while she sorted the letters into the order in which they had been mailed. Jake decided to explore the apartment while he waited.

"He did explain what happened, but the censors blacked it out," Rose reported, holding up the letter to show her the blacked-out lines of the text. The censors wouldn't allow soldiers to report anything that might be detrimental to the war effort, which meant anything that made the army look stupid.

Rose passed the letter to Elizabeth so she could read what the censors had considered suitable for those on the home front to hear.

"Oh dear, he got the flu," Rose mused as she read the second one. "He was very sick, but he recovered."

"That's wonderful news," Elizabeth said. That meant he'd been in a military hospital instead of on the front lines being shot at.

Rose passed her that letter and tore open the third one, the one that was only ten days old. "He's better, but they kept him at the hospital to help out because they had so many sick men to take care of and he couldn't get the flu again," she reported. "He really wants to be fighting with his men, but thank heaven he's at the hospital. At least he won't be shot."

"And he's alive, which is the best news of all. Do you know what that means, Rose?"

"It means Fred can't keep Tommy's money and

he can't cheat me anymore," Rose realized. "But it also means you did all that for nothing."

"Not for nothing," Jake said, coming back into the living room. "We uncovered a bunch of German spies."

"And you made some money and had a lot of fun," Elizabeth added. "We'll have to get someone at Gideon's law firm to write Fred a letter, notifying him."

"Maybe Gideon can do it himself," Jake said.

"I think he'd love to," Elizabeth said. "Why don't you take us over to his house, Jake, so he can see the telegram and the letters? He's still too weak to go to the office, but they can prepare the letter and bring it to him to sign. I think that will do more for his recovery than any medicine."

The letter from the draft board had come the last week of October. The flu epidemic was abating, and the army had reopened their training camps. Gideon was to report in two weeks. He and Elizabeth had spent as much time as possible together in the meantime. By some miracle, she never got the flu, although thousands of others had. The week after Gideon had fallen ill, New York saw four thousand new cases in one day. Black mourning wreaths hung on half the doors in the city, or so it seemed, including the home of his dearest friend.

The pain of losing David was second only

to that of losing his father, and his promise to Anna and her mother to stand in David's stead whenever they might need help was completely sincere. If only he could fill the void that David had left in all their lives.

The day finally arrived. He packed some essentials, although the army would be issuing him new clothes and probably new essentials as well, but he couldn't go off to war with nothing. Elizabeth had had her photograph made and given it to him as a farewell gift, framed in a leather folder that protected it from the weather and would slip into his pocket. She'd cried when he opened it, as she cried about most everything now.

They'd had a bit of excitement last Thursday, when some journalist at the front mistook a temporary stand-down for a cease-fire and reported that the war was over. The news arrived in New York at noon, and by one o'clock the word had spread and people left their jobs to celebrate in the streets. Elizabeth had cried especially hard when word came down that it was a false alarm.

She was being brave today, however. She and Gideon's mother had come to the station to see him off.

"I don't want you remembering me with red eyes and a runny nose," she said.

"Don't forget to write," his mother said. She, too, was being brave.

"And don't forget to duck," Elizabeth added without irony.

About thirty men had been assigned to his car, and they were all saying good-bye to someone on the platform. The noise above the hiss of the steam engines was nearly deafening.

"All aboard," the conductor shouted.

His mother wrapped an arm around his neck and kissed his cheek. "Take care of yourself, my darling boy. You aren't replaceable, you know."

Then he turned to Elizabeth, who threw her arms around his neck and held him tightly. "Don't die, Gideon. I won't care if you're wounded or crippled or anything. Just come back to me."

The lump in his throat made it impossible for him to say anything, so he simply kissed her. When he was done, he picked up his bag and backed toward the door where his fellows were slowly and with great reluctance boarding the train. He didn't want to lose sight of his mother and Elizabeth until the very last moment.

Once he was on the train, he found a seat on the platform side and opened the window. His mother and Elizabeth saw him and ran over. They both held his hands until the conductor came by and told them they had to leave.

A sergeant came down the aisle, checking each man off a list. Behind him, some privates were passing out blankets.

"What do we need these for?" someone asked.

"Shut up and take the blanket. You'll be glad enough later that you have it," the sergeant said.

With their loved ones gone, the men started to chat among themselves, sharing hometowns and draft stories and wondering what the training would be like. After a while, when the train didn't move, some of the men went back out on the platform to see if anyone knew what the problem was. No one did. They sat there for almost two hours before the sergeant came back.

"Listen up, men. I've got something important to tell you."

Elizabeth had planned to spend the rest of the day with Mrs. Bates. They were knitting socks, or at least Mrs. Bates was. Elizabeth was just knitting. She had finally mastered the basic stitch, so she was just knitting row after row in what, she hoped, might eventually be a scarf. She would send it to Gideon when it was finished so he could show it to the other soldiers, and they could tease him about what a poor housewife she was going to be.

Elizabeth had been trying to think of something to talk about to take their minds off Gideon leaving, but every subject she thought of was wrong. He still had three months of training before he'd go to the front, she reminded herself. Anything could happen in three months. Maybe all the Germans would die of the flu.

Someone rang the doorbell. Some of Mrs. Bates's servants had returned when Gideon recovered, but the young maid had also gotten the flu while she was away and died. Mrs. Bates could not bear to replace her yet.

"I'll get it," Elizabeth said. The house was quiet, she realized. When Gideon was here, she could feel his presence, even when he'd been sick. His strength seemed to vibrate in the very air. Now nothing vibrated. How would she survive if he didn't come home?

She opened the door, and there he was. She blinked, certain she had conjured him up with her imagination. But then he let out a whoop and scooped her up and spun her around.

"Did you desert?" she cried, laughing in spite of herself.

"I didn't have to. The war is over, for real this time. We sat on the train for hours, and then a sergeant came and told us we could go home because the war ended this morning. It's over, my darling. It's over."

AUTHOR'S NOTE

Writing this book was an educational experience. I discovered a lot I didn't know about the First World War, and I hope you had a few "I didn't know that!" moments, too. Everything I wrote about it in this book is true, especially the domestic spying done by the volunteer members of the American Protective League. President Woodrow Wilson was notoriously thin-skinned and could not tolerate any criticism. He also genuinely could not understand how any man of reason could disagree with him. He used his executive powers to censor the media and quash any dissent to his policies or decisions. Thousands of Americans, particularly Americans of German descent, were arrested on the barest of pretexts. Most of them were eventually released without charge, and even those sentenced to long prison terms were pardoned after the war. Still, the seeds of mistrust of authority were sown, and they continue to flourish a hundred years later.

German spies did operate in the United States, both before America entered the war and after. The Black Tom explosion on July 30, 1916 (almost a year before America officially entered the war), really happened and for decades was believed to have been caused accidentally. Only the work of dedicated investigators eventually uncovered the German plot and brought the perpetrators to justice in 1939. Several books have been written about this event and its aftermath. If you're interested, the story reads like a good mystery!

The Great Influenza Epidemic of 1918 is probably the worst worldwide epidemic in history. No one will ever know how many people died. Estimates range from fifty to a hundred million. The war and the movement of people it caused helped spread the deadly pathogen in ways previously unseen. Researchers believe that the pandemic began in one of the American military training camps, and gathering young men at military training camps proved a particularly effective way of spreading the disease. The camps were indeed closed in October of 1918 during the height of the pandemic. The masks people wore were not the least bit effective, and this flu did hit young adults the hardest, unlike every other type of flu. People often died very quickly, within a matter of hours from the first onset of symptoms, and a few died as suddenly as I describe David's death. The description of the deaths on the streetcar is based on an actual event in Philadelphia.

America entered World War I in April of

1917, but large numbers of American troops did not participate in a major battle until April of 1918, and the war ended only seven months later, on November 11, 1918. The reason it took a year for American troops to make an impact is because America had only a small active-duty military in 1917. They had to enlist a million young men, build lodging and camps for their training and produce uniforms (including shoes) and weapons for them as well as ammunition, tanks, supplies, food and everything else an army needs. Many early recruits practiced marching with sticks because they had no rifles. It took a year to get mobilized, but once they were, the American troops quickly turned the tide of battle and brought about the end of the war. Gideon's experience of reporting for duty on the last day of the war is based on an actual soldier's account of his military experience.

I did fudge on one thing. *Ali Baba and the Forty Thieves* wasn't released until November of 1918, but it seemed like the perfect movie for my characters to watch, so I sneaked it in a bit early.

Please let me know how you liked this book. You may follow me on Facebook at Victoria .Thompson.Author and on Twitter @gaslightvt and visit my website at VictoriaThompson.com to sign up for my newsletter so you'll always know when I have a new book coming out.

| Books are produced in the United States using U.S.-based materials | Books are printed using a revolutionary new process called THINKtech™ that lowers energy usage by 70% and increases overall quality | Books are durable and flexible because of Smyth-sewing | Paper is sourced using environmentally responsible foresting methods and the paper is acid-free |

Center Point Large Print
600 Brooks Road / PO Box 1
Thorndike, ME 04986-0001 USA

(207) 568-3717

US & Canada:
1 800 929-9108
www.centerpointlargeprint.com